A PRIVATE BUSINESS

Also by Barbara Nadel

The Inspector Ikmen Series

Belshazzar's Daughter
A Chemical Prison
Arabesk
Deep Waters
Harem
Petrified
Deadly Web
Dance with Death
A Passion for Killing
Pretty Dead Things
River of the Dead
Death by Design
Dead of Night

The Hancock series

Last Rights
After the Mourning
Ashes to Ashes
Sure and Certain Death

A PRIVATE BUSINESS

Barbara Nadel

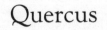

Quercus

First published in Great Britain in 2012 by

Quercus
55 Baker Street
7th Floor, South Block
London W1U 8EW

A CIP catalogue record for this book is available
from the British Library

HB ISBN 978 0 85738 773 8
TPB ISBN 978 0 85738 774 5

10 9 8 7 6 5 4 3 2 1

Typeset by Ellipsis Digital Limited, Glasgow

Printed and bound in Great Britain by Clays Ltd, St Ives plc

To all the east enders who inspired my life with their stories. To my grandparents, my dad, my aunts and uncles and to the long dead people they told stories about. To Oggy, Mrs Fawcett, the O'Malleys, Œ'Peggy' Dooley, Dr O'Dwyer, Mr Kopoloff, the Boleyn Bugler, the peddlers of rags and bones who kept their horses in their houses and all the other rich and varied real life characters I was privileged to grow up with.

Part One

I

The comedian is in full flow, effing and blinding in her usual style with the late Princess Diana as her target. She eyes a woman in the front row of the audience.

You look shocked, sweet? Not comfortable with speaking ill of the dead? Oh, please. That woman flung herself into the public arena when she told us all about her colonic irrigation. There was nothing that was private about her! Queen of Hearts? Diana was Queen of Chat. Empress of the Exposé! Let's face it, if she was still alive now she'd be on Jeremy Kyle *trailing a whole tribe of half Egyptian children, weeping because she can't get Disability Living Allowance.*

The audience laughs, all except one man who yells out, *At least Di never became some old has-been, like you!!*

The comedian leans forward into the audience and cups a hand at the back of her ear to hear better. *What's that? Is that Bloke with no Bollocks and a Theoretical Dick, I hear?*

The audience laughs and the man says something else but no-one can hear it.

Deal with it, mate. You're the sort of person who thinks the

Queen's got no ring-piece, that she can't fart and only burps rainbows. A British patriot who lives in a la-la land of ridiculous military uniforms and the divine bleeding right of kings. You're an arsehole. There's no divine anything. Babies are babies are babies. They're all like Joan Rivers when they come out of the womb, misshapen and screaming with fury. Even the royal ones.

The audience laughs but the comedian's face has turned to stone.

Nothing's sacred, people, nothing's divine. There's no such thing. Jesus was a crazy urban warrior crusty, with a bit of a Paul Daniels vibe thrown in. But he was just a bloke. He's not sitting on a cloud somewhere, blessing all the royal babies and twanging away on his harp. It's a fairy story! A fiction! It's like a white-hat, black-hat cowboy story for mad people. It's . . .

The comedian staggers slightly and looks confused as if she can't remember what she's doing. *It's . . .* She puts a hand up to her head, her eyes glaze over and then she collapses.

The woman, who would not give her name, was tall and elegant. A well-preserved fifty or so, she wore a beautifully cut trouser suit with a peacock-blue Hermès scarf wrapped turban-like around her head. Her slim face was almost completely eclipsed by large Jackie-O-style sunglasses which did not, however, manage to obscure her eyes. They didn't know how to be, those eyes; fearful and elated, ashamed and even possibly guilty and yet, at the same time, furious – intensely, madly furious too. Mumtaz had seen eyes like that before and she wondered what terrible thing was happening or had happened to this woman.

'Can I get you anything?' Mumtaz asked. 'Tea? Coffee?'

'No.' There was a pause. 'Thanks.'

Her voice was cockney with a veneer of 'proper' speech laid over the top. Mumtaz imagined that, given the good clothes and the general demeanour of the woman, she came from a 'nice' part of the borough, or maybe from somewhere outside, possibly the Isle of Dogs, Ilford or Chigwell. There was also something vaguely familiar about her but Mumtaz couldn't put her finger on what it was.

The woman stared down at her watch. Mumtaz looked at the clock on the wall and realised that she'd been in her awkward presence for just over an hour. Given her own comparative newness to the business, together with the feelings those eyes were evoking in her, Mumtaz didn't know whether she wanted to run away or somehow force the woman to tell a story that was clearly bursting to get out of her. In the end she opted for neither and just considered the old computer screen on her desk. She knew why Lee didn't invest in more modern equipment but it was still annoying to be forced to put up with such antiques. When Shazia had seen her office, she'd laughed. That was the first time she'd done that since her father's death, so

Lee's old rubbish served some sort of purpose even if the production of a professional-looking letter wasn't part of it.

Shifting in her chair, the woman looked as if she was about to say something but then she appeared to change her mind. Mumtaz went back to composing the letter Lee had asked her to write to Mr Savva, their landlord. He'd put the office rent up but, given the parlous state of the company finances, it just wasn't possible to pay him. Lee had told her to tell him to shove his rent 'where the sun don't shine'. She had translated that into rather more diplomatic language but was now struggling to read what she'd written on the cracked, scarred monitor screen. Looking at it produced a kind of double vision that made her feel vaguely sick, and not for the first time she considered bringing a laptop in from home. There were, after all, several about. Shazia had her own – it wouldn't be a problem – but just the thought of it made Mumtaz shudder. Those machines had been Ahmed's. The woman saw her body flinch, but she didn't say anything to her.

Mumtaz regretted not having brought any magazines in to the office for waiting clients. It had never even occurred to Lee, but then men didn't generally think about things like that. If they did, the magazines they chose were usually about cars or golf or caravans. The smart woman in the Hermès scarf probably liked to read rather serious women's magazines. True-life stories of people being incinerated by their ex-boyfriends and celebrities in 'crisis' were unlikely, Mumtaz felt, to be her thing. Her handbag was understated quality and she wore a small and discreet gold cross around her neck. In spite of her confusion she had nothing to prove; in some areas of her life, she was as she was and she possessed a degree of comfort with that. Only her eyes, trembling and shimmering with feelings she was clearly failing to cope with, gave her away – that and the fact that she was in that office at all.

'Mate, I'm not being funny or anything, but quite honestly, I don't give a flying fuck whether you get paid today, last week, next Thursday or when the saints go marching in. You owe me money.' Lee Arnold was calm, but the man sitting beside him wasn't. Lee smiled. 'Bob, mate, the rent's due on the office – just gone up as a matter of fact – the oven's crying out for Mr Muscle, I'm out of bird food and I could do with a diet Coke.'

'Oh . . .' The man, a small sort called Bob Singleton, got up, went straight over to the bar and ordered Lee a pint of diet Coke. The three old geezers sitting by the open door to the public bar looked at Lee. One of them flicked his cigarette ash out into Green Street while the other two laughed bronchitically.

'You wanna get money out of Bob the Builder you better

bring a crowbar with you next time, son!' the fag smoker said to Lee.

'Yeah, right,' Lee said gloomily.

Bob Singleton looked around resentfully at the men but he didn't say anything. He just paid for Lee's drink and then took it over to him. The Boleyn was quiet this lunchtime and so Lee's latest attempt at getting Bob the Builder to settle his bill was just about the only show in town. The three old men watched him sit down.

Bob moved in close to Lee and said, 'Look, I done this extension for this posh bird over Wanstead and she's, well, she ain't exactly satisfied . . .'

'So she's not paid you,' Lee said. 'At all.'

Bob, embarrassed, looked down at the floor and said, 'No.'

It was well known that Bob was one of the few sole-trader builders in the East End who didn't ask for any money up front. It was also well known that all his work was terrible, he suffered from appalling halitosis and was as tight as a gnat's arse. Was it any wonder that his wife had been having an affair with an Indian restaurant owner for the last six months?

'Well, you'd better go back and put whatever mess you left that lady in right, then, hadn't you,' Lee said. Then he pointed a finger up at Bob's face. 'Because if I can't clean that oven and, more importantly, if I can't pay my assistant, there will be consequences.'

Bob, who had known Lee Arnold for most of his life, knew when he was being serious and when he was not. He swallowed hard. 'You have to give me till Friday,' he said.

Lee Arnold looked down his long Roman nose at the small, grubby man at his side and he said, 'Friday morning and no longer. If I don't get it on Friday . . .'

'I know! I know!' Bob Singleton waved his hands in the air. 'It all comes on top and—'

'Pay me and you'll never find out,' Lee said in a voice the whole pub could easily hear.

The three old men opposite looked very seriously at each other, then two of them lit up cigarettes. Aware that everyone was watching him now, Bob the Builder muttered something to Lee about 'having confidence in him' and then he left.

The oldest of the three old men frowned and then said to Lee, 'You think you'll ever see him again, do you?'

Lee took a swig from his glass. 'If I don't his missus'll get a visit from me,' he said.

'Oh!' All three old men laughed.

'What's that then, Lee?' the shortest cigarette smoker said. 'You gonna help yourself to Tracey, are you?'

For the first time that day, Lee Arnold's face just barely cracked a smile. 'No, that'd be wrong,' he said. 'And anyway, Tracey's got enough problems of her own, without me. She's got Bob.'

'So what's the plan then?'

As Lee stood up to knock back his Coke, they all huddled around him like a pack of eager, wrinkled puppies. 'Bob's got the odd little secret that I'm sure Tracey would find of interest,' he said. 'It's up to him, really, isn't it. He pays me what he owes me and Tracey's none the wiser. He doesn't do that . . .' He shrugged.

The oldest old man shook his head appreciatively. 'You're a cool customer, Lee Arnold.'

Lee picked his coat up off the seat beside him and put it on. 'Thanks, Harry,' he said to the ancient. Then he turned to the others and added, 'Fred, Wilf, see ya.'

Parting like the waves of the sea as he moved through them, the old men all watched Lee's tall figure head towards the public bar door. Just before he actually left, Wilf, a fag hanging limply out of the side of his mouth said, 'Here, Lee, how's that new girl of yours coming along? She any good, is she?'

Lee turned, his face pulled into a frown now, and he said, 'Do you know, boys, I don't really know. Time'll tell I suppose.' And then he left.

Once out on Green Street, Lee properly considered what he had just been asked and he decided that it was a real puzzler. Mrs Hakim, Mumtaz, was a religious Muslim widow lady who wrote very good letters and made a mean cup of tea. Well-spoken and very polite, he nevertheless wondered how she'd cope hiding in the back of a van with a load of blokes and no access to a toilet.

As one hour dribbled over into two, she started to think that maybe going to the police would have been the better option after all, but then she pulled herself together. That was impossible and anyway it was too late now. She'd already invested too much time firstly tracking down this place and then sitting about for over an hour doing nothing. Also, it was a private matter. What she'd come to a private detective about was something the world did not need to know.

Every so often the Asian woman, who although not actually covered was well and truly headscarfed, looked up at her and smiled. She was very attractive, probably in her early thirties, and she had enormous moss-green eyes which she made up beautifully and with some skill. Slim and dressed modestly but very stylishly, she was rather a strange character to find working in a private detective's office. Women like her – from the look of her clothes and her make-up she probably had a wealthy husband – usually stayed in the home.

'I'm so sorry about the wait.' She smiled again. 'I'm sure Mr Arnold won't be long now.'

But she looked embarrassed, the Asian woman. What Mr Arnold was going to be like was both intriguing and worrying. With a tiny office up a rickety flight of stairs behind a dusty Greek barber's shop on Green Street, Upton Park, it was unlikely that he was earning enough to pay forty per cent tax. But did that mean that he wasn't any good?

She had a mental picture in her head of what a private detective was like but she also knew that it was probably very inaccurate. For a start she'd never imagined that any sort of private eye would have a headscarfed Muslim woman for a secretary, but then maybe that said more about her than it did about Mr Arnold's practice. Was Mr Arnold, in fact, Asian himself? Green Street had had a massive Asian presence for decades and even if 'Arnold' wasn't an obviously Asian name maybe it was the handle he'd taken for some reason best known to himself. Before she'd just turned up without an appointment, she'd had a few fantasies about what he was going to be like. Undoubtedly inspired by the cinema and TV, she imagined Arnold to be either some vaguely dusty East End geezer who smelt of beer and fags or some elegant and dashing Philip Marlowe creation. As it turned out he was something between the two.

The office door opened to reveal a tall, dark, handsome, forty something man with a pronounced Roman nose who smelt of pub and fags and who looked at her and said, 'Ah.'

She took her sunglasses off and watched his features recognise her.

'Oh, Mr Arnold,' the Asian woman said, 'this lady—'

'I know exactly who this lady is, Mumtaz,' Lee Arnold said, and then he turned to her and smiled. 'Shall we go into my office and have a chat? Assuming that's what you're here for.'

'I'm being watched,' she said baldly.

Lee offered her a chair opposite his desk and said, 'Let's pedal back a bit from that, shall we?'

'I'm really frightened.' She sat.

'Miss Peters, before we get into any of that, I have to know what a lady like you is doing in a place like this,' Lee said. 'First time I saw you was at the Hackney Empire back in the late eighties. Then suddenly every time I switched the telly on, there you were.'

She put her head down.

'You were a big star for a number of years and I liked your act,' Lee said. 'I've noticed you've been making a bit of a comeback on the comedy circuit.'

Maria Peters looked up. She remained the beautiful woman she'd always been, if a little older, but, so people said, she still had a mouth like a sewer. Although she'd suffered some ill health a little while back, after collapsing on stage, she seemed to be fully recovered now. 'I married in 1993,' she said. 'Leonard. We lived . . . I live in Forest Gate. No kids.'

Lee pointed at her. 'You're a local girl.'

'Plaistow.' She nodded. 'Me and my parents and my sisters all in a two-bedroom flat on Prince Regent Lane.'

He smiled; local girl done good. But how good? 'What you got now?'

'Five beds with landscaped gardens, outbuildings, new Merc on the drive.' She sighed. 'Got a couple of houses on Plashet Grove, three flats in West Ham, one old multiple occupation in Forest Gate. Inheritances from Len. Leonard Blatt, my Len, was a landlord – he died at the end of 2009.'

'I'm sorry for your loss.' Lee hadn't actually known Leonard Blatt but he had known of him. He'd had a reputation as a mildly dodgy geezer.

'Len left me well provided for and I'll be straight with you, I'm worth a lot of money,' she said. 'I don't ever need to work again if I don't want to. But I do. Len's death left me . . . We had a good marriage. I got back on the comedy circuit just under a year ago when my old manager took me on again. It's still rough out there but it's what I know.'

Lee leaned forward onto his desk. 'You were good,' he said. 'Controversial . . .'

'Bloody filthy.' She looked slightly ashamed at first but then she smiled. 'It was my selling point, that I'd say anything. I was young and pretty and I had no limits.'

'You were brilliant.' She looked away. 'So now I know something about your life, Miss Peters,' Lee said, 'what's this about you being watched?'

She frowned. 'Started about three months ago,' she said.

14

'Someone out in the garden. Thought it was kids at first and I still don't know that it isn't, to be honest. At night but sometimes in the day I see, or think I see, movement in the garden. It's not cats. There's a human figure, out the corner of my eye, you know. Then the other day I saw someone in the house.'

'Any idea who it might have been?'

'No. Like in the garden, it was just a flash, a corner of the eye job. I think it was a man.'

'Have you told the police?'

She turned away. 'No, I don't want to. Don't know if I'm . . . Been a bit dodgy, health-wise. Maybe, er . . . maybe no one's really there. You know?'

'Mmm.' Lee looked down at his desk. Of course it was possible that she was just seeing things. Sometimes people under stress, in this case bereavement, did experience hallucinations from time to time. But this was not exactly his area and he knew that he needed help. 'Miss Peters, would you mind if I asked my assistant to come in on this interview?'

'Your assistant?'

'Mrs Hakim. You met her in reception.'

'Oh. I thought she was your secretary.'

'No, she is my assistant,' Lee said. He mentally crossed his fingers against the almost-lie as he said it. Mumtaz Hakim had indeed been engaged to be his assistant even if, so far, all she'd done was make tea and write letters.

15

Maybe now was indeed the time to employ her expertise? 'Would you mind telling her what you've just told me?'

'As long as she takes what I say seriously,' Maria Peters said. 'Mr Arnold, this being watched thing, it . . . I get so scared, and I don't scare easily. Just recently my life's got a lot better. I don't want that to end, so I want this cleared up. Doesn't matter what you find, I can take it. And what it costs.'

Lee agreed to take Maria Peters' case. If someone was indeed getting into her garden and her house and managing to bypass her own outdoor security camera and internal alarms then that could be serious. And besides, she'd asked for 24/7 surveillance from the Arnold Agency and that represented a lot of much needed money. The only question mark was over her state of mind – although the good thing was that she seemed to be aware of that possibility. Lee sat back down behind his desk once Maria had gone and asked Mumtaz what she thought.

Sitting opposite, her hands wrapped around a big mug of tea, Mumtaz said, 'I don't really know, to be honest, Mr Arnold. Having only just met her, Miss Peters seemed to me to be quite a sane person. But that doesn't really mean very much, I'm afraid. Some people are sane for ninety per cent of the time but just have the odd delusory episode, usually when they're under pressure.'

Which could apply to Maria Peters. The main reason

why Lee had chosen Mumtaz above all the other candidates who had applied for the job as his assistant had
been because she had a degree in psychology. He knew
that he probably laid far more store by this than she did,
but the potential knowledge that she had about the human
mind and behaviour had seemed like a good investment
when he'd first interviewed her. She did also make a very
good cuppa and she was, he hardly dare acknowledge even
to himself, very beautiful.

'But you think I did right to take the case?'

'Oh, yes, Mr Arnold,' Mumtaz said. 'Undoubtedly. The lady
is alone. What if someone is trying to frighten her? Although
why she doesn't go to the police I can't really see.'

'Doesn't want them involved, I s'pose. She's rich and
famous and probably doesn't want some load of coppers
stomping around her home pursued by journalists. And
she wants someone to watch her back 24/7,' Lee said. 'They
won't do that, they can't; we're going to be stretched. I'll
have to tap up some freelance assistance and we'll have
to work shifts.' He leaned back in his chair and looked at
her. 'Course, this could be your big moment, if you want
it, Mumtaz.'

She frowned.

'You want to learn the business. I took you on to learn
the business. A gig like this is a good place to start. You
can come out with me to start with, then I could rota you
in.'

It was what she'd wanted. As well as needing the money, Mumtaz had actually been interested in learning about private investigation when she'd applied for the job three months before. By embarking on a new career it seemed as if she was symbolically turning a corner in her life and hopefully leaving a lot of things she didn't want to think about any more safely in the past.

'There'll be no evening or night work, not for you,' Lee said.

She'd told him about Shazia right from the start. *I have a daughter*, she'd said to him at the interview. *She's sixteen and she's just lost her father. I want to be there for her as much as I am able.* And Lee had taken her on knowing that and he'd met Shazia. He'd been, she'd felt at the time, like some sort of gift from God. Now he needed her and she couldn't let him down. 'That'll be fine,' she said. 'I'd like that.'

Lee Arnold smiled. 'Great,' he said. 'Bloody marvellous money, Maria Peters is minted!'

'Her eyes were very sad.' She wanted to say *You mustn't exploit her vulnerability, Mr Arnold.* But she didn't. Rightly or wrongly she found herself trusting him not to do that. 'You think she will be able to keep our involvement to herself?'

'She'll only tell her mum,' Lee said. 'I'm not happy about that but she insisted – the old girl's a right nosy cow apparently – and at least she isn't going behind my back

18

like most of my clients. I impressed it upon her, I hope, how to tell all and sundry would just mean she'd be throwing her money down the drain.'

It wasn't unusual for clients to undermine the agency's work by telling people they were either having someone watched or being surveilled themselves. Even in the short time that Mumtaz had been with Lee Arnold she'd learned that probably the biggest threat to the success of an operation was the client him- or herself.

Lee picked up his BlackBerry and began to work his way through his phone book. 'Have to get a few faces on board,' he said. Then he stopped, looked up and smiled again. 'But before I do, I think that we deserve a treat for this, Mumtaz.' He put his hand into his jacket pocket and took out a twenty pound note. 'Let's have a couple of cappuccinos from that Bengali-Italian place up by the station. Get yourself some of that chocolate sesame stuff you like . . .'

'Chocolate halva.'

'That's the thing. Oh, and get me a packet of Marlboro too. We'll close the office for the rest of the day and I'll have a fag at me desk for once.'

Mumtaz picked up the banknote.

'And when you get back,' Lee said, 'I'll tell you all I know about Maria Peters.'

'She was one of the most controversial comedians to come out of the comedy new wave of the nineteen eighties,' Lee said. 'They used to call her the English Joan Rivers, except that she was much younger and much prettier. Maria Peters, as you saw, is a beautiful woman. But she had a mouth like a toilet. One of her jokes I'll always remember was . . . I'm not sure I should repeat . . .'

'Mr Arnold, I am not made of glass.'

One thing that Lee had noticed about covered Muslim women was that people, and that included him, had extreme reactions to them. BNP thugs hurled abuse and dog shit at them, while some Asian men, as far as Lee could deduce, appeared to completely ignore their existence. He knew he personally tended to treat them with undue and unusual respect. Somewhere in his head they were ranked alongside nuns who were also pure and semi-divine beings. Except that really they weren't. No one was and some of them, like Mumtaz, were stunning. Lee took a deep breath and then did Maria Peters' joke. 'What do you call a bearded man with a wide mouth and a clitoris for a tongue?'

Mumtaz put what remained of her chocolate halva down on Lee's desk and said, 'A clitoris?'

'Yes.' Lee could feel his face start to burn with embarrassment. Mumtaz had to know what a clitoris was but he really wished he hadn't just said that word to her. 'A clitoris.'

'A clitoris?' She shook her head. 'I can't imagine,' she said. 'What would you call such a person?'

Lee's heart began to pound as his face achieved a sunburned look. 'Nothing at all,' he said. 'Poor bloke's got enough problems having a face like a cunt.'

For just a moment there was complete silence. Lee tried to fill it up by audibly puffing on his fag. He almost expected Mumtaz to either storm out or say that she didn't understand. But instead she said, 'Oh, I see. It's a sort of confounding of expectations thing.'

For a moment Lee held his breath.

'The audience think that the comedian is going to say that you call the man a c-face. So when those expectations are confounded it's funny.' She laughed. 'Clever. But then good comedy is clever.' She picked her halva up again and bit another lump off the side. Lee wondered how much comedy Mumtaz had actually seen and how much of that had been for the purposes of her degree. He doubted she'd grown up with *The Comic Strip Presents* . . . but then was that just him imposing a stereotype on her? He decided not to continue any further down that road.

'Maria Peters was one of the first comedians in the country to have a one-person show in the West End,' Lee said. 'She started out in pubs back in the eighties, went on to comedy clubs – I saw her at a comedy night at the Hackney Empire. Then she was in the West End, on telly, everywhere. She was a big star who made a lot of dosh.'

'And she's originally from Newham.'

'Plaistow. Went to school in the borough.' Lee drank his

cappuccino. 'I don't know much about her early life, she didn't really go into it. But she gave up her career in the nineties when she married a geezer called Leonard Blatt.'

'I know that name.'

Lee smiled. 'Forest Gate landlord,' he said. 'Mr Blatt used to own quite a bit of property up around your place.'

'He owned the house next to mine, which Miss Peters must own now,' Mumtaz said. 'I knew she was familiar. She comes sometimes to collect rent from the tenants.'

'Ah, could be useful.'

Both Lee Arnold and Mumtaz Hakim lived, in very different circumstances, in the northern Newham district of Forest Gate. Back in the nineteenth and early twentieth centuries, Forest Gate had been a genteel suburb of solid Victorian villas and ornate parks and cemeteries. But after the Second World War it fell into disrepair and became one of those areas characterised by multiple occupation. The twenty-first century, however, had seen Forest Gate re-emerge as a highly desirable location which was why the house that Mumtaz's late husband Ahmed had bought back in the nineties was now worth almost a million pounds. Leonard Blatt, the Forest Gate landlord who had married Maria Peters, represented the old, broken-down district, and the company he had bequeathed to his wife still owned one of the biggest and scruffiest multiple-occupation houses that remained. Everyone had known Leonard; fewer people knew his famous wife.

'As soon as she decided to ditch her career, Maria just retreated behind the walls of her house,' Lee said.

'Does she have any children?'

Lee shook his head. 'No, neither she nor Leonard. I have no idea why. She's a very private lady and getting even what I needed to know out of her was no mean feat.'

'What did you have to get out of her?'

'Who she thinks might be watching her.'

'Oh, right.' That, of course, had to be one of the first questions that a private investigator asked a client like Maria. *Who do you think is watching you?* Sometimes clients had ideas, sometimes they didn't, sometimes they had a notion of who their tormentor might be but they wouldn't say. Facing up to a threat from someone the client may have loved or even still did love, was hard. But the question, as Mumtaz had come to see even in her few months with the agency, was one that, if answered, often bore fruit. Often the watcher, the stalker, the sender of spiteful e-mails and letters was exactly who the client feared it was.

'Maria's best guess is it's some nut-job fan,' Lee said. 'She was dead pretty when she was young and that combination of a lovely face and a foul mouth was potent. Men used to chuck themselves at her.'

'She's an attractive woman now.'

'Exactly, so now she's back on the circuit she fears that some of her old fans may have re-emerged. She even gave me a couple of names, but I've already discovered that one of them's dead. The others are old men.' He shrugged. 'I doubt that's a goer.'

'Why?'

'Whoever is stalking Maria is managing to evade the CCTV outside her house and her alarms,' he said. 'I may be wrong but I don't see some sixty-something obsessive fan being able to do that. What do you think, Mumtaz?'

Mumtaz thought about her short conversation with Maria Peters and found it to contain nothing of interest. But then she thought about how her eyes had looked as she had waited for Lee to return. In light of that she said, 'She's probably hiding something from you, Mr Arnold.'

II

It was as the tide went out that the water made that special noise. When it flowed over old pieces of glass, it sounded like wind chimes crossed with the noise that glass makes when it breaks and falls onto a pavement. There was something both soothing and sinister about it. Whenever Maria heard it, it reminded her of Len. He had been just five years old when the Nazis broke all the windows belonging to Jews back in his native Germany. By the time he was seven, he and his parents had left the country for ever. Len had stepped through the glass shards to an entirely different life. But now the tide was in and there was no tinkling, no stepping through glass. The stone steps known as Wapping Stairs were almost completely covered by gently lapping Thames water that, in the darkness, looked like a great channel of crude oil. Developers could put up as many swanky apartments on the side of the river as they liked, the Thames and its environs would always bear the scars of the ruin it had been back in Maria Peters' youth.

Most of Maria's family had worked either in or around the London Docks. Her dad had been a docker in the old Royal Group just south of Plaistow where they'd lived, while her mum had worked in the Tate and Lyle sugar factory at Silvertown. But her mum's parents had come from Wapping. Wapping Irish, the Fitzgerald family had made its living on the river as lightermen and also, long ago, as mudlarks. Maria had loved visiting her grandparents in Wapping. While her grandad drank pints of thick, black stout in the Town of Ramsgate at the head of Wapping Stairs, her grandmother had taken her and her sisters down on the mud to see what they could find. Clay pipes, fragments of Roman roof tiles, little shards of brightly coloured and patterned pottery, nails from Elizabethan galleons. Once they had found something terrible. There were always dead rats but this horror had been beyond that – a tiny foetus in the remains of a cardboard box. Later Maria had learned that it was probably the product of an illegal abortion. Her grandmother had taken it to her priest for a decent burial and he'd blessed it, passed incense across its ruined face and placed a tiny holy medal in its hands. The past could be a malignant country but Maria always felt safe sitting atop Wapping Stairs. Down on the mud was another matter – the river was a law unto itself – but on the Stairs all was safe and dry and solid. The Stairs were stable in a way that the water, the mud and the sky, that shifted and moved, could never be.

Although it was dark now, Maria looked up, aiming her gaze above and beyond the ranks of brightly lit apartment windows on the southern shore. Once the site of abandoned, echoing warehouses, she wondered if the ghosts of old dockers still moved unseen amongst the chichi pot plants and the flat-screen televisions of the rich banker generation that inhabited these places. Nothing, as she knew only too well at fifty years old, ever really disappeared. All you had to do was look in the right place, pound on the right door and you were right back where you started.

Maybe it was this thought that made all the hair on the back of Maria's neck stand up. A shadow, just light and very fleeting, passed over her slightly bowed back and she turned quickly to see who or what it was. But there was nothing to see and Maria accepted the possibility that it was her own thoughts that had spooked her. But in spite of that she was still glad that she'd engaged Mr Arnold's firm to watch her and her property. They were coming in at six the following morning to install cameras and microphones in the house, and someone would always be monitoring her from then onwards. It was going to be costly, but reassuring, even if the thought of it made her cringe. Maria had to know the truth, one way or another.

Back in the eighties, she'd attracted a lot of flack. Moral and religious groups didn't like her act and she was actually banned by the BBC at one point – there had even been threats. All a long time ago now and she'd told Lee Arnold about them. Not that they were relevant any more. Her act was different, or rather it was *getting* that way. Five months before, in some pub in New Cross, Alan had insisted that she use *all* the old stuff modified for a modern audience. And, although the crowd had howled with laughter, it had been tough. Too tough for her, and she'd collapsed. Afterwards, Alan had issued an ultimatum. 'Get fucking smutty, give in to your cruelty, or get another fucking manager!'

Maria looked at the water, the sky and the Stairs once again and knew that even in this, one of her favourite places, she was still trapped. She was trapped all the time, whatever she did, wherever she went. She took a tranquilliser tablet with no water and then walked back to her car and drove home.

'Up the 'ammers!'

Lee closed his front door, put his keys on the telephone table and stared the chattering mynah bird in the eyes. 'Who's the patron saint of West Ham, Chronus?'

'Bobby Moore! Bobby Moore!'

Lee took a packet of bird seed out of one pocket and a tin of oven cleaner out of the other. He went over to where the bird sat on a perch connected to a feeding hopper and poured some seed for him. Chronus dipped his head into the hopper to feed while Lee rubbed his blue black back. Then, as quickly as he'd started, he stopped and said, 'That oven won't clean itself.'

The bird continued to feed while Lee went into the kitchen and began to remove all the racks from inside his electric oven. Had Chronus been able to apprehend such things, he would have wondered why Lee was again cleaning an oven he'd scrubbed only seven days before. Lee walked from the kitchen to his bedroom where he changed into a tatty pair of jogging bottoms and an old paint-spattered T-shirt. He then sprayed the empty oven with the cleaner and went into the living room to watch the television. The whole flat reeked of the harsh, comforting smell of ammonia.

The news was on and it was full of the sodding Olympics. Not quite eighteen months away, London 2012 was joyfully dominating much of the news while, in reality, making life for people who either lived near the site or wanted to move through it, difficult. Every day, or so it seemed, public routes around the site changed, and with winter still coldly entrenched, bringing with it mists from the river as well as concentrating the pollution from cars and factories, a hint of old London smog could now be discerned over the city from time to time. Around the still only partly formed Olympic site this lent an even more diffuse quality to the light. Lee didn't know from one day to the next how to drive around there. It was a good job that Maria Peters, who apparently attended a church just beyond the site up at Hackney Wick, was well accustomed to such things. Lee or Neil West, the freelancer he'd engaged to work with him on the case, were going to have to follow her. It was a bit weird to think about Maria Peters in church. Her act had always taken the piss out of religion and Lee wondered if she'd 'found' God. The most unlikely people seemed to.

Chronus, having had his fill of seed began to sing 'I'm Forever Blowing Bubbles'. It almost completely drowned out the news and made Lee regret, not for the first time, that he'd indoctrinated the bird so thoroughly in West Ham United chants and songs. It had been to impress Jodie, except that now she was 'off' West Ham and 'into' Man United and whenever she came to stay the bird just got on her nerves. Whenever Chronus went into his West Ham routine she'd yell at Lee, 'Can't you make him say nothing else? God, Dad, West Ham are so lame!'

According to her mother, Jodie had ambitions to be a Manchester United WAG. It was a long way from wanting to be a vet, which had been her choice of career all the way from primary school until she'd hit fourteen. Then, overnight or so it seemed, all her ambition had melted into demands for posh make-up, ridiculous handbags and a sunbed. Lee blamed his ex; silly cow spent most of her time chasing after blokes who looked like bit-part players from *EastEnders*. What kind of a role model was that for a young girl?

His landline rang. Only a very few people had that number so he picked it up quickly, looked at its LCD screen and said, 'Hello, Mum.'

His mother's thick, phlegmy voice coughed at him. 'Lee, sweetheart, it's our Roy, he's done it again. Can you come?'

Lee's eyes flicked over towards the door into the kitchen. He breathed in the oven cleaner ammonia and frowned, then he said, 'Course. Is he conscious?'

'Oh, yes,' his mother said, 'he's conscious all right. Conscious and locked in the khazi.'

'All right. I'll be over.'

'Thanks, darling.'

Lee ended the call and then threw the phone onto the coffee table.

He knew that he should phone Mrs Blatt and tell her about it, but he didn't like to. Leonard, Mr Blatt, had been one thing, but his widow, 'Mrs' as Martin liked to call her, was quite another. Why Len'd ever married her, Martin couldn't fathom; there'd been loads of nice Jewish women and girls who would have been delighted to marry Len Blatt over the years. Then he goes and marries some bloody Wapping Irish bird, some terrible comedian who thought it was big, clever and funny to say the c-word every five seconds. Martin had never got it – it had just been smut. Smut admittedly said by a very pretty girl with legs up to her armpits, but smut nonetheless.

Martin looked back down at the dormant gas fire lurking uselessly against his chimney breast. Bloody thing had to be from the nineteen seventies. When Len was alive he'd always sent some old frummer who could do a bit of DIY round to fix it. But now both Len and the frummer were dead and Mrs used all sorts of types, usually young and lairy. And they never did anything properly.

Not that he could blame Mrs Blatt for everything – Len had been no saint. Not only had he sold the houses either side to Pakis but all the rooms in number 35, except Martin's, were let out to them too. Men in long white robes with overcoats on top and women with their faces covered looking like long, black tubes, and there were babies everywhere. Depending upon who was in and who was out at any one time it was sometimes impossible to sleep, and then there was that wailing music they all liked, and the praying. The house on the left, the one where a load of old frummers used to live in what Len always said was a 'care home' now belonged to some long-bearded Muslim religious type and his family. Men in skullcaps and sandals were always in and out and there was Arabic writing on a square green plate on the front door. A prayer, he imagined, a Muslim mezuzah.

As the last of the old tenants, Len could have left Martin something in his will; he'd been in number 35 for decades, he must've bought the bloody flat many times over. But now Len was dead and one of the older Pakis had told him that Mrs wanted to sell up 35 and have done with having tenants altogether. Now that her career was up and running again she could do whatever she liked. Cow. Where was he supposed to go at his time of life if she did that? Ever since he'd heard the rumour, Martin had been down there many times, to confront her. Not that he had. He'd just stood outside that great big gaff of Len's and he'd stared. Oh, she'd been in there, Mrs with her foul mouth and her tits like Marilyn Monroe. Years ago he'd looked over the garden wall and seen her sunbathing naked on the lawn. He remembered she'd had no pubes and that had been exciting. He tried not to think about that when he gave her the rent.

The smell of frying onions followed by the sharp complex aromas of spice alerted Martin to the fact that people were cooking. It was nearly eleven o'clock. What was it with these people and cooking in the middle of the night? And yet Martin knew full well that it didn't have to be that way – the family who lived in the really big house on the right were Pakis too but they were very different. The woman covered her head but not her face and she always wore very smart, very Western clothes. Her husband, now dead, victim of an horrific knife attack so the papers had said, had been very Western too. They all spoke English and the daughter – the man's child, not the woman's – was just like every other teenager who liked fashion and was always plugged into one of those pod music things. She was very pretty, that girl. Martin liked that family. But then they, unlike all the babbling foreign sorts he had to live with, had money.

Even now that she was working, the bills were still a problem.

'Shazia!' She called from the kitchen into the drawing room where the girl was watching TV.

'Yeah?'

She was watching some stupid thing like *Hollyoaks* or *The Only Way is Essex*, some mind-numbing trash about young people having everything they wanted including lots of sex. Kids on such programmes were always glued to their mobile phones.

'Your phone bill is over seventy pounds,' Mumtaz said. 'That's over three times what mine cost.'

Shazia didn't reply. The TV banged on inanely and Mumtaz imagined the girl making a big 'W' with her fingers at her. 'Whatever!' Mumtaz hated that word – it was so casual, so dismissive. Mumtaz went back to perusing the bills on the kitchen table. Mobile phone bills came to ninety pounds, landline was a hundred and two, the gas bill was so huge she hardly dared look at it. Winter was still very much with them and so they had to have the heating on almost all the time when they were indoors. Mumtaz would have to switch radiators off in rooms they didn't use, and there were a lot of those now. The house was dominated by unused rooms full of overstuffed sofas, flat-screen TVs and onyx chess sets, which she'd have to get around to selling at some point.

'Amma, I'm eating the chocolate in the fridge.'

Shazia had known her real mother and at first she'd failed to address Mumtaz by any sort of title whatsoever. Now she called her 'Amma', Mum, and it softened Mumtaz's heart. But then it was designed to.

'Say please,' Mumtaz reminded her.

'*Please*,' she heard Shazia parrot.

The sound of oversized flip-flops flapping across the floor heralded the entrance of her stepdaughter. Tall, slim and sporting a very stylish asymmetric haircut, Shazia Hakim was an attractively gamine girl of sixteen. Wrapped up in a purple fleece blanket, it was impossible to see the vaguely Gothic clothes underneath; the short black and purple ruffle dress, the fashionable ripped up fishnet tights. Long hands topped off with slim, multicoloured fingernails briefly let go of the blanket and dived into the refrigerator.

'Yummy,' she said as she pushed a big chocolate truffle into her mouth.

Mumtaz looked up. 'Go easy on the chocs though, Shazia,' she said. 'Another tight month.'

The girl pulled a face. 'Oh my God, I thought it was all right now you're working,' she said.

'But it took me time to get a job. I have a lot of ground

35

to make up.' She didn't talk to Shazia about the debts; she hadn't told anyone about their full extent. 'I think we'll have to have fewer chocolates and more lentils.'

Shazia pulled another face.

'And I'm going to switch some of the radiators off and close up bedrooms. We only need two.'

Shazia said, 'Grim,' and then took another truffle from the fridge and went back to the drawing room.

It was ridiculous even trying to run such a vast house on not much more than minimum wage. But the job at the Arnold Agency had been the only one she had been able to get. Not that that was strictly true. Mumtaz could easily have gone back to her old job in her father's shop, working for her brothers, but the prospect of becoming a private detective had been so – tantalising.

She'd been so low when she saw that carefully printed little ad for a 'Trainee Security Operative – some Secretarial Duties' in the window of George the barber's. In the previous week, she'd had a lot of knock-backs, including one from a firm of solicitors who, she suspected, found her far too Muslim, and a shop on the Romford Road who considered her far too Western. By the time she'd arrived on Green Street, she'd all but given up hope. Quite why, apart from the fact that she had a sort of relevant degree, a white ex-police detective like Lee Arnold had taken her on she still didn't really know. As a Muslim woman who covered her head she wasn't the most obvious choice for

36

a potential private detective, but he'd taken her anyway and that was that. Maybe it was because she was cheap? Maybe it was because he found her attractive? But Mumtaz dismissed that thought immediately – that was silly. Why would he?

Shazia went up to bed at eleven thirty, leaving Mumtaz alone in the silent kitchen with the bills. She could only pay some of them and so it was no use just staring at the ones she couldn't even begin to tackle. It was just fortunate that Ahmed's ancient mother back in Bangladesh sent money to pay for Shazia's school fees. Had Mumtaz had to find the cash for that too, she would have been sunk. She wrote a cheque out to BT for the landline and put it in its envelope with the payment slip, then she got up and switched out the kitchen spotlights. But before she went up to her bedroom, Mumtaz walked over to the back door and looked out into the garden. Since Ahmed's death it had really gone to pot. No more gardener, no more Mercedes Benz on the drive, no more gold and silver and bright shiny bangles now that Ahmed had gone.

A fat, fast-food-stuffed urban fox ambled past the silent water feature in the middle of the lawn and made a loud coughing noise. They were everywhere. They probably even got into Maria Peters' no doubt very beautiful garden. Maria Peters, her client, the one that Lee Arnold would allow her to practice on. Just the thought of it made something inside her fizz with excitement. Then she thought,

37

Maybe Maria Peters is just seeing a fox? Maybe her fear is causing her to make that into a man? But even so, why was she afraid? Why was her fear making her hallucinate what wasn't there? To make a man out of a small, feral animal was quite a feat.

III

'I know, Paul, I know,' Maria said. Looking out of the front room window, she could see Alan Myers' car pulling up outside. It made her face crease with anxiety.

'I don't think that going back to what you did before all the time is good for you,' Pastor Paul Grint, the person on the other end of the phone, said. 'Not if you think about it in terms of where you want to be with God.'

'I know.'

'I don't want to lay a load of guilt on you, Maria,' Pastor Grint said. 'But you've some making up to do, you know.'

'Because of my act?'

'I guess. You know your own sins better than I do.'

She didn't want to hurt God, but she wasn't keen on hurting Alan either.

'Mocking God and blaspheming rots the soul, Maria,' Grint said. 'God is love and he forgives – he's a fantastic guy, which is why we love him, but we have to try and be better people ourselves.'

Maria watched Alan Myers get out of his car and begin

to walk up her drive. Soon he'd be in her house, telling her to do the exact opposite of what Pastor Grint was saying.

'But Paul,' Maria said, 'I have to do my old act tonight, it's what I've been contracted to do.'

She heard him sigh. 'Well, if you have to . . .'

'I—'

'Maria, just remember that God, though all great and powerful, can be hurt by humanity. You don't want to hurt the King of the Universe, do you?'

The front doorbell rang and Maria had to say 'goodbye' quickly and put the phone down.

When Lee called her later on that day, Maria Peters claimed to have had no idea about who was watching over her. All the surveillance devices were in place and Neil West – a retiree from Lee's old Met Police days, who now worked freelance – was monitoring them. He told Lee nothing untoward had happened so far. But then most of the sightings of the strange figure or man happened to Maria at night and by that time Lee would have taken over.

'A middle-aged bloke with red hair went in at ten thirty,' Neil told Lee. 'Alan Myers, Miss Peters' manager.'

'Yeah.' Lee scanned the list of people and appointments that Maria Peters had e-mailed to him the previous evening. He was still worn out – hauling his brother, Roy, out of their mother's toilet had been no mean feat, especially with Roy wielding an almost full bottle of vodka. Then, after that, there had been all the usual abuse. 'Miss Peters has a gig tonight at the Comedy Ringside in Camden.'

Neil laughed. 'You looking forward to it?'

Lee shrugged. 'A bit.' Enthusiasm for anything amongst coppers of a certain age could be misconstrued as weakness or even effeminacy.

'You know Myers wants her to get ruder,' Neil said. 'They had a little bit of a barney about it in her kitchen.'

'She didn't want to do it?'

'She wants to get cleaner apparently,' Neil said. 'Got no idea why. Fuck, shit and bollocks were like her catchphrases, weren't they?'

Lee looked across the office at Mumtaz who was carrying some women's magazines to the table in the reception area. Maybe Maria Peters' churchgoing was really serious? 'Yeah, and the rest,' he said. 'She's happy though.'

'Is she?'

'With us and what we've put in place. She's unaware, so she says, about where you're hiding your ugly mug, which is great.'

Neil laughed. 'Still the invisible man, boss.'

'Still the invisible man.' Lee cut the connection and replaced the phone on its stand.

'Going well?' Mumtaz asked.

'Neil was a good copper,' Lee said. 'Always knew how to keep a low profile.'

Mumtaz returned to her desk. 'You know, Mr Arnold, I was thinking about our client for a while last night.'

'Oh?' Where once he would have smoked a cigarette in the office he just fiddled with a pen instead. Hurrah, or not, for anti-smoking legislation.

'As you know, my house is next door to the multiple-occupancy place that she owns, and only two streets away from where she lives.'

'Yep.'

Mumtaz said, 'Last night I saw a fox in my garden. I expect you get them where you live too.'

'Sometimes.'

'It's just a thought, but if a person is anxious or maybe anticipating trouble of some sort, sometimes they can see things that aren't actually there. I don't mean they experience what we think of as actual hallucinations, not exactly. But movement in a garden, especially in the half light of dusk, can transform a creature, like maybe a fox, into something far more sinister and threatening.'

'Mmm.' Lee looked unsure. 'You think?'

'I know. The classic example happens with shadows. If you're in a house at night with another person, a shadow is a shadow, usually, but if you're alone and maybe tense because you're alone, a shadow can become a person with malicious intent, a ghost or even a monster.'

'Doesn't the person have to be imaginative or . . .'

'Suggestible rather than imaginative,' Mumtaz said. 'The two are not the same. Creative people can be suggestible, but so can those who are not imaginative. There's just rather more chance of someone with an active imagination spontaneously having an experience of this sort. I'm always amazed at what the mind can do. The eyes see one thing while the brain interprets that as something quite other.'

'A fox into a man?'

'At night all sorts of things are threatening, including foxes and men. Our brains process information from our environment and we don't even know it's happening, and that is especially the case if a person is under stress or experiencing anxiety. As I've said before, I feel Miss Peters may not be telling us the whole story of her situation.'

'But she's asked for our help. Why hold stuff back?'

'I don't know. I don't even know if I'm right, it's just a feeling.'

Mumtaz turned her attention to her poor, scarred computer screen, but Lee continued to watch her. Surely theories of the mind and religion had to be mutually exclusive, didn't they? Especially amongst Muslims. If such a thing could be said to exist, his old mum, Rose, was hard line C. of E., from what some called the High Church, some the Anglo-Catholic wing; Rose was all about original sin, Adam and Eve, God-given rights, anti-abortion

43

and she read the *Daily Mail*. Muslims, if anything, were even more religiously conservative. If God made man, how could his brain do such crazy things all on its own? Unless of course that brain was possessed in some way. A vision of Mumtaz waving her arms about over Maria Peters' head in an act of exorcism came and then, thankfully, went from his mind.

'Of course some of our senses evoke unlooked-for responses in us more easily than others,' Mumtaz said without looking away from her computer. 'For instance, can you smell that cumin coming from the samosa stall down on the street? I can and it's making me hungry *and* I've only just eaten.' Then she looked up and smiled. 'If I smell something even approaching curry I start to salivate.'

'Now look, love, you've a whole new generation of trendy Camden wonks out there, so give it all you've got.'

Maria Peters frowned. 'Alan, these kids are not like the kids back in the eighties,' she said. 'These are affluent, clean living, environmental activists . . .'

'And hippies too, there've always been hippies.' Alan Myers was, not for the first time that day, getting a little tired of his artist's objections. Either she wanted to revive her career or she didn't. And if she didn't, she could clean up her act as much as she wanted – but without him.

A tiny cupboard-like space painted dark red constituted

the Comedy Ringside's Green Room. Squashed in with a bloke who took the piss out of his own Parkinsonian symptoms, a woman with a stuffed Yorkshire terrier on her head, Maria and that interfering, churchy friend of hers, it did not do a lot for Alan's nerves.

'You can't bomb out again, Maria,' he said. 'Not like New Cross.'

'They were a much older crowd there, Alan. They really wanted the old stuff. I'm not sure about these kids . . .'

'You don't have to go on,' the friend said.

Alan felt his whole face explode with heat. 'Yes, she *does*.' The girl with the dog on her head was looking and so he lowered his voice. 'She's contracted to do so *and* they want all the old stuff.'

'Not if she's ill, she isn't. She has collapsed—'

Alan leaned across Maria's body and hissed at her tiny, boring friend. 'But she isn't ill! She had tests! She won't collapse!' He wanted to add in all sorts of abuse about how the woman, Betty Muller, looked a damn sight nearer the grave than his tall, beautiful client. But he held onto that. Some of the friends that Maria had these days – mostly religious sorts – were very odd, but she liked them. For some reason.

Maria put her hand on Betty's arm. 'I have to go on,' she said. 'Alan's quite right, I can't let people down. It wouldn't be right.'

Betty didn't look happy. But then Alan was beginning

to wonder whether she'd come along less to support Maria than to pander to her desire to radically change her act. It had, Alan thought, to be a noughties thing, this PC, religious, hemp skirts and saving-trees-from-McDonald's trend. The thing was that although young people were into all that, young people who went to comedy clubs were into what young people had always been into – sex, drugs, rock and roll, fags, booze and lots of swearing too. They'd come to see the Maria Peters who said 'cunt', not the Maria Peters who told nice little stories about mildly amusing antics performed by rather sprightly little old ladies. This was, after all, Camden, not bloody Midsomer Bumhole. 'Maria, love,' Alan said. 'The omens are marvellous. I've made sure. No peacock feathers in the place, no mention of the Scottish Play, everyone talking about "breaking a leg".'

Yes, the old theatrical superstitions were all covered, but still Maria had to concentrate to make her mouth smile.

Lee put an arm around the woman in the sharp nineteen eighties-style suit and whispered in her ear, 'Business or pleasure?'

Half the audience for the carefully ironically titled *Wot Larks!* – the comedy showcase at the Camden Ringside – were out on the pavement swigging bottled beer and smoking fags and other things. Detective Inspector Violet

Collins was just one of them. She turned her heavily made-up, heavily lined face towards Lee Arnold and said, 'I could ask the same of you.'

He smiled, kissed her on the cheek and then said, 'Ah, couldn't do that, Vi. If I told you what I was up to I'd have to kill you.'

She nodded her head. 'Likewise,' she said. 'But without the murder. We're the good guys, remember? The cowboys with the white hats.'

'So what does that make me?'

She took his arm and led him across the cobbles towards the wall overlooking the canal. It was dingy, a bit foggy and cold, but Vi still had a way to go before she got enough nicotine in her system to be able to get through the show. She leaned against the wall and lit up yet again. 'A private dick?' she smiled. 'Grey hat? Brown? Where d'you think you lot come in the moral colour code of the universe?'

Lee narrowed his eyes. 'Come on, Vi,' he said, 'don't keep a fella in suspense – how old is he and is he Moroccan or Tunisian?'

Vi Collins pursed her thin, red, wrinkled lips. 'Oh, no totty tonight,' she said. 'I've come to see our local girl. Why else would I drag my arse up to Camden?'

'Maria Peters?'

'Remember her from the old Comedy Store,' she said. 'Now that was a comic that was going at my speed.'

'She could swear like a sailor.'

'Still can – I hope.'

A couple of young girls walked past dressed in nineteen fifties-style dresses with lots of net petticoats underneath, all made up to the nines and sucking suggestively on lollies. As they walked past, Vi muttered, 'So much for the Women's Movement.'

'Some people think it's just a modern form of feminism,' Lee said with a smile on his face. He hadn't worked with Vi for over five years but he still knew how to wind her up.

'What? All these prats who reckon that these girls getting bling out of thick footballers are some sort of noble feminist army? Sisters with breast implants doing it for themselves?' Vi sucked hard on her fag and pulled a face. 'Do me a fucking favour.'

Lee laughed. 'Oh, Vi, you are such an easy mark.'

She laughed. 'And you're a cheeky sod.'

He put a hand out, ready to curl around her waist again, but then thought better of it and just lit up a fag. Vi had been his colleague, his best mate at the Forest Gate station and, for just one drunken night, New Year's Eve 1999, his lover. His lover from another century.

'So if you've come to see Maria Peters, you expecting a car crash?' Lee asked.

'You mean like New Cross? I hope not,' Vi said. 'Just collapsed apparently. Christ knows why.'

Maria had told Lee that she'd fainted during the New Cross gig, in part because of the stalking. That made sense;

one of the consequences of stalking was that the victim slowly but surely lost confidence in themselves, stopped eating, got sick. But he wasn't about to share that with Vi. Maria had come to a *private* detective and that was what she was getting.

Vi said, 'Why you here, then? Thought you spent most of your time with your parrot.'

'Mynah bird,' Lee corrected.

'Whatever.'

'You should know. Anyway, maybe I'm on the pull too,' he said with a twinkle in his eye.

Vi narrowed her eyes. 'I'm not on the pull,' she said. 'I'm here with our Ronnie. Don't be a funny bugger, Arnold, you know I'm a strictly holiday romance girl these days.'

'Up for a bit of Moroccan.'

Vi looked about her anxiously. 'Don't fucking say that! Ronnie don't know about any of that!'

'I bet he does,' Lee said.

'Oh, fuck off.' Vi laughed. Lee Arnold was a strange but sexy fella and she still carried a torch for him from way back in the twentieth century. 'Anyway, who you with then? On your Jack as usual?'

'Unless you want me to join you and your son, Vi . . .'

'Not a good idea.' Then she frowned. 'You really on your Jack Jones, Arnold?'

His face was open and innocent. It was a face Vi knew very well. 'What are you up to, Lee?'

'Having a night out at a comedy club, Vi. What's the matter with that? Am I not allowed entertainment or something?'

Vi rocked back on her high, spiky heels and said, 'No, you do what you like, love. But I know you, remember? And the Lee Arnold I know don't go anywhere just to entertain hisself. You, you little bugger, are here for a reason.'

IV

Catholic youth camp in Epping Forest – it was like a cross between a David Attenborough documentary and a porn fest for paedos. The life cycle of the centipede as witnessed on the front of Father Fernandez's cassock. Each tent contained at least ten plaster saints with terrible, suffering eyes which, if you put your hands inside your sleeping bag, would start flashing an eerie blue light until Father Richards'd come in and spank you till he could take no more. Masturbation alarm systems – what a great idea that was! Comedians need gimmicks. Ken Dodd has his tickling stick, I have a statue of St Augustine which flashes blue and plays the theme from The Omen *every time I come.*

Out in the audience, someone shouts, *Which isn't very often!* There's laughter.

Ah, Maria Peters says, *the gentle sound of spotty youth! One mention of masturbation and all the boys start to get nervous.* People laugh. *So Catholic Youth Camp was the first occasion I'd ever spent time away from home. Let's face it, I come from Plaistow, it was the first time I'd ever seen grass. I didn't know what the fuck it was. Or trees. As soon as the tents were put up, I went inside and I stayed there.*

Someone in the audience yells, *What? Your priest want a blow job, did he?* Maria laughs.

No. Actually, Father Fernandez, God rest his soul, wanted to take me up the arse. There's laughter but also a few gasps of shock too. *Not real sex, is it? Can't get pregnant doing the back door boogie, can you? Or can you?* Maria's face changes, her smile drops a little. She forces a laugh. *Mind you, bit of a dated view these days, isn't it. We're all down with sodomy now, aren't we?* The whole place becomes suddenly and strangely silent. *Can't say that anything's wrong any more, can we? However weird.*

Someone in the audience yells, *Fuck you, bitch!*

Maria's face twists with bitterness. *Not sodomy, not sado-masochism, not priests fiddling with children! It's all just a laugh, or your 'right' to do, because it makes you happy . . .* A sob brings her diatribe to a close and she runs off the stage, crying.

'You have to help me out here, Maria,' Lee said. 'I can't assist you unless you're a hundred per cent honest with me.' He passed her the glass of brandy she'd asked for and then sat down. They were in the now empty Green Room of the Comedy Ringside, the other performers, the audience, Betty Muller and Alan Myers having left over an hour ago. Maria took the brandy and downed it in one. She didn't so much as wince.

'I have to be honest,' Lee continued, 'I know you're holding back on me about something.' He failed to mention that had actually been Mumtaz's notion. 'So I'm sorry but I just don't buy that you're getting this upset about a *possible* invasion of your privacy just *glimpsed* out the corner of your eye. You can't concentrate and your career's going down the pan and you're turning on your audience!'

'I know.' She looked across at him with tears in her eyes. 'I know.'

Alan Myers had nearly lost his mind. He'd been the first one she'd bowled into when she ran off the stage. *You have one more chance and that's it!* he'd growled at her. *Do this to me again and I'll fucking finish you, darling!* Betty had been sympathetic but with an element of *I told you so* and so Maria had had to send her away. She'd offered to stay, of course, because she was a true friend but . . .

'I have to know about any threats,' Lee said. 'Real threats, not just some memory of some randy fan from 1989.'

'I haven't had any actual threats at all,' she said. 'I used to get them years ago.'

'Who from?'

'I told you. But then there were also people who thought I should be censored,' Maria said. 'Mary Whitehouse types, religious people. I offended everybody.'

'You still do, or you try to. That's still the point of the act, isn't it?'

She looked down. 'Yes.'

'So, you getting direct threats now, Maria, or what?'

'No! But I might do after tonight!'

He moved in so that he could see her face. She was only a few years older than him and she was lovely. There was something of the Katharine Hepburn about her. Lee loved the old movie stars, they were so much more glamorous than modern people. But she still wasn't telling him everything. Lee had been a good, instinctive copper and that hadn't changed. 'So if you're not getting threats, then what is going on? Why are you intimidating your crowd? Why are you alienating your audience?'

She looked into his eyes.

'Is it simply your fear? About what you're experiencing at home?' He didn't use the word 'imagine' or talk about what she 'thought' she might be seeing. 'That stuff you do about priests, is that true? Is it?'

She said nothing. Lee, helpless, shrugged.

And then she said, as if it were the most obvious explanation in the world, 'I've found God.'

'You go to church, I know,' Lee said. 'So do lots of people.'

Maria shook her head impatiently. 'No,' she said, 'I don't *just* go to church. As you say, a lot of people do that, paedophile priests do that. I'm not talking about Catholicism. No, I am being born again. I've committed to take Jesus into my life. I've found God and I know that he loves me. I also know that he wants what is best for me, and it isn't this act.'

*   *   *

'These fundamentalist chaps dishonour God.'

Baharat was holding forth again, distressed by the ten o'clock news. Some Muslim boys had been arrested in Manchester for apparently plotting to blow up a church.

'They think they're doing jihad.' Baharat shrugged his shoulders. 'What do silly bloody kids from Manchester know of jihad? Like those silly bloody buggers meeting at the café, talking nonsense.'

Sumita pulled her sari down across her shoulders and carried on folding the ironing. Ranting in English was one of her husband's very few pleasures and so she just let him get on with it.

'I mean, what do these sods think that the Brits will do now, eh? Islamophobia is what that character from the Muslim Council of Britain calls it. Islamophobia! But who can blame them? They see these silly buggers and their hatred and of course they think we're all the same!'

The television was turned up so loudly, Sumita could hardly hear herself think. Baharat was over seventy now and as deaf as a post. He shouted, always in English. His father, even though he'd never left Dhaka in his life, had always believed that English was 'civilised'. Sumita's grasp of it was at best adequate.

'They should hang them,' Baharat continued. 'That ridiculous bugger in the café and those boys he has with him too. Talking about beating up the girls who don't cover their heads. Modesty is what a Muslim woman should display, whether her head is covered or not. That is a choice. We are not fanatics in this society!'

Baharat made her tired, but Sumita couldn't charge him with hypocrisy, not exactly. Their only daughter, Mumtaz, had never been obliged to cover her head by her father. Her brothers had gone through a phase of thinking that this was shameful, but Baharat, as usual, had had the final say on the matter. 'If the girl wants to cover, then that is down to her,' he'd said. 'If she doesn't, that is her business too.' But he *had* kept her close. Working in the shop until she married that man that Sumita had never liked. She'd admired him, she'd wanted her daughter to marry him, but . . . A man with Savile Row suits, a Rolex on his wrist and perfume in his dyed black hair. She'd never liked Ahmed Hakim. He'd *made* Mumtaz cover her head.

'They want to close that café down, the police,' Baharat said. 'Bangla Town, it calls itself. Huh! A dishonour to the home country. And that ridiculous sod sitting in there all day telling silly boys he's some sort of sheikh. The man pours pure poison into people's ears. It's not right! It's not moral! It's not Islamic!'

He'd been stabbed, Ahmed Hakim. In front of her daughter. Only then had they discovered that all the wealth he'd dazzled Baharat with had been just so much smoke. Now Mumtaz had some job, now she made it her business to look after her husband's child. Alone. Far away from Brick Lane in that big, lonely house in Forest Gate. Sumita missed her so much she could feel her heart bleeding sometimes in her chest.

Baharat looked away from the television set and rolled himself a cigarette. He was a good Muslim who prayed five times a day, didn't eat pork, didn't drink, but he did smoke and he had a cough that was persistent and impressively loud. Sumita wished he wouldn't smoke, but then she also wished he'd give up going out six and a half days a week, and that wasn't happening either.

Baharat Huq had emigrated to London in the early nineteen sixties. He'd arrived with one suitcase from a country that was then called East Pakistan. He'd worked for an old Jewish man who sold women's clothes on Petticoat Lane Market and had lived with a group of other young East Pakistani men in a crumbling Huguenot house in Princelet Street, Spitalfields. It had been little more than a squat, really, and when Baharat's father had decided that it was time that he got married, he'd had to find somewhere more suitable double quick. Baharat and Sumita began their married lives in 1970 in one room above a fish and chip shop on Brick Lane. Tariq their eldest child had been born there but by the time they had their second son Abdul, and daughter Mumtaz, they lived in the house on Hanbury Street that they now owned. As the years had progressed, Baharat's idea that what Spitalfields needed more than anything was a shop that sold Islamic ephemera, had paid off. A lot of people had since emigrated from what by then was Bangladesh and they wanted prayer rugs, Qur'ans and tasbeeh beads. Baharat had been the first ever trader in the Brick Lane area to successfully import boxes for storing the Holy Qur'an in the shape of the Sacred Ka'aaba in Mecca, which had made him quite the famous chap in the community. And when his clever daughter had married an apparently wealthy and influential local businessman, Baharat felt that he'd made it. His dream of British streets paved with gold had, seemingly, come true.

But it had been an illusion. First had come the 7 July London bombings, Islamophobia as some called it, and then Mumtaz's husband had been murdered, leaving her his highly Westernised, privately educated daughter and a legacy of debt so enormous Baharat couldn't afford to even think about tackling. Ahmed Hakim had not been the man that Baharat thought he was. As if reading his wife's gloomy thoughts, he said, 'You know, I don't know which is worse: a misguided bugger who kills in the name of God or a liar who drinks and eats pork and has a gangsterly life.'

Sumita shrugged. 'Who can say?' she replied in Bengali. 'I just wish that our daughter would come home. That child of her husband should be sent back to his family in Sylhet. Then Mumtaz could remarry. There is no shame in widowhood.'

But Baharat did not reply. He looked back at the television and then began ranting about the economy. He knew as well as Sumita that there was no point in even talking about trying to make their daughter do something that she didn't feel right about. Not now.

Lee Arnold had not understood. He hadn't said anything, he was too professional for that, but Maria *knew*. Mr Arnold didn't believe in God any more than most of the people she came across. He was an ex-copper – not big on God, ex-coppers. Like most stand-ups really. Like Maria as she used to be.

Back in the day, she'd based a whole one and a half hour one-woman show around religion, or 'your invisible friends who are so much fun to be with!', as she'd put it. But then she'd been young and on coke and she hadn't even met Len, much less lost him. The isolation she'd felt after Len died had almost destroyed her, and her mother's dark Catholicism, the religion she herself had once loved, hadn't helped. Still praying to saints who had been roasted on gridirons, venerating relics – bones, bodies, beads, the words of discredited priests. She'd gone back on the circuit, not for the money but for the distraction. Then, suddenly, when she wasn't looking, Jesus had come into her life. Initially via leaflets through her door, then a booklet, picked up and read in the doctor's surgery; so Maria discovered the Chapel of the Holy Pentecostal Fire. And for the first time ever, she'd gone to a *real* church, a proper place of worship. Like Len, out of the blue, a man had arrived to save her – Jesus.

Lee, the man who was watching her, who believed that Jesus was a myth, looked after her because she paid him well. At massive expense he'd fitted cameras and microphones all over the house, and yet he probably thought that what she was seeing out of the corners of her eyes wasn't real. She'd asked him about evil and whether or not he believed in it, but he'd seemed unsure. All he would say was that he'd seen some things in his life that people might describe as evil. He was an atheist, what did she expect? Part of her brain, to her shame, was still in that world too.

It was the wee hours of the morning and Maria stood in her darkened living room and idly fingered one of her many ceramic cat ornaments. In spite of light pollution from the London monster that engulfed her, the sky was as black as a sky could get. Although illuminated by security lights, the garden was frigid with both lack of movement and with the onset of yet another bone-grinding cold snap. Eerie featherings of frost lightly touched the blades of her well-cut grass and not even a distant cough from a sick urban fox disturbed the night-time peace.

But Maria knew that he, she, *it* was out there somewhere. She could feel the tingling knowledge of it at the base of her skull. If she turned around suddenly and quickly she knew with her whole being that she'd see who or what was charting her slightest move, every variation in facial expression. She wanted to know what it was. That was why Lee Arnold and his colleagues were working for her. But then again she didn't want to know because deep down at the bottom of her soul just the thought of having that knowledge produced an urge to harm herself.

V

Words could reach right down into your core with or without your understanding. It had been the spikiness, the furious shape of the graffiti letters that had attracted Mumtaz first. What was being said only became apparent as she drew closer. *Filthy homosexuals get out* it read, and then a warning: *Allah will smite you*. People appeared not to notice it. But it made Mumtaz want to howl. She loved going back to her parents' house in Spitalfields but there was a dark side to it always and it wasn't just because of the odd religious nutter stalking the streets around Brick Lane.

Before the area became known as Bangla Town, Spitalfields had been home to generations of Jewish refugees. Their synagogues and ritual baths still appeared like shades from the past in back streets all over town. The Brick Lane mosque had even been a synagogue once and some people claimed that you could still occasion-ally catch a whiff of the smell of the kosher wine they had once stored in the basement. The Jews had co-existed with their Christian neighbours and some still remained.

They'd been grateful for the shelter from pogroms and oppression that London had given them. But there were written words in Spitalfields that indicated that this safe haven had come at a price. As Mumtaz passed in front of the whiteness of the great Christ Church on Commercial Street she recalled them.

She'd only been nine at the time and together with other children from her school she'd appeared in a musical concert at the church as part of the Spitalfields Festival. Their teachers had led them up the steps and into a sort of antechamber in front of the actual church itself where there had been some stone tablets high up on the walls with wordy dedications to people active in the 'Christian Hebrew' movement. Whether it was the possible forced conversions of Jews to Christianity, or the unfamiliar look of the few phrases in Hebrew written at the bottom of these tablets that had caused Mumtaz to shiver and sweat, she didn't know. But every time she'd been back, those tablets had made her feel exactly the same. Even only half noticed, their baleful presence was evident in the way she walked and in the pounding of her heart. To some extent the Jews had been under the cosh in this place even though they, like her own people, had been outwardly tolerated.

She didn't go straight to her parents' house, but stopped off at the other end of Hanbury Street and looked in the condensation-drenched windows of the Royal Raj Cafe (est.

63

1976). Predictably, her father was chewing the fat and drinking tea with another old, and remarkably pale-looking, man. Even though he went out every day, her father only worked in the shop when it suited him; Mumtaz's brothers ran things now.

'Hello, Abba.'

He looked up and smiled at her. Baharat's two sons had always honoured their father and did as they were told, but he knew that they only paid lip service to him. Mumtaz, however challenging she was, was always honest and Baharat liked that. He clearly and very obviously practised favouritism.

'Mumtaz!' he beamed. Then turning to his companion he said, 'Mr Choudhury, this is my daughter. She has a degree in psychology from London University. You know she was in the same set as the famous stage illusionist, Mark Solomons.'

The other man, who Mumtaz didn't know, looked impressed. She resisted the urge she always got at times like this to add that upon graduation her father had very passively aggressively made sure that she nevertheless didn't get to use her precious degree. She similarly failed to allude to the fact that she had also had a massive crush on magician Mark Solomons, a Jew.

Mr Choudhury said, 'It is a pleasure to meet you.'

'Mr Choudhury is a hajji,' her father said as she moved to the other side of the table.

Mumtaz nodded her head. Of course going on pilgrimage to Mecca was a huge achievement, but good Muslim as she was, she didn't envy Mr Choudhury in any way. By the look of him, he probably had a serious heart condition. Praise be to Allah that he had managed to go to Mecca before his death. While her father ordered her tea, Mumtaz sat down.

'Abba,' she said, 'I have good news.'

Her father leaned across the table expectantly.

'My boss, Mr Arnold, has promoted me,' she said. That afternoon she was going to do half of Lee's shift inside Maria Peters' house.

'So how much more money is he paying you?' Baharat asked.

Mumtaz suddenly felt stupid. Why on earth had she thought that telling her father about her try-out as a private investigator was going to be a good idea? She wasn't getting any more money. Mumtaz knew from long experience that elderly Bangladeshi gentlemen were generally only interested in academic qualifications, marriage, fertility and money when it came to their children, especially their daughters.

'So are you a proper detective now, Mumtaz?' Baharat turned to Mr Choudhury. 'Such a tragedy when a woman's husband dies! But see how my daughter, in spite of that, climbs the career ladder. What an inspiration, eh?'

Mr Choudhury nodded appreciatively while Mumtaz's

heart sank. The next thing to happen would be that her father would offer her hand in marriage to this grey old man.

Carefully easing her way past her father's awkward questions, Mumtaz said, 'Things will get easier now, Abba.'

It wasn't exactly a lie. True, Lee hadn't said that she could have more money if she went out into the field, but Mumtaz knew what he paid his freelancers and it was more than she earned. With luck she'd prove herself; with even more luck she'd get fieldwork more and more often.

'*Inshallah*,' Baharat said with a smile.

Mr Choudhury echoed with a whispered '*Inshallah*' underneath his laboured breath.

Mumtaz's tea arrived and so she had to sit with them to drink it. She wished she'd just gone straight to see her mother, but showing an interest in Mr Choudhury's haj was something she knew would very quickly and easily deflect all and any of her father's inquiries. He was always so happy to talk about religion. Baharat told her all about Mr Choudhury's travels without once including the old man himself in the conversation.

Nodding and shaking her head in all the right places, Mumtaz let her mind wander firstly into the realms of shopping she needed to do, then onto a damp patch she'd found on the bathroom wall until, eventually, it settled on the mythical manly face her mother had described to her many, many times in the past: the Silver Prince of her childhood bedtime stories. The handsome, good and faithful saviour of all Bengal who rode a flying horse and whose shoes and clothes were made from pure silver from the moon. Her mother had made him up, but Mumtaz had loved him. Once she became an adult, though, she had, like her father, considered such stories so much foolishness, especially after she married Ahmed Hakim. But then one day, quite out of the blue, she saw the Silver Prince in all his glory just north of her house, on Wanstead Flats. Beautiful and regal, he had stood with his head held high, his blue-black hair shining like a crow's wing. But then momentary elation had given way to such awful disgust that Mumtaz felt instantly sick. She felt sick again at the thought of it and so she drank her tea quickly, excused herself to her father and his friend and went out to take the air in the street. As she put her head down over the mud-and-fag-end-filled gutter, a white man passed by and looked at her with sympathy. But he didn't ask her what the matter was or whether he could help her or not. At times like this Mumtaz felt the scarf across her head wind itself tightly around her neck like a noose.

'There was always some bloke everyone called a flasher even if he wasn't,' DS Tony Bracci said. 'Turned out he was usually harmless.'

Vi Collins slid her lizard eyes across to observe his plump, still young-looking face. 'And everyone could leave their doors open day and night and we all had such a laugh singing round the old joanna down the pub? Do me a favour, Tone.'

They stood on Marshgate Lane looking across one of the many tributaries of the River Lee at the beginnings of Hackney. Behind them the Olympic stadium sat with a half jaunt in its demeanour, like a hat that can't decide whether or not it is stylish. A man had been seen here with his penis hanging out of his trousers.

'I know it doesn't always follow, but a bloke getting his knob out in public can be the first step on a career leading to rape,' Vi said. She sucked hard on a Marlboro and imagined what was going through DS Bracci's mind. *Just 'cause she's got some tin-pot degree in sociology . . .*

'I base that on thirty years coppering,' Vi added.

Tony Bracci hadn't been at the 'coppering' for many years fewer than Vi. 'Yeah, well . . .'

'Yeah, well, we need to apprehend this villain,' Vi said with a smile. 'All right?'

Tony looked over at Hackney and found it just as shabby and in need of attention as Newham; everything except the Olympic stadia and the massive great media centre was still shit. The whole area still reeked of shit from the old northern outfall, just like it always had, and once the games were over he, like most people in the borough, was prepared to bet that the whole lot would end up going to shit. Just another in a long line of attempts to 'regenerate' the old East End . . .

'He's whiteish, medium height, sort of middle-aged,' Vi said. 'Victim didn't notice what he was wearing except his CAT boots.'

'Could be a workman on the site,' Tony said. 'One of them eastern Europeans.'

'Couldn't be one of us then?' Vi said.

Tony bit his bottom lip. Vi could remember when his Italian father, Vincenzo, had sold ice cream out of a van on the streets of Barking, and he knew it. He also knew she'd almost certainly remember that Vincenzo had been able to speak only the most minimal amount of English at the time.

Vi put her cigarette out and then lit up another. 'You know what Lee Arnold's working on at the moment, do you?'

Tony Bracci hadn't been close to Lee Arnold since the latter had given up the booze. Going into pubs with a sober sort just wasn't any fun, but they still talked on the phone from time to time and Tony did get to hear things.

'I heard Neil West's got a gig with him,' he said.

Vi looked at a vast piece of graffiti on the wall of a half demolished factory. It showed a massive great face, its huge red mouth devouring the Theatre Royal, Stratford. Underneath someone had written *2012 Olympic Man*. 'Right.'

'Neil don't go out for just anyone nor for nothing,' Tony said. 'Why?'

'Because I saw Arnold last night,' Vi said. 'And he was up to something.'

'What?'

Vi raised her eyes to heaven. 'If I knew that, would I be asking you?'

'Why you so interested, guv'nor? Lee left years ago.'

A rat scuttled out of one hole and into another on the side of the riverbank. Vi Collins said, 'Because, DS Bracci, like it or not, former DI Arnold is now in competition with us. You know the old saying about keeping your enemies close? Well keep your competition closer. And never forget that private tecs like Lee Arnold are members of the public just like anyone else and if I think they know anything I should know, I'll have any one of them down the station as quick as hot shit falls off a shovel.'

And then, all of a sudden, what sounded like thousands of voices rose up to sing 'Abide With Me'.

Pope Benedict XVI looked sinister. Fully aware that this impression was probably just her opinion, Maria tried to keep it to herself but without success. Her mother had been baiting her all afternoon and now she just couldn't help herself.

'He looks like a paedophile,' Maria said. 'Just like his priests.'

Glenys Peters' mouth dropped. But then apparently pulling herself together she said, 'You've a gob like a toilet. Ah, what can be going on in your mind! My daughter, a woman who uses the c-word.'

'Cunt? I use it in my act. I don't generally toss it around in normal conversation.'

Maria Peters smiled, but her face reddened in what could have been embarrassment too. In spite of what Lee had told Mumtaz about the comedian having found God, clearly His influence had not yet stopped her from goading her mother.

Mumtaz had thought that Lee might be in the house with her, but he wasn't. He wanted to get her view on who came and went, and how Maria interacted with them, and with her surroundings when she was alone. She was something of a jumble. Apparently involved with an evangelical Christian group of some sort, she demonstrated nothing but contempt for the Roman Catholicism that she'd been brought up to respect which, to Mumtaz, didn't seem to make much sense. Weren't they both kinds of Christianity? But then there were different types of Muslim; Shia, Sunni. Nations had been to war over such differences. They mattered.

'Anyway, cunt is just a word,' she heard Maria say.

Mumtaz looked down at the floor plan of the house that Lee had given her and tried to concentrate on where the microphones and cameras he had installed were positioned. Ideally, no creak of a floorboard, nor vague shift in the quality of the light was to go unrecorded – not that that was actually possible. But he, she or it was hopefully going to be apprehended, if he, she or it actually existed. Out of the corner of her eye, Mumtaz observed the glee that Maria derived from goading her mother fight with the shame that uttering that word clearly made her feel. In her professional life, on stage, she broke down. She'd told Lee this was because her new-found faith made her feel guilty about saying words like 'cunt', about laughing at the misfortunes of others, about blasphemy. She was a comedian at war with her own material.

'I'll say something for them happy-clappies, they don't swear,' Glenys said. 'Can't be in their good books with your effin' this and c-ing that.' Her voice was what Mumtaz would have described as recognisably cockney but there was just a haze of some sort of southern Irish in there too.

Mumtaz noted that there were two microphones and cameras, both hidden in books, in Maria's vast lounge, and then she looked up in time to see the comedian's face fall into a bitter expression that made her appear much older. 'Don't call them – us – happy-clappies,' she said. 'It's insulting.'

Glenys's pale blue eyes flashed. 'Then don't call the Holy Father a paedophile,' she said.

Maria sat down. 'He is and he's a purveyor of superstition. All that Catholic superstition you brought us up with. I still can't get it out of my system, even now. Touch this statue of the Virgin and it'll bring you good luck. Beware of witches and jujus and nonsense. Father this, that or the other always knows best.'

'You used to love going to Mass,' Glenys said. 'Couldn't keep you away. Then you got into showbusiness . . .'

Maria ignored her and turned to Mumtaz. 'Would you like a cup of tea or something?'

'No.' Mumtaz smiled. 'Thank you.'

She saw Glenys looking at her as if she had a bad smell underneath her nose. 'What is it you're doing, love?'

'I'm looking at where Mr Arnold has sited the surveil- lance equipment,' she said. The principle thing about Miss Peters' living room was the amount of ornaments that were in it, mainly china cats; they all looked as if they had been very precisely positioned.

'She's learning,' Maria interjected.

'Oh.' Glenys took her eyes away from Mumtaz and said to her daughter, 'Anyway, once that church has been demol- ished, you'll lose interest. I know you. If it ain't on your doorstep . . .'

'The church is being rebuilt,' Maria said.

'Not where it is at the moment.'

'No. We'll have to move to a temporary building for a while.'

'Then where? This new church? Where's it being built?'

'Why do you want to know? You're not interested, are you?'

The older woman went silent. The ticking of a large baroque clock on the mantelpiece above the fireplace suddenly sounded almost deafeningly loud. This went on for at least a minute until Maria said, 'Barking.' Then, pointing at her mother who was now just beginning to smile, she added, 'Say nothing, Ma! Say nothing! The church, as in the people, are my friends, they support me. I don't know what I'd do without them.'

Her mother snorted. 'You managed before they come along. I'd put money on you still having your rosary and still saying it. They're just pulling you in so they can get your money. They're all the same these so-called "new" churches!'

Maria's fury bubbled over. 'I went to them, Mother,' she said, 'because I needed some support. You didn't give me any – ever! I learned not to even ask it from you. But they did. I sought them out, not the other way around!'

'Ah, have it your own way,' her mother said dismissively.

'If you don't like it, then don't bother to come here,' Maria said. 'Don't talk to me.'

Her mother stood up. 'Maybe I won't,' she said.

When she later reported back to Lee, Mumtaz said that she felt that some of Maria's responses to her mother were excessively confrontational. 'To me, she seems to be as much in conflict with herself as with anyone else,' she said.

'So could a person in a state like that imagine things, for want of a better word?' Lee asked.

'Yes, it's possible. Very possible.'

They both looked at the computer screen that gave them visual on the inside of the house and they watched Maria feed her cat in the kitchen. It was cramped and airless in the back of the surveillance van and Lee felt stiff and tetchy – people paid a lot of money for round-the-clock surveillance with good reason.

'So all this stalking thing could be in her head?'

'It's plausible.'

Lee looked back at the screen and wondered what to feel. If Maria Peters was unhinged in some way – and to him anyone in touch with God *had* to be a bit barmy – then she needed the sort of help only a doctor could give her. But, in the depths of winter, in a recession that the government was insisting was not a recession, she was paying him very well.

VI

'As you sit and you listen to the words of the Lord your God, I want you to bear in mind your prayer. This isn't a prayer that anyone has taught you. It isn't even a prayer that you have learned from the pages of the Holy Bible. This is your prayer, your conversation with your God and with His Son, Jesus Christ, our Lord. Eyes closed and heads bowed in supplication, you nonetheless know that the might of God is nothing for you to fear. Among the Elect you are safe, you feel warm and at your ease in the grace of His Holy presence.

'We all know that the glory of his Rapture is almost come upon us. We feel a yearning for it and yet at the same time we experience a deep sense of calm. Because we know it's coming. Jesus is coming, "as a thief in the night", to take all of those who have been faithful to His name, who have toiled and have witnessed and have given freely to the coming of His glorious kingdom. Safely gathered to His bosom, we will every one of us escape the Day of Trouble, the Apocalypse, when finally and completely the Lord Jesus Christ will rid the universe of Satan and all his manifestations of evil. When death and pain and blasphemy and perversion will be washed away for ever and Jesus will build a paradise on earth with us, his pure children.

'I want you to pray for that, pray for that now, Chosen People of Christ. Ask him to usher the time in now. You, me, all of us, we're all ready. Yearning, reaching towards the right words that will please Him, that will allow Him to pour His grace down upon us, to hasten His return. Mouths forming sounds that only God and His Holy Son Jesus can understand, words that . . .'

A boy of about fifteen convulsed in his seat, his thick blond hair flapping down across his face as he muttered, *'Ya Ha'Mashiach! Bethel! Da ach, waa kaarch, veton Israel!'*

And then in that cold, mist-shrouded place, people began to come to the boy and they all tried to hold him. Many of them wept, a few said they felt their souls begin to ascend.

Betty Muller was among them, but she didn't go to the boy. She made straight for Pastor Grint and she said, 'Oh, Paul, again you've called the Spirit and it has come!'

Her big, violet eyes burned with fervour and Paul Grint smiled.

'I love you, Paul!' Betty said, a blurt, pouring out of her mouth almost unconsciously. Then she blushed.

'But you love the Lord above all else, don't you, Betty?' Pastor Grint said.

'Yes. Yes of course I love Jesus,' she said. 'Of course I love him too. And we must get Marie to the Lord too, mustn't we, Paul?'

'Oh, yes,' he said, 'we must get Maria saved as soon as we can.'

The cold had hit Lee like a wall as soon as he'd jumped out of the van. Neil was on for the night shift, and so he began to walk home. He put his hands in the pockets of his overcoat and trudged towards the flat. Another evening with Chronus, the telly and Mr Muscle (bathroom) – the shower cubicle was a disgrace. The names of three local pubs – not his 'safe' bolthole the Boleyn – popped into his mind and so he called his mum.

'How's Roy?' he asked as soon as she picked up the phone. He knew full well how his brother was, he just wanted his mother to say it.

'Pissed,' she said.

Lee sighed with that weird kind of fearful relief he always experienced when he talked to her about Roy. There but for the grace of God went Lee himself. He'd been a drunk and shoved painkillers down his neck like sweets. He knew why Roy boozed, even if he didn't approve of how lairy it made him.

'Where is he?' Lee asked.

'Christ knows.'

It was dark already and a thin drizzle dampened his hair and his eyelashes. As he walked away from the van he turned and saw Maria Peters looking at him through her dining room window. She looked genuinely afraid. Even with Neil monitoring her every move from the van, she looked scared. He turned onto Capel Road and felt the wind from Wanstead Flats slap against the side of his face.

'Mum, you have to ask him to go,' Lee said.

Rose Arnold snorted. This was not the first time they'd had this conversation. In a minute he'd bring up the angina and then she'd have to put the phone down on him. 'Where'll he go to, Lee? Eh? Where?'

'That's his problem. He's a piss head . . .' He just stopped short of saying *like his father*.

'Oh, I know what he is,' Rose said. 'A piss head, a waste of space, a pain in the arse . . .'

'Mum, he makes you ill, iller . . .'

And there it was: the angina. Lee knew he'd blown it as soon as the words were out of his mouth. Rose liked to live in denial about her illness – it was the only way she could deal with it. She cut the connection and Lee said, 'Fuck!'

Fuck! Fuck! Fuck! Fuck! Fuck! It was enough to make you fall into the nearest pub and drink the bastard dry. Except that he wouldn't, couldn't. It was cold and wet and the bathroom needed a damn good scrubbing and anyway Chronus would be waiting. It was coming to something when your best friend was a bird, but at least he had the bloody thing. When he got through the front door of the flat he saw that the local paper had been delivered. On the front page was a large photo of the Olympic site over at Stratford with the headline SEX PEST THREATENS 2012. Then he caught sight of the name DI Violet Collins and realised that Vi was in pursuit of a flasher. Some poor sod addicted to waving his cock at anyone unfortunate enough to be in the vicinity was a bit of a low-level gig for Vi.

Lee sat next to Chronus's perch in the living room and thought about it. Mercifully, for once, the bird was asleep. Maybe it was the flasher in Maria Peters' garden? The Olympic site wasn't far away. But then in Lee's experience some randy old bollock with his dick hanging out was not the kind of person who stalked others with any degree of subtlety. Every flasher he'd ever nicked had been more interested in exhibitionism than in actually assaulting anyone. Getting the knob out in public was, for some, all of the thrill.

Lee picked up his phone and called Neil West in the van to check that everything was quiet on the Maria Peters front.

'Her friend Betty Muller, the pastor bloke and another woman called Rachel have just arrived,' Neil said.

Lee was aware that Betty Muller, Maria's grey little friend in Jesus, came and went frequently.

'Who's Rachel?' he asked.

'Rachel Cole. Another churchy type. They're all at prayer right now.'

'What? On their knees? On the floor?'

'In the living room. Yup.'

The picture that came into Lee's mind was, to him, odd. Maria, the comedian with a mouth like a bag of dirty washing, on her knees praying with dowdy women in a room that looked like it had been designed by some clueless Premier League footballer, but he didn't share any of that with Neil. 'Leave you to it?'

'Yeah,' Neil said. 'I'm on it.' He sounded resigned. Surveillance was generally boring.

Lee took his jacket off and began to make his way to the bathroom. That skanky shower was waiting. As he passed in front of Chronus's perch, the bird woke up and yelled, 'Goal!'

'You could actually see the moment the spirit entered the boy's body,' Betty said as Maria put a mug of tea into her hands.

'That's amazing.'

'It's a pity you couldn't be there, Maria,' the man with the long, ascetic face, Pastor Grint, said.

Maria had been obliged to spend time with her mother. 'Yes, it's a pity,' she said.

She gave Pastor Grint and Rachel mugs of coffee and then handed around a plate of biscuits. 'But it's really good of you all to pop in.'

They, or rather the pastor and Betty, usually did if Maria couldn't manage to make one of the services. Betty had been round the previous day as well. It was nice because it made Maria feel included and involved even when she couldn't attend.

'Young Peter Randall had a terrible fight when he first came to church,' the pastor continued. 'Satan had taken root in his soul and it was only due to the persistence of his mother that he is where he is with God today.'

'He spoke in tongues,' Rachel said.

Maria saw Betty close her eyes as if in the act of wishing for the power to speak in tongues too. It was the sort of thing Maria had done when she was a child – closing her eyes and wishing for something. 'The Spirit may descend upon any of us at any time provided we want it enough and are prepared,' Grint said. He looked at Maria. 'I think that you, particularly, want it badly.'

Instinctively Maria lowered her gaze. One never looked any priest in the eye back in the old days, even though she knew that Pastor Grint was very different from them. 'Yes.'

'Of course she does.' Betty put a hand on Maria's shoulder and smiled.

The sense of guilt that swept over Maria was instant. 'I'm so sorry about that gig in Camden.' She began to cry.

'Oh, there's no need for that. There's no need for that.' Pastor Grint put his mug down, walked over to Maria and placed his arms around her. 'You stopped. You couldn't carry on, God couldn't let you. He knows what you really want and he's trying to help you to achieve it.'

Maria put her arms around his neck and wept into his collar. Betty, who had been touching Maria too, whipped her hand away as if she'd just been scalded.

Martin knew what the score was with those Muslims! There was a young bloke who looked like he fancied himself rotten outside the house of that smart woman whose husband had been murdered. A right preening peacock with his gelled-up hair, big silver trainers, his shiny leather jacket and his jeans so tight you could almost see his sperm. Randy shit was lurking about after that young daughter of hers. Bloody Asians! They couldn't sniff about after women could they? Had to be little more than kids! The dead man's wife was far more of a catch than that gangly girl was, to Martin's way of thinking. She was a proper lady. The girl was just a bit of a kid. Pretty though . . . And sweet . . .

But still the bloke stood in the drizzle looking up at that house, hands in his pockets. Probably playing with himself. Martin smelt that familiar cumin-scented tang waft in from the room of the family who lived next door and he frowned. It was at times like this that he was sorry that pie and peas smelt of so little. How would they like it if they had to share the smell of his every meal?

The bloke lurking outside in the drizzle looked at his watch. What was he doing that for? That girl had been home from school for over an hour. Martin had seen her go indoors. Had she told him to wait for her? What were the two of them going to do? The woman would be home at any minute and she'd be none too pleased to see some wide boy like him hanging around the place.

The trees that lined the street were heavy with water and if Martin squinted he could see how each leaf groaned under the weight of so many days of accumulated drizzle. Night had already fallen and, if you ignored the modern street lamps and all the Asians' brand new Mercedes, you could easily think yourself back to the end of the nine-teenth century when the houses had been built. There was even a woman in a long skirt, rustling along under-neath an umbrella. Squinting still, Martin realised it was the smart Asian woman. Oh, now there'd be fireworks! She wouldn't like that man outside her house one little bit.

But to Martin's surprise when the woman saw the man she just stopped dead in her tracks and she stared. He saw her, the bloke, and Martin did think that he may have smiled. But if he did, then she didn't return it – she walked forwards, into her driveway, pushing past him as she went. She didn't say anything to him nor he to her. She didn't even ask him to leave or bugger off or anything. When she'd gone he just carried on standing there looking up at that house.

She had to know him. Maybe he was her brother? Most of the Asian men seemed to be obsessed with keeping their eyes on their female relatives. That lady was alone, which was unusual, but then if the man was her brother why didn't she invite him in? Why didn't he force his way inside the house? Martin returned to the idea that the bloke was there to ogle after the young girl. It was only then that he finally gave in and put his hand down his trousers to give his old fella a little bit of a tug.

A particular type of need brought Maria Peters downstairs at just after three o'clock the next morning. She wanted a drink of water but she didn't like to get it from the bathroom. Bathroom water tasted funny and was tainted, her mother had said so, and all through her childhood Maria had lived in fear of it. Bathroom water, like unwed sex, rotted your insides. She knew it was nonsense but she descended her staircase in the dark and then walked across the wide entrance hall to the kitchen.

Reaching around the doorpost, she flicked the switch to put on the kitchen spotlights. Like tiny stars in a dead white sky, the lights came on illuminating a vast chrome and granite room that looked like a cross between an operating theatre and a particularly cool restaurant. Even when Len had still been alive, she'd rarely cooked. Maria went over to the fridge and took out a jug of fresh cold spring water which she poured into a glass and drank. As the icy liquid went down her throat she began to feel more awake. That was a nuisance. She riffled around in the medicine drawer for a moment, looking for a sleeping tablet, but she knew all along that there wasn't one in there. They were upstairs with the rest of the junk.

Maria left the kitchen, walked back into the hall and then went into her living room. She imagined whoever was watching her from the agency was wondering why she hadn't just gone back to bed. She knew that she was being taken care of, that someone would come to her aid immediately if necessary, but still she couldn't settle. Thirst had woken her up, now an apparent and sudden lack of tiredness was keeping her awake. She walked around the largest of her two sofas and switched on the uplighter beside the TV. It took a few moments for the energy-saving bulb to do much more than cast a somewhat sepia gloom upon the ceiling, but then as the light grew stronger Maria was able to see the area around the television in detail. For want of anything else to do she leaned forward to switch the set on. It was then that Gog and Magog caught her eye.

Gog and Magog, like most of her ornaments, were ceramic cats. They lived behind the old grate at the bottom of the fireplace. Or rather that was where they always had been. Maria felt her heart begin to pound. She picked up her mobile phone and dialled.

VII

'So Betty Muller and Rachel Cole are friends.'

'They only came around briefly yesterday evening, with Pastor Grint. We talked and then prayed. I saw my mother for most of the day. Your . . . Mrs Hakim was here.' Maria Peters pulled her dressing gown tightly round her body and curled up into the corner of the sofa. First Neil West and then Lee Arnold had come to her aid as soon as she'd called. It was still only just after four in the morning with absolutely no sign of sunrise. 'I didn't ask you to come here to talk about my friends!' she continued. Then she pointed to the two ceramic cats underneath the television. 'I've told you, those cats have been moved. Gog and Magog always live in the fire grate.'

'Always?'

Her jaw became hard. 'Where the cats are, are where the cats are meant to be,' she said. 'OK, it's a bit OCD but it's what I do. I clean, dust, hoover every part of this house. *I* move things. Nobody else. Me.'

When Neil had first come into the house she'd been

completely hysterical. He'd called Lee to come and sit with her while he checked the surveillance data, but there was nothing of any significance on it. Neither her friends nor her mother had moved anything. The cats, though not directly in the line of sight of either living room camera, could nevertheless be detected. Since the equipment had been installed, they'd not been anywhere near the grate.

Lee asked Maria whether she thought she could have absent-mindedly moved the ornaments herself. She replied with a furious 'No!' And to be fair there was no evidence to suggest that she had moved them. 'Could you, or anyone, have moved the ornaments before we put our surveillance equipment in?' Lee asked. Someone, logically, had to have done so.

He knew that neither he nor Neil had moved them.

'I would have noticed. I would have!' Maria said, albeit with just a catch of uncertainty in her voice. 'This house is my palace. I know every inch of it because I have planned every tiny part of it! I didn't move Gog and Magog. I wouldn't. They live in the grate. Someone came in and—'

'Miss Peters, our cameras have recorded nothing,' Neil said. 'You said your mother was here yesterday?'

'Yes. Yes, but if there's nothing on record …' She shrugged. 'Don't get me wrong, my mother is quite capable of doing something evil just to piss me off. But as you said yourself, there's nothing …'

'As soon as the system went live the cats could be seen underneath the telly,' Lee said. 'What about your real cat? Could he have knocked them down or . . .'

'Caspar lives in the garden, occasionally I let him into the kitchen,' Maria said. 'I don't like him in here. He's only a stray anyway. He sort of adopted me.'

'I see.'

Maria looked at him. Without make-up she appeared far closer to her actual age than when Lee had first seen her in his office.

'They were where they are now this morning,' he said.

'They can't have been.'

'But they were. Now, Miss Peters, you talk about being a bit obsessive-compulsive. Do you check all your ornaments and whatever every day?'

She curled her lip. 'I'm OCD, not mad.'

'I didn't say that you were. I'm trying to find out whether or not you can remember checking on those particular cats yesterday.'

She did think about it. She thought about it hard.

'Because if you actively looked at those two cats in your grate yesterday afternoon or evening then we really do have a bit of a mystery on our hands. That or some seriously malfunctioning equipment,' Lee said. 'But if you can't remember seeing the cats then maybe you just didn't notice that they had been moved. They could've been shifted days ago.'

'I would've noticed,' she said. 'And anyway, who would have moved them except me?'

'I don't know. Your mum? You said yourself she likes to piss you off.'

'Not like that.' Maria hugged her knees up to her chest. 'Ma's all talk. She winds me up with words, but she's too cowardly to do anything.'

'What about your friends? Your manager?'

'Alan?' She shook her head. 'We have differences but he wouldn't try to send me round the bend. He's trying, to his way of thinking, to make me saner.'

'How?'

She looked over at Neil West and then said, 'He knows . . .'

'We share all our information, Miss Peters,' Lee said.

She took a deep breath in. 'Alan's upset about my conversion to Christianity,' she said. 'He says it takes the edge off the act, and to be truthful I don't find being the old Maria Peters that everyone knows and loves easy now. Christians aren't supposed to be cruel and cuss and make fun of God and His creation. And yet I still love being on stage. I feel wanted up there. Even with the heckling. I know it's arrogant, but up there I can forget for just a little while that Len's dead and I'm alone. But it breaks me up too.' She looked down. 'I keep on falling apart. As you know.'

Lee did.

'If it wasn't for the church and the people in it, I wouldn't be able to cope. I've put my life in God's hands.'

Lee had to say what was on his mind. 'Seems to me, Miss Peters, that it's the church that's giving you grief.'

Her face darkened.

'If it wasn't for this church you'd just be merrily doing your old act,' Lee said. 'No guilt. You'd be happy, Mr Myers'd be happy.'

'Once you've seen the truth, Mr Arnold, there's no going back, whatever the cost,' Maria said.

'The truth is important. But who arbitrates the truth?'

'God.'

There was a simplicity about her answer that spoke of an absolute sincerity. Lee heard Neil clear his throat and saw him look into some irrelevant corner of the room. For those without religion all this God squad stuff was embarrassing and incomprehensible. The first time Neil had seen Mumtaz – head and shoulders covered in scarves, admittedly very stylishly tied – he'd had what he called 'a moment'. *Christ Almighty*, he'd said to Lee, *what you doing taking on a nutter?* Religious people sometimes got a bad rap. Lee knew he had to be careful not to become infuriated with his client. But the notion that a woman who apparently put her life in the hands of God and yet paid him a mint to protect her, did not sit easily with him.

*   *   *

Mr Arnold wasn't due in until ten and so Mumtaz had a bit of time to tidy up the office. A woman who'd sounded as if she could have been Asian had called to make an appointment to see him and Mumtaz had booked her in for eleven. She'd given a very obviously false name, Danielle, and hadn't said what she wanted to see Lee about. Mumtaz hoped that the most obvious and stereotypical reason for the appointment – matrimonial issues – wasn't in fact true. But one's own experiences colour one's view and her marriage to Ahmed Hakim had been characterised by things that, even now he was dead, she could not easily think about. They were things she'd caught whispers of amongst other women over the years; good women, who prayed five times a day, looked after their husbands and their children and never left their homes without permission.

Mumtaz, anxious since she'd seen that young man outside the house the previous evening, took her phone out of her pocket. She should have told Shazia about him immediately, but she hadn't known what to say. She couldn't tell Shazia who he was – she didn't know his name herself – but she'd have to warn the girl somehow. He was, after all, very dangerous and as yet she had no idea about his motives. She called Shazia's number.

'Amma?' The girl sounded surprised and a little annoyed. In the background Mumtaz could hear the sound of young-sters milling around, laughing and talking. It was just before nine and they were lining up to go into their lessons.

'Hello, sweetheart,' Mumtaz said. 'Are you all right?'

'Yes. Why?'

She was thinking that this call was odd, which it was.

'Just making sure you took your lunch out of the fridge,' Mumtaz said. 'Did you pick up the strawberry lassi I put beside your sandwiches?'

'Yeah . . .'

Mumtaz knew that Shazia had taken the yoghurt drink. She also knew that Shazia knew that she knew. She'd even thanked Mumtaz for buying her favourite drink.

'Amma, you're being well weird, is everything all right?'

Mumtaz most certainly didn't want to discuss her own feelings; she'd barely slept. 'Of course!' she said. 'Just. . .' She heard Shazia's school bell ring and knew that she had to be quick. 'Shazia, there is a man exposing himself to women. . .'

'A flasher!' Shazia laughed. 'Oh, they are just *so* pathetic!'

That laugh was all bravado and they both knew it.

Mumtaz ignored the words and the laughter. 'Shazia, if you see any man you do not know hanging around our house, or following you from the bus stop you must call me immediately. It was in the paper last night, the police are looking for him.'

'OK.'

'There are bad people in this world,' Mumtaz said. 'Shazia—'

'Whatever. Amma, I've got history. Gotta go.' Shazia cut the connection, leaving Mumtaz holding a silent phone up to her ear.

In any great conurbation some people were bound to be watching others – the State was certainly watching. London had more CCTV cameras than any other capital city on earth, but in spite of that, things were missed. People with ill intent slithered through the system and sexual assaults, robberies and murders still happened way beyond the dead eyes of the State's surveillance every day. Mumtaz knew this to be an absolute truth.

Ahmed had never let her have a mobile phone of her own. He'd taken the one that Abba had given her, the one she'd used at university, and smashed it up with a hammer. When Ahmed was dying she'd had to use his phone to call an ambulance. She'd had to put her hand inside his blood-soaked jacket and pull it out. It had taken every gram of self control that she possessed to put it up to her ear. The ferrous reek of the blood had made her want to be sick. Dialling 999 had taken maybe as long as a minute, maybe more.

Had anyone seen them? Ahmed collapsed on the grass in front of her, Mumtaz putting her hand inside his jacket for his telephone and then holding it, doing nothing? Watching the handsome young man in the silver trainers who had just stabbed her husband run away across the

Flats towards Wanstead. Feeling nothing but disgust for her dying spouse.

It was one of those coincidences that Lee couldn't quite believe was a real coincidence. As he came out of Maria Peters' house, he saw Vi Collins getting out of her car. Fag on and reeking of Poison perfume, Vi walked over to Lee and then nodded towards the comedian's house. 'New woman in your life?'

'Couldn't possibly say.' Lee smiled.

Vi quickly clocked the van across the road and shrugged. 'Business?'

'And what brings you up here?' he asked. 'Thought you were supposed to be protecting the Olympic site from flasher attack?'

She leaned in close enough for him to be able to smell the tobacco on her breath. 'Believe it or not, Arnold, my job isn't all about blokes' dicks,' she said.

'So . . .'

'Can't tell you,' she said as she walked back across the road. 'If I did I'd have to kill you.'

He watched her walk around the corner and then disappear from sight. Mumtaz lived on that street. Lee jogged across the road in Vi's footsteps, but by the time he could see into Mumtaz's street, Vi had disappeared.

*   *   *

'I do apologise for the smell, DI Collins. Curry isn't to my taste, as you may or may not know, but the Asians who live here now, they love it.'

'It's all right, Martin, you don't have to apologise,' Vi said as she followed the old man up to his room on the second floor of the property. Leonard Blatt's boarding house had always been a bit of a tip. Compared to the rest of the grand properties in the street it was a positive disgrace. As Vi followed Martin Gold to his room, she could smell more damp than curry and whenever she touched the walls on either side she was made aware that they were only cheap plasterboard. Len Blatt hadn't been a bad sort, but he hadn't been the best landlord in the world and it looked like his missus was continuing that tradition. That or she was too distracted by whatever Lee Arnold was investigating for her. Oh, she'd put him coming out of Len Blatt's old house together with Lee's appearance in Camden and come to a conclusion. Whatever was going on, Maria Peters had been anything but her old self since she'd come back to comedy.

The old man opened a door which led into a room jammed with art deco furniture. There was a sink in the corner where something that could have been a load of underpants languished in soak, and the big bay window that allowed a view out into the street was cracked and filthy. The place smelt of feet.

As soon as he'd closed the door behind them, Martin said, 'I saw the story in the *Recorder*.'

'You understand I had to come and see you, Martin.'

There was a lovely old armchair she could have sat in but it was all piled up with books.

'That was 1975,' the old man said. 'You can't keep on harking back to 1975.'

'I'm not harking, Martin, I'm checking,' Vi said.

He sat down on his bed and wrung his hands. 'I never go anywhere near that Olympic site.'

'Neither do I unless I have to,' Vi said. 'Where the construction's going on they keep changing the road layout and it drives me bonkers.'

Martin Gold said nothing. He looked no different from the last time Vi had seen him which had to have been at least five years ago. But then Martin had always looked old even when she first knew him in 1975.

Vi sighed. She had to say it and he had to give her some sort of answer. 'Did you get your old bloke out and show it to a woman over the Olympic site?' she said.

'No!'

'I have to ask, Martin.' She looked around to see whether he had a pair of CAT boots somewhere on the floor. But he didn't appear to. Martin was more a brogue and dirty mac man.

'I don't . . . I never do that. Got no feelings for that now.' He didn't look at her, not once.

'Where were you, evening before last, round six?' Vi asked.

'Here.'

'Anybody verify that?'

He looked up and sneered. 'What? The Asians? They wouldn't know whether I was alive or dead in here. It was freezing, like today, and I'm old. Why would I be out?'

Vi raised an eyebrow.

Martin shook his head. 'I've not done a thing, like that, since '75,' he said. 'And yet you people can't leave me alone! Blimey, it's not like I touched any of 'em, was it?'

'You wanked off in front of women.'

Martin looked pointedly down at the covers on his bed.

'Quite a lot of women,' Vi said. 'Took us a while to get you, didn't it, Martin? No cameras or DNA back in those days.'

'So why're you bothering me now? That Olympic site must be bristling with cameras. Why would I go over there to do that, *if* I was going to do that? I'd have to be stupid, wouldn't I?'

'Nothing clever about being a wanker, Martin,' Vi said. 'It was lucky for you old Len Blatt wasn't too fussy about who he put in his places.'

Martin's lips peeled back and he bared a set of brown and broken teeth. 'I lost everything because of you people!' he said. 'My job, my home, me kids!'

Vi knew Martin of old and had seen and heard it all

before. 'So it's nothing to do with getting your old bloke out and tossing yourself off in front of people who didn't want to see it? All my fault? Martin, to be truthful, I couldn't give a flying fuck what has and has not happened to you. My only concern is that you're not wanking in public.'

'I'm not!'

'Good.'

Vi hadn't really believed deep down in her soul that Martin Gold was the same person as the flasher over on the Olympic site. Apart from anything else he was too old and, to be fair to the mystery man, all he was doing was getting his penis out. He wasn't actually doing anything with it. Martin Gold had masturbated, he'd come at women at night in and around the East London Cemetery and he'd taken delight in ejaculating near them. He'd worn a hood and he'd frightened them and Vi had had no sympathy with him then or now.

'So how you getting on with Len's widow?' Vi asked. She hadn't seen Martin since Len Blatt's death.

'She comes and picks up the rent. Sometimes, when it suits her, she gets some maintenance done.' Martin was still fuming. 'One of the Asians said she might want to sell up, now she's back on the stage.'

'Must be worrying,' Vi said.

The teeth bared again and he said, 'What do you care?'

Vi shrugged. 'I don't.' Then just to be certain she said,

'Now, Martin, don't take this the wrong way, but I need to have a bit of a poke about for a minute.'

Martin Gold's face blanched. 'What are you looking for?' he said. 'What now?'

'Martin, mate,' Vi said, 'we can do this the easy way or I can go and get a warrant. It's up to you.'

Once Pastor Grint and all the others at the blessing service had left Maria's house, the comedian and Betty made eggy toast together and then sat down at the kitchen table to eat it. There was a message on the answerphone from her mother, but Maria just deleted it. She had nothing to say to her. Every so often, when Maria caught a glimpse of Betty, when she wasn't looking, she found herself hardly able to reconcile the girl she'd once been with the woman she was now. Betty Muller had been very pretty. At school she'd had lots of boyfriends, but not, it was said, any sex. Her family had been Christians and she of course still was, although now with a different church from the one she'd gone to with her parents.

At seventeen Betty had married a boy from her church and everyone had said that soon she'd have a baby, but she hadn't. Betty had never had any children, and now divorced, alone, fifty and decidedly beige, she was never likely to have them. When, after reading their booklet, Maria had first gone to the Chapel of the Holy Pentecostal Fire, seeing Betty there had initially made her heart stop and then dance. She thought she'd lost her years ago.

'I tell you, I felt like I was going crazy last night,' Maria said. She sprinkled some cinnamon over her toast and then took a bite. 'I'm so grateful everyone came here to pray with me today.'

'The church cares. That's why Pastor Grint and the rest of us came to bless the house.'

'I know.'

Betty thought for a moment. 'But if the cats are always there . . .'

'They are! You know how anal I am about this house.'

Betty chewed. Everything about her was small and that included her tiny mouth and little, bride-white teeth.

'But the private detective guys couldn't see anything on their tapes,' Maria said. She frowned. 'Betty, do you think that there's really something in what Pastor Grint says?'

Betty's thin face coloured. 'You know I do.'

Maria put her knife and fork down on her plate. 'Don't get me wrong, I feel the peace of Christ growing in me every day of my life, but when Pastor Grint talks about demons and spiritual attack . . .' She raised her arms in the air and then let them drop loosely by her sides. 'I don't know what to think! Logic tells me that such things are just not possible.'

'But Marie, you know that evil exists, it's around us all the time. Only Jesus can deliver us from it. And until you are truly born again, your soul will be fought over by the powers of good and evil.' Maria and Betty had been best friends at school. Betty had always called her 'Marie'. It was terrible that they'd lost touch for so many years. It turned out that Betty had been living less than a mile away from Maria all the time. 'But Pastor Grint has cleansed this house now, for the time being.'

'Mr . . .' Lee had told her not to tell anyone his name. He'd told her not to tell anyone, apart from her mother, that she was being surveilled, but she'd told Betty almost immediately. 'The private detective guy I told you about, he isn't comfortable with the spiritual.'

But Betty made no response.

Demons, exorcism and possession were things that Maria was still unsure about. Her lack of belief in such things was one of the reasons why she had not as yet testified and been born again. Maria had seen Pastor Grint perform exorcisms, she'd just watched him cleanse her house. However, decades of first Catholic terror and then scepticism had left her with a nagging feeling that the people involved had to be deluded in some way. She was certain that what the pastor and the church as a whole was doing was done with good intentions but sometimes she cringed at it nevertheless. In a way, and in spite of feeling quite oppressed by him at times, Maria could see why Lee Arnold was a sceptic; such things made no sense. Except that when she found the church and saw Betty that first time and then Jesus came into her life she knew that His presence in her heart was real. His presence was changing her, making her into a better, more authentic person. He and His church were becoming part of her family – better than her family.

Maria looked out of the kitchen window into her rain-soaked garden and Betty's eyes followed her. 'This house is beginning to feel like a prison.'

'You miss your husband. You loved him.'

Maria felt a tug of pain in her chest. When the word 'heartache' was used in the context of loss it really did describe what happened. Her heart hurt for Len. He'd been years older than her, in no way physically attractive and he'd had terrible trouble with wind, but he'd been funny and generous, irreverent, clever, he'd loved her and he'd made her life work. He'd kept at bay the psychological demons that she knew for certain were real.

'The memory of your husband has to be everywhere in this house,' Betty said. 'When you have a good marriage you do everything together; choosing the furnishings, the decoration. I can tell that you put this place together with great care, Marie. If you feel it's a prison then it's a very beautiful one. You've been very lucky because God has given you this place to enjoy and to use for good if you so wish.'

'Use for good?'

Betty smiled. 'It's a big place, Marie, there are lots of

things you could do with it that would help you and others. If you wanted to.'

Maria looked from granite worktop to brushed steel fridge to star-like spotlights. Opulence. Betty lived in a rented one bedroom flat in Manor Park furnished out of second-hand shops. She had no husband, no money, no job. Betty was plain and quiet and yet her face glowed because Jesus had entered fully into her life and Maria was, if not envious, ambitious for that peace, that serenity.

'I've been very lucky,' Maria said. 'I should be more generous.'

'You've worked very hard.' Betty put her knife and fork down and reached across the table to take one of Maria's hands. 'You're over-strained, Marie. You need peace, a bit of time to reflect and be with Jesus and with the soul of your dear Len.'

Maria knew that she was right. And she knew that as well as Jesus, she needed Len to be there too. Betty was very perceptive about that. She understood why Maria went to Len's graveside as often as she did. She knew that, really, Maria wanted to be with him.

VIII

What Neil was saying wasn't anything that Lee hadn't come across before. In fact when they'd both been in the police they'd had problems with people they'd been ordered to watch for their own protection. Most people had this desire to be completely alone from time to time, and so what Maria Peters was doing now was not out of the ordinary. She'd given the agency a list of places she visited regularly and East Ham Jewish Cemetery had been on it. Neil West, however, would rather have gone in there with her.

'So you're parked outside?'

'Yeah.'

'Anyone else in there with her?' Lee asked.

'There's another woman.'

'Visiting a grave.'

'I guess. It's hard to know. Jews don't put flowers on graves, do they?'

'No.' Fred up at the bar, mouthed at Lee. Did he want

a drink? 'Coke,' Lee said. 'Diet.' Then back into his phone, 'Clock anyone?'

'No. Blue Ford Ka, old style, followed into Sandford Road but then headed off up towards High Street South. Got a Fiesta in front of me here but a bloke got out and walked into the house opposite. Otherwise, quiet as the proverbial. But then it would be. It's cold, drizzling, dark. I thought these places shut up early in the winter.'

'Usually.' The barmaid with the thalidomide arm came over and cleaned his table with her one manicured hand. Lee briefly looked up and smiled. 'What did Miss Peters say to you about it?'

'Said she needed some time alone at her husband's grave. I said I'd follow at a distance. She wasn't having it.'

Lee shrugged. 'You can see inside though, can't you?'

'Yeah, course I can see her.' Neil knew better than to actually comply with a client's request for solitude. It was generally just whimsical. 'She's walking down the central pathway. If she starts to disappear from view, I'll nip through the gates.'

'Let me know when she heads back and I'll take over when she gets home. Rung around a bit earlier and I've got a couple of other old faces interested in taking on some shifts.'

'What about your new girl?'

Old Fred put a diet Coke down in front of Lee and Lee winked at him. 'I'm putting her on a new client,' Lee said to Neil. 'Lady wants her teenage daughter watched. Reckons she could be in to drugs.'

'You think that what's-her-name is up to it?'

'Mumtaz? Well the client's covered, so's her kid and so's Mumtaz. So of all of us, she's the one least likely to stick out like a sore thumb.'

'Mmm. Funny, you know I never think of Muslim girls being on drugs.'

Lee rolled his eyes. Neil was a good enough bloke but he did tend to think in stereotypes. 'You wanna get out more,' he said.

'Oh! Client slipping out of sight,' Neil said. 'Call you later. Putting the phone on vibrate.'

'OK.'

Old Fred sat down next to Lee and smiled. 'So what you done about Bob the Builder?' he asked. 'He still owe you money, does he?'

'Oh, yes,' Lee said. He didn't look too bothered about it.

They were joined by Fred's mates, Harry and Wilf. All in their late seventies or early eighties, they'd known Lee's late father and, like him, they'd been drinking in the Boleyn since the nineteen forties. Wilf, who had emphysema, rasped, 'How come?'

'How come he still owes me money or . . .'

'How come I just see him walking about down Upton Park Lane,' Wilf said. 'He never had a broken leg or nothing. What's up with you, boy?'

Lee looked into Wilf's concerned, watery blue eyes and smiled. Even though he didn't drink any more, this pub was his second home – he'd known it, and these old men, all his life. 'But did he look worried, Wilfred?'

'Worried?'

'If he didn't, he obviously hasn't seen his missus today.'

Harry supped his pint and said, 'Tracey? Why?'

Some young lads with skinhead haircuts barrelled through the public bar doors, already pissed as parrots. Lee watched them lurch over to the bar and made sure they were polite to the barmaids before he continued.

'I told Bob. I warned him,' Lee said. 'My money this morning or there'd be consequences.'

The old men leaned forwards in their chairs, their ancient eyes big with their desire for a good old mouthful of gossip.

Lee bent down across the table and lowered his voice. 'You see, lads, Bob, as I told his Tracey, has a little bit on the side. Name of Kerry, she works out of an old container in Rainham. Entertains gentlemen callers, if you know what I mean.'

'Oh! Never!'

'My dosh aside, in the interests of safe sex, I had to tell poor Trace,' Lee said. 'Phoned her up this afternoon. She was none too happy.'

'Don't s'pose she was,' Harry said.

But Fred, who'd sucked on his bottom set of dentures and furrowed his brow when Lee told him what he'd done said, 'Bit of a low blow though, ain't it, boy? Grassing on a geezer about his tart to his missus?'

'Depends,' Lee said.

'On what?'

'On how many tarts a bloke actually has.'

Wilf coughed and then spat mucus into a large, tattered handkerchief. 'You ain't telling me that Bob . . .'

'Four, not counting Kerry. She's the best of 'em,' Lee said. 'All on the game. One's as rough as fuck, looks like she hasn't bathed for a month. Bob the Builder, my friends, will give me what he owes me because if he doesn't I'll tell Tracey about the others and if Tracey gets to know so will her Indian restaurant-owner boyfriend. Now he is a heavy geezer! The thought of possibly getting a dose of the clap off Tracey via Tracey's husband's rough old toms will not please him at all. Bob'll work that one out quick enough.'

'Mmm.' Wilf looked down into his pint and shook his head.

Harry just sat saying nothing. Then Fred said, 'It's like that morning show in the East End these days, ain't it?'

'What morning show? What do you mean?'

'*Jeremy Kyle*,' Fred said. 'The whole world's like *Jeremy Kyle* now, ain't it?'

Lee drank his Coke straight down and said, 'Always has

been actually, boys.' Then he smiled. 'Thank God. If it wasn't I'd be out of business.'

The picture showed a slim young girl wearing a hijab. She was almost the same age as Shazia but she went to one of the local comprehensives. Not for her the wilder reaches of Woodford Green and the delights of Bancroft's. Her name was Anjali and when her mother 'Danielle' had come to the office she had been wearing a niqab.

Lee had been a bit taken aback, but Mumtaz had half expected it. When she'd first spoken to the woman on the phone, she'd gathered from her tone and the fact that she whispered that she probably came from the sort of family where full veiling was not going to be a surprise. She wanted Anjali watched because she feared that the girl was getting involved with drugs.

'Her school grades have slipped and she's always tired now,' she'd told Mumtaz. 'And she is sometimes disrespectful to me.'

Mumtaz had, gently, tried to point out that tiredness, slipping grades and the odd bit of disrespect for her mother were really rather small crimes for a teenager to commit. When she had first met Shazia and the girl had gone on a full-scale offensive against her, it had been bad. But then Shazia had had a very good reason.

'Anjali was always such a good girl,' her mother had continued. Then she'd added, 'I don't want her father to know.' She'd turned her veiled face to Lee. 'I have some money of my own so I can pay you. Just . . . discretion. Please.'

Looking at Anjali's photograph, Mumtaz struggled not to experience an overwhelming feeling of gratitude. Her father had been so different from everybody else's father. She'd gone to university, he'd left the covering or not covering of her head up to her. He hadn't forbidden her from working outside his shop even though he'd employed a good, solid dose of emotional blackmail, which had worked. Then Ahmed. But Ahmed had lied to her father, he had tricked him as surely as he had tricked and cheated everyone.

From the sound of it, Anjali was just being a teenager. Her family were religious and had high standards and so they saw what was quite natural in a girl of her age as worryingly divergent – maybe. Mumtaz had thought that Shazia's crazy tantrums were just teenage angst allied to the inevitable protest a child would make at the prospect of a new mother coming into its life. And Shazia with her fashionable clothes, her private school and her every material whim catered for had looked like a very typical spoilt little princess. It was only when Mumtaz actually witnessed Shazia's pain that she discovered the truth.

Mumtaz bit down on any tears she may have left inside her and concentrated on Anjali. The child was to be her first real case out in the field and part of her relished it.

Lee Arnold was trusting her to put into practice techniques she had only observed and talked about – and he was going to pay her a bit more to do it. It was a pity that she hadn't been able to carry on with the Maria Peters job but she also saw the sense in it. Unlike Lee and Neil she would not look out of place waiting outside school gates, following young girls along the street.

Downstairs she heard the front door open and then close.

'Shazia!' she called down. 'You OK?'

'Yeah. Why?'

She wanted to ask her whether or not she'd seen anyone, any man wearing silver trainers lurking around the house, whether anyone had followed her back from the bus stop. But she didn't. She'd warned her, now she had to leave it at that. To do anything else would raise the girl's suspicions and Mumtaz didn't want that.

'I'll be down in a minute,' Mumtaz said. She put Anjali's picture back inside her file and then went over to her bedroom window. It was dark but by the light of the street lamp outside, she could see that there was no one out there. If not with words, she had warned him to go on his way and she prayed with all of her soul that he had heeded the pleading in her eyes last time she'd seen him. He was not wanted. He never could be. She just wanted to forget about him, for both their sakes.

It had been late, after four, when Maria had driven to East Ham Jewish Cemetery. But it had still been open. Maria didn't tell the Jewish lady she saw on the path that she was going to pray to her messiah at Len's grave. This woman, like all the Jews, still waited for their deliverer. Except that He'd come.

Maria put her hand in her coat pocket and felt for the stones that she'd brought from her garden at home. Len had never had much interest in the garden and had once even suggested that they concrete part of it over. But it had been his and she hoped that putting the pebbles she'd carefully selected on his grave would please him. Pebbles placed on a Jewish grave indicated that the dead had not been forgotten; they were calling cards.

As Maria bent down she saw that Len had two other stones. One had probably been placed by his cousin, Karl – an old man himself now, he was the only blood relative, apart from his parents, that Len had ever been able to find after the Holocaust. They'd loved each other in that intense way that those who are stuck with each other do. And then there was another stone which, as Maria began to pray, she saw had a piece of paper underneath it. Maybe that was from Karl? Maybe some private message to Len in Yiddish or German or Hebrew?

'Dear Lord Jesus Christ,' she murmured. 'Please have mercy upon Leonard Blatt and . . .'

Aware of slipping into the Catholic prayers of her youth

from time to time, she was entirely sincere, but she was distracted. She wanted to see what was on the piece of paper underneath the stone. Even if she couldn't understand it, she still wanted to see it; Len had been her husband. She said 'Amen' and automatically crossed herself. Then she bent down and took the piece of paper from underneath the stone. Something was printed on it but, because of the darkness of the evening and her own increasing long-sightedness, she had to dig in her bag to get her glasses before she could see it. It was in English and it said *Not funny*. And in spite of knowing what a common expression that was and how it could be used in any number of contexts, Maria's first thought when she saw it, when her hands began to shake was, *How does anyone know?*

IX

His name had been Dave Delmonte and he'd started what he called a 'fun pub' down on the Custom House/Canning Town border. Years before it had been an old dockers' gaff, and after that it had lain derelict for years. Dave had bought it in the late seventies and when he renamed it Dave's Fun Palace, Maria had gone down there to audition for a resident comedian spot.

The whole alternative-comedy thing had only been in its infancy then and so a lot of the young comedians, like Maria, were just gingerly feeling their way. They went from clubs, to pubs to strip joints – anywhere that would have them, testing the water.

Maria, so nervous she shook from head to foot, turned up for the comedian auditions on a grey day in January. Half of London's comedy scene arrived with her and so she joined a queue that went outside the old pub and along the Victoria Dock Road. So many were on the dole then that even some folk who were not comedians had come along, chancing their arms. She remembered easily how terrible she'd felt; just trying to concentrate on remembering her material had completely filled her mind.

The first half hour was spent outside in the drizzle and so by the time Maria got inside the pub her hair was plastered down flat on the top of her head and her make-up had run. When she finally got into the wings of the tiny stage that she hoped might be hers in the near future, she looked out from behind the curtains. Some rough sorts plus Dave Delmonte were in the audience. He was fat, middle-aged, and he was pissed, knocking back pints of lager – he gave each act less than a minute. There were four people in front of her when she first saw Dave and he dismissed them all with the same, growled out words, *Not funny!*

The place had smelt of stale beer, of smoke-soaked curtains and carpets and of toilets that were only used by men. Maria had felt sick even before she'd started her set, but as she walked onto the stage, looking scraggy, misshapen, scruffy and unattractive, she began to feel acid rising up into her throat. It wasn't easy looking straight at Dave Delmonte anyway, but when she heard him say, 'Not exactly Bernard Manning, are you, love?' she just fell into a blind panic. Bernard Manning was old school, mother-in-law and Paki jokes! People who liked Bernard wouldn't like her! But she'd only prepared one small set and so she had to do that because she didn't have anything else. It had been about periods.

She heard Dave Delmonte mutter the word 'lesbian' underneath his breath less than thirty seconds in. Then he waved his pint in the air and he said, *Not funny! Not funny! Not funny!*

As far as Maria could tell, no one else had had three *not funny*s. Only her. She must have been *really* not funny. Oh God. She'd only just started out, she was young, she was also, unknown to her at the time, pregnant. Maria threw up on the stage then and there in front of Dave Delmonte and to the sound of laughter from some of the auditionees behind. Dave snapped his fingers and two blokes with faces like smashed arseholes came on and dragged her off. As she passed him, Dave said something about being 'up the duff' and then he'd yelled again, *Not funny!* She'd run home immediately, alone and weeping.

Her confidence was so knocked that she almost gave up. And then there was the pregnancy. That time, when the pregnancy and everything that both preceded and superceded it was so intimately connected to her failure as a comedian, was far too painful to recall. It was why those two words on that little scrap of paper on Len's grave hurt her so much and frightened her.

How she held back her tears and got back to her car, Maria would never know. She dropped the awful little paper and ground it into the mud with her foot and then she left. That was not her life – not any more.

*　　　*　　　*

Lee watched Maria cry. She knew where the cameras in the living room were and he saw her turn away from them. But he could still see her shoulders heaving and hear her sobs. She'd been to visit her husband's grave and so she was bound to be upset. Neil hadn't seen anything untoward happen at the cemetery. The viewing screen started to go on the blink and so Lee did what he always did and hit it. Normal service resumed immediately.

Working with a load of second-hand, ancient surveillance kit hadn't been a problem when he'd first started the agency, but four years on, it got on his tits. He still couldn't quite believe that he'd been stupid enough to go into business in the first year of the recession. He'd spent the first six months living on chocolate and fags and then when the work had started to come in, it had been all about serving writs and following gangsters' girlfriends. On more than one occasion during that time, he'd wished he'd stayed on in the police. But they were making redundancies now and so that probably wouldn't have been for the best.

Ever since he'd left school, Lee had been looked after by someone. First the army, then the police, with his missus doing the caring back home. When Denise left him and took baby Jodie away with her, he threw himself not only into his police work but also into the arms of booze, plus the codeine painkillers he'd found so comforting at that time. Only Vi Collins had ever known about that and that was just because they'd slept together at his place one night. She'd seen him neck a whole load of them as soon as he got up and she'd had a right old go about how easy it was to kill yourself on them, how they dissolved your liver, turned you into a junkie. He hadn't listened. That hadn't happened until Vi had turned up with a birdcage containing what had looked at first like a scraggy blackbird. 'If you top yourself then this poor parrot or whatever it is'll starve to death,' she'd said. Then she'd left without another word and Lee had found himself alone with the creature that he eventually named Chronus. The same handle as the god of time was a good one for a bird that, though young, looked as old as stone. But Lee had taken to him and had stopped the codeine that day. Chronus had done nothing wrong; he didn't deserve to starve.

Maria Peters switched on her television and began to watch some sort of comedy show, but she didn't laugh once during the whole course of the programme. Someone, Lee couldn't remember who, had told him years ago that all comedians were miserable buggers. He wouldn't have gone so far as to say that in relation to Maria himself, but she was certainly a worried woman. Whatever she was seeing and hearing when she went about her daily business was real to her. Lee just wished that he knew who or what, if anything, that was. Maria scratched the back of her head and the diamonds on her fingers sparkled into the camera. One worry she didn't have was money. That he envied her.

Anti-terrorism laws had cost Lee Arnold dear. They'd come in in the wake of the attack on the World Trade Centre in America and then after the 7 July attacks on London, they had only got more stringent. Lee had worked out of Forest Gate police station at the end of Green Street all his coppering life and so, even before Mumtaz's appearance, he'd known a lot of Muslims. Green Street was where Muslims, Sikhs, Hindus and Asians of all stripes went to create businesses, shop, pray and socialise. Suddenly people who had known their Muslim neighbours for years were looking at them with suspicion. The law itself, it seemed to Lee, was doing that too. Rounding up lads he knew, who were justifiably angry and upset, was not his thing and by 2007 he'd had enough.

Lee's phone began to vibrate in his pocket. He took it out and answered it.

'Roy's buggered off with that Scotsman from Walthamstow,' Rose Arnold said.

'Fitzy? I can't go out after my idiot brother and that tosser,' Lee said. 'I'm working.'

'I know, love,' his mum replied. 'I'm just saying in case you see the stupid dollop on your travels.'

Roy was so like their dad it was almost painful. Harry Arnold had drowned his sorrows in booze, mixed with arseholes, got violent. Lee had spent much of his young life looking for that stupid dollop in his travels. Usually, like Roy, he was in some boozer or other with a load of other losers. Sometimes he was in some gutter, thrashing around in his own piss.

Resisting the urge to tell his mother, yet again, to chuck Roy out, Lee said, 'I will.'

'I'm off round Auntie Annie's,' Rose said.

'Yeah, you do that,' Lee said. Auntie Annie was his mum's older sister. They liked watching *Coronation Street* together. They could both remember when it had first started back in 1960. Roy had been two years old. 'Have a good time.'

'I will.'

Suddenly something on the monitor made Lee lean forward and look hard at Maria Peters watching television. 'Night, Mum,' he said, and cut the connection.

In Maria Peters' living room something that wasn't the television was catching her attention. It was in the corner to the left of the TV and, from what Lee could see of it, it appeared to be a shoebox.

The dream never featured Ahmed as a viable person. He was always dying on the ground, with her just waiting and waiting and waiting for his breathing to stop. The moon was silver and liquid-looking in the sky. Then she had his bloodied phone in her hand and she was calling the ambulance, all the time thinking about what she was going to tell Shazia, worrying about how Shazia was going to know what to feel. She began to cry. She'd started to cry when it had really happened. But even through her tears she'd still watched Ahmed's attacker's back as he ran away so quickly from the scene, the light just catching the silver trainers as he'd headed north towards Wanstead. Even in her dream, especially in her dream, she didn't know whether she was crying because her husband had died or because her beautiful saviour had run away. Who was he? Why had he done what he'd done? Why did he keep on coming back just to stare at her?

When Mumtaz eventually managed to wrestle herself out of the dream, Shazia was sitting beside her on her bed. The reading lamp was on, illuminating the girl's pale, worried face.

'You were screaming,' Shazia said.

Mumtaz, still breathing heavily, put a hand on her chest and then said, 'I'm sorry, Shazia.'

'Was it about Dad?'

She'd stopped calling him Abba while he'd still been alive. It had been a way for her to rebel against him.

'Did you dream about Dad dying again?'

Mumtaz didn't want to tell her. She wanted to make up some innocuous horror that the girl would be able to just dismiss and then go back to sleep. But she couldn't. There were far too many lies still floating on the air without that.

'Yes,' Mumtaz said simply.

Shazia put her arms around Mumtaz's neck and hugged her. 'It's all over now, Amma, you must try not to think about it.'

'Bad things come sometimes in dreams.' Oh, she was such a loving girl! Such a contrast to the awful madam she'd been when Mumtaz had arrived! She hugged her back. So tightly!

'It must have been just . . . I don't know!' Shazia said. 'You were like covered with blood. There were two policemen with you and I wondered what had happened. I thought that maybe . . .'

Mumtaz hugged her still more tightly. 'Sssh! Sssh!'

Holding hard onto each other so that their knuckles became white they sat in silence for a few moments. Only when Mumtaz began to feel her own panic subside did she gently relax her grip on her stepdaughter. Shazia reluctantly moved away a little and sat back and breathed out. Her face wasn't so pale any more and she began to smile. 'I thought for a moment that something terrible was happening to you,' she said.

'Just a dream,' Mumtaz said.

'Yes.'

Briefly Shazia hugged Mumtaz again and then, still with a smile on her face, she said, 'But at least he really is dead, Amma.' She got up to leave and then she added, 'He can't do stuff to us any more, can he. Not even in dreams.'

'We can wake up, Shazia,' Mumtaz said.

The girl blew her a kiss and then she left the room, closing the door quietly behind her.

Maria Peters hadn't moved for nearly an hour. The television banged away of its own accord, but she just kept on looking at that box in the corner. Lee wondered what, if anything, was in it. Had she been really distressed she would have cried out, maybe even asked him to talk to her over the phone, but she didn't. Much as the box appeared to be holding her attention, she did not seem to be visibly distressed. But then why would she be? It was just a shoebox.

Then again it probably wasn't. The thing with the ceramic cats apparently moving about of their own accord had only happened the previous night. Had this box moved from, perhaps, her wardrobe down to this corner by the telly? He'd have to check through the tapes and see what he could find. The house had been rammed full earlier on in the day for some sort of bloody exorcism or blessing or something. If he could catch her in the act of moving things around herself . . . It wasn't that he believed she was doing so consciously; in reality Lee didn't know what he believed or didn't believe about Maria Peters. So far he'd seen nothing untoward. Only her – and her weird churchy mates.

Lee had a problem with religion and he knew it. Try

as she might, Rose Arnold hadn't been able to enforce the Anglican values that Lee and Roy received at Sunday school and at church, because no one at church had made any sense. They'd had a 'traditional' vicar which meant that worship had been heavy on the fear of God and anti-abortion, and light on joy. When he grew up, Lee had left the church with the abiding impression that religion was all a load of malignant bollocks. How a sharp woman like Maria Peters could be taken in by it he couldn't imagine, but then Mumtaz was no fool either and she was all headscarfed up. He'd taken a risk employing her. Although the old Boleyn crew didn't say anything, he knew they thought he was barmy, that it was weird. But even before she told him about how she was a widow with a child, he'd seen the need in her. Her eyes, if not her mouth, had begged him to give her a chance. Beyond having a big house and a kid at private school, he didn't know what the state of her finances were exactly, although he could infer that they weren't good. Her husband had been murdered by, as the police would have it, 'a person or persons unknown' and so not only did she have her grief to deal with, she had the horror of that experience to try and live around too. She'd been there when her husband had been stabbed – they'd been walking across Wanstead Flats together going to visit a doctor.

Mumtaz hadn't told him that they'd been going to see a gynaecologist. That had come out when the crime had been reported. They'd been two people, doing an ordinary thing, and one of them had been murdered.

Looking back at the screen, Lee noticed that Maria's head had slumped forwards. There was a faint buzzing sound, a snore like a light cat's purr. Still looking at the box, she'd dropped off.

X

Early Sunday mornings were always busy in Maria Peters'
house. First Betty arrived, then the rather younger and
prettier Rachel Cole. Then the slim man with greying
blond hair, wearing a cheap brown suit, who Neil now
knew as Pastor Paul Grint.

'We always go to church together every Sunday, it's
nice,' Maria had told Neil. 'It also saves on petrol.' She
didn't mention the cardboard box that had apparently
been taking up so much of her attention. Neil was
surprised she had time to get upset or even go to church,
given all the prayer meetings and blessings that seemed
to go on at her house.

Betty, Rachel and Paul Grint all walked to Maria's place
so they could go in her car. Neil wondered whether they
gave her petrol money. Not that the church was far away.
Over at Hackney Wick, the Chapel of the Holy Pentecostal
Fire was in an old industrial unit on Roach Road. Prior
to becoming a church, it had been first a bathroom factory

and then a tyre warehouse. In order to allow more access to the Olympic site, it was up for demolition sometime during the coming months.

Neil had never been to the church before but found it hard to imagine these lower-middle-class white people in such a place. Churches with hellfire names in old factories and wholesale outlets were usually the preserve of African Christians. They all had names like The Tabernacle of the New Life, or The Holy Church of the End of Days. Generally focusing on the Book of Revelation and the end of the world, the so-called Rapture, there was usually a lot of shouting, of 'testifying' and a great many people just talking gibberish, which they called 'speaking in tongues'. That was something to do with being inhabited by the Holy Spirit. To Neil, an atheist, it all sounded a bit like something out of *The Exorcist*.

Maria Peters and her party pulled out of her drive and down to the Romford Road. She was going to go through Stratford and, briefly, onto the A12, then she'd turn off onto the old industrial site. Neil knew the area. He was in a car he hadn't used before, his brother's old Nissan Micra which had no turn of speed whatsoever but it was anonymous and it never broke down. He had the route and so he let Maria get almost out of sight before he followed. It was a grey, drizzly, misty London morning and although there was a fair bit of traffic on the roads they were hardly packed so it was all plain sailing until Neil reached the A12.

It wasn't mist, it was fog, getting denser by the second as he followed a white van down from Stratford High Street and onto the roundabout that would take him onto the A12. He wasn't old enough to remember the London smogs of the nineteen fifties but his dad had told him enough for him to be able to imagine what they must have been like. There had, his dad had always said, been a sort of a green tinge to them, like a whiff of arsenic. The stuff he was driving through was faintly green. Or was he just imagining that? He followed the van, secure in where he was going, where he had to be. Maria's car, out of sight, was up ahead.

Leaving the van on the A12, Neil took the Old Ford exit and negotiated the awkward Tredegar Road junction. Turning on to Wick Lane he was almost there. Strangely for such a short journey in familiar territory he felt nervous. It was probably the fog – that or the notion of going to a church. Neil knew so little about religion. When he was a kid some Catholic boy at school had told him about the Holy Ghost and he hadn't slept for a week. Apparently it was everywhere.

The car in front, an Astra, turned right into Monier Road and Neil allowed himself a second to take in all the breakers' yards and empty warehouses on both sides of the road until, facing front, he found himself looking at a metal barrier and a pair of very cold blue eyes. 'What the . . .' Neil slammed his right foot down on the brake, bringing the car to a halt in front of the temporary metal barrier. The Astra in front was already on its way. Neil wound his window down. 'What's going on?' he asked the man with the bright blue eyes. The man shrugged.

'That's no bloody answer!' Neil said. 'What's going on?'

'Is bad holes in road,' the man said. Probably some sort of eastern European. Where the fuck had the Olympic jobs for the locals gone? Neil fumed. 'So fucking what?' he said to the man. 'This is Hackney Wick, it's full of holes.'

'Is dangerous. Cannot see.' The man placed the barrier on the ground and put a hand up to the grey sky, tinged with green.

Neil pointed to the retreating Astra. 'You let him go!' he said. 'Why you stopping me?'

The man shrugged again. 'Boss tells me only now. Your bad luck, I think.'

Neil, red with fury now, looked at the barrier, the fog and the blank-faced man and remembered just how scared he had once been of the Holy Ghost.

Maria was still shaking. Although he'd very patiently sat in the back of the car and just waited, she'd been able to feel how worried Pastor Grint had been. He'd kept on fiddling with his scarf, taking his gloves on and off nervously. At one time he'd handed her his sermon while he rearranged his coat and then he'd taken it back again.

She didn't want to let him down! But all the road prior-
ities had changed so none of them had known where on
earth they were going. The satnav had been completely
useless. She'd taken what had proved to be a silly detour
and there'd been a real danger of not making it in time
for the service.

She jumped out of the car quickly and looked around
as discreetly as she could for any sign of Neil West, but
there was none. Although she was amongst friends she
felt exposed and alone. It had taken her two days to open
the box down by the side of the TV. Two days! It had of
course been empty, but it had also been a Clarks shoebox
and that indicated knowledge. Like *Not funny*, it came from
a time she would rather forget. Lee Arnold had seen her
looking at it, must have seen her open it. He'd asked her
about it twice, but she'd just played it down and said it
was nothing.

'Marie! Are you coming?'

Maria turned around and saw Betty standing at the
back of the queue to go inside. The last Sunday in every
month was Sunday Lunch Fellowship Day and Betty was
struggling to carry a cake tin full of sausage rolls she'd
brought to add to the meal. People brought all sorts of
things. Often they cooked them themselves which Maria
admired enormously. But she couldn't do that and so her
own contribution consisted of a range of sweet treats from
Marks and Spencer.

'Come on!' Betty said. 'We're late!'

The mist split as Maria walked through it towards her friend. She put a tranquilliser under her tongue and swallowed hard. Sunday Lunch Fellowship was always well attended and so there were a lot of people clutching food and bottles of soft drink in front of them. Maria joined Betty, aware of a pervading smell of sour bodies on the air. More of the local homeless than usual had come for a blow-out, but then that was part of the point. As Pastor Grint always said, to feed a person's soul one must first ensure that his body is fed. Hungry people could not concentrate.

'A lot of cars here today,' Betty said as she looked at the large piece of waste ground that constituted the car park. 'A good turnout considering the difficulties with the roads changing and that. I know I shouldn't be, but I'm always amazed at how thirsty for the Word people are, especially from Pastor Grint.' She turned her one remaining beautiful feature, her startling violet eyes, on Maria's face and she smiled. 'It's truly the end of days, isn't it? The Lord draws near in all his wrath and all his mercy. Can't you just feel the shimmer of the Rapture in the air, Marie?'

Maria fought to suppress a shudder. Time was short. The Rapture, the taking up of Jesus's own into heaven was coming and she had to do what was right soon. Maria knew what that meant.

*　　　*　　　*

The Archers. He'd driven what felt like all over East London in the fucking fog and all Neil had to help him calm down was the tale of some bunch of touchy farming folk somewhere just outside Birmingham. He turned the dial on the Micra's antediluvian radio and found the racket that was Radio 1 – not that Radio 2 was any better. Some sort of love songs request show. Ugh. Maria didn't want him in church with her so Neil wished he'd brought some CDs to help pass the time – except that the car didn't have anything to play them on. Oh, for an iPod! But then at just over fifty, Neil always felt a twat when he listened to his in public. The oldest fucking swinger in town.

The happy-clappies had gone in by the time he'd arrived. What had been the front door of the old factory had been well and truly closed and now they were all singing. He could also hear guitars, which reminded him of that terrible church social his mate Steve had taken him to when they were kids. Steve's family had been born-agains and they'd been forever inviting him to one church thing or another. He went just the once. There'd been two young blokes in tank tops playing 'modern Christian music' up on a stage at the back of an old chapel in Ilford. They'd all been so bloody smiley, it had made Neil want to open his veins. When, he wondered, had born-agains become almost exclusively black and African? This Chapel of the Pentecostal whatever had to be some sort of freakish exception to attract its mainly white congregation. Neil wondered what else apart from singing was going on in there. He wondered if they had a secret stash of dancing girls somewhere, or booze or drugs.

He gave up on the radio and turned *The Archers* off. The only book he'd managed to grab before he left the house was some load of old pony about vampires his daughter kept banging on about. Neil didn't 'do' newspapers, even on a Sunday. He got out of the car and lit up a fag. His brother Dennis had given up three years ago and he wouldn't allow smoking within a ten mile radius of him or his family, and that included his cars. Through the mist he could see the outline of the massive Olympic media centre; it almost over-shadowed the main stadium. If size had anything to do with it, then the Olympics themselves were almost an irrelevance. It was the spin that was important, how the thing was presented, which media organisations got the biggest cuts of the Olympic cake and how much merchandise could be shifted off the back of the games. The athletes themselves had nothing but Neil's admiration, but the rest of it? To blast Hackney Wick almost off the face of the earth for the sake of two weeks in 2012 . . . No. Neil looked around, remembering how the old Wick had been, anticipating the emptiness that would follow on from the demolition of all the old factories and industrial units, including the church. He began to walk.

The area had needed some sort of redevelopment, but had it needed this? A load of artists had moved into all the old empty factories, pubs and yards some years back and although Neil didn't exactly understand modern art, he applauded the young artists' gumption to get up and do it for themselves. It wasn't right that so many of them were having to go. It wasn't right that the old allotments had gone or that the smoked salmon plant had had to relocate. All for some sort of prestige only a very small minority gave a toss about. Neil wandered around the church – he couldn't go too far away. He heard a load of voices shout 'Hallelujah!' and he smiled. Just like Steve's old church. A load of people with their arms in the air, listening to guitars, waiting for the end of the world. Neil leaned up against the side of the building, finished his fag, lit up another and waited. They were all going to have lunch together after the service. It was going to be a long old shift.

All the food had looked and smelt really lovely, but Maria hadn't been in the mood. In a strange sense, in just this one respect, she wished that she was still a Catholic. She could understand, and actually wanted, formalised confession. This ridding of the soul of sin in preparation for Christ's love and the Rapture that Pastor Grint talked about just served to confuse her. How did you do that? Did you speak directly to Jesus? Did someone in the church help you in some way?

Everyone was still eating but Maria needed some fresh air. It had been a very emotional and upbeat service during which many people had been saved and two women had been healed. She never got over the sheer amazingness of the miracles. Christianity had never been like this when she'd been a child. All the Catholic miracles had taken place in dark grottos; they'd all been performed by saints who had flagellated themselves for decades. There had been no worlds beyond that one could actually imagine. Just gold-covered bones and darkness and waste and fearful, awful sex. There had been no Rapture. Jesus was coming – soon – and everyone had to be ready. All clean and ready.

Maria looked down at the cracked and filthy pavement and knew that she could murder a drink – or a joint. She looked up and saw Neil West leaning against his car. Even though she was alone she didn't let him know that she'd seen him. Neither he nor his boss or anyone could really help her. All these shadows which may or may not be real had to be faced and they had to be faced alone.

Maria walked over to her car and put the bag she'd brought the cakes in in the boot. When she moved around to the driver's side her eye was caught by something white on her seat. She could see that it was either a piece of paper or card. She opened the car door and took whatever it was in her hands. *DEATH ISN'T FUNNY.*

Maria dropped the card on the ground and started to scream. She found that in spite of herself, she couldn't stop. Neil West ran over to her and, when he saw what she had seen, he started dialling a number on his mobile phone.

XI

'Did you lock the car up when you went into the church?' Vi asked.

'I don't know! I've been trying to tell you!' Maria Peters said.

'All right,' Vi said. 'Let's put it this way. When you came out of church did you have to unlock your car to put the bag you brought the cakes in into the boot?'

But Maria couldn't remember that either. She was still too traumatised by what she'd found in her car and by the police. Neil West had given her no choice. 'This has to be a police matter now,' he'd said. 'This could be perceived as a death threat.'

'No it isn't!' she'd insisted. But she couldn't tell him or anyone else why that was. She couldn't tell them about the note on Len's grave, about the shoebox . . . She wasn't ready. She knew it was wrong, but she just wasn't. She'd thought that she was only being stalked – or going mad – but it was worse than that.

'I don't want any of this!' she said when the forensic

people arrived. That hard-faced woman copper was talking about interviewing everyone in church – it was ridiculous! 'I want you all to go away!'

Neil West was hanging around with the other police officers, blending in. Maria wanted to ring Lee Arnold and tell him to call the whole thing off, everything, but she couldn't do that in front of all these people.

Betty, at her side, said, 'Marie, you should let these officers help you or let them get on with something else. They're busy people.'

She didn't know what had happened. Maria hadn't wanted anyone to see what she'd seen. The police had taken the note and now they were looking in the car, asking her questions about whether or not she'd locked it up. She didn't know!

'We have to check any CCTV footage we can get,' Vi Collins said. Maria Peters was looking even rougher than she had done when she'd seen her break down in Camden.

'Can't you leave these people alone?' Maria asked Vi through her tears. 'They haven't done anything wrong.'

'I'm not saying they have,' Vi said. 'But if you've been threatened, ma'am, I have to try and find out who's doing it. Do you see?'

'Yes . . .'

Neil West hadn't seen a thing, but then he'd arrived late and he had gone for a bit of a stroll around the side of the building. There'd been enough time for someone

to put something in the car provided it had been left open
... or whoever did it had a key. At first Neil had thought
that this real piece of hard evidence proved that Maria
was not delusional or manipulative, but it didn't. She
could have planted the sheet of paper on the seat herself.
Why she would do such a thing was another matter.

'I don't want to take this any further.'

A young copper was taking down details from Pastor
Grint and Maria couldn't bear it. She ran over and pushed
the policeman aside. 'Leave him alone!'

'Miss Peters!' Vi gently but firmly pulled her away.

Pastor Grint smiled. 'It's all right, Maria,' he said. 'No
one here has done anything wrong. We're all happy to
answer questions from the police. We all need to be law-
abiding, Jesus would want us to be.'

Maria's eyes stung with tears.

Vi nodded to the young copper and he took Grint to
one side again. She turned to Maria. 'Now look here,' she
said, 'if you want to drop this then that's up to you. But
if anything happens later it'll be on your head, not mine.
Do you understand?'

'Yes.' Maria, through tears, looked down at the ground.
'But it wasn't me who called you. It was Mr West.'

'If you're involved with Lee Arnold's firm then you're
worried about something.'

'That's a private matter.'

'If someone's threatening you then that's a legal matter,'

Vi said. God but Maria Peters had gone down the pan! Vi
was both shocked and disappointed. If this was what religion did to you, she wanted none of it.

Neil joined them. 'Thanks for covering up for me, guv,'
he said to Vi.

'Don't worry, it's all on my mental balance sheet. As
the Godfather would say, "If I need to call on you . . ."'

'I want to go home,' Maria said. 'I want everybody to
just go home.' Still crying, she walked away.

Neil moved in closer to Vi. 'Can you do forensics on
that sheet?'

'Not unless she wants to proceed. Why?'

'I want to see how much of her is on it,' Neil said.

'You think she might have done it herself?'

'I'm saying nothing,' Neil said.

'Client confidentiality.'

He didn't reply. There was no need.

'Forensic analysis costs.'

'I know.'

They looked at each other. Vi had known Neil for a very
long time. 'If laughing girl doesn't ask for it back, I'll do
it,' she said. 'But as I said, if I need to call on you . . .'

'Yeah. Yeah.'

Vi leaned in very close to Neil's ear and said, 'And we'll
need something for comparison. Nick her toothbrush, a
used glass, something.'

Mumtaz spooned the oil over the Yorkshire puddings and then put them back in the oven. Her mother, frowning said, 'It's lovely of you to invite us to dinner, but . . . Mumtaz, I'm not sure that your father will like it. It seems very bland to me.'

The sound of her father's voice, shouting at the television, floated in from the living room. Shazia, sitting opposite Baharat on the sofa was plugged in to her iPod. The old man said, 'Bloody Olympics! Look at all those bloody men from eastern Europe working in those construction jobs. What about jobs for local people, eh? That's what we were promised by Lord Snooty Coe.'

'Shazia loves a roast dinner,' Mumtaz said. 'Her mother always made one, every Sunday.'

'But her mother was from Bangladesh!'

'She was from Birmingham,' Mumtaz corrected.

'Yes, but her family were from Dhaka.'

Mumtaz turned the heat down on the frozen peas and put a lid on the saucepan. 'They were very English,' she said. 'That was the way they wanted to be.'

Shazia's mother, Fatima, had been the last child in a family who had moved to Birmingham back in the nineteen fifties. Her mother had been well over forty when Fatima was born and the girl had grown up knowing nothing about anywhere east of Peterborough. The very few pictures she'd seen of Fatima were enough to convince Mumtaz that she'd been very beautiful. She'd also been very obviously uncovered. Fatima Hakim had not worn a hijab and her clothes had been exclusively Western. Not for the first time Mumtaz wondered whether Fatima's spirit of independence had cost her her life. She'd died from a blood clot on the brain when Shazia was eight and Mumtaz could all too easily imagine how such a thing had formed. Ahmed had probably hit her. Or maybe he'd pushed her, probably forcing himself upon her, and she'd accidentally banged her head on something. Mumtaz had been hurt that way herself by Ahmed. That had been the least of it.

'So how is the new job going?,' Sumita said. Using Mumtaz's best cutlery she began to lay the kitchen table.

'OK.'

'So how is it being some sort of detective now. Does that mean that you have to follow people around?'

Mumtaz smiled. 'Sometimes.' On Monday morning she'd have to walk along with all the other mothers to Anjali Butt's school in Plaistow, watching.

'Mmm.'

Her mother clearly didn't approve. Wandering about looking into people's private business was hardly a digni-fied thing for a Muslim lady to do.

Mumtaz left the cooker and went over to her mother and hugged her. 'Amma, I have to make a living. For Shazia and for me.'

Sumita pushed her away. 'The girl's own family should

143

take her,' she said. 'Then you could sell this house and come home.'

'Amma, we've had this conversation!' Mumtaz, angry, walked away and stood over by the kitchen window. All but one of Fatima Hakim's immediate relatives were dead. Her brother, Faraj, worked in America. Ahmed's mother paid for Shazia's education but nothing else. Mumtaz had been through all that.

'I'm not selling the house, Amma. Not until I have to.' That wasn't too far away but it was all she had, all that terrible man had left her. She deserved it – if she could hang onto it. Shazia deserved it too.

Sumita shrugged. 'Remarrying under such circumstances will not be easy,' she said. 'But you're clever, Mumtaz, and this house is worth money, but the job and the girl . . . You know your father has some very well placed friends with lovely sons.'

Mumtaz always saw red when the subject of marriage arose. She'd been down that avenue once before and she didn't want to go there again. 'Amma, my view of marriage is a lot different to yours,' she said. 'You have Abba. I had a monster.' She moved closer to her mother again and looked her in the eyes. 'He wasn't the Silver Prince, was he, Amma, he was a monster. A monster you and Abba chose for me.'

Sumita lowered her head. Her daughter's words hurt because they were true. She wanted to say that marriage didn't have to be the way it had been for Mumtaz. She would find a man just like Baharat for her – somehow. Mumtaz would see.

'Oh, fuck, not this again!' Roy Arnold took a swig from his bottle of cheap cider.

Lee looked at him with disgust. 'Mum wants to watch it,' he said. 'So it stays.'

Roy was eight years older than Lee. But he looked more like a seventy-year-old than a man of fifty-two. Being permanently pissed for thirty years would do that.

'Fucking *Columbo*!' Roy waved a wet roll-up at the telly. 'We've all seen it a million times before.'

'Yeah, but Mum wants it on!' Lee persisted. He grimaced at his brother, that useless carbon copy of their useless father. 'And it's her house.'

'I live here too!'

He did and although Lee didn't like that one bit there really was no answer to it. His mum let Roy stay on whatever he did to himself, the house or her, just like she'd done with their dad.

'Oh, let him watch what he wants,' Rose said. She pointed the remote control at the TV and changed the channel to motor racing. 'It's only bloody Sunday afternoon drop off to sleep telly.'

Roy smiled. 'Handsome.'

Lee knew better than to argue. When he went, Rose

would be left alone with him and if Roy had had a bad time with his brother, he'd take it out on her. Rose Arnold was a tough old bird but she was getting on and she didn't need a beating from her son. Not that she'd ever told Lee about Roy's violence towards her, but he knew. He'd seen her put make-up on her face just to do the housework.

As ever, Rose had cooked her boys a nice Sunday dinner. Roast chicken, roast spuds, carrots, onion gravy, all the trimmings. Then hot rice pudding with raspberry jam. Lee had wiped his plate clean while Roy had fitted in the odd spud between booze and fags. Rose sat in her favourite chair over by the window and closed her eyes to the sound of screeching car tyres. Lee had to put up with this almost every Sunday! Spending time with some alcoholic arsehole just so his mother could have a few hours free from worrying about what he was going to do next.

Lee's mobile began to ring and so he slipped out to the kitchen to answer it. As he left, he heard Roy say, 'Who's that? Dr Watson? Mrs Colombo?'

Prick!

Lee closed the kitchen door behind him and answered the phone.

'Boss?'

It was Neil West. 'Yeah?'

'I'm at Miss Peters' place,' Neil said. 'Can you get over here?'

Lee frowned. 'What's happened?'

'She wants us to pull out,' he said. 'Completely.'

'What! Why?'

'Good question, boss. There's just been an incident and if you ask me, I think she needs protecting more than ever now. Can you leave what you're doing and get over here?'

She knew they were only really bothered about her because of all the money she represented. Potential earnings. 'I don't want to have my every move monitored any more,' Maria said. 'I'm sick of it.'

She sat on one of her huge, overstuffed sofas while the two men stood. Later, Pastor Grint was going to come over and so she knew she'd have to dispense with these two soon and she wanted it over with. Hiring a private detective agency had been stupid. She wanted it finished before anyone apart from her mother and Betty got to know.

'Miss Peters,' Lee said, 'you received a hate note, a threat of death today.'

Maria looked at her polished fingernails. 'Just a prank.'

'*Death isn't funny?* I don't think so.'

'A lot of people know that I'm a comedian. It was a joke.'

'Miss Peters—'

'Mr Arnold, I know that this job represents a lot of money for you—'

'You came to me, Miss Peters, you asked for my help.'

147

She didn't say anything. She just watched his face turn red.

'If you recall,' Lee said, 'we're only in your life because you came to my office because you thought you were being watched. Now, correct me if I'm wrong, but we've actually had no concrete evidence of anything untoward, apart from a pair of apparently mobile ceramic cats and some box you were fixated upon but wouldn't talk about, until today. Now I'm worried, you're apparently not. You have to help me here. What's going on?'

'Nothing.' But she looked away as she said it. 'I'll pay you until the end of next week and you can keep the retainer. I just . . .' She looked up into what she now noticed for the first time were his very green eyes. 'I don't like men watching me. It's nothing personal.'

'That box you were looking at appeared after that prayer meeting—'

She held up a hand. 'I've no interest in it!'

It was bollocks. No one whose life was in danger ever cared a toss about who was protecting them. Lee sat down on a pouffe in front of the television. 'Miss Peters,' he said, 'Neil has told me you sent the police away too.'

'Yes.'

'Why?'

'Because they were questioning entirely innocent people.'

'In your opinion. Even church people can be wrong 'uns.'

'These people aren't,' Maria said.

'Coppers have to start somewhere,' Neil added. 'Your mates were at the scene. Coppers start with the scene.'

But she ignored him. 'I would like you to switch off all your surveillance equipment now and then come and remove it as soon as possible,' she said.

'So you were mistaken about being stalked all along?'

'Clearly.' Her eyes looked wet and she bit her lip. 'I'm sorry to have wasted your time.'

Lee shrugged. 'You've paid for it,' he said. 'I'd be more worried about the coppers if I were you.'

She looked at him and frowned, as did Neil West. But not for the same reason. Neil'd told Lee about the little deal he'd done with Vi Collins as well as how he'd nicked some of Maria's hair from the brush in her bedroom, in confidence – or so he'd thought.

'The coppers sent that note of yours off for forensic examination before you called the whole thing off,' Lee said. 'It's in the system now. We've been coppers ourselves – we know. They'll look for fingerprints, DNA. If we're lucky we'll get a known face. Each and every incident has an incident number and this'll be no different. Whether you like it or not, the police are officially aware of it.'

Lee could see the way her confusion settled across her face in deep crevices. He felt as if he was watching some sort of internal struggle. She so clearly didn't want this church she'd become involved with to get embroiled in anything potentially unpleasant even at a distance. She wanted, apparently above everything else, to protect them. But she was still scared, Lee could see that. Would now be the time when she admitted that she'd just stalked herself? He couldn't imagine why she'd do that unless it was to raise her profile with the public. But she'd been, so far, very discreet about the stalking as far as the public were concerned. Falling apart on stage was what people knew her for. As yet it was hardly enhancing her career.

'You can waste our time, but you can't waste the coppers',' Lee said.

'I didn't,' Maria said. 'Neil—'

'Neil called the police out to what was and is a police matter,' Lee said. 'Apparently concrete proof like that? With the possibility of nabbing the perp on the spot? I'd've called them myself! We watch and we gather information and we protect on request. But when something becomes a criminal matter a time will come when we have to hand it over to the police. Do you see?'

She said nothing.

'Miss Peters, if you've anything you want to tell us . . .'

'You think I'm crackers, don't you?' She looked up at him with hatred in her eyes. 'Think I'm a mad woman doing all this to myself.'

Lee didn't want to lie to her but he didn't want to make her even more angry either. But before he could formulate a reply she shouted. It sounded just like the old Maria.

'Oh, just get out the both of you! Send me your fucking bill, take your fucking stuff and leave me alone!'

Paul put his hands around Maria's in the position of prayer.

'Jesus, we thank you so much for giving our sister Maria the strength to tell us the truth,' he said.

Maria's closed eyes leaked tears. As soon as Pastor Grint had arrived with Betty, Maria had told him about the agency, the surveillance, the stalking. In return he'd told her something strange which nevertheless made sense.

'This is not the work of man,' he'd said. 'This stalking as you call it, Maria, is the power of Jesus at work in your life.'

'The power of Jesus? Attacking me?'

'In a way, yes.'

She'd looked up at him and he'd smiled at her.

'But why?'

'Because he knows that you are both vulnerable and ready.'

'Vulnerable? How do you mean?'

He smiled his gentle smile again. 'You are still in sin . . .'

'You mean my act?' She ran her fingers through her hair. She'd known all along it had been wrong; she'd tried to tell Alan, but he just hadn't listened. 'I'll give it up.'

Paul said, 'Giving up your act will be a beginning on the road to being reborn . . .'

'A beginning?' If her act went then in terms of sin what else was there? But then there was the past . . .

'Other sins,' Paul said. 'You have other sins, Maria. Everyone who is not reborn does.'

Maria felt her whole body go cold. Did he mean *Not funny*? How could he know about that? She'd never told anyone. He couldn't. But then someone had to know because of the notes and the shoebox.

'I had to fess up to my rotten past before I could move on. I had to leave a lot of people behind to do that, even my family,' Paul said. 'Jesus wants us to lay *all* of our sins before him if he's to make us born again and so ready for the Rapture, his kingdom and an eternity with those we have loved. You have to give it all up or the Holy Spirit'll just keep on using your own fears to prod your conscience into a breakdown for your own good. You're not being stalked, Maria, you're being begged by Jesus to come to him. You have to stop using man's solutions, like these private detectives. You've got to give it all up to God.'

'Then I will.' Maria began to cry again. 'I'll never go on stage again. Never!'

'As I said, that's a good start,' Grint said. 'We'll get rid of the comedy and then we can work on other things, in time. Don't worry, Maria, the church will support you. Tell us what you want to tell us when you want to. Jesus is always eager for a new soul, but he'll wait for you. I know he will.'

Part Two

XII

Even though it was night-time, it was out in the open where anyone could see. But what choice did he have? Jacob was running like a rabbit and if he didn't catch him, who knew what would happen?

Matthias pounded the pavement hard, only just aware of how painful the stones were against his bare feet. His heart was so loud he could hear it in his head and when Jacob turned around to look at him with massive, frightened eyes, it became even louder. Why wouldn't the stupid boy just stop and talk about it? But Matthias had no breath left to call out to Jacob, who rounded the corner that led into his own street. He was nearly home and if he got there, it was all over. Matthias pushed himself so hard his lungs felt like they were bleeding.

Round the corner, racing after Jacob, he was running so fast he almost missed the body on the ground over by the wall in front of Amin's Grocery. Jacob had tripped. Instantly Matthias went down on one knee and leant on the other boy's rapidly rising and falling chest.

'You know what you must do!' he gasped.

Jacob shook his head.

'You got to be sensible, man!'

'You too late now, Matt.'

There were people in Amin's, shopping, but no one was coming in or going out. Jacob shook his head again.

'You are . . .' Matthias began. But then he stopped because Jacob had taken something out of the pocket of his jeans. Matthias looked at Jacob's knife and said, 'Don't do that!'

But Jacob stabbed the blade into Matthias's arm and blood came out in a river. For a moment Matthias could do nothing but watch his own blood flow down onto the pavement. Then in a last-ditch attempt to stop Jacob yet again, as he tried to get away, Matthias took his own knife out and slammed it deep into the other boy's chest. Tears in his eyes, he twisted it, hard. Just before he staggered away to the side of the road and was sick, Matthias saw the light in Jacob's eyes die.

It was the last time that they would gather in what had once been the old bathroom factory, then a tyre warehouse in Hackney Wick. The actual service had come to a close and Pastor Grint was going through the practicalities of where the new, temporary church was going to be.

'The building was a public house, many years ago,' he told the congregation. 'The nearest station is Custom House which is on the Docklands Light Railway. As you come out of the station you turn left along the Victoria Dock Road until you come to a turning called Munday Road which is on your right and the building is on the corner. I know that a lot of you might be disturbed that it's an old pub, but until our new centre is completed, God has provided this.' He smiled. 'Glass half full. At least we won't have to worry about this man who has been exposing himself around the canal any more.'

People murmured, 'Praise God.'

'But we still must pray for him and for his victims too,' the pastor said. 'There are a lot of unhappy people who have lost their way out there and remember, guys, it's our mission to get as many folk saved as we can before the Rapture. The more souls we can bring to Jesus the more pleased the Lord will be with us, and His pleasure is all we want, right?'

Some said 'Yeah', others 'It's the truth', while others still just prayed.

'So it's a priority to get the new centre up and running as soon as we can. Easter's on our doorstep, guys, we all need to make that little extra effort. Let's do it for the souls of the lost sheep we're gonna save, people!' He began to clap his hands. 'Let's do it for the Glory of God! Come on!' He waved his hands, encouraging everybody to clap, and almost five hundred people smiled and then complied. Grint walked up and down the front of the stage, a look of pure joy on his face. 'Let's do it for all the people hungry for the love of Jesus! They are starving, people, starving for the Word, the Love, the Peace of Almighty God! We gotta give it to them! We gotta take that soul nourishment to them!'

'We have to save everyone!' a woman yelled. The whole crowed swayed in time to their clapping.

'Yes, we do, Sylvia!' Pastor Grint said. 'You are ambitious for the Lord and that is a good thing, my friend!' Again he threw his arms out and waved his hands in the air. 'Let's all be ambitious for Christ! There is no soul so lost, so blackened and corroded by sin that it cannot be washed clean by Jesus. His love is endless, it is mighty and it can be seeded in the hearts of everyone in the whole world. All we need is the will, the ambition as Sylvia said, the faith, the glory and the sheer courage to build our chapel high, build it strong, build it so great it can take in each and every soul that each and every one of you goes out there and saves!'

Maria Peters put her head in her hands and silently screamed.

'Still being given the runaround by your flasher?' Lee asked.

Vi Collins looked at him and scowled. 'What you doing here, Arnold?'

Two bulldozers revved their engines in front of the Chapel of the Holy Pentecostal Fire. The happy-clappies didn't usually meet on a Tuesday morning, but the pastor had wanted to have just one more service before the developers reduced the place to rubble.

'Don't worry, I won't bother Miss Peters,' Lee said.

'I should hope not, she sacked you. She sacked us an' all,' Vi said.

'Your boffin proved that only Maria touched that death threat note,' Lee said. 'Either whoever put it in her car had gloves on or she did it herself. Personally I'm inclined towards the latter. There's something well adrift with that woman. You could do her.'

'For what?' Vi lit up a cigarette and then smiled at one of the young men sitting in the cab of one of the bulldozers. 'Neil West called us in, and *he* gave us the sample we needed for comparison, not laughing girl. Anyway there's no CCTV footage to back it up. Sod all cameras in this area that work.'

'I still think she did it herself,' Lee said.

'Then she must be ill, which is not my problem.'

Lee looked at her and smirked. 'You just don't want to get old Sid in trouble for using his lab inappropriately. Still doing him favours are you, Vi?'

She pulled her coat closely around her shoulders. It wasn't cold, it was late March, but it was damp and what with all the churned up dirt on the roads from the construction, it got into your bones. 'The last time me and Dr Smith had relations, Princess Diana was still happily married to Charles,' she said. 'Fucking grow up will you, Arnold! I did you a favour, it came out how you predicted it would. What more do you want? The woman's a nutter and she sacked you, deal with it.'

She was right, of course, but Lee had never been sacked before and although that was over four weeks ago now, it still irked him. Mumtaz had even tried to explain why he should feel sorry for Maria Peters, but he couldn't. Everything that had happened had done so because she had made it happen. On the day that she'd sacked the Arnold Agency, Maria herself had been dropped by her manager Alan Myers, for cancelling a gig he'd had lined up for her at the Comedy Store.

And yet questions still remained. Lee had checked the security tapes from the house again and again and he hadn't once been able to record her putting items where they shouldn't be. He hadn't caught anyone else doing that either. But then nothing, as far as he could tell, was moving on its own. No stalker had once been detected in Maria's garden or following her anywhere. The only slightly dodgy thing was the way that shoebox Maria wouldn't talk about had definitely turned up at the end of one of the big prayer meetings she sometimes had at her place. But that didn't mean that she hadn't put it there. Maria had been at the prayer meeting as well as all the other weirdos. Vi was right, she was cracking up. She was a poor mad comedian who was attempting to make some sort of pathetic comeback but it was all too much for her.

From inside the building, voices shouted 'Praise the Lord!' Lee rolled his eyes. Sounded like one of those African churches. The older of the two blokes up on the bulldozers lit a fag and then leaned onto his steering wheel looking bored. To Lee, he looked like a foreigner of some sort – a Serb or an Albanian – there were a lot of them about on the Olympic site. Poor sod! All he probably wanted to do was get the job done and then go back to lie down in whatever rancid little room he'd managed to rent.

'So what about your flasher then?' Lee asked Vi again. She was on site, together with Bracci and a load of uniforms, to supervise the safe destruction of the church and the derelict building next to it.

'I'm not here about that.'

'Yeah, but I read in the *Recorder* some old dear had an eyeful last Wednesday. You got a description?'

'From a myopic eighty-five-year-old?' Vi threw her dog-end onto the ground and then lit up another fag. 'I'm still not sure she even saw a knob. Could've been wishful thinking. He, whoever he is, was lucky she didn't just walk past him.'

'What about known faces?'

'I've a few on the bubble,' she said. 'Nothing useful. I give old Martin Gold a nudge a few weeks back though, remember him?'

'Bit before my time. Wasn't he the cemetery wanker?'

'In the mid-seventies you couldn't walk safe in the East London, no,' Vi said. 'Not if you were a woman. It was Martin Gold I was going to see that morning I saw you outside Miss Peters' place. Martin's one of her tenants.'

'In the Forest Gate multiple-occupancy place?'

'Yeah.' She looked up at him and smiled. 'Old Len Blatt never gave a toss, if you'll excuse the expression, about who he put in his rotten old dumps. He was a nice enough bloke, but he was a slum landlord and his missus seems to be continuing the tradition. Place is a shit hole. But then Martin said that one of the Asians had told him Maria Peters was thinking of selling up the rental places.'

'She never mentioned anything to me,' Lee said.

The old double doors of the bathroom factory opened and what looked like a load of people about to go on a particularly jolly trip spilled out onto the street. The bull-dozers both revved their engines, but the happy-clappies didn't seem in the slightest bit fazed by this. For some reason, in spite of the fact that their church was about to be demolished, and that many of them were poor, they appeared to be in very good spirits.

'Just look at them!' Lee said with contempt. 'Happy as Larry, silly as arseholes!'

'You're just jealous,' Vi replied.

Lee looked down at her and scowled. He hated it when she told him the truth about himself.

*   *   *

Young Anjali Butt was not, as far as Mumtaz could tell, taking any sort of narcotic substance. Anjali Butt was distracted from her school work, vague and not very communicative because she was in love. This was a very big love that encompassed her entire mind, body and soul, and contemplation of it left her little time for anything else. But it was also Anjali's great and very guilty secret because the object of her affections was a boy called Bipul, from a very nice family from Seven Kings who were all devout Hindus.

Now Mumtaz was waiting for Mrs Butt to come into the office to talk about Anjali and she felt terrible. Good Muslim woman that she was, Mumtaz knew more than people would have guessed about infatuation and desire for someone 'unsuitable'. Anjali and Bipul were just having little conversations, kissing, looking longingly into each other's eyes. They weren't having sex, they weren't even indulging in heavy petting. They were just kids who had fallen in love for the first time and it was really quite sweet.

When she'd first told Lee about it, he'd seemed sympathetic too. But then when she'd said that she was reluctant to tell Mrs Butt about her daughter, he'd become angry. 'We have to be honest with clients!' he'd said. 'Otherwise what's the point? Whatever you find out, you have to pass that on to the client. That's why they're paying us.'

'But if Mrs Butt thinks that Anjali has dishonoured the family, if she tells her husband then it could go badly for the girl!' she'd said. 'I don't know this family, but some families, they can do terrible things!'

Lee had known about honour killing but he'd told Mumtaz it was none of their concern. Provided Mrs Butt didn't actually say that she or her husband were going to harm their daughter, they couldn't call the police. What the Butts did with the agency's information was their own affair.

But Mumtaz still dreaded Mrs Butt's arrival. She was clearly an extremely religious woman. No one ever wore the niqab lightly and so she had to have very high moral standards indeed. What was she going to say? What was she going to do? Anjali was almost Shazia's age, she couldn't bear to think of what a furious father might do to her.

The office door swung open and the black pyramid that was Mrs Butt entered. She smiled at Mumtaz with her eyes and then sat down. Even her hands were covered by thin, black gloves, her feet swaddled in men's socks and what Mumtaz saw as the obligatory open-toed sandals. Even her mother wore them, just like this lady probably, all through the winter and into the spring. These were spattered with street mud and there was an old cigarette end sticking to one of the straps.

Mumtaz got straight to the point in case her courage

failed her. 'Your daughter is not taking drugs,' she said. 'But she is seeing a boy sometimes after school.' Knowing that the woman would view kissing and touching as highly undesirable, she attempted to soft pedal. 'Nothing sexual or inappropriate. Just young love.'

The woman's eyes narrowed. 'Do you have photographs?'

'You wanted photographs and so I have them,' Mumtaz said. She'd had the file ready to view on her screen. Now she turned it around so that Mrs Butt could see it. Anjali and Bipul were holding hands and smiling at each other.

'Do you know his name? The boy?'

Had he been a Muslim, it would have been bad enough, but this . . . 'He's called Bipul Banergee,' she said. 'He comes from Seven Kings.'

Mrs Butt did not reply. Her eyes, stilled now, could have been expressing anything from disappointment to grief. The name was so obviously Hindu.

'Where do they meet?' she asked.

Mumtaz's stomach turned. Was Mrs Butt going to get her husband to go out and find them? Beat the boy and do who knew what to the girl? But what could she do? She had to give the client the information that she'd paid for.

'Mrs Butt—'

'The information – please.' She lowered her gaze.

Mumtaz had never thought that this job would involve something as painful as this. Working in the office only gave one a distant, academic view of the job, but private investigation was about real people and their real, messy lives. It was grubby, boring, pathetic and visceral. Mumtaz hated herself. 'They meet on Wanlip Road, beside the sixth-form college,' she said. 'They only spend at the most fifteen minutes together.'

'I see.' Mrs Butt sat silently for a few moments, her gloved hands clasped nervously in her lap. Then slowly she put her hands inside the folds of her chador and took out a wad of banknotes. 'You have my thanks,' she said. She put the notes onto Mumtaz's desk and then withdrew her hands quickly. Mumtaz looked down at the money and began to feel sick.

'Could you keep the photographs here on your system for me?'

'I have taken copies, you may have them,' Mumtaz said. She pushed a large brown envelope across the desk at the woman.

Mrs Butt pushed it back. 'No!'

'But you've paid for them,' Mumtaz said. 'They're yours.'

'My husband mustn't see them.'

'You're not going to—'

'I used my own money for a reason. If it had been drugs I would have used more of my money to cure my daughter. My husband is a good man, but ...' She stood up. 'Your part in this is now over.'

She moved towards the office door and Mumtaz

jumped up. 'What are you going to do?' she asked. 'With Anjali?'

The woman turned, her chador sweeping the old office carpet. 'I will talk to her,' she said calmly. Then she added, 'I will tell her how love has to be duty. I will cry with her.'

Betty and Rachel went back with Maria after the service. Unlike many of the other church congregants, all three women were subdued. Betty said that even though it had been a terrible old building, she would miss the church at Hackney Wick.

'Shall we have a cuppa?' she asked Maria when they walked into the kitchen.

'I could do with something a bit stronger than that,' Maria said. On top of the shock of finding out where the temporary church was going to be, she'd seen Lee Arnold. He'd been watching the bulldozers from over by the canal. Her blood had frozen, she hadn't wanted to be reminded of that time. As soon as she'd sacked him, all feelings of being stalked and haunted had just vanished. She'd felt instantly relieved and Pastor Grint had said how much more peaceful she had appeared to be with herself and with Jesus. But then she had also been dealing with her sin. So nothing had 'moved', she'd had no mysterious notes or letters, no boxes. Only now that she learned that the new church was to be in Dave Delmonte's old Fun Palace was she horrified. But she knew she had to keep her nerve.

She'd made her decision back in February. Pastor Grint had been right: it had all been her own guilt. The stalking, the notes, the box. She'd done it all herself. She'd had a breakdown, a God-given breakdown.

And yet that terrible feeling of threat she'd experienced when she first went to the Arnold Agency had been very real and she had been desperate. She'd only been back on the comedy circuit for six months. Had the pressure of that been too much for her? The look on Alan Myers' face when she'd told him she wasn't going to do the gig he'd got her at the Comedy Store still stuck in her mind. The same went for what he'd said.

You cancel the Comedy Store, you're finished!

It had been a few hours after the *Death isn't funny* incident. She'd sacked Lee Arnold and his firm but that didn't mean she wasn't still frightened. She'd actually been more frightened than ever for a while, thinking that someone might, *had to* know. But Paul Grint and Betty had soothed her and later she'd told Alan that she couldn't even think about leaving the house and he'd asked her why, but she couldn't and wouldn't tell him. He'd called the Comedy Store to tell them she was ill and then he'd resigned. No more Alan, no more comedy and for a while it had felt like a relief. For a while it had felt like the old days. But then Len hadn't been there and so it couldn't be.

Maria poured herself a glass of port, took two codeine painkillers and then drank the alcohol down immediately.

Inside she could feel her viscera shaking. She wanted to sit down, preferably on her own, but then she remembered that there was something she had to do. Stupidly she'd promised the old creep in the multiple occupancy she'd go and see him. 'One of the tenants down the road has had a new gas fire put in,' she said. 'I need to go and check it's OK. I won't be long.'

'Don't you have an agent or someone to do it for you?' Rachel asked.

'Yes, but . . . Well, this man . . .' Maria said. 'Well, he's quite old and Len always used to go and sort his problems out himself, collect his rent in person. It's not a problem.'

But that wasn't strictly true. Maria hated having to go and visit Martin Gold in his smelly, old man's room. He gave her the creeps. If she were honest with herself, Martin had been one of the first people to come to mind when she'd thought that she was being stalked. Not that she'd told Lee Arnold; she'd hoped that he'd find that out without her help. She did not, after all, want to actively point the finger at any of her tenants. That could be very legally dodgy if said tenant was innocent and took offence, and although Martin Gold was an old flasher, an easy target, and she didn't like him, Maria didn't want to actually put him out on the street unless she had to. For the time being her only profession was that of landlady and so she wanted to do that fairly and well. But Martin Gold's oily manner was hard work and by the time she got back to the house, Betty said that she looked pale.

'Did that tenant give you grief?' she asked.

'No, I'm just tired,' Maria said. And to be truthful, Martin Gold hadn't been a problem. His room had smelt, as usual, but he'd been pleased with his new gas fire. Maria had been relieved that it worked properly. Problems with tenants on top of everything else was not something she needed. Wondering just how she was ever going to be able to go to church again was what had made her face lose its colour. Dave Delmonte's place was just too full of memories. How could she go and pray in a place that was so tainted? How could she be sure, given her recent experiences, that her mind would not just crack apart completely? Was Jesus asking too much, pushing her too hard this time?

XIII

She looked exactly the same as the last one had to Lee, but Mumtaz knew Mrs Malik and she knew Mrs Durrani and, most importantly, she could tell them apart.

'They both wear dark blue burqas, how do you know?' he asked her when he came back in after Mrs Durrani had left. None of the excessively covered women would say a word while he was in the office and so, for the duration of their visits, Lee had to sit outside on the stairs.

Mumtaz shook her head. Did he do this ignorant thing deliberately or was it just to wind her up? 'Mrs Durrani is a good five centimetres taller than Mrs Malik and Mrs Malik walks with a limp. What's so difficult about that?'

'Nothing.' He didn't want to say *they both look like walking fabric rolls to me actually* to Mumtaz and so he shut up. To complain about the clients was unprofessional and churlish and besides, since Mumtaz's success with Mrs Butt and her daughter, Anjali, word was clearly out about her amongst the Asian ladies of Newham. Whether Mumtaz actually did the surveillance or security work that the ladies required was sometimes irrelevant; they could talk to her about it without embarrassment and they knew she was discreet. And although the demography of who did and who didn't use the Arnold Agency hadn't changed completely, it had shifted. Whereas before Mumtaz's arrival most of their clients, such as they were, had been white men, now they had a lot of Asian women too. Lee had to wonder just how much, or how little, the ladies' husbands, fathers, brothers and sons knew about all this. They always paid their bills in cash. For women, basically in purdah, they were proving themselves not only financially independent but also very far from being pushovers. It was not all plain sailing, however.

'I may be wrong, but I do not think that Mrs Malik has good intent towards her daughter-in-law,' Mumtaz said. 'I tell her that Nazneen never leaves her marital home except with her husband, but Mrs Malik doesn't believe me. Now she wants that I mount the surveillance myself. Amy, I think, is too European for her. I hate prejudice like that.'

Lee nodded in agreement. He'd put one of his free-lancers, Amy Reichs, on the Malik job and she had indeed seen nothing untoward in or around Nazneen Malik's house. She'd only actually seen the girl outside the house with her husband.

'I think that Mrs Malik thinks that Nazneen isn't good enough for her son,' Mumtaz said. 'I think she's seen some other young girl she wishes she'd married him to.'

Lee, who was casually looking at a pile of flyers that had come through the door earlier that morning said, 'You got any evidence for that?'

Mumtaz shook her head. 'Not directly.'

Lee looked up from three separate fried-chicken take-away menus and said, 'OK.' He didn't know that what was happening to Nazneen had happened to Mumtaz's cousin Farah. But he had, in a very short space of time, learned to trust Mumtaz's judgement. After all, what did he know about Muslim women?

'I'll do as Mrs Malik asks,' Mumtaz said. 'For the business. But I trust what Amy has said and I don't think that Nazneen is doing anything wrong.'

'Mmm.' Mrs Malik was paying them and so Lee couldn't really get too worked up about it all either way. If the girl was mucking around with other men, then she was mucking around with other men. If she wasn't, she wasn't. What did grab his attention, however, was a flyer that wasn't for fried chicken. He frowned. 'Look,' he said, 'there's a thing here for that church that Maria Peters went to. They've moved down to Custom House, not far from my mum, actually.'

The whole Maria Peters saga had left a very bad taste in Lee Arnold's mouth and Mumtaz, if nobody else, knew that in Lee's mind it hadn't gone away. Like the good copper he had once been, he wanted to know the truth. She'd sacked him, she'd apparently given up her career and yet, as far as Lee knew, she was still going about her business in the same way that she always had. She hadn't apparently had any sort of breakdown that had necessitated hospital admission, and yet the last time he'd seen her, she'd looked and sounded mad. She'd just received a death threat, albeit probably from herself, but she'd been well and truly through it that day and he had wondered how she had survived.

Mumtaz walked over to Lee's desk and looked over his shoulder at the flyer. 'It is called closure,' she said.

He looked up at her. Her beautiful oval face was quite impassive.

'The Maria Peters case is still really a mystery,' she said. 'You need answers.'

He sighed.

'You feel that she took us all for a ride and you don't know why,' Mumtaz said. 'It certainly wasn't to enhance her career, so what was it about?' She sat down again.

'Still too much of a copper to let it go,' Lee said. 'Maria Peters paid for our time and so there's nothing I can do. Had I still been on the force I could.'

'Or not. DI Collins came out when Maria found that death threat in her car and then Maria told her to go. If the victim doesn't want to be helped what can you do? Even if you do suspect them of wasting police time?'

Mumtaz had met Vi Collins just once since she'd been working for the agency. She'd, as she'd put it, 'popped in' to see Lee. They'd worked together up at Forest Gate and remained friends. Mumtaz had freely offered to cover the office while they went to the Boleyn together. DI Collins had been what Mumtaz regarded as a typical white East End woman; in other words she was loud, tough, stylish and genuinely kind. She did, however, wear a very odd necklace. It was a gold chain from which was suspended both a cross and a Star of David. How one could display both these symbols of faith, Mumtaz couldn't imagine. She couldn't ask either. DI Collins was not a client, she was Lee Arnold's friend, it would have been rude.

Lee flung all the flyers into his waste paper bin and said, 'You're right. Nothing I can do.' He yawned, stretched and then stood up. 'I'm gonna go out and get some fags.'

'OK.'

He walked towards the door. 'You want anything?'

'No, thank you.'

He left. She heard what he liked to call his 'whopping size twelves' running down the stairs at the back of the barber's shop and fade into the distance. Only when she was sure that he was unlikely to come back did she go to the waste paper bin and take out the flyer for the Chapel of the Holy Pentecostal Fire. There was a picture of a lot of smiling people on it.

Martin Gold had a secret – or he thought he had a secret. He wasn't sure. The young Asian girl next door was bunking off school every Thursday: from about midday onwards she'd be at home doing goodness knew what. It was a mystery to Martin. The kid went to Bancroft's, a fee-paying school. Surely they would report such a thing to the girl's stepmother, who was obviously paying a lot of money for her education? But then she herself was hardly at home any more and so maybe the whole thing had just, somehow, gone out of control. The young girl, as far as Martin knew, never had a boy in there with her although there were other girls. There were always other girls.

Sometimes that young Asian man he'd seen lurking outside the house in the winter, the one he thought was probably the woman's brother, passed by the house, but he never stopped. He just looked at it as he walked down the road, sometimes even turning his head to keep on looking after he had passed, but he didn't appear to have anything to do with the kid.

In theory, he told himself, Martin liked to think about how he might turn the young girl's naughty behaviour to his advantage. Her stepmother was a very proper sort of lady, quite different from the girl's actual mother, and indeed the girl herself. The girl wouldn't want the woman to know that she was probably sitting indoors on her mobile phone, watching telly and maybe even smoking and drinking with her mates every Thursday afternoon. He'd tried to find a way to look into the house when the woman was out to see exactly what the girl was doing, but he couldn't. If he was going to do anything at all, he'd just have to wing it. The first thing would be to talk to her. Martin shuddered. In theory the girl could just shop him to the police straight away and then he'd have that rough old bird Vi Collins on his back for evermore. But all of this was *in theory*; he'd never *do* any of it.

The rumours that Mrs Blatt was selling up all her rented property wouldn't go away. Martin felt that they could be, in part, to do with her appearance. She'd given up the silly comedy thing some time ago, but she had also become thinner and ill-looking in that time. Luckily, so far, those magnificent breasts of hers remained impressive, but she was pale and was starting, he felt, to look her age. She'd said nothing at all about selling up to him, but the Asians seemed to be fretting about it constantly. Mrs Blatt was not, he hoped, the sort of person who would just bung them all out on the street. Len had certainly not been like that. But it was a worry. Martin thought about the young girl next door again and wondered whether he'd be able to drum up the courage to talk to her before Mrs Blatt sold up. He thought about this only *in theory*, of course.

'Sebastian Coe, as he was when I was girl, and me are of an age,' Vi Collins said. 'Fucking "lord"! Honestly, I'm telling you, you dignify any of these celebrity types with a knighthood and they think they're bloody beatified.'

Vi was 'on one'. It wasn't anything that DS Tony Bracci

or anyone else in Forest Gate CID wasn't used to. Someone on the Olympic Committee had called the station super-intendent to check up on what was happening about the so-called 'Olympic Flasher' and Vi, who made absolutely no secret about her revulsion of all things Conservative, was convinced the complaint had come straight from the Tory peer.

'Who needs the bloody Olympics anyway?' she continued. 'A load of people exerting themselves to the point of aneurysm isn't my idea of fun.'

Tony ignored her and looked at his computer screen. 'Last complaint was last week, guv,' he said. 'Anonymous call from a woman in a phone box at Canning Town tube.'

'Nowhere near the Olympic site!'

'She said it happened on Marshgate Lane.'

'So if it happened all the way up there, why didn't she call from her mobile?'

'Maybe it was out of charge. Maybe she doesn't have one.'

'Don't be daft!' Vi said. 'Everyone's got a mobile. And anyway if she called from Canning Town there must be CCTV.'

Tony Bracci wanted to say *I told you all this at the time,* but he managed to stop himself from doing so. Vi just didn't seem to get any more that the Olympic Flasher was important – she'd changed her tune. But then he'd not hurt anyone as yet – and in a way, Tony himself could see why she didn't care. In the past week they'd had two stabbings – one fatal – both in Manor Park. A flasher who just got his dick out was nothing.

'There is CCTV, guv,' Tony said, 'but it's impossible to ID. She's white, she's little, she's got long dark hair. Interesting thing about it' – he wanted to add *as you may recall* but didn't – 'is that she said that the flasher was Asian.'

'Yeah, I remember,' Vi said. 'She the first to ID him IC4?'

'Yes, guv, although a couple of the victims plumped for IC2.'

Vi crossed her arms over her chest. She put the last inch of a Curly Wurly in her mouth and chewed. It was no real substitute for a fag. 'So he's dark then,' she said. 'Dark European, Asian, could be an Arab of some sort, or a Turk maybe.'

'He's circumcised.'

Vi raised her eyebrows. 'Can't get a decent ID on his face, but his knob . . .'

'Guv, I've—'

'Tone, I know you've strained every nerve,' Vi said. 'But, if you remember, a boy called Jacob Sitole has just recently died on our patch – he was stabbed. He was fifteen. I'm sorry all these women keep on getting an eyeful . . .'

'They're all white.'

Vi frowned.

'All the women who've seen the flasher have been IC1,'

Tony said. 'No black girls, no IC4s, 5s . . . One I'd describe as IC2 – that woman with the Spanish surname. But he, whoever he is, likes fair skin and likes 'em a bit older too.'

'Oh, well then, I'll have to keep topping up me tan then, won't I.' Vi shook her head. 'Tone, we keep on it. Keep his lordship happy but—'

'Guv, it was you who said flashers' behaviour can escalate, not me.'

Vi knew that Tony Bracci, as well as quite a few other officers in CID, viewed what she had learned on her Open University Sociology and Criminology course as just south of useless. But she'd picked up enough on her degree course as well as on the streets of Newham to know that flashers who just stopped at flashing were rare. Eventually an opportunity would arise for actual contact with a woman; that, or the urge to masturbate in front of a particularly frightened victim would become overwhelming. Fear could be very erotic and, in the mind of the flasher, very provoking. Vi was aware that the Olympic Flasher could just take off at any minute. But one boy had been killed and another wounded in a fight between two Zimbabwean lads in Manor Park and that was her priority. Vi stood up. 'Tell the super we're on it and throw in the stuff about all the victims being white,' she said. 'I'm off out.'

'Where?'

'I've got an appointment to see Murderer,' Vi said. 'At the Royal Pie and Mash.'

'Murderer? What do you want to see him for?'

Vi smiled. 'Murderer tells me that he has some intel on Jacob Sitole's death.'

Tony Bracci pulled a face. 'Yeah and I'm Johnny Depp.'

Vi raised a warning finger. 'Now, now, DS Bracci, we cannot discount any possible source of information, however peculiar.' Then she leaned down and whispered in his ear. 'And if you were Johnny Depp I'd've had your trousers round your ankles long ago.'

Jesus was more than just nudging her now and there was no way she could have engineered this herself. There was a big cloth banner right across the front top storey of the building which said *Jesus is Alive! Come and meet him here every Sunday at 10 am.* Then in smaller letters underneath were listed other meeting times and days and a website, www.chapelofpentecostalfire.com. The mission was growing in strength and yet still just the look of the old Fun Palace made Maria shudder. Dave Delmonte had had her thrown out of there like a bag of rubbish. Guessing she was pregnant when she chucked up all over the place, he'd said, *You up the duff?* in front of everyone. She'd just managed to mutter *No* at the time, but of course she had been and Dave Delmonte had said, *I think you are, love!* Then he'd laughed and in the days and weeks that had followed she'd realised that he was right. Then she'd given her soul, free, to the devil. Could even Jesus forgive such a thing? Maria turned away and looked across the road towards the ranks of brand new apartment blocks that now ringed the old Victoria Dock. In comparison to the vast brick and concrete structure that was the old Millennium Mill on the other side of the dock, they looked very flimsy and impermanent. Her dad had worked in the dock next door, the Albert, until the industry came to a halt in the nineteen seventies with the advent of shipping containers. Then the whole thing had moved down to Tilbury and that had been that. Maria wondered what her dad would have made of the blocks and blocks of tiny, flimsy flats. She knew what he would have made of her pregnancy had he ever found out about it.

Girls who go with boys outside of marriage are no better than common tarts, was all she'd ever heard him say about women who 'got into trouble'. Her mother hadn't been quite so condemnatory but she'd had no sympathy with such behaviour either. She'd always favoured the word 'loose' in that context.

Maria walked back towards Appleby Road where her car was parked. At the side of the building she saw the door Dave Delmonte's men had thrown her out of. They'd said she should consider herself lucky that Dave hadn't wanted her to pay to have the sick cleared up. Maybe the presence of the church on the site of that awful place would somehow negate its former evil? Perhaps it would take away the visions of Dave and his awful henchmen, of Maria's own humiliation at their hands? Maybe, but it would never take away her crime.

With thick, green liquor running down his chin, Eric Noakes looked like a man locked in a life or death struggle with really bad snot. Vi Collins, sitting opposite, tried not to take her eyes off her plate of jellied eels and said, 'So, Murderer, what you got to tell me?'

Eric 'Murderer' Noakes had once been a Hells Angel. He still wore all the leather, still showed his tattoos of demons and of famous hangings to anyone who was interested, but he hadn't walked since he came off his motorbike on a run down to Brighton in 1979. Paralysed from the waist down, Murderer used an electric wheelchair to travel round the streets of Upton Park. Except when he was eating, he always had a roll-up in the corner of his mouth and a stick in his hands to swipe pedestrians out of his way. As he delighted in saying to women who tried to be nice to him and asked after his health, 'I haven't had a shag since September 1979, how the fuck do you think I feel?'

He turned his cold eyes on Vi. 'It's all to do with God,' he said.

'What is?'

As a person, Murderer was pretty much straightfor-wardly odious, but as an informant he could have his uses.

'All this malarkey up Manor Park. With the blackies,' he said.

'You mean the Zimbabweans.'

Murderer lobbed a large lump of meat into his mouth and said, 'I don't do political correctness, DI Collins. I'm too old and I can't be arsed.'

Vi sighed. Her eels were lovely, her company not so much.

'Them two boys what fought; it was over God,' Murderer said. 'One of 'em belongs to one type of happy-clappy church and the other lad to another one. One of them churches says the other lot are all witches. Dunno which one.'

Murderer wasn't the most articulate person in the world, but Vi had got the gist. One of the churches that one of the boys belonged to adhered to the notion that witches existed among them. Said witches were always evil and needed to be either exorcised in some way, or killed, or both. Sometimes witches could even be children, like Jacob Sitole. As yet, they didn't know for certain who had stabbed the boy but Vi had a very good idea that it was probably the other, injured, lad, Matthias Chibanda. Other sources had it that the two families had some sort of feud going, but no one seemed to know what it was about, or they weren't saying.

'So you're telling me this is a witchcraft death?' Vi said.

This wasn't the first and probably wouldn't be the last African witchcraft death in London. Just because people emigrated thousands of miles to another continent it didn't mean that their beliefs would change in line with their location, and Vi had read several accounts of young African girls forced to work in the UK as virtual slaves because, supposedly, some ju-ju man back home had said if they didn't they would bring bad luck on their families.

'All religion's magic at the end, isn't it?' Murderer said.

'What do you mean?'

'Bloody belief in spirits, waving incense about, all that,' he said. 'Smoke and mirrors. And I don't mean that stuff that Mark Solomons does on the telly. They get people under their spell, these religious types, and make 'em do things 'cause God says so. They do exorcism at them churches and all sorts of mad shit.'

'Why you never joined up, Murderer?'

A single middle-aged white woman came into the shop and ordered pie, mash, peas and a cuppa. It was lunchtime and the place was like a tomb.

'I had the chapter,' Murderer said. 'As well you know.'

Vi remembered the Hells Angel chapter that Murderer had belonged to. She'd nicked at least five of its members in the past. 'How does an old racist like you know about these Africans then?' she said.

Murderer, who didn't mind in the least bit being called a racist, said, 'No names, no pack drill. I have women all colours, shapes and sizes in and out my place. Know what I mean?'

He was talking about the small army of carers who went into his ground floor flat on Plashet Grove to put him to bed, change his inco pads and look for pressure sores on his bum. So one of those girls had said something to him.

'Wouldn't take me long to track down any African ladies who work for you, Murderer.'

'She'd deny it.' He shrugged.

'If you're pulling my plonker . . .'

'Why would I do that?' he said. 'You're the only copper I've ever known with a full set of nuts.'

Vi would have to go softly-softly on this whether it was a witchcraft killing or not. To explore 'difference' too closely could smack of racism, while ignoring it completely helpfully opened the door to every fascist, send-'em-all-home nut on the manor. For the first time since she'd sat down, Vi looked up into Murderer's dry, cold face and she said, 'Jerk me around and I'll make sure that you think that being paralysed from the waist is a holiday.'

He didn't even bother to shrug. 'So you gonna pay me or what?' he said.

Vi, who had already bought Murderer his lunch, pushed two twenty-pound notes across the table. He scooped them into a battered old bumbag on his lap and said, 'Religion's ruining this country, you know.'

'Some people reckon it brings them peace,' Vi said. 'Gives meaning to their lives.'

He pulled a sour face. 'What, like the Asian women dressed up like dustbin bags? The Sikhs with their heads in bandage? The happy-clapping Christians staying virgins for *the Lord*? Do me a favour!'

Vi Collins didn't have a religion. Her mum had been an Irish Catholic while her father had been a Jew. The kids had ended up nothing.

'Religion's a magic trick,' Murderer said. 'And like any magic trick it can go wrong and it can kill you. Look at Houdini.'

XIV

'Maria?'

She felt her stomach turn over. But she made the effort to smile into the telephone receiver. 'Alan.'

'Love, I thought it was time I called a bit of an old truce,' Alan Myers said. 'Don't like to be at odds with my artistes, whatever may have happened.'

He was still angry about the Comedy Store, but he was doing his very best to suppress it.

'I'm not one of your artistes any more, Alan,' Maria said. 'You sacked me.'

'Oh, yes, well . . .'

He wanted something; probably someone to fill in for a sick comic somewhere. 'What do you want, Alan?'

It was Saturday night and she had to spend time alone, praying for the strength to go to the new church in the morning.

'Do you want me to fill in for someone somewhere?' she asked.

There was a moment of silence, then he said, 'No.' He

sounded vaguely hurt but then Maria knew of old what a good actor Alan could be.

'Alan, get to the point.' She heard him take in breath and then sigh. 'Do you want me to do something for you or what? Because if you do I've told you I've finished with comedy. When Len died I needed something familiar in my life so I went back to comedy but it was a mistake.'

'But you were good, love. When you started back out on the circuit you were great.'

He was right. When she'd first gone back, she'd been brilliant. But because he was right she became flustered because she didn't want to be that person any more. 'So you do want . . .'

'You out on the circuit? No.' Now Maria was shocked and she was hurt too – but why was that? 'After all your performances breaking down and that, and then the Comedy Store cancellation, your name's a bit, well, poisoned at the moment.' He must have heard her sharp intake of breath but he didn't give her a chance to speak. 'Maria, people are saying you look ill and I'm worried.'

Her name was poisoned? When she did manage to speak she just said, 'People?'

'Well, Beppo actually,' Alan said. 'Still lives with his ancient mother up Odessa Road. He saw you at one of the chemist's on Woodgrange Road. He said you looked thin and pale and he didn't like to talk to you because he said you looked like you wanted to be on your own.'

'Did he say what I was buying, by any chance?' Now she was cross. Beppo was a nosy, old-fashioned, queeny old clown who Alan still managed for some bizarre reason. She'd never liked him.

'Painkillers,' Alan said. Of course Beppo had seen what she'd bought. 'Some of those with codeine.'

Maria saw which way this was blowing. 'Oh, so now I'm a codeine addict.'

'You used to stick all and sundry down your throat in the old days!' Alan said.

'I had a headache, Alan, a bad one. I know you'd love to ascribe my behaviour to something as sexy as addiction, but it just isn't true, not this time. You know full well why I can't perform the kind of comedy I used to any more and it's your problem if you won't accept it.' Jesus. Alan Myers couldn't even bring himself to allude to her religion. In the past he'd tried to ignore it, but maybe he'd been wrong to do that. Maybe he should have talked to her about it when all the Jesus stuff had first started.

'Maria, if you're ill you know that you can count on me to help you. All professional stuff aside, you're a lovely girl and—'

'Alan, I don't need your help. I have all the help I need.'

'God.'

'Yes, God,' she said. 'I've finally come to my senses, Alan. I'm not the mess you discovered back in the year dot any more. I'm not in thrall to the Catholic Church like I was when I was a kid. This is real.'

It took a lot to make Alan Myers lose his cool. But he, like Len Blatt, had seen Maria battle addiction before. And addiction came in many forms – not all of which were substance based. 'Maria, these people, this church, they're manipulating you.' He could almost hear her sneer down the phone. 'It's all fairy stories, what they're telling you. I've seen it all before. Trust me on this!'

'Oh and how is that?'

'They're drawing you in. Changing you. They just want your money, love.'

'No they don't! No, I sought them out, Alan. I needed God. I went looking for Him. Trust me on this and deal with it. Goodbye.'

Maria replaced the receiver to the sound of Alan Myers still wittering away about her 'health' at the other end. Then she went over to the dining room window and looked outside through the drizzle into the street. Evening was beginning to drift over into night and people were hurrying home to get in front of televisions dominated by cheesy talent shows. When she'd been young every artiste, whether a comedian, a singer or a dancer had had to serve their time in dodgy pubs and clubs for years before TV stations came knocking. That was probably why just about everyone had been on something back then. Now, people just seemed to pop up from nowhere all the time. Without even thinking about what she was doing, Maria poured herself a glass of port from the decanter on the dining table and threw it down the back of her throat. Then, for just an instant, she stopped.

Outside in the rain a familiar figure stopped in front of her house and she only just avoided making eye contact with her. It was that Asian woman from the detective agency. Mumtaz. For just a second that terrible time when she'd engaged the Arnold Agency came back to her and, not for the first time, she wondered how she'd managed to put that note on Len's grave for herself. She had no memory of doing that – or of putting the Clarks box next to the television.

It was a truly horrible feeling to be so conflicted. Mumtaz wanted to tell Lee about seeing Maria Peters – how sick she'd looked, how she'd been knocking back booze – but she also just wanted to let all that lie. It was Saturday night and Lee would probably be out with friends, and besides, Maria Peters wasn't their business any more. Except that to Lee she kind of was. She kind of was to Mumtaz too. She still had that flyer for the Chapel of the Holy Pentecostal Fire in her handbag. Mumtaz wondered if Lee fancied Maria; slim or thin, she was a good-looking woman, even if she was older than he was.

Her mother took a tray of samosas out of the oven and put them on the kitchen table. 'When will you be able to come home again?' she asked.

'What?' Mumtaz hadn't been listening. Now she felt bad. 'Amma?'

'Home, child,' Sumita said. 'It would be nice if you could come and eat with us for a change sometimes. All you do these days is just pop in for half an hour occasionally, it's not enough.'

At some point almost every weekend Mumtaz's parents would eat at her house, mainly because Shazia didn't like having to drag all the way over to Spitalfields, which she hated. And if Mumtaz worked on a Saturday, Sumita and Baharat generally came over to look after the girl. On Sumita's part that was mainly as a favour to her daughter although Baharat did actually seem to get on quite well with Shazia even though she wasn't his real granddaughter. He also felt sorry for her as a child without parents whereas Sumita saw her more as an inconvenience. Without her it would be much easier to find a man for Mumtaz.

'Yes, but Shazia—'

Her mother dismissed her with the wave of a hand. 'Ah, she can make Brick Lane her playground for once, it won't kill her.'

Mumtaz, who knew how scornful Shazia always was of the 'losers' on the streets of Bangla Town, nevertheless bit her tongue. She took her phone out of her pocket and looked at it again. Her mother saw her and frowned. 'Waiting for a call?' she said. Her voice sweated suspicion and Mumtaz knew why.

'I'm waiting for no one to call,' she said. 'I am wondering if I should call someone myself.'

'Who? A man?'

Mumtaz breathed deeply and attempted to remain calm. After all, her mother couldn't help it if her entire thinking had always been dominated by either hoping for a man for herself or her daughter, keeping men, weddings, and children. That was how she had been raised.

'Yes and no,' Mumtaz eventually said.

'What is it?'

'Something to do with my job, Amma. Nothing romantic, I promise.'

Sumita placed a selection of samosas on a plate and said, 'You should not be alone, Mumtaz. It isn't good for a woman. People talk about such women.'

Mumtaz didn't say a word. Suddenly, wiping out the microwave was something she could no longer ignore.

'You're an educated woman who keeps a nice home,' her mother said. 'A nice, quiet gentleman would be very happy to care for you.'

Apart from the fact that Mumtaz had decided as soon as Ahmed died that she never wanted to be 'cared for' again, the implication behind the words 'nice, quiet gentleman' made her shudder. Her mother meant some old man, some venerable widower who wouldn't mind, too much, that she wasn't a virgin any more. Someone like poor, heart-diseased Mr Choudhury. Mumtaz stopped wiping the microwave and began to scrub it. For the moment, she quite forgot all about Lee Arnold and Maria Peters.

A tall, skinny, white girl with thick purple dreadlocks looked down at Vi's stiletto-shod feet and very obviously turned her middle-class nose up. This part of Hackney Wick, the area around Forman's smoked salmon place, was stiff with people like her, too cool for school. She was probably an artist, which was code for a trustafarian who until very recently had been Head Girl at Roedean. Vi Collins was aware that she was probably the most cynical and judgemental person in the known universe but she didn't much care. She'd come down to the Wick to talk to a bloke called the Reverend Charles Manyika, pastor at the Bethel Revival Church. It was where Jacob Sitole had worshipped and where his family still went.

In common with most of the 'churches' around the Olympic site, the Bethel Revival was housed in an old warehouse. Opposite a tarpaulin-covered corner shop and next door to a place called the Happiness Club, which Vi knew for a fact was an S&M hang-out, it looked almost the same as the now demolished Chapel of the Holy Pentecostal Fire. But then the happy-clappy places did all tend to be out of the same mould. Around the corner was a church that called itself the Peace in Jesus Foundation. That was where Matthias Chibanda, the boy who she now knew had killed Jacob Sitole, worshipped. She'd been there already.

Vi knocked on the door nearest to the sign outside and waited. After a few moments a tall, bespectacled, black man answered. Smiling, he introduced himself as Charles Manyika. As he took Vi through into a big, draughty hall filled with what looked like almost a thousand chairs, he said, 'We are all very distressed about Jacob, he was a good boy.'

'Mrs Sitole says the church is being very supportive,' Vi said. An elderly lady, dressed entirely in sunflower yellow asked the reverend if they both wanted tea and Manyika said that they did. He took Vi over to some soft easy chairs beside the large stage at one end of the hall and they both sat down.

'That two Christian boys like Jacob and Matthias should fight until one of them dies is beyond appalling,' Manyika said.

'Matthias worshipped at the Peace in Jesus Foundation,' Vi said.

'Yes, he did.'

'Do you know the Peace in Jesus Foundation people?'

'I know Pastor Iekanjika,' Manyika said.

'What do you think of him?'

Manyika frowned. 'Inspector?'

It wasn't an easy subject to broach but, while Vi couldn't go straight to the subject of witchcraft just on Murderer

Noakes's say so, she did have to attempt to follow up what he had raised. And Pastor Iekanjika had been . . . difficult.

'Reverend, there's no point my beating about the bush. There's been a suggestion that Jacob may have been killed because of a difference of opinion between your followers here and the people over at Peace in Jesus.'

'But that's ridiculous! We are all Christians! Murder is anathema to us!'

The old lady put two large mugs of tea on the table together with a bowl of sugar and a plate of what looked like cheesecake. As she walked away she muttered something that Vi couldn't hear.

'As I understand it, the boys had a fight,' the reverend said. 'I have no idea what it was about but it ended badly. Young men carry knives these days to defend themselves, the streets are not safe. What can I say to make them stop? There are gangs in this city and I preach against such things. What do you do about the gangs, DI Collins?'

Vi had imagined he'd be defensive. And who could blame him? In all likelihood he was a committed Christian and a decent man and he probably felt that she was being racist.

'I do what I can too,' Vi said. 'But sir, I'd be negligent if I didn't follow up all and every lead . . .'

'Who says we are bad people?' He took a piece of cheesecake and nibbled nervously at one side. 'We are not bad people.'

'No one is saying . . .' Vi leaned forward, took a sip from her teacup, bunged a load a sugar in and said, 'Because it's said that you practise exorcism—'

'Everyone practises exorcism! The Catholic Church, the Anglicans . . .'

'Sir—'

'Because we are charismatic, born again, is that the problem? I suppose you think we practise witchcraft too?'

He was furious now and Vi didn't know what to say. She hadn't even directly mentioned the concept of witch-craft – even though Manyika himself had – but then she had no evidence for it. This man, unlike Iekanjika, seemed very reasonable and he would at least, talk. Vi's own antipathy towards religion meant however that she remained suspicious. But taking it any further with this man was pointless. Other more subtle methods would have to be employed to find out what, if anything, was happening in these churches.

'People fear what they do not understand. Inspector, in my eyes it is a good thing that so many people come to the Lord these days. Now we even have more white brothers and sisters too. Churches rising up, thirsty for Christ. Jacob's death had nothing to do with religion, or with any witchcraft. I know what you people think about that! But young men, even good young men, they fight . . .' He bit into the cheesecake in a robust fashion. 'Even if one chooses a certain church over another, that is no cause for violence or bad feeling.' He looked up at her. 'What does Matthias Chibanda say?'

'Nothing. He won't talk to us,' Vi said.

'And Pastor Iekanjika? Have you asked him to talk to the boy?'

'Of course.'

'And?'

'And, nothing. Pastor Iekanjika says that the boy's crime is between him and God. He says he does not recognise secular authority.'

And that was really the nub of the matter. What Murderer Noakes had said had been of interest but it had been Vi's interview with the hostile and unhelpful Iekanjika that had really roused her suspicions. He'd answered nothing, had thrown faithism, racism, every-thing at her.

Manyika took a deep breath, put his cake down and attempted a small smile. 'Well, that is clearly wrong,' he said. 'I don't know why Pastor Iekanjika is behaving in that way. In my experience he is a most zealous man of God, not always an easy man, but ...' He sighed. 'Sometimes, DI Collins, people immersed in the Spirit can be a little bit blind to life ...'

'What do you mean?'

He leaned back in his chair. 'Knowing, as we do, that God will ultimately judge all souls, we can sometimes forget that man too has a need for justice. We are human and we feel anger and sorrow and hurt for all sorts of reasons. Myself, I am upset that the Pentecostal Fire Chapel has had to move from this site. For our congregants it was good to have so many mostly white British people close by. We don't seek to live in a ghetto, Inspector. All nations are equal under God. More and more of your people are coming to the Lord.' He smiled. 'But in the end of days that is what will happen.'

Vi groaned inside. End-of-the-world shit. Fuck! People had been predicting that for millennia. Didn't any of these happy-clappies ever read history? But she smiled, she hoped, not too indulgently.

'You talk about rivalry between churches?' the reverend said. 'DI Collins, we go in and out of each other's churches all the time. We are a brotherhood, a fellowship, we bathe in the Word of the Lord whenever and wherever we can. Churches here on this site, Pastor Nwogu's Divine Light Church, the Nigerian People of the Book, we are all strong in the Lord and so to lose that contact would not be a good thing. Ma'am, I encourage our congregation to take fellowship with others whenever they can.'

But he didn't mention Iekanjika and his Peace in Jesus Foundation.

Vi left having hit what was basically another brick wall. But she did now at least know that the surmised antipathy between the two churches had some basis in the silence that appeared to exist between the Reverend Manyika and

Pastor Iekanjika. Or was that just her interpretation of things? But if it were the case then so much for Christian charity, she thought. Then she wondered what Iekanjika had done to upset Manyika, or vice versa. She walked out onto White Post Lane and saw a man run past her towards Hackney Wick Station. As he passed he looked at her and the sight of his grey, terrified face made her heart jump.

Automatically, Vi shouted, 'Hey, stop!' And then she began to run after him. 'Oi, you, police!'

The man, though clearly overweight, began to run faster. Whiteish and frightened, he could be the flasher. He could be almost anyone, but Vi had a strong feeling that he wasn't. Over the years she had come to trust such notions. Vi's attempts to run in stilettos came to nothing and so she took them off and then legged it after him, shoes in hand. Thirty-odd years of smoking didn't help as she tried to make a call on her mobile back to the station. But then by the time she actually reached Hackney Wick station the man could not be seen or even heard any more. No footstep noises clattered through the night and Vi was left in the middle of White Post Lane panting, her shoes in her hands, her tights in tatters.

XV

'Marie, what's wrong?'

Betty must have thought she'd lost her mind. But she couldn't go inside, her legs wouldn't move. Slumped against the wall that Dave Delmonte had had built around the car park of his fun pub, Maria fought with sickness as well as with the way everyone kept looking at her. The service was due to start in ten minutes' time and people were clearly conflicted as to whether to help Maria or go inside.

Maria wanted to confess. People did it all the time, they called it 'testifying'. But she couldn't. In spite of what she thought about the Pope and Catholicism, she wanted, she needed, formality – a confessional – and she wanted a penance and then punishment that lasted for ever. But Pastor Grint didn't do that Catholic stuff. He was a good man and formal confession, as he always said, was just an exercise in futility. God wasn't some sort of simpleton who could be placated by a few Hail Marys. But that didn't stop Maria wanting it.

'Come into church, we can look after you there,' Betty said.

'No!' Her breathing had gone and her mouth had dried up. She thought about a routine she'd done years ago about Victorian women fainting and it made her feel even sicker. *It's said they fainted because their corsets were too tight,* she'd said, *but I reckon they had men up inside those crinolines. Men with moustaches. Licking.*

'What *is* it, Marie?' Betty reiterated. As people she knew and liked looked on, Maria clung to the wall with all of her strength. She couldn't go in there. That was where it had all first come to light.

'Come inside with me,' Betty said. 'Come to church.' Her voice took on a sudden hard edge. 'It will do you good.'

'No!'

The large crowd of people around her all looked at each other, and that included Pastor Grint. He hadn't actually seen her collapse but he'd come out immediately when some of the others had called. 'Whatever is it, Maria?' he said.

'I'm too dirty!' she said, shivering as she spoke. Some congregants were confused by this apparent incongruity. 'I can't go in there! I can't go *back* in there!'

'But it's our new church,' Grint said. 'For the time being. I know it's not exactly what we want . . .'

She heard someone whisper, 'Maybe she used to get

drunk in there years ago,' and it made the dam inside her crack.

'I got pregnant!' Like liquid spilling out of an overfull mouth.

'In there?' The pastor pointed to his church.

'No.' Her voice was just a whisper now. 'I realised in there. That was where I found out. In that building. There.'

Martin bided his time and then he struck. To hell with *in theory*! The headscarfed woman went out to get some shopping, leaving the girl in the garden – alone. He went out into his own mattress-and-dirty-disposable-nappy-filled garden, and he caught her eye.

'Better day today, isn't it?' he called across the fence. 'A little bit warmer.'

He couldn't quite make out whether she was afraid of him or just appalled that he, an old man, had spoken to her. She said, 'Yeah.'

'Summer coming.'

'Yes.' She turned away.

'You must have your exams coming up soon,' Martin persisted. 'What is it? O levels?'

'GCSEs.' She smirked. He was showing his age talking about O levels and she was amused by that. Little cow! She thought he was old, past it, a right coffin-dodger. Martin felt his face darken.

'Studying hard, are you?'

She shrugged.

'Must have a good future in front of you going to a posh school like Bancroft's. Bet they make you work hard, don't they?' Again she didn't respond and so Martin just went for it. 'Give you a lot of home-study time do they, your school?'

She looked up at that!

'Noticed that you always seem to have Thursday afternoons off,' he said. 'Bit of group study with your mates?'

She was pale for an Asian and so he very clearly saw her face flush. It was good because it unequivocally answered his question about Thursday afternoons. That girl was not supposed to be at home. No sir!

'Well, see you,' he said, smiling. Then he went back inside. He'd leave her to think about that for a while. He'd leave her to wonder whether the old man next door would tell her mother about her Thursday afternoons or not. He suspected that next time they met she might actually instigate the conversation.

Something wasn't right and it went beyond the fact that she was upset. She felt . . . violated. It was almost as if returning to that terrible place, even if it was now a church, had reactivated the feelings of dread she'd experienced before. But then it would. What she'd felt when she'd engaged Lee Arnold's firm to surveille her house was not what she'd imagined it had been back then. Now she knew that no one was watching her, that somehow she'd moved Gog and Magog from the fireplace over to the TV, that she'd put the old Clarks shoebox in the corner herself. She had been haunting her own life because finally the guilt had come back and it wasn't going away. She hadn't admitted her crime and so she still wasn't right with Jesus. He was pressing her because she needed to be right with Him. The location of the new church just served to underline it. Soon, she knew, she would have to tell everything. The congregation knew she'd had a child but . . . She felt it being forced out of her like icing out of a piping bag. She longed to be empty, to fill the space left behind completely with God.

And yet because that old feeling of being observed had returned, Maria couldn't completely convince herself that its perpetrator wasn't either herself or another, human, being. She walked from the hall into the kitchen and took a bottle of whisky out of her drinks cupboard. It could still be a person, couldn't it? Someone who knew her secrets and wished her ill will? She poured a small amount of booze into a glass, put a pill on her tongue and knocked both back while standing up looking into the garden. The sun was out and she could hear the sound of her neighbours mowing their lawns and cutting their hedges. Normal life was still going on. That was all she'd ever really wanted: normal life. Had God not given her that because of what she'd done? And had the subsequent boozing and drug-taking and all the vile stuff she'd put into her stand-up routines made that impossible?

In the great silence that roared into her life after Len died, a little voice demanding justice had wheedled. She'd tried to silence it with flip jokes about God and sex and all sorts of shit she'd shut it up with years back, but it wouldn't go. It just got louder. It had been then that she'd started to notice things – about God.

A random, tattered poster on a railway arch wall, leaflets through her door, a booklet. It had been as if Jesus was beckoning her. But then she'd always known she'd have to make amends some time. She went to the Chapel of the Holy Pentecostal Fire and there she discovered her old friend Betty and she found Jesus with her.

Here at last was a measure of peace and security that mirrored, in some ways, what she'd had with Len. But then the feelings of being watched began to roll in, the dread and then, of course, the terrible, terrible guilt.

Maria walked into her living room. It was so beautiful outside in her gardens, but she wasn't interested. If she went outside there was always a chance she'd be obliged to talk to some neighbour over the fence and she didn't want that. Betty had offered to come home and spend some time with her after the service, but Maria had wanted to be alone.

She sat down on the sofa and scanned the *Sunday Times* culture supplement for the TV pages. Usually on a Sunday afternoon there was some sort of crime show on one of the channels. An old *Columbo* or *Murder, She Wrote* or something. Eventually Maria found a programme that appealed to her on a distant cable channel. She leaned across to the sideboard behind the sofa and was about to pick up the remote control when she saw something she should have seen as soon as she came into the room. On top of the sideboard, tied together with a great big purple ribbon, like a bunch of flowers, were at least twenty perfect peacock feathers. Maria pulled her hand back and away from them immediately and only just managed not to scream. What were they doing in her house? Where had they come from? Who, *who* had put them there?

Glenys, her mother, had always been and remained a superstitious woman. It was something she had passed on to her children. Peacock feathers brought bad luck. To have them in a house was tantamount to inviting ill fortune across the threshold. Maria knew it was bollocks, but as she looked at the feathers she felt her throat begin to close and her eyes start to water. She would never, ever bring such things into her house, not even in her sleep, not even in her nightmares. With trembling hands she grabbed the phone and called Pastor Grint. But he was 'temporarily unavailable', as the electronic message had it. Maria felt alone and let down, although she knew that was irrational. Why should Paul Grint be at her beck and call all the time? Her legs shook as she stood up and stumbled back towards the hall and the front door. The feathers were seeping malice – she could almost see it. She had to get out.

Much as she would have liked to have cooked Shazia a traditional English Sunday meal, Mumtaz just couldn't justify the expense this week. It was going to have to be dhal and to that end she'd had lentils soaking overnight. But she lacked cinnamon and also one of the most basic ingredients of *mitta dhoi*, the sweet – and cheap – baked yoghurt treat she would use to try and take the edge off Shazia's disappointment. For that, as well as the yoghurt, milk and sugar she already had, Mumtaz also needed a tin of evaporated milk. There were several convenience stores up on Woodgrange Road and so she headed off to get what she needed at just after midday.

Mumtaz spent rather longer in the Sylhet Convenience Shop than she had imagined that she would. Because the day was warm and bright, people were encouraged to talk as they went about their business in the good weather and Mumtaz stopped to speak to several ladies she hadn't seen for months. As she suspected they would, these women all knew about her job and one of them even suggested that they should 'talk' at some point. The world of Bangladeshi women could be, at times, very small.

Mumtaz walked back from the shop down Osborne Road and into Richmond Road. All these streets were quiet and leafy and it didn't take much to imagine how elegant they had been in the past. Mumtaz's own house was one of those that even had an old coach house in the back garden. Not that her house was actually *her house* in reality. Most of it belonged to the bank that had given Ahmed a very dodgy mortgage. It was a mortgage he had extended several times. She paid them what she could, when she could, but recent telephone conversations had involved the word 'repossession'. As calmly as she was able, Mumtaz had asked only that they restrain themselves until after Shazia had finished her GCSEs. The girl knew nothing about any possible repossession and Mumtaz wanted to keep it that way for as long as she could.

She crossed the road at the junction of Richmond Road and Claremont Road. There was no traffic and so she didn't hurry. Had she done so, she wouldn't have heard the crying. But she did and, although she had to wrestle with her 'nice-Muslim-lady-don't-get-involved' thing, she eventually gave in to her much more recent private investigator's curiosity. The sound was coming from her right and so she turned into Claremont Road and began walking back towards Woodgrange Road. Vast, tree-screened houses, just like her own, gently basked in the unseasonable warmth. Most of them were quiet. A lot of people had probably taken advantage of the weather to go out into Epping Forest or down to Brighton for the day. Maria Peters, half sitting, half lying on her doorstep crying, was an exception. Mumtaz walked up to her front gate, pushed it open and then closed it behind her.

'Miss Peters,' she said once she'd reached the front step and put a hand on the woman's shoulder. 'Whatever is the matter?'

They both looked across the room at the bunch of peacock feathers. They had all been tied, very artistically, together with a purple silk bow.

'They bring bad fortune,' Maria Peters said. She bit her own lip and frowned. 'I know it's all bollocks, but it's an old tradition – in the theatre – and it's what my mother taught me.'

'What our mothers teach us, stays with us,' Mumtaz said. When she leaned forward to touch the feathers, she heard Maria wince.

'You don't think they bring bad luck?'

'No.' Mumtaz smiled. 'I think only God gives and takes away.'

Maria wanted to say that that was what she tried to believe too, but she didn't. She said, 'The point is, I didn't put them there, I wouldn't and I don't know who did, or would.'

'You think that someone is trying to frighten you again?'

She didn't want to say 'yes'. But this time she *couldn't* have done this to herself. She would never have been able to bring herself to touch those . . . things.

Mumtaz picked up the feathers and turned to look at her. 'If you want me to dispose of these, I'll do it gladly,' she said.

'That would be nice.' Maria smiled. But then she put a hand up to her mouth and chewed down on a fingernail.

Mumtaz put the feathers into her blue plastic shopping bag. She couldn't be sure that Maria Peters hadn't put the feathers there herself, it had to be a possibility. But it was only that. No one had ever really got to the bottom of her last bout of persecution fear.

'Would you like a friend or a relative to come and be with you?' Mumtaz asked.

Maria sat down. 'Like my mother? I need her in my life like a hole in the head. If she calls I ignore her.'

'The police?' Mumtaz offered.

'No.'

'If you feel that your house may have been broken—'

'There's no sign of any sort of break-in.' Maria rubbed a hand across her face, smearing what was left of her mascara out towards her temples.

'Maybe whoever put these feathers here has a key.'

'No.' She shook her head. 'No one else has a key but me. I love my friends and even my mum, in a way, but I wouldn't want them to be able to just come in when they felt like it.'

'You're sure?'

'Yes.'

But Mumtaz wasn't. Even when people didn't give keys away, people still managed to get hold of them. Her oldest brother Tariq had stolen their mother's key when he was a teenager, had a copy made and then put it back in her handbag before she noticed. For almost a year it had allowed him to come and go at will from the family home whether his parents approved or not.

'Whatever's going on here, I don't want people that I care about and who care about me, involved,' Maria said. 'Not this time.' Sitting out on the doorstep she hadn't tried to call Grint or anyone else again.

Mumtaz sat down next to her. 'But don't you think that people who love you would like to help if they can?'

The comedian looked into Mumtaz's eyes. 'You've a background in psychology; do you think that I'm doing these things myself? Do you think I'm losing my mind?'

Unknown to Maria Peters, these were not easy questions to answer. Neither Lee, nor Neil nor Mumtaz had been able to actually witness Maria placing objects and moving things around back in February. But that didn't mean she hadn't been doing it. She was genuinely afraid of what she seemed to genuinely feel were the actions of an outside agency of some sort. But clearly some anxieties about her own sanity were present too. An honest answer in either the affirmative or the negative was impossible. Mumtaz said, 'I don't know.'

'You don't *know*!'

'Miss Peters, things have happened in this house that no one as yet has got to the bottom of. But peacock feathers, which you hate, do not just appear out of thin air. Well, not *really*. I think that someone could be getting into your house somehow. I think that you should call the police.'

But Maria Peters shook her head.

'Why not?'

She didn't answer. She didn't need to. Last time the police had got involved with Maria it had ended with her not just dismissing them but also sacking Lee and the agency too. It had been something about not wanting to upset her friends, about not wanting to be watched 'by men' any more. Lee was still of the opinion that her reasons had been bollocks. He really did think she'd lost her mind.

'Miss Peters, if you'd like the agency—'

'Oh, no, no, no, no, no!' She shook her head violently. 'Men outside my house looking into every corner! No, no, that was awful dreadful, like a nightmare!'

'You engaged—'

'Oh, I engaged Mr Arnold and the rest of you, yes, but . . .' She slumped against the back of the sofa. 'That wasn't the answer, was it.'

Mumtaz said nothing. The more time she was spending with Maria Peters the more she became convinced that what she needed was a doctor. But how to even begin to say such a thing? She wasn't the woman's friend or relative and although Mumtaz's confidence had grown considerably since she'd been working for the agency, she still couldn't quite get to the point of telling strangers they were bonkers. She was lost in these thoughts almost completely when she heard Maria Peters say, 'I'd employ you though, alone.' Mumtaz looked up and frowned. 'If you would come and stay with me here, I'd pay you well,' Maria said. 'I trust you.'

Mumtaz, taken entirely by surprise said, 'I don't know if that will be possible. I'd have to speak to Mr Arnold.'

'Don't hit him!'

Vi blocked the heavy fist of Luther Chibanda as it attempted to make contact with his son Matthias's head. Thwarted, Luther reeled away into the corner of the room, weeping.

'You must tell the police what has happened!' he shouted.

The boy, lying in the hospital bed, turned away.

'However bad and whatever it is, you must tell them.'

But still Matthias didn't speak.

Luther looked across the small hospital side room at the tall, impressive man standing over by the door and said, 'Pastor, you must help us to get Matthias to speak. Please! He and Jacob were like brothers. We do not understand why this has happened.'

Vi saw how unmoved Iekanjika was and it made her skin crawl.

'Luther, I can pray for the boy only,' he said.

'Pastor, maybe he is possessed!'

'If that becomes apparent, then I will cleanse him. But at the moment—'

'You think that Matthias killed Jacob because of some, some earthly thing, some thing of greed or ...' Luther Chibanda broke down in tears again.

Vi, at a loss amid so much that she didn't understand, put a hand on Luther's shoulder and said, 'Mr Chibanda, we will get to the bottom of this.' Even though she really didn't know whether that was possible.

'He must be possessed,' Luther Chibanda said, as much to himself as to anyone else. 'He must be.'

Vi just caught, as she quickly glanced away from Luther Chibanda, a brief look that passed between Pastor Iekanjika and Matthias Chibanda. It was not a look of complicity or collusion or amusement or even disapproval. It was a look that told her that Matthias was terrified of Iekanjika.

XVI

'I told her that even if I could do it, she'd have to pay the agency and not just me,' Mumtaz told Lee. It was Monday morning and, after a truly awful Sunday afternoon with his mum weeping over Roy, who was missing again, Lee had needed the subject of Maria Peters landing back in his life like a hole in the head.

'But what about your other work?' he asked. 'There's that dodgy husband over East Ham, and what about the woman who thinks her daughter-in-law's up to no good? You can't just walk out on them for some gig babysitting someone who's bonkers.'

'I know. But she'd pay us an awful lot of money.'

Mr Savva, the landlord, had been completely deaf to any entreaties from Lee. So the rent on the office had gone up, as had the utility bills. Cars and vans needed servicing, insuring and taxing and although the agency was making more money than it had ever done before, income was still not keeping pace with expenditure – or Lee's debts.

Frustrated, Lee said, 'But the woman in East Ham as well as the one with the daughter-in law want you because they trust you as an Asian woman,' he said. 'I can't bowl out there and do what you do for them!'

'I told Miss Peters I would have to get your approval,' Mumtaz said. 'I also said I was busy, that maybe for a while I could only spend part of my time with her.'

'She won't have surveillance equipment again?'

'No. She says she doesn't like being watched. I think she may have an issue about being observed by men. I've no idea. She was married and she seems to like men on some level.'

'So what about Amy, then?' Lee said.

Mumtaz shook her head. 'I tried that tack,' she said. 'She wants me. She trusts me.'

Still looking distinctly disgruntled Lee said, 'You are very trustworthy.'

'Thank you.'

Then he shook his head again and said, 'But what about Shazia? You can't expect her to just go and live in the house of some woman who might be mad.'

Mumtaz frowned. She'd made various suggestions to Shazia about how Maria Peters' plan might work, but she'd hated them all. She didn't, quite rightly, want to leave her home under any circumstances and she certainly didn't want Mumtaz's parents to move in, in order to look after her. It left Mumtaz feeling torn. If she did live with Maria

Peters for a while then she would get a lot more money in overtime payments which could help to mollify the bank. Leaving Shazia alone in the house at night, however, was not something she was comfortable with. But then, as Lee had said, she couldn't take her to Maria Peters' house either because the woman was not right. And what if she discovered that she was actually raving mad? What then? Maybe it was time for Mumtaz to tell someone just how deep her financial problems were.

'I haven't paid my mortgage for six months,' she blurted. 'I need the money.'

Lee had known that she was hard up but he thought that the house she'd shared with her husband now belonged to her. He was shocked. 'Mumtaz! Didn't your husband have life insurance?'

She felt ashamed. Even though what had been done had been none of her doing. 'He took out a mortgage with a proper bank and then he took it away and gave it over to a bunch of criminals. Then he remortgaged. Then he remortgaged again,' she said. 'You know, Lee, it was my husband who made me cover my head because he was supposedly such a good Muslim and I did it gladly. It is a good thing. I can't imagine my life any other way now. But in my religion we are not supposed to either pay or take interest payments. What kind of a Muslim was he?'

Lee didn't have an answer. He wanted to put his arms

around her and give her a hug, but instead he said, 'Why didn't you say?'

She began to feel her eyes fill up. 'For what reason? You have financial problems all the time! What good would it do?'

Now she'd told him, she still didn't feel any better.

'Does Shazia know about it?'

'No.' She shook her head. 'How can I tell her? It's her home. She's never lived anywhere else. It's full of memories of her mother.'

'And her father.'

Mumtaz didn't answer. Lee didn't know about Ahmed. Nobody really knew about Ahmed except herself and Shazia.

Lee Arnold took a deep breath in and then stood up and went over to the front office door. He turned the Open sign at the window to Closed and then sat down again.

'Sorry, Mumtaz,' he said, 'I'm going to have to smoke to think this one through.'

'There's nothing you can—'

'Listen.' Lee took his cigarettes out of his jacket pocket and then lit up. 'You need Maria Peters' money, I need Maria Peters' money and, I'll be honest, I need to know what's going on in that house for my own peace of mind. At the moment, what's going on in there, or not, is like a cross between *One Flew Over the Cuckoo's Nest* and the bloody *Amityville Horror.* Then seeing the look of confusion on Mumtaz's face he said, 'One's a film about nutters, the other's a supernatural horror flick. I need to think. You have to meet one of your ladies this morning, don't you?'

'At ten thirty in East Ham, yes.'

Lee sighed. 'Could be a bit of a chain-smoke problem,' he said.

'Lee, you don't have to—'

'I need the dosh too, Mumtaz,' he said. 'Rent's due and I'll be honest, I ain't good for it.'

'Oh, no!' As well as feeling sorry for him, if her job disappeared now she'd definitely be out on the street.

Lee held up a hand. 'But listen, don't fret it now,' he said. 'Go out to your meeting, let me have a smoke and something'll come to me. The main thing is we need to get Shazia safe and looked after in a way that won't upset her and we need to keep you in with the Asian ladies of Newham.' Then he looked up and smiled. 'Bit of thought, couple of fags, it'll be a doddle.'

'He was maybe about forty, possibly older. Darkish, guv,' Vi said to Superintendent Tom Venus.

'IC4?' He didn't even bother to look up from his paperwork. Vi couldn't decide whether it was because the paperwork had come from Lord Coe or whether it was because she was over fifty and therefore invisible. Venus liked young and pretty women almost as much as he loved all the Olympic nonsense.

'I don't know for certain,' Vi replied. 'IC1? Maybe, more likely, IC2. To me he looked more grey than anything else.'

'No recognisable skin tone is grey, DI Collins,' he said. He still didn't look at her.

'No, sir.' *Fucking prick!* she thought. *What do you know with your sexy little secretary and your posh Surrey accent.*

'You gave chase.'

'Yes, sir.'

Now he looked up at her and muttered, 'Mmm.' She saw him look at the thick lines that radiated out from her mouth and she knew he was thinking *dirty, unfit smoker.* But then he changed the subject. 'And the revivalist churches, DI Collins?'

'I definitely detected some tension between Jacob Sitole's minister Reverend Manyika and Matthias Chibanda's pastor, Iekanjika,' she said. 'I also think that Iekanjika may have some sort of hold over Matthias.'

'What do you mean?'

She shrugged. 'I'm not sure yet, sir. But when I was at the hospital I noticed that the boy looked afraid of the pastor.'

'What about witchcraft?'

'I only got that off my snout, guv.'

'You followed it up?'

'Of course. But we've had no other reports about it on

the manor and I didn't pick up anything from Manyika that made me skin crawl. Iekanjika, as I've said, was another matter though.'

Venus creased his otherwise smooth brow into a frown. 'In what way?'

'Doesn't recognise what he calls "secular authority",' Vi said. 'Won't talk, just like Chibanda.'

'So something dodgy's going on,' Venus said. 'Think we've got enough to pull this Iekanjika in?'

'What for?' Vi said. 'He was nowhere near when Sitole got killed. The whole thing about Iekanjika revolves around his silence and my feelings about him.'

Venus sighed. 'But just as the devil makes work for idle hands so, sometimes, I think God does too. Run a check on this Iekanjika.'

As far as Vi was concerned Venus's only saving grace was that he had little time for God squads of any stripe. Apart from that he was an arrogant berk in the grip of a mid-life crisis. It was said that he did some dance/exercise thing called Zumba.

'Yes, sir. Nothing was removed from Sitole's body,' Vi said. 'Often in witchcraft cases it is. Body parts are used as talismans. Not always but—'

'We don't need this in the run-up to the Olympics, whatever it is,' Venus said. 'We don't need this and we don't need a flasher. By the way, did he actually get his tackle out for your benefit?'

'No, sir.'

'Mmm.'

Vi thought he was probably thinking that he could understand why. But what did Venus really know about the flasher anyway? He went for white women, generally older, didn't matter to him what they looked like.

'There have been a couple of cases of fraud concerning some of these charismatic churches down on what is now the Olympic site,' Venus said. 'They take their parishioners' money, ostensibly for charity, and then they do a bunk. Maybe we should have a look at exactly where these churches stand in terms of finance. Perhaps it's money rather than God that keeps Matthias Chibanda's mouth closed.'

'Yes, sir.'

Vi had only just left when her mobile began to ring. She listened to the voice at the other end for about a minute before she said in a tone much louder than she had intended, 'You what?!'

The rope was thick, like nautical rope, and it hung on the back of the kitchen door handle like a long, blond braid, but it had a neck-shaped loop at one end. Maria, slumped against the door frame, covered in milk and glass, couldn't move. She owned nothing, had never owned anything, like it, and yet here it was, materialised on the back of the kitchen door. Brought out of nothing, just like the peacock feathers: a hanging noose. She could hardly breathe. What was it doing there? What was it saying?

In her phone she had Mumtaz Hakim's number but she couldn't remember where she'd put her BlackBerry, even if she had wanted to call anyone. Because she hadn't. Because she knew. She'd been alone all night and she'd only got up half an hour ago. Only she could have looped that thing around the kitchen door handle. Or rather, *logically* only she could have done so. In the world of the unseen anything was possible and God, who was love, was also, as even Pastor Grint sometimes said, a God who made those who sought him confront their misdeeds by force.

Did the noose mean that she wanted to kill herself? That Jesus wanted her to confess or die? Surely not. Suicide was a sin.

Somewhere upstairs, her BlackBerry began to ring and Maria Peters screamed. She could no more move to answer it than she could stop looking at the terrible anomalous *thing* on the back of her kitchen door. The only way forward was just to sit quietly where she was and not interact with anyone or anything. She didn't want to horrify Betty or appal the pastor with her madness and Mumtaz Hakim was never going to call! She had a daughter and a job and a life and she'd never killed anyone.

*   *   *

All she had to do was tell Amma that she was doing private study at home on Thursday afternoons and everything would be OK. It wasn't a lie. Private study was scheduled for Thursday afternoons and Year 11 GCSE candidates did have the choice of studying in school or going home. It was when Shazia didn't actually study that it was a problem. When Hilary and Adele came home with her and they all had a bit of a laugh. Did the weird old white man who lived next door know about that somehow?

The brief conversation Shazia had had with the man on Sunday had bugged her all day. He'd been slimy and looked like he smelt and his whole approach had seemed to be based around the idea that he knew things about her that Amma didn't. But then Amma didn't know that Hilary and Adele came round to the house almost every Thursday. Now that she was working all the time she didn't seem to take a lot of notice of much. Fancy suggesting that her old parents come and take care of her while she went off to guard that old comedian woman. It was terrible! The old woman, there all the time making endless samosas, while the old man sat in that chair in front of the television coughing his guts up every five minutes. It'd be a nightmare.

Shazia walked past the house next door while scanning every window for the old white man's face. What could he know and how? She always pulled the curtains and shut all the windows. Unless he had X-ray eyes he couldn't have seen anything. He was just playing with her.

But if he was just having some sort of game with her then why was he doing that? He hadn't after all said anything about the other girls or that he intended to tell Amma at all. But she'd just felt that he would. It hadn't been what he'd said but the way that he'd said it; it had been oily and suggestive and it had made her feel uncomfortable in a way that she hadn't been for a very long time. Shazia felt the hairs on the back of her neck rise and she shook her head as if trying to get them to lie flat again. Confronting the old man was not something she wanted to do even if she did really, really want to find out what he did or didn't know. In the months since Amma got her job, things had been better than they had been for years, since her own mother had died.

Shazia let herself into her house and put the television on. When bad things happened and no one seemed to know what to do next, Hilary always quoted her mother. Hilary's mum always said, 'Go for the do nothing option first. Always. Do nothing, see what happens, then act.' Shazia flung herself down on the sofa and let herself be engaged by some silly kids' programme. She gave herself over to the 'do nothing' option.

XVII

The front door was not only unlocked, it was open. Given Maria Peters' nervousness as well as the number of burglaries that took place in the borough, that was worrying. Mumtaz took her phone out of her handbag and plugged in 999 just in case she had to call the police. She walked into the large entrance hall and called the woman's name, but she didn't reply. There was a strange, fusty and yet acidic smell to the place that she hadn't noticed before. Walking slowly, her ears straining to capture all and any noises that may come her way, Mumtaz moved into the living room. It was empty. She came out again and went into the little corridor that led past a row of cupboards and a bathroom into the kitchen. The door was open and opposite it, slumped down against the door frame was Maria. She was wet, covered in what looked like glass and she was looking fixedly at the kitchen door or rather at something hanging from the handle of the door. It took Mumtaz a moment or two to actually register the noose.

She squatted down beside the comedian and took one of her hands. She was cold and, now that she was closer to her, Mumtaz could see that the liquid she was covered in was milk. She had also, by the smell of her, wet herself. She wanted to ask her what was going on, what had happened and why, but Mumtaz knew that Maria would not be able to talk. Other things would have to be done before that was going to be possible.

'I'm going to get you a blanket and then I think a drink of some sort,' Mumtaz said.

Maria Peters couldn't even move but her eyes looked as if they agreed with that plan. Mumtaz went upstairs to one of the many bedrooms and pulled a duvet off one of the many beds. She went back downstairs and carefully moving as much broken glass to one side as she could, she wrapped the duvet around Maria's shoulders. Now all she had to find was a drink, and by drink, she meant alcohol. Maria Peters wasn't a Muslim, so what she was about to do wasn't a sin. She went back into the living room and grabbed the decanter she'd seen Maria drink something or other from before. She took it into the kitchen, poured a large amount into a glass and held it up to Maria's lips. 'Drink.'

The woman looked at her with both growing recognition and apparent astonishment.

'I can give you alcohol,' Mumtaz said. 'Don't worry, just drink.'

The port felt good and warming, even if she spilled much of it out from the sides of her mouth. She saw Mumtaz smile and thought again how beautiful she was.

Once Maria had managed to swallow a couple of mouthfuls of alcohol, Mumtaz put the rest of the port down beside her and stood up. 'I'm just going to clear up some more of this broken glass so that you can stand up,' she said. 'You just stay there and I'll get rid of it for you.'

She was so kind. Maria felt so unworthy, she began to cry.

'I must have failed to close the front door properly after I took the milk in off the doorstep.'

They were in the living room now and Maria was sitting on the sofa wearing a clean dressing gown and drinking tea. Mumtaz, sitting opposite, had cleaned both the comedian and her kitchen up as much as she could.

'I walked into the kitchen and there it was, looped around the door handle.'

'The noose.'

Maria screwed her eyes up against the memory of it. 'Yes.' She opened them again. 'I dropped the milk bottle and then the next thing I knew I was down on the floor. That . . . that thing on the back of the door, it is real, isn't it?'

Mumtaz had left the noose exactly where it was.

'Yes,' she said. 'It's real.'

Maria put a hand up into her hair. 'Where did it come from?'

'You've no idea?'

'I don't have anything like that,' Maria said.

'In your coach house . . .'

'I don't even put the lawnmower in there any more. Certainly not since Len died. The place is shut up. And anyway I can't remember ever having rope in there even when Len was alive.' Then she asked, 'Why are you assuming that I put it there myself?'

'I'm not.'

'You asked if I had rope in the house. You think I'm a lunatic.' She looked down into the depths of her tea. 'You may be right. Maybe this means I want to kill myself. Maybe part of me does.'

Mumtaz said, 'Maria, I came here to tell you that if you still want me to move in and be with you, I can do that. But if you want to call the police—'

'No!' She looked up quickly. 'No.' She smiled. 'So you came and the door was open . . .'

'Yes.'

'That thing, the rope. It felt like a threat. Like the peacock feathers.'

'Do you have a particular horror of hanging . . .'

'Well, I'd be a bit of a weirdo if I didn't!' Maria said. 'Who doesn't? All that struggling for breath and kicking out in agony. I can remember when my parents used to talk about how criminals used to hang in this country. They approved of it. Hanging always was ...' She swallowed. 'It was a murderer's death.'

'And a suicide.'

'Sometimes.' Maria looked out of the window and into the warm, leafy street beyond. There were times when she hated it. Specifically she hated the niceness, the comfortableness of it. Or rather since Len's death, that was how she had felt.

'I am not going to say whether or not someone is doing these things to you,' Mumtaz said, 'because really, I just don't know. But if you want me to be with you to observe, then I can, in part, do that.'

At 'in part' Maria frowned.

'I am currently working on some other cases and so from time to time I have to go elsewhere,' she said. 'But for the most part I will be at your disposal and I will be able to be here at night. I will just have to go home and see my daughter and prepare food ...'

'Your daughter can come here, it's—'

'It's not appropriate, Maria,' Mumtaz said. 'Not for anyone. No, arrangements have been made so that my daughter will not be alone at night, although this will have to be reviewed from time to time. My daughter is soon to take her GCSEs and so I cannot neglect her.'

'No.' But Mumtaz could see that Maria was disappointed.

She'd wanted her to be with her all the time. She trusted her, which was gratifying, but 24/7 just wasn't practical, not unless she'd let someone else in. Maria looked up. 'What if I am doing these things – the noose, the feathers, the notes – to myself? Will you tell me?'

Mumtaz looked into her eyes. 'Of course,' she said.

'But that'll mean that I'm mad.'

'No. It might mean that you're ill.'

They sat in silence for a moment, looking at each other.

'And if you recall, Maria, when you first came to the agency all of your fears revolved around another person maybe being involved in frightening you. And that may indeed be the case,' Mumtaz said.

'But that means that someone is getting in and I'm the only person who has a key. It's impossible.'

'When you manage to leave your front door open after collecting the milk, it isn't impossible,' Mumtaz said. 'You didn't realise that you'd even done it. And you know, Maria, with or without permission, people can get hold of house keys. Believe me, I know. Now later on this afternoon I will go home and get some things and return here to be with you tonight. Is that OK?'

'Yes . . .'

'And then I will have to ask you about your visitors, the church, your friends. Betty for instance . . .'

'Betty?' she smiled. 'I first met Betty when I was ten, at school. We were close. But we lost touch, or rather she disappeared from my life. Then when Len died I found her again, through the church.'

'What made you go to that particular church?' Mumtaz asked.

Maria hesitated for a moment and then she said, 'I was brought up a Catholic and I loved it. I wanted to be a nun at one point. But for ... for many reasons I couldn't go back to it. I needed something when Len died. God? I didn't know. But then I began to notice God, wherever I went.'

'How?'

She shrugged. 'Random things. Posters, leaflets, my own thoughts. I found a booklet at the doctor's surgery.'

'For the Chapel of the Holy Pentecostal Fire?'

'Yes. I felt I had to go there, you know? God moving in mysterious ways and everything.' She smiled. 'It was meant to be. Like the universe was telling me something. Seeing Betty there just served to confirm those feelings.'

That Lee Arnold had a fucking nerve! But then that was one of the things that had first attracted Vi Collins to him. He wasn't backwards in coming forwards with what he wanted and that was probably why he had his own business while most of his contemporaries at Forest Gate were either retired or out in the professional wilderness. But still, babysitting was a bit harsh.

'I don't even know the bloody kid!' she'd said when Lee

had phoned her up and suggested that maybe free and easy single girl Vi would like to spend her nights in Mumtaz Hakim's house watching over her stepdaughter.

'She's a nice girl,' Lee had replied. 'Studious. And Vi, you'd be doing me such a favour. You know how skint I am. If Maria Peters wants Mumtaz to watch over her and I can give her what she wants she'll pay us handsomely.'

'Oh? And what do I get out of it?'

She'd heard Lee smile at the other end. 'Apart from my undying love and respect, Vi, what can I say? You're a copper – I can't do anything that might make it look like you're bent.'

She'd wanted to say *I'll settle for a shag*, but she'd managed to stop herself. Moroccan boys young enough to be her grandsons were nice, but older men, like Lee, were more *practised*.

So he offered her nothing and she agreed to do it anyway. She moaned and she grumbled but when she finished work for the day, she packed a bag and drove over to Mumtaz Hakim's great big pile of a house and rang the doorbell.

'I've come for the sleepover,' she said as Mumtaz opened the door.

'Oh, DI Collins,' Mumtaz said, 'I can't tell you how grateful I am.'

Vi stepped over the threshold. Nice. The hall was wide and very white and the flooring was an old and venerable parquet. 'No problem,' Vi lied. 'Lee Arnold's already told me how wonderful I am once today. Oh, and Mumtaz, it's Vi, not DI Collins.'

Mumtaz smiled and then said, 'Vi,' in a small, slightly embarrassed voice.

'So where's . . .'

'Shazia?' she smiled. 'She's in the kitchen.'

Vi followed Mumtaz into a vast, slightly shabby wooden fitted kitchen. In it, sitting at the breakfast bar was a thin, very resentful-looking teenage girl. When Vi smiled at her, she turned away. *This*, Vi thought miserably, *is going to be a laugh a minute.*

A lot of people had asked about Maria. Now that the new, if temporary, church was up and running, a full programme of events had been reinstated. Just like the old days. But Maria wasn't coming and people were concerned that her own feelings about the new location had put her off. She'd only attended the new church once and then she'd had to be almost carried in, shaking, on Pastor Grint's arm. When asked about her, Betty had just said, 'She's not very well at the moment. She's had a lot of problems lately.'

It wasn't untrue, she had. But then Maria had had problems for thirty years, give or take. And now was the time, finally, to put it all right. Paul would do it. He was strong in the Lord and he understood Maria's heart far better than she knew. Things were happening to Maria that no one but a man steeped in the Lord could help her with. Things those outside of Paul and herself – certainly not empty headed little Rachel, who'd quit the church now it had moved – could not understand. Cruel things. But necessary.

Maria had to testify and be delivered in order to be right with God and take Jesus fully and finally into her heart. So far she'd given time and money, but that wasn't enough, she had to be sorry too, for everything. Really and truly and in front of the whole church. In front of God. Again, Paul would help her. He helped everyone. He'd helped Betty, and just his presence in her life continued to support her every day.

Maria had to be ready. Casting around to find solutions via the world of men – private detectives – was not going to fix her life. That way led only to death. The way all her pills and potions were leading her if she wasn't careful. Still deep in grief, she could die so easily and if she died in sin that would be bad. It would upset Paul.

Mumtaz was exhausted by the time she eventually got to bed. It was gone midnight, unusually late for her, and the bed was unaccustomed and strange. Much firmer than her mattress at home, it made her back ache.

They'd talked. She'd enjoyed Maria's company and talking about trivial things had been relaxing. Settling Vi

Collins in with a resentful Shazia earlier had not been so easy and as she lay staring at the ghost of the full moon through Maria Peters' curtains she wondered how they were getting on. Shazia's face had still been bright red with fury when she'd left her. Mumtaz turned onto her side and closed her eyes. If she was going to sleep at all, she'd have to make an effort. Exhausted she may be, but she wasn't actually tired. As well as all the problems she'd had with Shazia, Mumtaz had found her meeting with old Mrs Malik in East Ham worrying. When she'd presented her with what amounted to a complete vindication of her daughter-in-law's wifely behaviour, the woman had become angry.

'That girl is rotten!' she'd insisted. 'I know it as surely as I know light from dark.'

Mumtaz had been so tempted to ask her just who she had in mind for her son once Nazneen was out of the way. She ached to know how rich the girl's family was as well as who they were related to. But she didn't say anything. As calmly as she could, she'd asked Mrs Malik whether she wanted to carry on using the Arnold Agency and the woman had said no. It was all right. She still had other clients and, sadly, Mrs Malik could probably find another firm of private investigators who would discern something about poor Nazneen if she paid them enough. Sorry as she was for the girl, there was nothing that she could do for her.

Somewhere outside some boys shouted something she couldn't make out. Leafy and tranquil as the street was, they weren't far from the Romford Road and lots of crazy things happened up there. Kids out on their own, on bikes, on skateboards, rolling around outside McDonald's. Boozed up, some of them, some of them on drugs. Mumtaz used to think that if she ever had children of her own, she'd never let them do things like that. But that had been years ago and now she knew that all she could ever do was guide. Living with Shazia had taught her that. Sometimes children did things for reasons that needed less blame and more sympathy. Some kids lived lives of absolute hell, that was just fact. Anyway, she was never going to have any children.

Mumtaz turned over again. She'd opened the bedroom window earlier to let some fresh air in, which meant that the double glazing wasn't keeping out noise, which wasn't helping her to sleep. And so after a brief wrestle with fresh air versus soundproofing, she got up and went over to the window to close it.

She put her head underneath the net curtain and put her hands onto the bottom half of the sash to push it down. It was as she looked down into the garden that she saw something move in the hedge behind the fish pond. At first she thought that it was a cat but, although she didn't actually see a face, she definitely made out a form that was human. As far as she could tell, although she had seen it, it hadn't seen her. Heart hammering with fight or flight hormones, Mumtaz nevertheless reasoned that the figure was probably a kid just mucking about. But he or she wasn't with any other kids and that was weird. Kids mucking about generally did so with others of their kind. Frozen, Mumtaz didn't close the window until she was sure that he or she had gone. Then she went downstairs to make sure that all the doors and windows were secure. They were.

XVIII

'What you told my old woman was bang out of order!'

It was really too early for Bob 'the Builder' Singleton, but Lee couldn't bring himself to even start to get angry. Some figure had been seen in Maria Peters' garden in the early hours of the morning and his brother Roy had rocked up at his mother's house again. Lee had bigger fish than Bob to fry.

Lee paid for his fags and then pulled Bob out of the newsagent's after him. Wearily he said, 'Bob, do you or do you not bang many tired old toms on a regular basis?'

Bob's face went red. Lee lit up a fag. 'You do.'

'Yeah, but my Trace—'

'You and your Tracey have both screwed around for years,' Lee said. 'But some of the tarts you go with, Bob, as you know, fuck for Britain. They've had most creatures living or dead and as you've got older, mate, you've stopped worrying about safe sex, haven't you?' Bob looked as if he might explode. 'So Tracey knows who all your tarts are now and so does her Prideep. He don't want a dose of the clap or worse and neither does your missus. Tell you what is a scandal though and that's that you still owe me money.'

'You never found no evidence of industrial espionage!' Bob protested.

Two men in shalwar trousers and old Murderer Noakes on his mobility scooter enjoyed the escalating yelling between two well-known local characters.

'That's because there weren't any!' Lee shouted. 'The reason you were and are losing business, Bob, is because you're shit. I gave you the truth, and that is either stop wrecking people's fucking roofs and their conservatories or go and do something else! Nobody is nicking your business. You're undermining yourself.'

For a moment Bob, who could usually handle himself in a fight, looked as if he might take a pop at Lee, but then he appeared to change his mind.

'Just fuck off and get me my fucking money,' Lee said. Then he walked away from Bob. Everyone looking on knew that not only did Lee Arnold have the moral high ground, he was also more than just handy in a scrap. Lee Arnold could half kill a man, as he'd demonstrated on several occasions.

Back in the office, Lee steeled himself to speak to his mother. Before he did that though he briefed Amy on the phone about an errant-husband job he'd got for her in Leytonstone. The Arnold Agency didn't usually do honey-trap work, but Lee needed the money and so did Amy.

The Prime Minister could bang on as much as he liked about reintroducing morals to 'broken Britain' but while the recession was on people were going to carry on boozing, drugging and shagging their way out of their misery and there was nothing anyone could do about it. Two weeks of Olympic 'glory' in 2012 certainly was not the answer.

As soon as he'd finished with Amy, there was a buzz at the door and Lee got up to answer it. Doing everything himself was like being back in the bad old pre-Mumtaz days. 'Yeah?'

'Lee, it's Tony Bracci.' Vi's DS. 'Let us in.'

Lee pressed the button to unlock the door and Tony Bracci walked in. They'd only really been drinking pals when Lee had worked at Forest Gate police station and after he'd given up the booze and then left the force they'd just had the odd phone conversation or two. So they greeted each other as ex-colleagues and not as mates. It was cordial but Lee knew that Tony Bracci wouldn't come to see him without a good reason and so he was glad when the DS got straight to the point.

'We've got a situation with some black happy-clappy churches,' he said.

Lee nodded. 'Kid got knifed.'

'Jacob Sitole, he belonged to a church called the Bethel Revival. He was spiked by a kid called Matthias Chibanda who went to another happy-clappy place called Peace in

Jesus. Both down by the Olympic site. You had Neil West down there a few months ago, didn't you, at the Pentecostal Fire place.'

'Toasting crumpets, yeah.' Lee laughed. 'But seriously, that's a mainly white set-up. We never got involved or even close to any of the black organisations.'

'Your Mrs Hakim's still working with the well-known comedian who is, I believe, a little bit fond of a bit of Pentecostal Fire from time to time,' Tony said.

Vi had to have told him. But then, Lee thought, *fair dos*, DI Collins hadn't had to go and babysit Mumtaz's step-daughter. She generally had far better things to do with her evenings. But she'd agreed to it and Lee, without doubt, owed her.

'Can't give you any details, Tone,' Lee said.

'Ditto, mate,' Tony said. 'But, Lee, what I can tell you is that we've been looking into the finances of these churches and we've found a connection between Pastor Iekanjika's Peace in Jesus church and Paul Grint's Chapel of the Holy Pentecostal Fire.'

'A connection?'

'The Pentecostalists rent their new Canning Town church, what used to be a pub, from Iekanjika. Bit of a rough old building. In need of TLC, I'd say.'

Lee shrugged. 'Yeah?'

Tony Bracci smiled. Then he delivered the punchline. 'For seven grand a month!'

'Fucking hell!'

'Lodged as IOUs, official IOUs, with Iekanjika's bank.'

'So Grint can't just welsh on it?'

'Not easily. But Pastor Iekanjika won't talk to us because he says he doesn't recognise "secular authority". The kid that killed Jacob Sitole, Matthias Chibanda, one of Iekanjika's parishioners won't talk to anyone and looks shit scared, particularly of Iekanjika. Now I don't think that it's just DI Collins and myself who smell the faint honk of possible financial shenanigans but I think it might be helpful to both of us if your Mrs Hakim watches more than the famous comedian.'

'Watches the church?'

Tony shrugged. 'No pressure.'

'But . . .'

'But I'm sure I don't have to tell you, Lee, that almost anyone can set up a church in this country. And, under EU human rights legislation, they can do some things that may or may not make sense to the likes of us. The DI received some intel that the Sitole murder could be an African witchcraft affair, but to be truthful there's no actual evidence to support that. All we've got is this weird little bit of finance stuff which might mean something, might mean nothing.'

'But you have to tread carefully,' Lee said.

'We all have to do that,' Tony said. 'We live in strange

times, Lee. Times some, like the happy-clappies, would say prefigure the end of the world.'

Lee Arnold laughed. 'You do talk a load of shit sometimes, Tone!'

Something very strange and also alarming was going on in the house next door. The older Paki woman seemed to have moved out and had left the girl in the care of that bitch DI Violet Collins. Why? Martin Gold racked his brains to try and remember exactly what he'd said to the girl on Sunday. He hadn't threatened her, had he? He'd been a bit suggestive about what he may or may not know about her Thursday afternoon activities, but then if she'd had nothing to hide then she would have had nothing to fear, would she?

Martin couldn't believe that she'd gone to the police. What with, for God's sake? As far as he knew the young girl didn't know anything about his past. That said, he did remember noticing at the time that she hadn't looked exactly happy when he'd first spoken to her. He watched the girl leave for school and then Vi Collins get in her car to go to the station. She didn't look up at his house at all, but that didn't mean anything much. Ever since he'd got out of Wormwood Scrubs the coppers had wanted to somehow put him back in again. But Martin had been good and then he'd been clever. This was a pattern that he followed by turns and at the present time he was in a 'clever' phase. That was one of the few benefits of being what his mother had always called 'nondescript'. Old Len Blatt had once said he looked a bit like ex-Prime Minister John Major, grey.

Mumtaz worked her way through the messages on her phone. One was from Lee who wanted to have a meeting at three, another was from a client thanking her for finally confirming that her husband was indeed being unfaithful. There was a resentful little 'Good morning' from Shazia and then there was her mother.

'Mr Choudhury and his son are coming to eat with us on Thursday night,' she said. 'Your brothers are coming. Mr Choudhury's son is just fifty and he has his own accountancy practice.'

Her mother was hopeless at even pretending to conceal her motives.

'You must come,' she continued. 'And you can bring Shazia. Mr Choudhury's son is most open-minded.'

Mumtaz sat down on Maria Peters' linen basket and wound a towel round her wet hair. The comedian's shower room was bigger than most people's main bathrooms, and it was also one of the few places in the house where Mumtaz could be alone. She hadn't told Maria about the figure she'd spotted in the garden the previous night. Maria was very needy and was having panic attacks every few hours and so to cause her further alarm seemed unwise, especially in view of the fact that the person Mumtaz had seen in the garden could easily have just been a wandering kid. She looked down at her phone and resisted the urge to text back a bald 'No' to her mother. But then her mother only just about knew how to answer her mobile phone. If she left a text her mother would have to involve her father in order to get it and that would open her up to conversations with both of them. Much as she loved her parents, Mumtaz most definitely didn't want that. Her father could bang on about her single status just as effectively and irritatingly as her mother. Mumtaz put the phone down, walked over to the sink and began to brush her teeth. She looked at her face in the bathroom cabinet mirror and decided that she could no longer really go out in public without make-up. Not that she ever actually did. But now, to Mumtaz's way of thinking, that wasn't even a viable choice. To her, her eyes looked heavy and washed out and her face was pale and she had a few spots on her cheeks. She didn't look old, she just looked worn out. A set of good cosmetics would help. Maria Peters, for all her distress and her age, always looked attractive and Mumtaz wondered what kind of cosmetics she used.

Brand names like Yves St Laurent and Clarins came to mind and Mumtaz opened the bathroom cabinet to see if she could discover any cosmetic clues.

There was a slightly dusty Max Factor lipstick in a vibrant shade of pink but what the cabinet mostly contained, what it had been designed to hold, was medicine. Loads of it. As well as the usual aspirin, paracetamol and ageing sticking plasters there was a whole raft of products that contained codeine. One wet afternoon back in February, Lee had told Mumtaz how he'd once had a problem with codeine. He'd started taking it for a pain in his shoulder but when his wife had left him he'd found that it had helped him to sleep. DI Collins had, apparently, been instrumental in getting him off it. But Lee now hated the stuff and Maria Peters had enough of it to kill half the street.

But that wasn't all she had. There were boxes and boxes of the antidepressant fluoxetine. Mumtaz looked at the dosage and saw that it was high; twenty milligrams three times a day. At University she'd specialised in what they called 'abnormal psychology' and so she knew quite a lot about psychiatric pharmacology. Amongst the fluoxetine boxes there were however also some loose strips of a drug called Ranflutin which made Mumtaz frown. Quite what that was she didn't know, but she made a mental note to look it up online. Then there was diazepam too. She knew exactly what that was; a tranquilliser that used to be known as Valium and it was in great big ten milligram tablet doses. Again it was loose. Unlike the fluoxetine, neither the Ranflutin or the diazepam appeared to have boxes that would allow her to check whether the tablets had actually been prescribed for Maria Peters or not. The fluoxetine had been prescribed by Mumtaz's own doctor on

Woodgrange Road and, although the dose was quite high, it was a reasonable response to the acute grief Maria was clearly still experiencing. But if one included all the other medication, this was a fearsome and potentially lethal pharmacy by anyone's standards.

'Betty.'

Maria hadn't been expecting her. It was barely eleven o'clock which, apart from Sundays, was early for Betty. In this instance it presented Maria with a bit of a dilemma too. Mumtaz was upstairs in the shower room and so theoretically she could come down at any minute. Maria had been told yet again, this time by Mumtaz herself, that the surveillance was to be kept from everyone – and that included her mother. Everyone had to be treated with caution and some suspicion. But Betty was her oldest friend.

The best thing to do was just to get it over with. Maria took Betty into the living room and said, 'I've got something to tell you.'

Betty, concerned, said, 'Nothing horrible I hope.' She sat down.

Maria took a deep breath. 'I've been having . . . trouble again,' she said. 'In the house. Things . . .' she coughed, 'turning up.' She put her head down.

Betty stood, went over to Maria and hugged her. 'Oh, Marie,' she said. 'You must call Pastor Grint immediately.'

'No—'

'Marie, this means you still have problems with sin. Paul can help you.'

'I didn't mean to tell you, let alone . . .'

They sat down side by side on the sofa, Betty's arms encircling Maria's shoulders.

'There were peacock feathers and . . . other things, just appeared,' Maria continued. 'Bet, I don't know if I'm going mad or what. I would never have put things like that in this house.'

'Because they're unlucky? But they're not really, are they, Marie,' Betty said. 'That's just silly old superstition, isn't it?'

'Maybe. But how did they get in here? They just appeared.'

Betty looked away as if she was nervous about what she was going to say next. 'Marie . . . You know I worry about you. You know I feel that, whatever this is, what you need is to testify and take Deliverance . . . You may have been doing these things yourself, guided by Jesus, but maybe you're not. Maybe Jesus is forcing the issue.'

Exorcism. The casting out of demons by bell, book and candle. Paul Grint would gladly do it. But how could she let him? Exorcism only worked if the source of some evil was exposed for all the world to see, and that couldn't happen. She wasn't ready. But did God or Jesus really care about that? No, they just wanted her soul. The Rapture was coming.

Maria, unable to think about it, changed the subject. 'I've engaged a private detective again,' she said. 'A lady, from the same agency that I was with before.'

Betty frowned.

'I can't be alone, Bet.' Maria stood up and then paced once around the sofa. 'Maybe I don't know what I'm doing.'

'God does,' Betty said. 'You shouldn't have gone back to those people, Marie, there's nothing they can do.'

'They can watch and tell me if I'm doing things to myself, going mad,' Maria said.

'You should trust Paul. You should ask him to come, and put it all into his hands.' Betty was angry.

Maria said, 'I may be sick, Bet.'

'Well, have you been back to the doctor?'

'I have but what can he do?' She sat down again.

'He gave you pills?'

'Yes, but I've got pills coming at me from every direction. I need help.'

'But what can this lady do?'

'She's staying with me,' Maria said. 'Monitoring what happens, what I do.'

Betty was quiet for a few moments, then she said, 'Marie, why didn't you get me or someone else from the church to come and be with you when this first happened? I imagine you're paying this lady—'

'Bet, money isn't a problem!' Maria said.

'No.'

'I don't want to burden you with this. I don't want to burden anyone.' Maria wiped her hands down her face. 'If I'm just going crazy . . .'

'You're not going crazy, you just need—'

'Need what? Deliverance?' Maria shook her head. 'I can't do that, Bet!'

'Because you don't truly believe in the unseen? In demons? In the corrosion of sins unrepented? How can you not believe in evil if you do believe in Christ?'

'I do believe in evil and all that, it's just . . . I don't know. Some of it just doesn't make sense to me.'

Maria's eyes were full of tears now and, from her hiding place just outside the living room door, Mumtaz heard her reiterate, 'Doesn't make sense.'

'But Marie, if you talked to me then I would be able to help you,' Betty said. 'Or Pastor Grint. There's a terrible sorrow in you, Marie. I don't know what it is, but Jesus does and I think he's trying to get through to you . . .'

'No!' Maria sat down again and repeated, 'No.'

Mumtaz heard her breathing hard as she clearly tried to calm herself. Then she heard her say, 'I'm sorry, Bet, I'll have to go and get something.'

As she moved towards the door, Mumtaz ran upstairs and went to her room. Not that hiding herself from this Betty mattered, the woman knew she was installed in the house now. But she didn't want either of them to know that she'd been listening in on their conversation.

Mumtaz saw Maria go into her shower room and then come out again almost immediately. When she'd gone back downstairs, Mumtaz went into the shower room and saw a strip of diazepam pills on the side of the sink. One tablet was missing.

XIX

'Traffic warden,' Vi said as she flicked the ash from her cigarette out of the car window.

'Nah.'

She turned to face Tony Bracci. 'Why not?'

'Traffic wardens are hated but it ain't necessarily boring, is it, guv?'

They were on surveillance across the road from Pastor Iekanjika's house in Silvertown. A bog-standard Edwardian terrace, it backed onto the City Airport and so every few minutes they had to put up with noises from jets heading off to Paris and Amsterdam. They were playing a game they often played which was called 'What jobs are more boring than surveillance?'

'I don't know,' Vi said. 'Not sure I could walk about all day looking at car windscreens.'

'Hated by millions.' Tony picked his nose and stuck the bogey on the roof of the car. He always did this. Vi had long ago become sick of telling him to stop it. 'What about magicians?'

Vi turned to look at him and said, 'Magicians?' Tony Bracci had an odd mind.

'Yeah, like Paul Daniels,' Tony said. 'I can't stand Paul Daniels, he's an annoying little shit. And then there's that American wanker. David something. The one in the plastic box over the South Bank.'

'David Blaine.'

'That's him. People were throwing burger buns at him. Tosser. That had to have been boring, sitting up in that box all day and night.'

A battered old Renault 5 pulled up two cars in front of them and the Reverend Manyika got out. Vi shuffled down a bit in her seat. 'Now that, I didn't expect,' she said.

'None of these holy Joes are all sweetness and light,' Tony said.

'I never said Manyika was.' Vi waited until a white woman had admitted Manyika into Iekanjika's house and the door had closed behind him, then she said, 'I'm going in.'

Tony Bracci shrugged. 'Leave me here like Nobby No Mates . . .'

'Venus himself ordered this obbo, Tone,' Vi said. 'Let's not fuck it up by stomping around in our size twelves, shall we?'

Vi got out of the car and knocked on the front door of the house directly opposite Iekanjika's. A Constable Moss let her in. She nodded briefly to the elderly owner of the house and then followed Moss upstairs to the front bedroom. Two DCs, Tim Holland and Gazi Hussein, were in situ. Tom monitoring the house through a long-lens camera, Gazi listening in. Iekanjika's house had been wired for sound the previous evening when the pastor and his family had been out at a prayer meeting.

Vi murmured, 'Cosy,' as she looked around a bedroom that had probably last been decorated in 1968. The swirling psychedelic wallpaper was faded but it was, unfortunately, still all too recognisable. It wasn't unlike the bedroom Vi had shared with her sisters back in the early sixties.

Gazi Hussein, listening in through headphones via his laptop said, 'Ah, crap.'

Vi and Tim Holland looked at him. Gazi pulled one earpiece to one side and said, 'Talking in their own language, guv.'

Vi raised her eyebrows. 'But you're recording.'

'Oh, yeah,' Gazi said. 'And when Manyika first went in they spoke in English.'

'Anything I need to know about?' Vi asked.

'Pleasantries aside, Manyika was a bit lairy, ma'am,' Gazi said. 'A bit exercised.'

'About?'

'Before he went off into their own language he asked Iekanjika what kind of Christian allows killing. Iekanjika replied that Manyika was talking rubbish.'

Vi sat down on a candlewick bedspread that was

definitely older than she was. 'So Manyika knows or suspects that Iekanjika is involved in a death of some sort then,' Vi said. 'How do we get him to share that intel?'

'Ah! Speaking English again.' Gazi listened intently while Vi and Tim Holland looked on.

Gazi frowned.

'What is it?' Vi asked. 'What they saying?'

'Iekanjika just said that if Manyika doesn't drop it then Harare will suddenly get a lot closer,' he said.

'I thought they were both supposed to be refugees from Mugabe's regime,' Holland said.

Vi narrowed her eyes. 'Maybe only one of them is,' she said.

Mumtaz had just laid out a small sample of the medication she'd managed to take from Maria Peters' medicine cabinet on Lee's desk when her phone began to ring. Thinking it was probably Maria, she answered it without looking.

'Your father would be very grateful and pleased if you would come and have dinner with us on Thursday night,' her mother said. 'Did you get my message? I said that you could bring Shazia.'

Mumtaz looked pleadingly across at Lee and said, 'My mother.'

'So take it,' he smiled.

Mumtaz turned aside while Lee riffled through the pills

on his desk. She spoke to her mother in Bengali. 'Amma, I am at work.'

'But Mumtaz, I have to know for the catering,' Sumita said. 'With you and the girl we will be eight, without, six. I need to know. Mr Choudhury and his son—'

'I know full well that Mr Choudhury and his son, who is an accountant, are coming and I do know why, Amma.'

'Because Mr Choudhury is your father's friend.'

'Yes, well, you just keep on telling yourself that,' Mumtaz said in English.

'What?'

'Amma, I have to work on Thursday night,' Mumtaz said, back in Bengali once again. 'It's just not possible.'

'Working at night? What are you doing working at night? What's happening to Shazia while you work at night?'

Mumtaz sighed. 'Amma, we have a big job on. I have to watch someone, a lady. This lady could be in danger.' And then remembering just how nervous her mother could be she said, 'But you don't have anything to fear on my account, I am just watching, I am perfectly safe.'

'And . . .'

'Shazia is being looked after by a friend. A nice woman.' She didn't add that Vi was not only not Muslim but clearly not anything. That would have been way too much. 'Amma, you know I need the money. Please don't be difficult about this.'

'But Abba—'

'And Abba can stop trying to marry me off too,' Mumtaz said. She felt her face go hot and red. 'Amma, I don't want to be married off to anyone. Not Mr Choudhury's son, not that Pakistani dragon man from the television, not even Imran Khan.'

Mumtaz ended the call. Lee looked at her quizzically for a moment but he didn't ask her anything about her conversation. Hands amongst the tablets, he said, 'So Miss Peters takes a lot of medication.'

Mumtaz, still a little wound up, said, 'I saw her take ten milligrams of diazepam and it barely affected her. I assume that she is taking the sixty milligrams of fluoxetine that her doctor has prescribed for her but I don't know about the Ranflutin – which incidentally is the same as fluoxetine, I looked it up – or the codeine meds.'

'You asked her about it?'

'No.'

'Mmm. She doesn't present as drugged up,' Lee said. But then neither had he all those years ago. Not until it got really bad.

'If the diazepam incident is anything to go by then she has built up tolerance,' Mumtaz said. 'Ten mils is a lot and she just carried on as normal. But Lee, any of these drugs, or the interactions between them, may explain some of her experiences. They can make you forget things you've done, make you fearful, they can even induce hallucinations.'

'And yet you saw an actual figure in her garden last night.'

'There were lots of kids out last night, I heard them,' she said. 'It could have been one of those.' She shrugged. 'But then maybe it wasn't. If Maria is, in effect, stalking herself then she is doing it in a way that has to be increasing her drug dependence. Those peacock feathers had her in bits.'

'What's she doing now?'

'Her friend Betty is with her,' Mumtaz said. 'They're baking.' She shook her head. 'One of the first things Maria did when Betty arrived this morning was to tell her about me.'

Lee raised his eyes to the ceiling. 'Christ.'

'Betty felt that Maria would have been better served having someone from the church, preferably Pastor Grint, to be with her. I think they, the church, feel that all Maria needs is exorcism.'

Lee put his head in his hands. 'They would.'

'But she was very against that, Lee,' Mumtaz said. 'And I was surprised. For a woman who is as religious as she is, who has given up her career for this religion, well, it is odd.'

Lee looked at her. He knew little about Islam but he did know that some of their beliefs were kind of parallel to some Christian traditions. He wanted to formulate some sort of question that was not either stupid or offensive, but she beat him to it.

'It's like me covering my head and yet at the same time eating pork,' she said. 'It's strange. It doesn't make sense.'

'You think maybe she's a hypocrite?'

'I don't know, I don't think so. I think she's sincere. But she's also afraid.'

'Obviously.'

'No, not just of whatever or whoever she believes is watching her, but of something else too,' Mumtaz said.

'Like?'

'I don't know.' She shrugged. 'But all the medication . . . She's damping her grief down, I know, but what else? You know, Lee, the fact that fluoxetine and Ranflutin are the same thing makes me uneasy. Why have Ranflutin if she has fluoxetine, and why all that possibly unprescribed diazepam too?'

'She could have the boxes they come from elsewhere or she could have thrown them away.'

'True. But the fact remains, Lee, that Maria has a huge amount of medication in her house and I heard her say herself that she gets it from "all directions". To me, that means not just the doctor, and I am going to have to ask her about it. If she is, in effect, frightening and haunting herself then she has to know that. And if someone who isn't a doctor is supplying her with extra medication then we need to know who that is.'

Lee shook his head. 'You know I took you on, in part, because of your psychology background. These meds are of interest but I wouldn't ask her about them just yet. I'd keep that in reserve,' he said. 'This client seems to be turning you into some sort of therapist.'

Mumtaz didn't reply. Had she done so, he would have been able to see the really quite unseemly delight she was taking in her new role. After all, while she was thinking about Maria she wasn't thinking about herself – or anything else.

Lee cleared his throat. 'Anyway,' he said, 'that to one side for a moment, I've been asked by DI Collins to ask you to keep your ear to the ground with regard to the Chapel of the Holy Pentecostal Fire.'

'Maria's church.'

'Yeah.'

'Why? You think that the people . . .'

'I don't think anything,' Lee said. 'But the coppers have their eyes on the place. They think there could possibly be some sort of financial scam in the offing.'

'But by keeping an eye on the church . . .' Mumtaz began.

'You're her minder, follow her,' Lee said.

'To a church service? She feels safe there. She never actually wants to be watched in church.'

'Of course to a church service,' Lee said. 'Coppers can't get in there. I can't get in there. But you can – with a few modifications.'

'But her friend Betty knows who I am.'

'Follow her without her knowledge. Go in late, sit at

the back. Assume another identity. You're smart. You can do that, can't you? See what you can pick up from the worshippers. That's what this job's about.'

'Assume another identity?'

He quite deliberately didn't allude to her headscarf. But Mumtaz knew that was what he meant. She couldn't go into that church with her headscarf on, it wasn't negotiable.

'Oh, and put those meds you nicked back,' Lee said. 'Don't want Miss Peters to know we know about them just yet.'

Betty left before Mumtaz returned from her meeting. Afraid of what she might do or find or see, Maria sat on her doorstep waiting for her to return. Whether it was some person tormenting her, her own mind falling apart or Jesus, she still didn't know. But what she was very well aware of was that being alone was no good. When she was alone, bad things happened and the past crashed into the present like a curse.

A couple of the tenants from her house in the next street passed by and she had to make a conscious effort not to catch their eyes. It was a fine afternoon but sitting on her doorstep was not something that Maria did. It wasn't what a landlord was supposed to do, she felt.

She saw Martin Gold, the flasher Len had always liked for some reason and she let him catch her eye. Creepy though he was, she was prepared to be a little less aloof with him. Was it perhaps because his native language was English, because he was white? It was an uncomfortable thought but one that was probably true. Even with Mumtaz there was a distance that went beyond the professional. There were things between them, like Mumtaz's headscarf, like Jesus, and Maria's yearning for the audience she had now twice lost but still, in spite of everything and to her shame, hungered for. She watched the old Jew cross the road and then she saw him stop. A young Asian girl, thin and leggy, caught his attention and she watched him watch her as if he were mesmerised.

Although she'd never met her, Maria recognised the girl; it was Mumtaz's daughter. Martin Gold watched her with hungry eyes and Maria saw the girl cringe underneath his gaze. Did he fancy her? Did he maybe want to get his penis out and show it to her, knowing it would induce revulsion? Or fear?

The girl ran while the old man made his way towards the shops on Woodgrange Road with a smile on his face. Maria knew that had Mumtaz seen the incident it would have disturbed her. No one wants their children to be letched over like that. If one has children. Maria imagined that the girl would probably tell her mother and then Mumtaz would have words with Martin Gold. And if that was indeed the case, which it had to be, then there was no need for her to tell Mumtaz too. After all, someone else was looking after the kid while Mumtaz was at Maria's. The girl would surely tell that person. It wasn't her business. When she did finally see Mumtaz walking down the road towards her, Maria waved and smiled and she immediately forgot all about Martin Gold.

XX

Alone, or when Maria was just with Betty – Rachel Cole seemed to have left the church now – they prayed quietly. When there was a group of them, as now, they were more voluble. On her own in her bedroom, Mumtaz listened to Pastor Grint lead about ten people in a made-up prayer that, to Mumtaz, sounded like a conversation. Shazia had been subdued when she'd spoken to her earlier, but she'd said she'd been OK. She and Vi Collins had apparently shared a vast take away pizza the previous night which had made her happy, even if she still wanted to know when her stepmother was going to return home. But then that was only natural. The girl's life had been, albeit temporarily, turned upside down. Shazia had had quite enough upheaval and uncertainty in her young life, she didn't need any more. Mumtaz's thoughts turned to the subject of her late husband.

Whatever Lee Arnold might think, making her cover her head had been the least of Ahmed's faults. In fact it hadn't been a fault at all, because before Ahmed had even been a thought in her father's head, Mumtaz had wanted to cover. A level of modesty made her feel better, more secure, more engaged with her religion. It gave her a sense of belonging and everyone needed to belong somewhere. After 9/11 some women, in light of a level of anti-Islamic sentiment in the Western world, had abandoned their headscarves out of fear. They didn't want to attract hostility or abuse and Mumtaz couldn't fault them for that. But her own stance, though quietly pursued, was more positive. She hadn't flown a plane into the Twin Towers, she'd been appalled by that act. Why should she hide who and what she was?

Lee Arnold had treated the removal of her headscarf so lightly. In order to do her job she had to be able to change her identity from time to time and she'd known that was a possibility right from the start. But that didn't mean that her emotions were quiet about it. To go into a Christian church was fine, but to pretend to be someone else in what was a holy place for some people, felt less than fine.

Suddenly, from the living room where Pastor Grint was holding his prayer meeting, a sound that Mumtaz half did and did not recognise emerged. Beyond words or even recognisable human sound, it came to her ears in the same way as the sound of the *dhikr*, the ecstatic ritual that holy dervishes performed when they danced their way into remembrance of Allah. She'd only ever heard it one time when, years before, her parents had taken them all to visit her great-uncle Sharif back in Dhaka. He had been a dervish and once, late at night, a group of his spiritual brothers – including some of her young male cousins – had come to dance and commune in the way the Christians were doing now. Back in Bangladesh, the unaccustomed sounds of the holy ecstasy had unnerved Mumtaz. Her father and indeed none of her British Bangladeshi relatives did that and she had found it strange. Now was no different to that and her body, in spite of itself, shuddered. In fact, if anything, this experience was even more chilling than it had been back in Bangladesh. Now with her psychologist's hat on she knew that spiritual ecstasy could be both divine and malignant, both real and horribly manufactured.

Vi, as she liked to be called, was going to be late. Amma had come back briefly to make her some dinner but now Shazia was alone. Just her, some maths homework and the telly: *Come Dine With Me*. A woman whose tits were way too big for her dress was putting on a dinner party for a girl who was allergic to everything, an elderly gay man and a boy with spots. But Shazia was finding it difficult to engage with either *Come Dine* or her homework. She was thinking about the next day. Hilary and Adele had said that they were coming round in the afternoon and Shazia didn't know what to do. The old man next door knew something. She didn't know what, but something. The way he'd told her had made her skin creep. Why had he done that? Did he want her to give him money to shut up about what he knew? Or did he want something else? Shazia closed her eyes just as the woman with the massive breasts served up a trio of puddings. One was chocolate, the others not even worth mentioning. Did the old white man want *that*? She couldn't even think about it. Sex on any level was violent and disgusting.

Shazia felt a familiar sickness rise in her throat. There was no way that she could put Adele and Hilary off. That would be just, social death! But if they didn't come here then where could they go? They came to hers because their mums were always at home. Amma's job had been, like, amazing! Sort of. She couldn't put the girls off but she couldn't take the stuff into school with her either; it was far too risky. Mrs Reed, who was just an old bitch, had a thing about girls bringing make-up to school and so she searched bags regularly. It was too random to be safe. Shazia's heart beat fast. She'd seen the old white man in the street earlier and he'd looked at her in that weird, creepy way that he had.

The girl who was allergic to everything on the telly was throwing a massive strop about cheese. Shazia couldn't stand it. Not the allergic girl on the TV but the uncertainty about the old man next door. He knew something and she had to know what it was. She'd hardly slept since he'd spoken to her on Sunday. What if he just appeared on the doorstep or even in the garden when Adele and Hilary were around? That would be like a total disaster!

Shazia looked at her watch. Vi had said it was unlikely she'd be back before nine. It was now seven thirty. She'd have to go and see the old man. She'd have to. Shazia threw her maths book to the other side of the sofa and stood up. She walked determinedly to the front door, closed it behind her and then lost her nerve. How was she going to go to that house and knock on the door and ask for him? Who was he anyway? He was the only white man in a big house full of Bangladeshis and what were they going to make of her asking to see a white man on her own and unescorted by her mother? Wouldn't one of them tell Amma?

Although it was warm, Shazia trembled in the soft spring air. She was caught. Stuck in a terrible place that, while not entirely of her own making, was a position that she felt had been exacerbated by her own weakness. What was she going to do? But then the matter was taken entirely out of Shazia's hands. The old man, smiling, was walking down the garden path towards her.

'I don't know what you're talking about,' the Reverend Manyika said.

'You went to see Pastor Iekanjika,' Tony Bracci said.

'He is a brother in Christ, why shouldn't I? Why are you watching me? I have done nothing wrong!'

'Last time I spoke to you, Reverend,' Vi Collins said, 'I got the impression you and he didn't get along too well.'

'Then you were wrong. We do.'

She knew that they didn't. But Vi also knew that now was not the time to let on that Iekanjika's house was wired for sound. According to the translator who'd listened to the tape, Iekanjika had said nothing to actually incriminate himself with regard to Jacob Sitole's death. But he and Manyika had talked about money. Manyika had said that he didn't want his own practices to be tarred with the same brush as Iekanjika's. Iekanjika had just laughed. According to the translator, all through their exchange Manyika had sounded afraid. Then at the end of the meeting, Gazi Hussein had heard Iekanjika threaten Manyika by alluding to Zimbabwe, the country they had both apparently run away from.

'Reverend, Matthias Chibanda, the boy we know killed Jacob, still isn't talking to us. He's terrified.'

'Of you.'

'Only in part, I think,' Vi said. Then she moved in closer towards him. 'I think poor Matthias is afraid of something far more scary than the British police.'

His face didn't move. But she could see that he was sweating.

'Don't know what. Some spiritual terror?' Vi said.

'You're watching me!'

'We're keeping an eye on both the Bethel and the Peace

in Jesus churches,' Vi said. 'A boy from one church killed a boy from the other. We don't know why. We have to know what's going on. You'd tell us if you knew why, wouldn't you, Reverend Manyika? Even if it meant falling out with your mate Pastor Iekanjika?'

'I am a Christian man of God.'

Vi glossed over the fact that to her that was no kind of answer.

'Because if you don't tell us and later on we find out that you knew, you'll have God and us to deal with,' Vi said.

Manyika said nothing.

'Keeping Pastor Iekanjika happy could come at a price,' she said.

'Pastor Iekanjika didn't kill Jacob Sitole.'

'No, but I think that he knows why Matthias Chibanda killed him and I think that Iekanjika is making sure that the boy keeps his mouth shut about his motives,' Vi said.

'Why?' Manyika looked into her eyes. 'Why do you think these things?'

'Reverend, are both you and Pastor Iekanjika refugees from the Mugabe regime?'

'Yes, why else would we be here?'

'I don't know,' Vi said. 'You tell me.'

But he just shook his head and said, 'I can't. I don't know what you mean.' But his eyes were frightened.

Vi said nothing. Manyika looked at Tony Bracci. 'Why

don't you ask Pastor Iekanjika these things? Why are you asking me?'

'Pastor Iekanjika won't talk,' Vi said. 'And anyway, Reverend, you ever see a television programme called *The Weakest Link*?' Tony Bracci smiled. 'Why would I put myself through trying to speak to Iekanjika – who won't talk – when I can speak to you, who will? You are my weakest link, Reverend, get used to it.'

Maria had emerged from her prayer meeting exhausted. Whether the participants had danced as in the *dhikr*, Mumtaz didn't know. But she recognised the heavy, almost drugged-looking quality around the comedian's eyes and it made her wonder how the regular services at the church were conducted.

The comedian, exhausted, went to bed. Mumtaz watched TV and then she went out into the garden for a while. This night was much quieter; she couldn't hear any childish voices yelling text-speak into the night. And yet there was still a feeling of tension. Earlier in the year, people, including a lot of very young people, had staged sometimes violent protests in central London about the government's policy of increasing university tuition fees. In all but name (the government insisted upon calling it a 'downturn') the country was in recession and a lot of people had lost their jobs. What some called 'traditional' Conservative policies allied to an international economic crisis were fuelling fear and unrest. And in her own community Mumtaz remembered very well how the immense amount of sympathy for the US and the West in general just after 9/11 had turned into something else when the Americans and the British had invaded Iraq. Now the divisive elements shrieked loudest. The fascist British National Party, the Muslim boys who daubed homophobic slogans on the walls of shops on Brick Lane, the kids who dreamed about joining al Qaeda. She called Shazia, hoping for a light chat about school and make up and handbags.

But the girl was subdued, almost monosyllabic. Eventually Mumtaz had to ask, 'What's the matter? Did you have a bad day at school?'

'No.' Her failure to expand made Mumtaz even more anxious. Usually if Shazia didn't want to talk about school, she just changed the subject.

'Shazia, can I speak to Vi, please?' Mumtaz asked.

''k.'

The next voice she heard was Vi Collins. 'Hi, Mumtaz.'

'Vi, I'm sorry,' Mumtaz said, 'but is Shazia all right? I know she's a teenager but . . .'

Mumtaz heard Vi tell Shazia that she was going to take the call in the kitchen so as 'not to disturb you watching your programme'. Noises of first the living room and then the kitchen door closing behind her ensured that Vi could not be heard by Shazia. 'She was quiet and red-eyed when

I got in,' Vi said. 'That *Come Dine with Me* thing she likes was just finishing and she was sitting down next to a load of homework. I asked her if she needed any help – not that I could do much I don't suppose – but she said she was OK with it. I know you said she does well at school, but do you know how she is with friends or . . .' she hesitated a little, 'boyfriends?'

Mumtaz thought for a few moments. Shazia always said she had friends and sometimes she went off shopping with other girls to Ilford. She was pretty sure that Shazia didn't have a boyfriend.

'Because this age can be a bitch,' Vi continued. 'I remember my boys. All arguments and fights and some really nasty little mind games going on. And girls, of course.'

'Shazia only talks about Daniel Radcliffe, you know the Harry Potter boy,' Mumtaz said. 'Her father . . . she is still, I think, maybe nervous of talking about boys because her father, my husband, he disapproved . . .'

That was putting it so mildly it was almost a lie.

'Maybe it's just a mood,' Vi said. 'John, my eldest, had them something rotten when he was a teenager. One minute he was the best kid in the world, the next he was like that cartoon of the Tasmanian devil.'

'Shazia can be moody,' Mumtaz said. 'But she isn't usually quiet about it. If she's upset she tends to stomp around and—'

'Oh, hang on, she's coming!' Vi interrupted. Then Mumtaz heard her say, 'Shazia, sweetheart.'

'I'm going to bed,' Mumtaz heard Shazia say.

'You all right, love?' Vi asked. 'Feeling unwell?'

'No, just tired.'

Mumtaz heard the kitchen door close and then she said, 'I must make some time for her, I think. Make her some food like a good Bangladeshi amma. Food is love."

'I reckon that's a good idea.'

'I'll tell Maria I have to go and make tea for Shazia after school tomorrow. She'll understand.'

'That'd be favourite.'

'I'm sorry, Vi, that things are like this. I can't think why she's so subdued. Maybe it is just the fact that I am not there.' And then she added by way of explanation. 'But we really need the money. If I wasn't—'

'You don't have to explain it to me, love,' Vi said. 'My old man had an allergy to work so I had to keep five people all on me own when the kids were at home. I like Shazia, she's a lovely girl, but this is all new to her and she might, as you say, just need a few hours alone with you.'

'Yes. Yes, I'll organise that. Thank you, Vi. I can't tell you how much I appreciate what you're doing.'

She heard Vi make that crackly smoke-dried laugh of hers. 'Me and Lee Arnold go back to the Flood,' she said. 'Any friend of his is a friend of mine.'

Mumtaz was genuinely touched. She ended the call and

went back in the house again with a feeling of, if not well-being, some confidence. Vi Collins would look after Shazia until Mumtaz herself could find out what was wrong. The girl was safe in the police officer's care. Mumtaz walked through the living room and into Maria's considerable dining room. The street outside was quiet and still and it took her a few moments to realise that someone was actually outside the garden gate. He was tall and young, his trainers were silver and he made her heart miss two beats. Months ago, for a few seconds, out on Wanstead Flats he had almost blinded her with his beauty. He had been her Silver Prince and he had killed her husband. He was also the man she had not given a description of to the police. What did he want? Did he want to silence her? Mumtaz toyed with the idea of going outside and telling him his secret was safe with her. But then her nerve failed her and she just sank back into the living room shadows until he eventually walked away.

XXI

A lot of the old Hackney Wick drinking dives and strip clubs had been cleared away in preparation for the Olympics. But some remained and there was one, a swingers club, that was just simply called Jollies. To Lee Arnold, who had been standing outside the place since just after midnight, it looked about as jolly as a bout of dysentery. But he was waiting for a bloke he'd seen go in there, and photographed, eight hours before so that he could discreetly take his photograph again when he came out. The man in question, an apparently model husband, was no longer wanted by his wife and with what seemed to be some good reason.

Coincidentally, Jollies was just three doors away from the old warehouse that was now known as the Peace in Jesus church. Someone who could have been the possibly dodgy Pastor Iekanjika that Tony Bracci had talked about had gone in at about two and hadn't come out. As far as Lee could tell he'd been alone. Not that he'd spent the long dark hours thinking exclusively about happy-clappy churches. First he'd thought about his brother, who usually invaded his mind when he was alone. There'd been more scenes back at his mum's place and Lee was rapidly coming to the conclusion that the only thing that Roy was ever going to understand was a bloody good hiding. It's what he'd often wished he'd given his father. Not just a duffing up, a proper beating. He didn't like the idea and had no desire to do it but Roy couldn't just go on making their mother's life hell. After that, he'd thought about other things – anything. Then, at just after six am, Mumtaz had called. He'd told her he'd be watching some dodgy man for an indeterminate amount of time. The phone had vibrated against his leg and because it was her he'd answered it. Maria Peters, Pastor Grint and some of the other Pentecostal Fire people had had a prayer meeting at the comedian's house the previous evening. Mumtaz, although unaware of what had actually been said during the meeting, had described it as hypnotic. She'd said they'd all entered some sort of trance while they prayed. That, together with the fact that she was still grieving for her husband, and all the meds that Maria seemingly took, didn't appear to Mumtaz or Lee to be a healthy combination.

A couple of Hasidic Jews, on their way to Forman's, the salmon smokery, as well as a slightly plump Asian bloke walked past Lee without looking at him. They didn't look at each other either. It was as if they lived in parallel

worlds. Which in a sense they did. If a Hasid and a fundamentalist Muslim spoke it would, Lee felt, probably be a
bit like infidelity.

He looked at his watch and wondered how much longer
his client's husband could 'swing' for. He was one of those
shitty little city traders who'd wrecked the economy and
so it was difficult to have any sympathy with him, or his
wife. In spite of what had happened, he was still employed,
and she still did bugger all except get her nails done, have
fake tans and have glitter sculpted round her vagina. They
lived in a massive, ugly house out at Ongar and both of
them drove Ferraris. And he chose to spend his time with
a load of wrinkly, dodgy couples in an old factory office
down at Hackney Wick.

A sound like thunder made Lee jump and he saw the
big black guy he'd seen go into the church earlier come
out. He was talking, or rather shouting, into his mobile
phone. It was in English and it was about money. He said,
'Get it to me, cash, or there will be consequences!'

She had dreamed about the child, what she would have
been, what she imagined she would have looked like. Maria
woke up crying in a cocoon of sweat and when she took
the cup of tea that Mumtaz had made her from the kitchen
unit, her hand shook. She only just about managed to
concentrate on what Mumtaz was saying when she told
her she needed to go home for a few hours. It was a

Deliverance night at the church and Maria was going to have to make a decision.

Mumtaz had put fruit and cereal out on the worktop for her but Maria didn't want it. Yesterday, Mumtaz had cooked some sort of curry which she'd only pretended to eat. But she wasn't hungry. She couldn't actually remember when she had last been hungry.

Maria phoned Betty who was due to arrive to get a lift with her to church at six thirty but then, just before she put the phone down, Maria remembered that Mumtaz was going to go and spend a few hours with her daughter at four. The thought of being alone when she might do anything, when anyone might do something to her, was too much.

'You can't get here a bit early, can you?' she asked Betty. 'At four?'

'I don't see any problem with that,' Betty said.

'Oh, thank God,' Maria said. The relief was enormous.

Betty turned to Paul Grint as she put the phone down and he noticed there was a slight smile on her face. He frowned in disapproval. 'Don't be judgemental, Betty,' he said. 'It's a sin.'

'She's in pain,' she said.

'For the good of her soul.'

She gazed up at him, trying to soften the look in her eyes because she didn't want to shock or frighten him. 'Of course. Even if she does deserve it anyway.'

'Even if she does deserve it,' he said. 'Everyone has the potential to have a beautiful soul, Betty. Maria is a beautiful person and we must bring her to Jesus as soon as possible. He wants her soul badly and so do I. Now I'd like you to stop giving her your pills. I know you're still doing that.'

Betty shrugged. 'She asks me,' she said. 'She's always afraid of running out.'

'We mustn't build her tolerance up even more,' Grint said. 'That would be wrong. We don't want to hurt her, do we?'

Betty's small mouth tightened. How could he, a virtual saint, say such a thing about *her*?

'He was in there from 02.05 to 08.10,' DC Gazi Hussein said.

'Alone?'

'Seemingly, ma'am.'

Vi Collins frowned. What had Iekanjika being doing at his church alone, in the middle of the night? 'And he came out ranting at someone?'

'Demanding money,' Gazi said.

'Did he say a name?'

'No. When he went into the church he locked the door behind him. I tried the door at the back, but no joy. Couldn't see much through the windows, most of them are covered with screens. He didn't make a sound.'

'Anything else?'

'A couple of Hasidic Jews waiting for Forman's to open and a bloke outside Jollies spending hours on end trying to decide whether he wanted to swing or not.'

Vi shook her head. Men were such ridiculous creatures! Her ex-husband had always said he'd suffered from crippling guilt whenever he'd been unfaithful. She'd put up with it for the kids' sake until they'd left school and then she'd told him she really didn't give a shit. She looked at DS Bracci. 'Tone?'

'Difficult to get a lot of intel out of the Zimbabwean authorities – some of them, including their president, still see us as the colonial enemy – but I spoke to a woman who told me that that nice Reverend Manyika is most definitely not welcome back in Harare.'

'Why not?'

'Witchcraft,' he said.

'Witchcraft?'

'A right dab hand with the bones and the children's body parts, apparently,' he said. 'Came here claiming political asylum which was granted back in 2003.'

'Did you find anything out about Iekanjika?'

'Been a British citizen since 2005, but he's got a British wife. Couldn't get a thing out of them about his politics, his status or nothing. No comment.'

'So both of them could be dodgy.'

'Yes, guv.' Tony paused for a moment and then he said, 'But you rate Manyika, don't you.'

'I don't rate him, Tone, I just personally don't have reason to suspect him of involvement in Jacob Sitole's death.' Then she raised her arms in the air in frustration. 'If only bloody Matthias Chibanda would speak!'

'But, ma'am, haven't we got enough forensic evidence against him to put him away for Sitole's murder anyway?' Gazi Hussein said.

'Yes, but I want to know why he killed Jacob,' Vi said. 'Don't you?'

'Well, yes . . .'

'Two boys, who had been friends, who both called themselves Christians. Different churches, I grant you. But where does a fatal stabbing fit into that?'

'Boys can get carried away,' Tony said. 'Hormones.'

'That I understand, Tone,' she said. 'But if that was the case why doesn't Chibanda just say so? The kids had a fight, he was wounded himself. And he knows he's going down whatever. Why doesn't he speak?'

'I don't know.'

'When he was laying in that hospital bed and I went to see him, he was terrified. I questioned him and it was like there was a stopper in his mouth physically preventing words from coming up. Part of him wanted to speak, I know! But he couldn't,' she said. 'I'd also like to know why he looked particularly terrified when Iekanjika looked at him. There was real dominance going on there.'

'But if he doesn't speak then how can you know what he's thinking?' Gazi asked.

Vi turned to Gazi and stared him hard in the eyes. 'Not been with us long, have you, love?' she said. Tony Bracci smiled. *Here she goes!* he thought. 'One way or another I'll find out why Jacob Sitole died and I'll get whoever is frightening the life out of Chibanda – up to and including Iekanjika. Whoever's doing it there's a whiff of superstition and magical wotnots in the air and I don't like it. Each to his own when it comes to religion but there can be a dark side to unquestioning faith and I won't have none of it!'

'But ma'am, we also have the Olympic Flash—'

'Oh, I've not forgotten him either, Gazi,' Vi said. 'But just at the moment I'm a bit more bothered about a dead kid than I am about a bloke getting his todger out down by the canal. Know what I mean?'

Martin watched Shazia open the French doors into the garden as he'd instructed and he heard one of the other girls say, 'Pull the curtains across, someone'll see!'

Shazia said, 'No they won't! It's just, like, our garden.'

'What about your neighbours?'

'They can't see anything,' Shazia said, shakily Martin thought. 'There's a hedge. Anyway, look, the windows have to be open or the place'll like, smell. And if I get grief from my mum that will be, like, horrible, you know.'

The other girl went quiet. In one fluid movement that surprised even him, Martin slipped through the hole he'd made in the hedge and walked behind the flower beds until he found the 'sweet' spot. This was the place where he'd worked out he could see into the house without himself being seen.

All three girls were inside and they were all sitting where Shazia had said they would be. They hadn't done anything yet but it wouldn't be long before they did. Martin unzipped his trousers and began to tickle his penis. He'd have to be quiet when he did finally come, but then he was used to that. He'd had years and years of practice at that.

Her mother just had to have another go!

'Not only is Mr Choudhury and his son and both your brothers coming but so is Mosammet with her husband Rejan,' she said to Mumtaz. 'Can't you come?'

Mosammet had been Mumtaz's best friend at secondary school and she would have loved to have seen her. But it just wasn't possible. It was four o'clock already and she needed to get back home for Shazia. 'No, Amma,' she said as she waved goodbye to Maria, 'I told you I have to work.'

And how dare her mother invite Mosammet! Using her as temptation just to get her home to meet Mr Choudhury's son. Poor Mosammet would be so disappointed. As she walked down the road towards her house she said, 'Amma, please stop trying to find a man for me. I don't want one!'

'Yes, but—'

Her mother didn't understand. How could she?

'Amma, I'm going to switch my phone off now,' Mumtaz said. 'Goodbye. I'll phone you soon.'

She finished the call just as she opened her front garden gate and took her keys out of her bag. When she went in the house it felt like a gale was blowing through.

'Shazia!' she called. 'Good grief, have you got the back door wide open or something?'

It had been a warm day but it was still early in the year and there was a rather chilly wind. Mumtaz walked into the kitchen but found that the back door was closed. She went into the living room just in time to see Shazia shutting the French windows.

'Oh, Amma,' she said, 'you're . . .'

'I thought it would be nice to spend some time together,' Mumtaz said. 'Make dinner, eat together.'

'Yes.'

She looked pale but the skin around her eyes was dark as if she hadn't slept. Mumtaz walked towards her, but Shazia, oddly, began to move away.

'Is everything OK?'

'Yeah, why shouldn't it be?'

'Not overdoing the homework? You get on with Vi OK?'

Shazia smiled, but she didn't look Mumtaz in the eye. 'Homework's boring but OK and I like Vi, she's cool.'

'Good.'

They stood opposite each other, neither doing nor saying anything for a few moments, then Shazia said, 'I've got geography and maths I have to do.'

'Oh. Oh, I thought, because I'm away a lot at the moment that we might spend some time—'

'Geography's due in tomorrow.' She smiled, but she still didn't look at Mumtaz. Then very quickly, almost at a run, she left the room.

Amazed and a little bit hurt too, Mumtaz watched her go. Then for want of anything else to do, she called after her, 'What do you want for dinner?'

The answer came back breezily, 'Whatever.'

Annoyed, Mumtaz felt stupid, as if Shazia had duped her in some way into coming home. But then the girl's behaviour was odd, shifty. But what could she do? Mumtaz herself needed to change her clothes before she set off for the Chapel of the Holy Pentecostal Fire. It was a Deliverance night, exorcism. However weirdly Shazia was behaving, somehow she had to get herself together for that. Once in the church she'd have to have her wits about her in all sorts of ways. Believe in it or not, exorcism was frightening and if the people behind the church were, as Lee believed, possibly criminal in some way too, she'd have to be careful. Whatever her thoughts and feelings about what she was going to see might be, she'd have to keep them to herself.

XXII

The place was rammed with the poor. They smelt of damp pavements and cigarettes, cheap cider and dogs. For every ten of them there was one like her. But that was the point, wasn't it? Looking after the needy? Maria sat down next to Betty on a chair that looked as if it had once belonged in a hospital.

In reality the new church wasn't any more or less squalid than the old one. The people were the same. It was Maria herself who was different. Her response to this place made her so. Not that it looked anything like the way it had done when it was Dave Delmonte's old fun pub. The bar was long gone, as was the old stage where a thousand mother-in-law jokes had once been told. There was a sort of a stage but it was one that Pastor Grint had built himself and the walls, rather than being grimed with fag smoke, were covered with colourful posters and pictures that people had painted of Jesus and His miracles. The building had become a good place and yet still Maria quaked. As discreetly as she could, she took a diazepam tablet and wished that she'd asked Mumtaz to come with her. But then if she wasn't safe, even from herself, in church, where was she safe?

'The Devil's going to get a right old beating tonight,' Betty said. 'Lots of people will testify and have the Devil cast out.'

Others could feel it too. There was an excited hubbub amongst the poor and the dispossessed. Looking for new lives or just a spark of hope, they speculated about whether or not the Spirit would fall upon them, whether they would be blessed by Deliverance. Maria looked around the vast space and knew for a fact that she was the only one in that room who actively feared it. In order to be delivered one had to want to free oneself of sin and push the Devil out. Of course sometimes the Devil had to be forcibly cast from a person – she'd seen that done twice now – and that could be violent and traumatic. But whatever happened, people always had to confess all their sins first and she couldn't do that. But then maybe that was her punishment. Maybe this limbo state of yearning for Christ whilst at the same time being unable to completely enter His kingdom was a kind of protracted penance.

'Brothers and sisters, let's make a start shall we?' she heard Pastor Grint say. She looked up and saw his sweet, thin face behind the stage microphone. He looked a little worn. But then the prayer meeting they'd had the previous night had been intense and it must have taken it out of him.

People stopped talking and began to take their seats. Grint smiled. 'Hey, everyone,' he said, 'we are going to have a banging Deliverance service tonight! We are going to make our beloved Jesus jump for joy! Let me hear you say "Jesus is just!"'

'Jesus is just!' They all cried out, even Maria. It was always like this. Once a service started she got caught up, like everyone else.

'Jesus is just what I need!' Grint said.

'Jesus is just what I need!'

'Jesus is just what you need!'

'Jesus is just what you need!'

'Jesus! Jesus! Jesus! Jesus!'

'Jesus! Jesus! Jesus! Jesus!'

The man to Mumtaz's left smelt of beer while the woman to her right just hadn't bathed for a while. In the final row of seats, right at the back, Mumtaz was glad there was a small breeze coming from underneath the front door. Unused to wearing trousers – Ahmed had hated her in them – and especially unaccustomed to an uncovered head, Mumtaz felt totally odd, both in this context and in herself. Her hair was almost down to her waist! When had it got to be so long? Why hadn't she noticed that?

'Jesus! Jesus! Jesus! Jesus!'

Everyone around her was standing, swaying, smiling and clapping to the beat. A man she recognised as a local solicitor was slightly more reticent than others. She could see Maria, down at the front, swaying along with the rest of them, her eyes, like everyone else's, firmly on Pastor Grint. Mumtaz stood, but she didn't sway, nor did she chant. No one seemed to notice.

'Let me hear you say, "Give it all up to Jesus!"' Grint yelled. 'Let me hear you!'

'Give it all up to Jesus!' they all said. 'Give it all up to Jesus!'

'Let me hear you say, "Sacrifice to the Lord!"'

'Sacrifice to the Lord! Sacrifice to the Lord! Sacrifice to the Lord!'

Somewhere, music played. It sounded to Mumtaz like music from that old film *The Blues Brothers*. There'd been a preacher in that, she remembered. That part of the film had ended in all sorts of dancing and ecstatic craziness. Mumtaz knew about repetition and how it could affect people. She stood still and silent and looked at the pictures and the slogans that lined the walls. They were rough and amateurish but their message was clear. Someone giving someone else what looked like a piece of food was accompanied by the slogan *The meek shall inherit the earth*.

'Sacrifice to the Lord!'

A man with long, light brown hair and a beard, who could have been Jesus, had light coming out of his head.

A speech bubble had him saying *Give and you shall receive.*
There were children in lots of the pictures, most of them
poor and hungry-looking.

'Sacrifice to the Lord! Sacrifice to the Lord!'

The hairs on the back of Mumtaz's neck began to stand
up. Light coming through a single window up high in the
roof illuminated the stage and Pastor Grint had now changed
the chant to 'Lord don't love a liar! Jesus Lord of Truth!'

'Lord don't love a liar! Jesus Lord of Truth!'

Someone had scrawled the words *Bring on the Rapture*
above a tattered picture of a rose, a slogan referring to
the Apocalypse some Christians believed was coming soon.
Mumtaz began to feel her head lighten so she moved her
gaze around the building. The chanting had been going
for a good fifteen minutes and if she allowed herself to
go with it, she wouldn't be able to see what was going
on any more.

'Jesus loves His family! Oh, yes he does!'

'Jesus loves his family!'

Grint was smiling and sweating, his face looked red
and cherubic. The smell coming from the woman standing
next to Mumtaz became intense. Everyone clapped in time
to the music now which was also repetitious. Some people
closed their eyes.

Grint pointed one arm up into the air. 'Tonight we are
going to deliver those afflicted by the Devil to Jesus!
Hallelujah!'

'Hallelujah! Hallelujah! Hallelujah!'

A woman she'd not seen before gave a bag to the man at the end of the row. He took the bag, put his hand in his pocket, took out some money, dropped it into the bag and passed it on. Christian worshippers, like most religious people, took collections. Mumtaz took fifty pence out of her purse and when the bag came to her, she dropped it in. The smelly woman put in a five pound note which was both surprising and not surprising. Her eyes shone with ecstasy.

Hallelujah, as a chant, almost as a song, went on. Mumtaz fought to keep a handle on how much time had passed but she found that she couldn't. She began to relate one of her mother's old stories about the Silver Prince to herself. *In Bengal, many centuries past, an immortal Silver Prince was born to a humble washerwoman and her husband. Though poor, the lady and her husband were good Muslims. Allah rewarded their piety with* . . . She looked up at the ceiling again and saw the slogan *Come the Hour, the sinners will perish!* written in red paint. Her stomach curdled and Mumtaz began to shiver.

'Who is hungry for the Lord?' Grint asked.

Everybody yelled out, 'I am!'

'Who wants to renounce the world, kick out Satan, testify, confess, be DELIVERED?'

Mumtaz's heart beat fast.

'Lord, forgive me, I took a man who was not my husband

295

to my bed!' The woman who said this threw herself at the stage, smashing her face against the flimsy wooden panelling as she lay down at Grint's feet. 'I took another man and I had sex with him and I can't be right with Jesus! I—'

'Sister.' Grint bent down and raised her up to her feet and then onto the stage with him. Her face was bleeding and she was crying.

'Oh, God!'

Grint put his hands underneath her armpits to support her. She was limp with emotion and her eyes were glazed and rolled around wildly in their sockets. 'Sister, if you are truly remorseful, if you truly can offer your sorrow, your life and everything you are in this world to the Lord then he will forgive you! Do you want that, sister?' He shook her. 'Do you?'

She made a noise like a wounded cat, a yowl of pain, and then he forced her to the ground again and put his hands on her head. 'Leave this woman, Satan!' he shouted. Grint had a loud and, now that he was yelling, rough voice, almost like Vi Collins's. 'She's confessed her sin! She says she wants no more of you and your works! You have no power over her now!'

The woman began to buck and shake and red blood-tinged spittle flew out of her mouth.

'You hear me, Satan, you old hypocrite, you old liar, you old tight-fist, you old enemy of love! Get out of this woman in the name of Jesus, Lord of Light, Lord of the Truth, Lord of Generosity, of Brotherhood and of Life!'

He leaned forward, digging his fingers into her back and the woman howled. A long, deep, almost orgasmic sound that took with it every tiny breath from her body. Mumtaz's mind fought to hang on to what was real, what she had been trained to *know* about things like this.

'Get out!'

Everyone, including Mumtaz, watched as something invisible, intangible appeared to leave the woman and she stopped bucking and heaving and lay flat and silent on the floor. Pastor Grint, still sweating but now also panting like a runner, bent down on one knee and put his hand, gently this time, on the woman's head. 'The truth,' he said, 'in Jesus, has set you free.'

Everyone fell to their knees except, Mumtaz thought, herself. But then she saw that Maria Peters was also still on her feet. She put her arms out towards the stage and she said, 'Help me! Help me!'

Grint looked round and smiled. 'Maria?' He beckoned her to him while the woman on the floor still lay flat and motionless. 'Are you ready for ...' He took one of her hands as if to shake it, then he tapped her forehead with a finger and whispered something to her.

Maria took one step forwards and then she just collapsed.

Pure instinct made Mumtaz rush down the aisle and kneel

down at Maria's side. She hadn't seen Maria eat for at least twelve hours and she dreaded to think about what drugs she'd consumed in that time. She also knew she'd seen Grint do something to her as well; something she, probably alone in that church, recognised.

'Maria?' Mumtaz took her pulse which was slow.

'Who are you and what are you doing?'

Mumtaz looked up into Pastor Grint's livid face and saw Betty recognise her all in the same moment.

'What are *you* doing here?' Betty Muller asked. Then she turned to Grint and said, 'She's that private detective!'

Maria began to groan and splutter and Mumtaz sat her up so that she could cough. Grint and a few other people talked quietly to one side. Everyone else either tried to see what was going on or just stood about looking concerned. Quite a few of them looked dazed.

Mumtaz said, 'I think I should call a doctor . . .'

'Mumtaz?'

She looked down into Maria's face. Her eyes were only just able to focus.

Betty Muller's face appeared from one side and blocked Mumtaz's view of Maria. 'What are you doing here?' she asked again. 'What?' She was angry but then church had always been the one place that Maria had wanted to go to alone. For a moment Mumtaz thought about lying her way out of her dilemma but then people had already seen her at the back.

'I came because . . .'

She heard the words 'private detective' but she didn't know where they came from. Maria Peters, though still ashily pale, was sitting up now and looking at her. 'Mumtaz?' she said. 'Mumtaz, I'm OK in church.'

'Yes, I know but—'

'So what are you doing here?'

She didn't know what to say. *I came to check your church out because the police think it might be dodgy? I came to see what these people do to your mind when you're full of drugs and half starved? I don't like what I've experienced here today?*

'Mumtaz, when I'm at church or at prayer meetings at home, I don't need you,' Maria said. 'This is my private life.' And then she noticed that Mumtaz's head wasn't covered. 'Were you trying to disguise yourself?' A look that Mumtaz didn't like came over Maria's face. 'Why?'

'Why—'

'Yes, why? I didn't ask you to come here. You went home to your daughter. I would have called you when I got back.'

Neil West had followed Maria to the old church back in the winter but he hadn't gone in. Flustered and angry with herself for not even planning what she might say if she was recognised, Mumtaz felt her face turn red. She looked up and saw that they were all staring down at her with suspicious, hostile, sometimes glazed eyes. When she did speak, she just blurted. Pointing to Grint, she said, 'He just tried to put you in a hypnotic trance. I saw him.'

'What? What total nonsense. You're crazy!' she heard Maria say. 'I will need to speak to your employer, right now!'

Part Three

XXIII

Matthias Chibanda had pleaded guilty to the murder of Jacob Sitole in a hearing that had lasted just under ten minutes. Vi Collins and Tony Bracci went out onto the grass outside the honey-coloured courthouse and had a smoke. Snaresbrook was a funny old place. A great graceful Victorian pile as often as not surrounded by groups of heavily tattooed gangsters, their women and their kids.

'I don't call this summer,' Vi said as she pulled her coat in close to her body. 'Bloody July! If this is global warming I can't be fucking done with it.'

'At least Chibanda did the right thing,' Tony said.

'Yeah.' But Vi didn't look convinced. Matthias Chibanda had only actually spoken about what had happened between himself and Jacob Sitole in early June. So silent he had become almost catatonic, Chibanda had been sectioned under the Mental Health Act for a month so that a psychiatrist could assess his fitness to plead. For weeks, nothing had happened and then one day he'd said to one of the nurses, 'I killed Jacob because he wouldn't give me his phone.'

It wouldn't be the first time that someone had been killed for their mobile phone and Jacob Sitole had indeed just been given a new iPhone by his mother. But Vi wasn't buying it. One thing the psychiatrists at Basildon Mental Health Unit had discovered was that Matthias Chibanda had a mental age of just twelve. Apparently his thinking was magical and animistic; in other words he saw the world in very superstitious ways. And he hadn't had Jacob's iPhone on him when he was taken to hospital. Even wounded, someone who really wanted something that badly would take it.

'Still got it in for Iekanjika, guv?'

Vi pulled a face both of disgust and against the sharp wind. 'He makes my skin creep,' she said. 'What's he doing making seven grand a month out of that old pub in Canning Town?'

'Potentially. If Paul Grint's now paid . . .'

Vi laughed. 'One bloody crook fleecing another!'

'Ah, but Grint's had a religious conversion, guv,' Tony said.

'Yeah, and I'm Cheryl Cole.' Vi shook her head. 'I know it was a long time ago but Grint went down for fraud,' she said.

'He makes no secret of it.'

'No. And being originally from the West End, we haven't followed his career,' Vi said. 'But I have a bad feeling in my water about him and not just because of what Mumtaz

Hakim reckoned he was doing. Bloody holy men! Most of them turn out to have feet of clay. I don't like Iekanjika for the same reason. Maybe it's because the Zimbabwean High Commission suddenly like him now he's apparently off the hook for any sort of involvement in Jacob Sitole's death. Or perhaps it's because their attitude towards poor old Reverend Manyika seems to be in such marked contrast. But then maybe I just can't bring meself to believe a word any representative of Robert Mugabe says. Him starving his own people is a story that seems to have slipped off the news radar. But then he doesn't have any oil, does he?'

Vi had had a bad time wrestling with her conscience during the build-up to the second Iraq war. She hadn't approved and when she'd been sent to help police the anti-war march in London in February 2003, her heart had wanted to take off her uniform and join in. But she hadn't. She'd done her duty in spite of the fact that she believed then, as now, that the only reason for the invasion of Iraq had been because the West wanted its oil. Tony Bracci she knew disagreed, and so she changed the subject. 'But in the meantime, we still have that fucking flasher threatening the Olympics,' she said.

They both laughed. The inflated importance of the 2012 Olympics was something they did agree on. That said, Vi didn't really take the Olympic Flasher lightly. He could, she knew, escalate his behaviour to assault at any time.

Plus Chief Inspector Venus was distinctly unamused by their lack of progress and Vi had wanted to tell him that given the fact that the Met as a whole was facing job cuts, and possible pension cuts too, motivation and morale across the entire force wasn't exactly high. Going the extra mile for a flasher was not at the top of anyone's agenda, in Forest Gate or outside Forest Gate.

'Could be to do with being anxious about her exam results,' Lee said.

It was a slow day and he and Mumtaz were in the office together for all of it.

'I wish my daughter cared at all,' he continued. They were talking about Shazia and Lee's daughter Jodie and their very different attitudes towards their upcoming GCSE results. Shazia, according to Mumtaz, was not a happy girl and had lost weight she couldn't afford to lose.

'I can't get her to eat,' Mumtaz said. 'Even when my mother comes over laden with sweets, she doesn't eat them. Shazia has always loved chocolate. I don't know what's going on.'

Lee shrugged. 'My Jodie wants to go on *X Factor*. Doesn't see qualifications as anything she needs. Just the right handbag, the right tan, the right shoes . . .' He shook his head. 'Kids!'

It had been nearly three months since Maria Peters had fired the Arnold Agency for a second time. She'd made a vitriolic accusation about Mumtaz prying into her private life and making 'groundless' accusations against Paul Grint and then, after paying up by post, she'd just disappeared. Lee had tried to talk to her about what had happened, but she never returned his calls. Of course he couldn't tell her that Mumtaz had been in the church that evening partly because he owed a favour to his old colleagues up at Forest Gate. But he had wanted to tell her that no offence had ever been intended. Now it was July and half the country was on holiday, in spite of the recession, and so the agency was quiet. Yet again, Lee was worrying about how he was going to pay his bills. The departure of Maria Peters still rankled, not just because she was a complete mystery – who was possibly being manipulated – but because she had brought good money too.

'I don't know why Shazia might be worried about her exams,' Mumtaz said. 'She worked very hard for them. Her predicted grades are all As or A stars.'

'She's a bright girl. You're lucky.'

'Am I?' She didn't feel lucky. The bank had called her three times already that morning about the mortgage. But why bother Lee with that? There was nothing he could do about it. Mumtaz walked over to the tiny kitchen in the corner of the office and put the kettle on. 'Tea?'

'Brill.' Lee leaned back in his chair and rested his head against the wall behind him. 'Shazia thinks,' Lee said. 'Kid's got some sort of inner life going on. All my daughter ever goes on about is stuff. Clothes, make-up, iPhones, jewellery. She's on my case all the time.' He didn't say anything about his ex-wife who chose not to work. That was private business. 'And yet some parents are shelling out for things for their kids all the time. Little sods won't leave them alone.'

The kettle began to boil. 'Your daughter will grow out of it,' Mumtaz said.

'You think?' Lee was far from convinced. 'When it comes to kids nowadays I don't know what to think.'

Vi Collins's case with the two Zimbabwean lads had finally resolved. Matthias Chibanda had admitted that he'd killed Jacob Sitole for his new mobile. How pathetic! And how very, very sad for a death to occur over something so trivial. But it was also good that it hadn't signalled some sort of feud between the two respective churches – even if Vi still distrusted Pastor Iekanjika.

'Even religious kids get involved in crime now.' Lee was aware that he was making himself sound like some sort of grumpy old git but he didn't care.

'You mean like the Zimbabwean boys?' Mumtaz poured boiling water onto teabags in two cups and then stirred them around with a spoon. 'People still want things even if they are religious.'

'Like Pastor Grint?'

Grint's fraudulent past had involved a property scam in his native Shepherd's Bush. Twenty years ago he'd sold houses he didn't own to immigrants.

'Part of his appeal is that he's come through all that and found God,' Mumtaz said. 'Supposedly.'

'And yet you think that he's hypnotising those people in his services.'

Mumtaz poured milk into the cups and then hooked out the teabags. She spooned two sugars into Lee's cup and put it on his desk. 'I definitely saw a well-known technique at work when he took Maria's hand and then tapped her head. He was confounding her senses so that she would shut down. He told her to sleep, I think. He was trying to put her in a trance.' She took her tea back to her desk and sat down. 'All religious ceremony and ritual has an element of hypnosis within it. There is repetition, there is meaningful imagery, there is enhanced emotion. All these things can lead to states of heightened consciousness. So she was halfway there already.'

'And you're religious yourself? Knowing all that?'

She smiled. 'Just because ritual worship encourages a heightened state of awareness doesn't alter the central tenets of a religion; it doesn't mean that God does not exist.'

'But if we're basically animals just responding to—'

'So what if we are? Just because we are animals that doesn't disprove God. God made us whatever we are.'

Lee was really happier listening to old punk records and cleaning up than he was with philosophy. Although he was intrigued as to where Mumtaz stood on the theory of evolution. He'd never met a religious Muslim yet who believed in it. He did play about with the notion of asking Mumtaz what she thought about dinosaurs, but then thought better of it. Christian fundamentalists claimed to believe that God had put dinosaur bones in the earth to test man's faith. Lee thought it was bollocks and it made him cross and so he held his peace.

Lee thought about his brother Roy and wondered where he was. It was nearly three months now since he'd chucked him out of their mother's house. She'd been out. Lee had found Roy pissed as a fart, shitting on the kitchen floor. He'd beaten what crap had remained inside his brother out of him and then thrown him into the street. Amazingly he'd gone and stayed gone. *Maybe*, Lee thought without any emotion whatsoever, *he's dead.*

If she looked for long enough at the cats in the fireplace, she could make them disappear. Had Mumtaz still been in her life, she would no doubt have been able to explain that scientifically. But Mumtaz was not in her life because Mumtaz had betrayed her. She'd watched what went on in church and no doubt mocked and she'd managed to prevent her from testifying and accepting Deliverance. That moment of clarity and grace she'd felt on that evening, now almost three months ago, had disappeared never to return. Maria despaired that it ever would. She put a pill on her tongue while Betty was out of the room and swallowed it.

Betty knew that she had to take medication; sometimes she went and got it from the chemist for her. Sometimes she even gave her some of her own pills when she was in danger of running out.

'Would you like a cup of tea?'

Maria jumped. She hadn't heard Betty come in from the kitchen. 'No. Thanks.'

There was a look on her friend's face that could have been pity but then she smiled, said, 'OK,' and went back into the kitchen. If Betty did pity her, then Maria could understand it. She was still outside God's grace, how could she not be pitied? And Betty didn't even know why.

Betty came back into the living room and Maria listened to her talk about 'designated charities'. Every month, the church nominated a designated charity to give a proportion of its donations to. This month it was some organisation to do with rehabilitating child soldiers in Africa, but Maria didn't really listen. Distracted by her own problems, she cut into Betty's explanation and said, 'I'm going to ring Mr Allitt. Could you get me the phone please, Bet?'

Betty looked at her questioningly, as well she might. The phone was on the coffee table, only a short stretch of the arm away. But everything ached and she felt sick and tired and she just didn't want to make any effort. Betty handed her the phone and then left the room. Maria dialled Mr Allitt's number and instantly began to feel relieved.

*   *   *

It was Adele and Hilary! Shazia slumped down underneath her bedroom window and wondered what to do. The old man next door was in and so he'd know they were there. He'd guess she was in, even if he didn't know.

She heard Hilary call, 'Zia, hon, where are you?'

They would have brought fags and enough of Hil's mum's fridge cake to sink a ship. Shazia bit her bottom lip. Now it was the school holidays they were always round. The landline rang and she knew that she was going to have to leave it. But she didn't want to ignore them! When they did finally catch up with her they'd want to know where she'd been and what she'd been doing. The phone continued to ring until the machine cut in. She heard Mumtaz's voice ask callers to leave a message and then a long beep.

Outside Adele yelled, 'Oh, come on, Zi, shift your arse!'

Shazia heard someone on the other end of the phone take a deep breath and instantly she knew it was *him*. 'Oh, Mrs Hakim, this is most respectfully Mr Aziz Choudhury.' He took another vaguely asthmatic breath. Shazia pulled a face. He sounded like some sort of comedy Paki, this man her stepmother's parents wanted so much for Amma to like! 'I would be very grateful if you could call me at your earliest convenience. Thank you.'

As well as talking like a comedy Paki, Aziz Choudhury was completely hideous and old and wore horrible, stinking shalwar kameez. Ugh. Shazia didn't want a man in the house with them, not ever again.

'Zi!'

They weren't going away. Shazia looked out of the side window at the house next door and then, keeping low so that she couldn't be seen, she ran to Amma's bedroom at the back. Being careful to remain down and out of sight, she looked out into the back garden just in time to see the old man slip through the hole in the hedge and hide himself amongst the plum trees. What was she going to do? She felt her eyes tear up but quickly wiped them away with her sleeve. She'd already hidden from her friends once that week. If she denied them again they'd really make her life crap. As for the old man, well who knew what he'd do?

XXIV

He walked along beside her, making them look like a couple, smiling his lime-white smile. Through a mixture of guilty desire and absolute disgust Mumtaz made herself look up at him. Then she said, 'I don't know what you want with me. I don't know why you killed Ahmed, but you must realise by now that I'm not going to give you to the police.'

'Why not?'

'That's my business,' she said. 'Go away.'

It was the first time he had ever spoken to her and his voice was very deep and very posh British-sounding for an Asian boy of his age.

They were just turning out of Windsor Road and into Claremont and she was beginning to suspect that he might be walking her home. She didn't understand why and she didn't want it. 'My stepdaughter will be in,' she said. 'I don't want her seeing you. Whatever the ... You killed her father. Please go.'

For just a second his eyes flickered in a way that could

have signalled some sort of conscience. But then he smiled again and she knew that really he was a reptile – a cold-blooded silver lizard.

'I will not expose you and I am grateful, but you also disgust me,' she said. She began to walk faster, but he lengthened his stride just a little and very quickly caught up with her.

She hadn't seen him for almost two months. His appearance, seemingly waiting for her outside the police station, had come as a shock. She'd just walked past, avoiding eye contact as she did so, but he'd followed her. She didn't know why any more than she knew why he'd lurked outside her house in the past. Surely he had to be afraid she'd call the police even if she said that she wouldn't? Now she was almost home and she wondered what he would do. Head down, she powered forwards. Intent upon just getting away from him and into her own house, she didn't notice the thin, elderly man walk out in front of her.

'Oh, I'm so—'

Flustered, she looked up at him. 'I'm sorry, I . . .' He was old, thin and white and she recognised him.

'No, no, no,' he said. 'It's my fault, I wasn't looking where I was going.'

He smiled. He was the solicitor who worked near to her office on Green Street – the one she'd seen at Maria Peters' church. Mumtaz looked up and, suddenly aware of her surroundings, saw that he'd just come out of Maria's house.

'Are you all right?' She'd made him stumble slightly.

'Oh, it's nothing, my dear,' he said. 'Nothing at all. Are you all right?'

'Oh, yes, I . . .'

'Well, that's jolly good then.' He smiled again and then walked, large briefcase in his hand, to a Bentley that was parked across the road.

Once the solicitor had gone, Mumtaz looked around for *him*. But he'd gone. Feeling grateful for that, if nothing else, she put her hand on her chest and then stood still for a moment while she caught her breath. Then just for the smallest of seconds she looked at Maria Peters' house and saw a thin, white face that could have been the comedian looking back at her.

His dad had called it ligging – turning up in a pub with no money and expecting to be bought drinks. But he was skint. Bob the Builder still owed him a ton, but no one seemed to know where he was. Depressed, Lee tried to kid himself that because he didn't drink booze his ligging wasn't 'real'. But it was and when the old men, his dad's old mates, who usually haunted the outer reaches of the Boleyn had gone, Lee was left alone with a pint of ligged diet Coke, the bar staff and a load of strangers. He looked around, half hoping and half dreading seeing Roy. But his brother was nowhere – unlike what looked like a random selection of Newham's indigenous white tribes who sat and drank and flirted, laughed and sometimes shouted. Contained in the pub they were, Lee thought, a bit like a band of well fed refugees. Many of them, and that included his mother and his brother, saw themselves very much as an endangered minority. For some reason the coming of the Hindus and the Sikhs back in the sixties had gone on almost without comment. But first the Pakis and then the eastern Europeans had struck some sort of nerve with the locals that Lee didn't entirely understand. In a sense he could see that some of the Pakistanis and Bangladeshis kept themselves to themselves but then so had some of the Sikhs and the Hindus. As for the eastern Europeans, many of the Jews who still lived in the borough had come originally from places like Poland and they were just part of the community.

That said, and as old Reverend Murkoff the rabbi once told Lee, 'Trouble is, son, a lot of these Poles and Lithuanians have anti-Semitism stamped through them like Southend rock. Some of their ancestors worked in the camps during the war.'

That something that had happened such a long time ago was still having an effect upon the present was both understandable and horrendous at the same time. It made Lee feel bleak and he knew that had he actually had any money he may well have bought a pint.

'On your own?'

He didn't recognise the girl at all. He saw a curtain of straightened blond hair, a face and shoulders unusually brown for an English summer and he smelt a very strong waft of perfume. 'Hello.'

Lee Arnold didn't need some young Essex girl to come on to him to confirm that he was attractive to women. But he looked at her with a slightly crooked half smile and asked her her name.

Her laugh was pleasantly deep and throaty even if her make-up was thickly appalling. She said, 'I'm Foxy.'

'Are you now.' If she came from Romford or Basildon or Southend-on-Sea that was probably her real name. 'And what can I do for you, Foxy?'

'A WKD and Coke?'

He laughed. Somewhere at the bottom of his left-hand jacket pocket there was a twenty pence piece. 'And if I can't buy you a drink?' he asked. 'What then?'

He knew how avaricious girls of her age were. He was prepared for the abuse, the imagined slight she would make to his manhood. But strangely Foxy just kept on smiling.

Back at the flat Chronus went into a frenzy of excitement when Lee walked in with a visitor.

'Bobby Moore!' he shouted. 'Geoff Hurst! Bobby Moore! Trevor Brooking!'

Lee and Foxy took their clothes off in the living room and then went to the bedroom and shut the door on the bird's endless yelling. After almost a year without sex, Lee was both happy and grateful that Foxy was an enthusiastic and proficient young lady. His phone rang once just as he was about to come and so he threw it across the room, much to Foxy's delight. It was only later, when the girl was on top of him, that Lee wondered if the call might have been from Mumtaz. And although it was a thought that didn't cool his ardour in any way it was distracting because from then on he could only continue if he closed his eyes and completely cut himself off from the girl having sex with him.

'I was just passing,' Vi Collins said.

Mumtaz knew that was probably a lie, but she was still glad to see her. Shazia had gone to bed early and she was lonely. 'Come in.'

Vi put the mobile phone she'd just attempted to call Lee Arnold on back in her bag and went inside. She'd actually fancied a shag if he'd been up for it, but obviously he wasn't.

Mumtaz led Vi into her living room and the two women sat down. 'So finally the one Zimbabwean boy who killed the other has explained what happened,' she said. 'That must be a relief to you and to the victim's family. All over a mobile phone.'

'Mmm.'

'Sign of the times.'

Vi could have said that she didn't believe Matthias Chibanda but she didn't. In all probability his version of events that night would be accepted by whichever jury tried him and what she still believed would be lost for ever in one boy's fear. Or maybe she was just so anti-religion she couldn't bring herself to believe that the happy-clappy churches were not involved in one way or another. Or perhaps it was because all these churches seemed to have so much money?

'Tea?'

Vi looked up. 'Oh, er, yes, ta, Mumtaz. Lovely.'

Mumtaz went into the kitchen and put the kettle on. She was, Vi sensed, a little tense.

'Shazia's gone to bed,' she heard her say from the kitchen.

It seemed very early for the girl to have gone to bed but there it was. Vi was actually rather more distracted by a slight musty smell that she'd never noticed in Mumtaz's house before. Big Forest Gate gaffs like this one often had cellars which could get damp. Maybe it was that? Vi didn't really care. For the first time in ages she'd wanted some comfort sex, with a man as opposed to a boy, with a mate and not a stranger. She'd wanted Lee Arnold. But she couldn't have him. And so instead she talked about not much at all to a woman whose head was covered with a scarf because of her religion.

Only as Vi was leaving did Mumtaz's tension seem to

lift. Vi was at the front door when she said, 'I saw Maria Peters today. At least I think so. She was staring out of her living room window and she looked awful. She had a solicitor at the house with her.'

Vi sighed. 'Up to her who she sees and why, love,' she said. 'I know she's unfinished business for you ...'

'Those church people are with her all the time now. I see them coming and going. Whatever they're doing, her health seems to be suffering. I'm sure she's ill.'

'Possibly.' Vi put a hand on Mumtaz's shoulder. 'But we're not doctors. Unless she commits some sort of offence or makes a complaint against someone there's nothing I can do.'

Betty didn't seem to see the shoebox at all. But then Maria didn't bring it to her notice. Lurking in the corner by the television, stinking of death. Even when she wasn't alone, Maria couldn't clean in that corner any more. In comparison to the rest of the room that area looked unkempt and dirty.

Maria stared at the box. Clarks. Her mum had always taken them to Clarks, in Ilford, to buy their school shoes. They'd all hated going, Maria and her two sisters, Ursula and Teresa. Urs had been particularly vocal about it, going on about how ugly the well-made but unfashionable shoes were. Now she was a nun and went about in shoes that made Clarks' school range look like Jimmy Choos. Maria hadn't seen either Ursula or Teresa, who had a ton of kids and lived in Edinburgh, since Len's funeral. She'd chosen a Clarks box because it had been all that she had and because, down on the mud of the river, it was what people did. Now it was all coming back because what goes around comes around. You couldn't have the charmed life she'd had in recent times and not expect to pay a price for it. Pastor Grint was right; she couldn't be at peace with Jesus until she'd properly admitted her sins and she couldn't do that. She took some codeine.

Betty had left her food, but she'd just chucked it in the bin. Everything she ate hurt as it went down inside. It was as if there were sores all the way along her intestines.

XXV

The preparations for the Choudhurys' visit started early. Baharat woke up to the smells and the sounds of Sumita preparing a feast. His wife had talked of nothing else for over a week. His daughter, the actual object of the visit, had not spoken a word. Baharat felt a thread of anxiety tighten in his stomach. Last time Mumtaz had been introduced to a man for the purposes of marriage it had ended badly. Ahmed Hakim had turned out to be a handsomely wrapped parcel of trouble whose terrible influence still lingered in his daughter's life in the shape of her poverty.

Baharat knew that the only boy she'd ever really had feelings for had been that Jew she'd gone to university with, the magician. Mumtaz thought that was her secret, but Baharat noticed things. The boy, Mark, had visited them a few times. He'd been a nice boy. Something between him and Mumtaz had of course been impossible, but yes, he'd been a good boy – nicer than Mr Choudhury's son. And now Mark Solomons was on television. When Ahmed Hakim's death had hit the national headlines, Mark had called to ask for Mumtaz's number so he could offer his condolences and Baharat had given it to him. But he'd never called. He was a busy man. All that was gone now.

Maybe it was because of Ahmed Hakim, but Baharat was finding he was suspicious of Aziz Choudhury. Sumita was completely captivated by him – or she said that she was. Baharat found him nondescript and it was just that lack of definition that worried him. The man was like a blank slate – he could be anything! Around his own father and his friends he was a deeply respectful and loving son, even when Mr Choudhury senior behaved like an arsehole. But how was Junior around his own friends? If he had any. Baharat couldn't actually see Aziz Choudhury out and about with other people. As well as having no personality he didn't even have his father's cache. Mr Choudhury senior was a respected man, a hajji, which was something that no one could take away from him, and he had money too. But he was an arsehole. He believed the most ridiculous nonsense about people. He actually believed that Hindus mated with cows! Hindus worshipped cows. How could anyone believe such insanity? It was pure blind prejudice and Baharat had no time for it. If only Mumtaz hadn't married that awful Hakim man. Now as a widow and over thirty, her options for remarriage were limited.

Baharat put the radio on and lay back on his bed to listen to the news. Some man had been shot by police up in Tottenham. They said he was a drug dealer who had been armed but his family said that he was innocent. Baharat found himself thinking *well, they would* and then he felt how uncharitable that was and turned the radio off. It was all bad news lately – bad economy, cuts, unrest all over the place! Greedy bankers and gangsters like Ahmed Hakim had leeched all the money out of the world and just thrown it away on rubbish. People were awful. He'd been cornered by one of those jihadi types in the street the night before. He'd made the 'helpful' suggestion that maybe Mumtaz could become his second or third wife. Baharat had told him to bugger off! It was clear that he just wanted to have sex with her.

She was a beautiful woman, his daughter, but some people were talking about her. Alone with a child that was not hers in that great big house in Forest Gate – and working every day alone with an Englishman. And even though Baharat knew that Mumtaz was a girl of pure and honourable heart, he feared the gossips and the troublemakers. Married, she would be protected against such people. But was Aziz Choudhury the right man to do that?

Foxy, and that had turned out to be her real name, had proved to be quite a difficult girl to shake off. She'd stayed the night with Lee, which had been fine, but then she'd made a bit of a song and dance about leaving, which had been a pain. She'd wanted breakfast, which had been a total non-starter unless she liked old fag butts and sour milk – which she hadn't. With no job to go to, she would have liked to have hung around the flat and have more sex, which was a nice idea – in one way. But Lee had to go to work and besides, in the cold light of morning, he just wasn't that impressed any more. Foxy wasn't a bad girl – she was pretty in a plastic sort of a way and she wasn't in any sense dim – but she was hardly brain of Britain either. She was also twenty-four, which was bloody ridiculous. Under some childish protest, he took her to Upton Park tube station and made a mental note to avoid the Boleyn in the evenings for at least the next week.

When he arrived at his office Mumtaz was already with a client. It was a white man. From the back he looked thin and a bit down-at-heel, but Lee had no notion of who he might be. It was only when he turned around that he realised it was Roy.

Vi felt ashamed of herself. Last night her mind had been clouded by her need for sex and it had apparently adversely affected her nasal passages too. Mumtaz's house wasn't musty! What it was was something she very much doubted had anything to do with Mumtaz at all. Shazia, however, was, or could be, quite another matter. Kids did that stuff.

Even if she hadn't had a day off, Vi would have made time to go around to Mumtaz's place. Shazia Hakim, as far as she could tell, was a basically good, clever girl who shouldn't be jeopardising her own future. When Vi approached the house, Shazia was putting rubbish in the dustbin.

'Hello, love,' Vi said. 'Got a minute?'

'Yes.' She smiled but she also turned pale. 'Would you like a cup of tea?'

They went inside the house which smelt of something Vi couldn't exactly define except that it was probably some sort of air freshener. As they walked into the kitchen and Shazia began to boil the kettle, Vi considered how she might broach the subject gently, but then decided that she might as well just go straight for it.

'So how long you been smoking dope, Shazia?' she said as she sat down at the kitchen table.

For a moment the girl just stopped what she was doing, with her back to Vi, and said nothing.

'I smelt it in the house last night,' Vi said. 'I've worked on enough drugs busts to know what it smells like, love. And I am a mother.'

Shazia turned. Vi very easily saw the fear and she stuck a knife right in it. 'Your mum'd be horrified,' she said. 'She's a good person, your mum, she don't need this.'

'But I don't smoke weed.' It was said softly and was accompanied by a sudden reddening of the girl's cheeks.

'Oh, so if I order a search of this house you'll be all right with that, will you? If I went through that bin outside ...' Vi left that thought hanging in the air and just sat and waited. Shazia was exhibiting every sign of guilt in the book and so it was only a question of time.

'I don't smoke dope, I . . .'

'So you'll be happy to take a drugs test then, will you?'

The anger burst onto Shazia's face like a smashed egg. 'You can't make me do that! You can't make me do anything!'

Vi took her warrant card out of her handbag and held it up for Shazia to see. The girl knew she was a police officer but now she needed to really think about what that might mean. 'Oh, yes I can.' Then she took her mobile phone out of her pocket and held that up too. 'I can organise all of that right now.'

As quickly as Shazia's anger had exploded so did the tears behind her eyes burst out and flood onto her cheeks. Vi put her bag, her phone and her warrant card down and went to her. Shazia didn't even try to stop her as she put her arms around her shoulders and rocked her gently from side to side. Really sobbing now, Shazia was unable to speak and so Vi just held her and kissed the side of her face until eventually what looked like the pent-up tears of many weeks and maybe even months began to subside.

Once the girl's head was upright again, Vi took her over to the kitchen table and sat her down. While Shazia hiccupped and gasped through what remained of her tears, Vi made them both tea and then sat down herself. She looked at Shazia and said, 'So what's been going on?'

There was a whiff of coercion around this situation which Vi had seen before. She didn't know who was involved but she felt the presence of someone apart from just Shazia in all this.

'Will I go to prison, Vi?' the girl asked.

'Not if you tell me the truth.'

'About my smoking weed?'

'About why you do it, who you do it with and where you get it from.'

She looked frightened again and then she looked away. 'I do it on my own.'

'Do you?' Vi didn't believe her and she could see that Shazia knew it. 'Not much fun in that. Where'd you get your gear?'

Shazia just shrugged.

'You don't know, do you?'

Still looking away she said, 'I get it from a boy.' Then she did looked at Vi and she said, 'You won't tell my mum, will you?'

Vi ignored her. 'What boy? Where? At school? On the street?'

She didn't answer. Had she had any more tears to cry she would have wept again, but she didn't.

'There is no boy is there, Shazia?' Vi said. 'There's no boy because I don't believe that you get the gear yourself. I think someone else does it. Who is it, love? Is it a schoolfriend? A boy you fancy?'

Shazia remained silent.

'Is it someone you're afraid of?'

The girl looked up.

Vi said nothing but she noted it. 'Shazia, whatever you may think about dope smoking it is a criminal offence and so you shouldn't do it. Personally, I don't think the odd joint is the end of the world, but that all depends on why you're doing it and I'm not sure you're doing it because you want to.' She put her hand on Shazia's hair. 'I know you've had a hard time, love. You lost your dad and—'

'I don't want to be split up from Amma! I don't want to be taken away from her!'

Oh, there was a fierceness here, a connection to Mumtaz that was desperate. With luck it gave her a way in. 'Then tell me,' Vi said. 'Tell me the truth and I swear to you on my children's lives that you and your mum will not be parted.' She hoped to Christ that she wasn't going to be told something so bloody awful that she'd have to break her oath.

The pause that followed seemed to disappear into the far, far distance. Time extended and then pushed out still further and then, just as Vi was beginning to feel she couldn't bear it any more, Shazia said, 'Since my dad died, I haven't been able to do anything.' She cleared her throat which was threatening to close up on her every time she spoke. 'When he was alive, he gave me money. I could have anything I wanted: clothes, holidays, anything. Amma does her best but it's . . . different. I used to go everywhere with my friend Adele . . .'

Another silence opened up which Vi filled. 'And now?'

Shazia lowered her head. She was ashamed of what came next. 'I couldn't go shopping all the time any more. Then Hilary Proctor invited Ady to go to Bluewater with her and her mum and then they were, like, joined at the hip. Ady didn't drop me or anything like that, it was just that I couldn't do much stuff any more.' She swallowed and then she blurted, 'But then they both started smoking, you know . . .'

'Dope.'

She looked away. 'Yeah. But they had nowhere to keep it. Their mums don't work so they're always in the house when everyone else is out. Ady and Hilary were afraid their mums would find their weed and so I said they could keep it here. They were really made up, you know.'

Vi moved her head so that she could look into Shazia's frightened eyes. Poor kid. She'd so wanted to keep in with her old friend! 'When did you start smoking it in the house then?'

Shazia shrugged. 'Don't know. Back in the spring . . . I don't like it much. Ady says it helps her to forget her troubles. But it doesn't do that for me.'

'Has Ady lost her dad?'

'No, her parents are divorced,' she said dismissively. 'It didn't help me to forget that Amma was having to work so hard. And I was scared.'

'Scared she'd find out?'

'Yeah. She'd be so, like, disappointed! But once I'd started, I couldn't stop. Ady and Hilary come here to smoke. They expect it, especially now it's the holidays.' She shook her head. 'And it's nice for me to be with Ady again.'

'What do you think the girls would do if you said they couldn't keep their dope here and come round to smoke it?'

Shazia shook her head. 'I don't know.'

'Have they ever threatened you, as in maybe not being friends with you any more if you don't carry on with this?'

There was a slight pause before she said, 'No,' but again Vi took note. It sounded like Shazia was, at the very least, having pressure exerted on her by what sounded like two over-privileged little madams. Of course the kid had been vulnerable after her father's death, which had been compounded by the fact he'd left both her and Mumtaz potless. Rumours had floated around about Ahmed Hakim and his somewhat dodgy business dealings for years.

'So do you have any dope in the house at the moment, Shazia?'

She nodded her head. 'In my jewellery box in my bedroom.'

Vi sighed and then she stood up. 'Better have a look then.'

'Oh, but Ady and Hilary are coming this afternoon and then there's Mr Gold,' Shazia said. And then suddenly realising the full import of her words she put her hand over her mouth, her eyes wide and frightened.

Vi's eyes, by contrast, narrowed. She leaned down towards Shazia and she said, 'Mr Gold? As in Martin Gold, your neighbour? Now where the fuck does *he* come into this?'

'That's no fucking way to talk to me, you scabby cunt!' Roy Arnold roared at his brother.

Lee, appalled almost beyond words to be in Roy's presence again, flung him through the door of his office and said to an amazed Mumtaz, 'My brother. Sorry. Try not to be long.'

'It's OK . . .' She hadn't known that the man was Lee's brother. There was obviously a problem though. But then Mumtaz, full of dread about her mother's upcoming meal with the Choudhurys, had problems of her own.

In Lee's office, Roy lit up a fag. Lee joined him. To hell with legislation about smoking in the work place. 'What fucking rock have you slithered out from under?' Lee said. 'I told you to fuck off and I expected you to do just that.'

'Or you'd kill me?' Roy laughed. Oddly he didn't stink of booze and although not exactly tidy, he no longer looked like a tramp. It was weird.

'Go back to Mum's and I'll break your fingers,' Lee said. He spoke more softly now, aware that Mumtaz was only in the other room.

Roy, who could be a very perceptive man when he wanted to, picked up on it immediately. 'Frightened your girlfriend'll hear you?' He laughed. 'You fancy her.'

Lee ignored him. He was used to this sort of behaviour. 'What do you want, Roy?' he asked. 'If it's money you're after, I'm skint.'

But Roy just looked at him, smiling. Usually if Lee said he had no money, Roy flew into a rage and then had a tantrum like a two-year-old. Out in the other office, Mumtaz's mobile rang and Lee heard her answer it. 'So what is it?' he said to Roy. 'What do you want with me?'

Still smiling, Roy looked down at the fag between his fingers and said, 'It ain't what you can do for me, but what I can do for you.'

Lee's eyes went heavenwards. 'What? What can you do for me, Roy? And how much is it going to cost?'

'I can put you on to a scam,' Roy said. 'A fucking great big one.'

'What an illegal—'

'Oh, it's illegal all right.'

'Well then go to the police. It's what they're there for.'

'I don't like police stations, I'm a bit allergic, like,' Roy said. Then he leaned forward onto Lee's desk and he said, 'And anyway, this scam I've come into contact with is one I know that will interest you, Lee.'

The door to the office suddenly flew open and Mumtaz,

obviously flustered and red-faced said, 'Oh, Lee, Mr Arnold, I'm so sorry, I have to go home, it's Shazia—'

Lee sprang out of his chair and went to her. 'Is she ill?'

Mumtaz shook her head. 'I don't know, but something's wrong. Can I just—'

'Go! Go!'

'I have an appointment, a lady coming in at three. Hopefully I should be back by—'

'Go!' Lee waved her out and then said, 'Hope she's OK. Let me know. Don't worry about anything here.'

He saw her pick up her handbag and then shoot out through the front door. He went back into his own office where Roy was cackling gently to himself. 'Cosy.'

'Oh, shut up, you fucking freak!' Lee said. 'Now what's this thing, this scam you think I might be interested in?'

'Well, it concerns a church called the Chapel of the Holy Pentecostal Fire,' Roy said. 'And I know that people there know you.'

Lee felt his face turn white. 'How do you know that?'

'Because people told me. Talk of the town, this firm is down there,' Roy said. 'See, I've become a Christian, Lee.' He laughed. 'They've been very good to me, the Pentecostals, given me food and money and all sorts. But them at the top, they're a little bit dodgy and I think you should know about that.'

Lee looked at his brother and felt, for the millionth time, nothing except complete disgust. Roy always found someone or something to latch onto when he went walk-about. This time it was Maria Peters' church. 'So why you ratting on people who helped you?' he asked.

'Because fraud ain't Christian,' Roy said, with a definite light in his eye.

Lee, knowing to the bottom of his soul that his brother was ligging said, 'So what did you do to piss them off, Roy? Did you boil up their floor polish to make a little drink?'

Roy's face darkened immediately.

'Chuck you out, did they?' Lee shook his head. The last thing he needed was Roy back in his life, and the thing he needed only a little less than that was further involvement with Maria Peters and her band of happy-clappies. The whole affair still bugged the crap out of him. He wanted none of it.

Roy looked like he was about to spit but then he leaned in towards Lee again and said, 'They're into dodgy money, you stupid twat, and I found out. You ain't the only fucking Sherlock in the family. But if you don't want to know . . .'

Lee looked up into Roy's eyes in the full knowledge that he couldn't help but be intrigued by the notion of dodgy money – especially given what he already knew about Grint and his church. He knew that Roy would know this too. He sighed. 'So what do you want?' he asked.

Roy smiled again then and said, 'A place to kip.'

XXVI

Maria woke up with crawling flesh. Someone was in the room, but when she looked around there was no one. Briefly, she wondered what the time was, but it was irrelevant. The news was on the telly and people were shouting but Maria switched it off before she could see the time. The Clarks box was still in the corner, that was the main thing. Had an hour passed or a day? If she called Betty or Pastor Grint or someone and they came over, it might disappear. Accepting, of course, that she could even bring herself to talk about it. But then, whatever happened, it would come back again. She thought about calling Mr Allitt and checking on the progress of the paperwork, but she knew it was too soon. He was quite aware that she wanted her business concluded with some speed, but it had to be done right too, and besides, if she had to wait she had to wait, and maybe that was a good thing. Maybe that was part of her punishment.

Feeling herself begin to panic, Maria took some diazepam and then, when it began to take effect, she slumped back down on the sofa. She hadn't washed for days but it didn't really bother her. When she'd first been on the circuit, driving around between obscure pubs and clubs in the north and in the Midlands, she sometimes hadn't washed properly for ages. A bit of perfume under the armpits, dry shampoo raked through her hair – mainly it just made her look as if she had a bad case of dandruff. She'd gigged anywhere and everywhere, the relentless travelling together with the endless writing had kept her sharp and thrilled and had forced her mind to be forever off herself. She'd played the universities and had been the first entertainer ever to use the word 'cunt' on stage at a Cambridge University college May Ball. She couldn't remember whether it was King's or St John's. One of the two. But it made her smile.

If only she could write again. But Alan had only taken her back on condition she rehash her old material – about the royal family, about Catholicism – for a new generation. 'You can't really lose, dear,' he'd told her when they'd first discussed her relaunch. 'Your old fans will be delighted to see you back again and you, an old gal, can just appal the youngsters, they'll love it!' And they had.

Out on the road she'd heard the few old stagers that remained from her glory days say that a lot of the new, young comics didn't write their own material. They were 'products', like the weirdly appealing plastic singers that came to prominence through awful talent shows on the telly. She'd found that depressing, although whether that had actually been the exact moment when she began to have doubts about comedy, Maria didn't know. She'd got a spot on Radio 4 to do *Woman's Hour* round about that time, to speak about her comeback. She'd talked about a lot of positive things, about her website and her use of technology that hadn't even existed when she began on the circuit. But she'd also criticised the 'product' comedians, without mentioning any names, of course. Had that exposé of what was going on in comedy, in public, caused her to begin to fall out of love with what she did? But had she ever, really, fallen out of love with comedy at all?

Alan, simplistically, blamed the church. And yes, the church had made her think about whether or not it was right to make fun of people because of their looks, their state of health or their religion. The swearing had begun to grate and she could no longer really get behind all the sexual stuff in the way she had before. But was all that really just to do with the church? Wasn't that more just growing up? Finally facing up? She looked at the Clarks box through a haze of tranquilliser and wondered whether she should open it. She'd done so once before and of course it had been empty.

Maria knew that her responses were blunted by the drugs but there was also a sudden feeling of *what do I have to lose?* as well. She slithered over the carpet rather than getting up and walking. She was on her own, it didn't matter.

The carpet near the box was filthy. She pulled herself over on her elbows and then found dust bunnies and bits of crisp and what looked like chocolate stuck to her arms. When she got close to the box, she knew she should really pray or at least say something. But she didn't know what to say or how to formulate her own prayer and so she said nothing.

Maria took the lid off and put her hand inside the box without looking. She didn't feel a thing, not even a sensation of wetness, until she took her hand out again and saw the blood running in long thin streams down her fingers. Then she passed out, or something hit her, she didn't know which.

Shazia looked awful. She'd been crying and her eyes were red and puffy. Even as Vi was telling her about the dope, Mumtaz was trying to put her arms around her step-daughter's shoulders, but Shazia kept pulling away. Her shame was great and it was genuine. Mumtaz, on the other hand, was just angry, not at Shazia, but at her so-called friends and their not-so-innocent elderly neighbour.

'The important thing here, above everything else, is to catch Martin Gold in the act,' Vi said. 'He was up to all this exposing himself lark back in the seventies and I think he might well be flashing over on the Olympic site too. He's a slippery sod.'

Mumtaz looked at Shazia. 'Why didn't you tell me?'

'Because I thought you'd go mental.'

'About the drugs? Well, I'm not pleased, Shazia, but I would have understood.'

'Ady was going off me,' Shazia said.

Vi's phone rang and she left the kitchen to go and answer it.

'Vi's sending policemen round to Ady's house and Hilary's,' Shazia said. 'They'll never speak to me again! I'll be called a grass.'

Mumtaz pushed a lock of hair that had come down in front of Shazia's face back up onto her head. 'Sweetheart, there really is no other way,' she said. 'Vi has to do her job. As she said, if we all cooperate no one will be arrested. Well, only Mr Gold. I'm sure Vi's colleagues will explain everything very sympathetically to Ady and Hilary's parents. It'll be OK.'

'No one will ever speak to me again!'

Mumtaz hugged her close. 'Darling, there's no choice. I can't second-guess what the girls will say, or anyone else at your school, for that matter. But we have to do what is right.'

Shazia hung her head. 'I've not been this unhappy since just before Dad died.'

Vi, who had just come back in on the tail end of their

conversation looked confused but then rationalised that she had probably misheard what Shazia had said. 'DS Bracci is at Adele's house now. Apparently Hilary is round there too, but we'll have to catch up with her parents. We won't be able to do anything today. Does Mr Gold know the girls are supposed to be coming this afternoon?'

Shazia nodded.

'Well, if he's watching the house, as I imagine he is, he'll know I'm here, and your mum, and so he'll realise he's out of luck today. We're going to have to plan how we do this carefully,' Vi said. 'Martin Gold is no fool and so I want to make sure that there's no way he can wriggle out of a conviction. With everyone's cooperation, I'd like to catch him red-handed.' She looked at Mumtaz. 'What are your plans today?'

'Well, I'm supposed to be at work. I've an appointment at three that Lee can take, although it is a woman and so . . . Shazia and I are supposed to be going to visit my parents this evening.'

Shazia pulled a face. 'Oh, Amma, do we have to go?'

'Be better if you're home in case we need to talk again today,' Vi said. 'And we are going to watch the house next door tonight. Just to see what Martin does, if anything.'

Although what was happening was shocking and upsetting, Mumtaz couldn't help but be a little jubilant about not having to go and have dinner with the Choudhurys. Aziz Choudhury was a pale, soft and uninteresting man who had absolutely nothing, bar money, going for him. She didn't have any intention of marrying him. She had no intention of marrying anyone.

'I'd better let my parents know we can't come,' Mumtaz said. She got up to go and find a phone. 'They'll be disappointed but . . .' She shrugged. 'I would like to keep my appointment with this lady I'm supposed to see at three, though.'

Shazia looked suddenly frightened again.

Vi said, 'Well, in theory it's my day off so how about you and me, Shazia, go off to Lakeside for a while and do a bit of shopping this afternoon?'

'Oh, Vi,' Mumtaz began, 'that's very nice but we really don't have—'

'My treat.' Vi smiled and put a hand on Shazia's shoulder. 'I've only got great big lumps of sons. No fun to shop with. I could do with a trot around some proper clothes shops. How about it, kiddo?'

According to Roy, Pastor Paul Grint was potless.

'He don't even have his own gaff and he don't own that old pub he calls a church,' he said.

'So where does the dodgy money come into it and how do you know about it?' Lee asked. He'd agreed to let Roy come and stay with him for a week provided he didn't try to contact their mother. It was a massive sacrifice and Lee knew he was going to resent every second of it. But getting the dirty on ex-con Paul Grint had been just too tempting, for Maria Peters' sake, if for no other reason.

'I heard him talking to that black geezer.'

'What black geezer?'

'Some black pastor. I don't know his name. Anyway, he owns the old pub and so Grint pays him money. Or rather he owes him. Like IOUs, you know.'

'So Grint pays rent to this black pastor, but he doesn't really.' Lee already knew this. Tony Bracci had told him that Grint put an IOU in the bank for a Pastor Iekanjika every month.

'Every month he gives the geezer an IOU for fucking thousands,' Roy said.

'OK. So what's your point?'

'What's my point? Because he's got a job coming along,' Roy said. 'That's the point! That's the hooky bit. He knows he's gonna have money and so he keeps this black bloke hanging on with IOUs.'

'So how does he live?' Lee asked.

Roy shrugged. 'I dunno. Out the collection plate? People don't half give generous at them services.'

'Not you.'

Roy shrugged again. 'I'm the deserving poor. They have to try and save my soul, not empty me wallet.'

Lee leaned back in his chair and put his feet up on his desk. 'So what kind of job is Grint planning?'

'I dunno. He was done for fraud years ago. But who

knows? He told the black guy he was still up for the job and it was worth a mint. That's what I heard.'

'How did you come to hear them talking?' Lee asked. 'What were you doing at a church?'

Roy helped himself to another of Lee's fags and then said, 'When you beat me up and told me to fuck off I went where I usually go.'

'The hostel down Poplar.'

Roy smiled. 'Couple of blokes there said you could get good tucker down some new church in Canning Town.'

Lee remembered the group meals the Pentecostal Fires had had when they were over by the Olympic site.

'I went down and it was true. All I had to do was wave me arms in the air and shout "Jesus!" every so often and the job was a good 'un. Most of 'em seemed to be bonkers, but I knew the name Paul Grint and he weren't backwards in coming forwards about his past. I figured that once a crim always a crim and so I hung about to see if I could find out what his game was.'

'And eat his food.'

'I had to be as near to sober as I ever want to get to do it,' Roy said with a scowl. 'I'm fucking sober now. Credit where credit's due.'

'I still don't know how you came to hear them talking, or how you know I'd been involved with someone at the church ...'

'People told me about your Paki lady dashing up the

aisle to go and help Maria Peters,' he said. 'They ain't got no lives, none of 'em. Still banging on about it now.'

'You never let on you were my brother?'

'Why would I jeopardise tea, cake and the odd buffet just to drop you in the shit? Do you know what the food's like at the Seamen's Mission?'

Lee looked up at the ceiling. Clearly Roy knew something. 'How'd you come to find out Grint's up to something?'

'Like I say, he was talking to the black bloke—'

'How come you were there?'

'It was last week. We were all washing up after a meal. You have to do that, it's part of their community fucking doo-dah. Anyway . . . Just outside the kitchen there's what used to be the old pub bogs. I thought Grint was going outside but then I heard him talking to someone. I put me head round the door and saw this big black fella.'

'Was anyone with you?'

'No. Out collecting plates and cups and that in the church.'

'So you were alone at the sink.'

'When they began to talk, I kept quiet,' Roy said. 'That black geezer looked moody and so I thought I'd see what the score was.'

Roy was the sort of person who thought that anyone of Afro-Caribbean origin was automatically dodgy.

'They talked about all these IOUs Grint had outstanding

and how the black bloke wouldn't wait for ever. Then Grint talked about the job and how it was coming along nicely. The black geezer said it had better had as he had need of it. Then Grint said that so did he. To use his exact words, he said, "I need to get out of here." I need to get out of here! How about that?'

Paul Grint, as far as Lee knew, was having a new building done up in order to make a permanent church in Barking. Maybe he meant that?

'So if you thought that Grint was dodgy, why didn't you try and get some cash out of him? Some shut-up money?'

Roy looked offended. Lee knew it was an act. When he needed a drink he'd do just about anything to get money and that included blackmail.

'Oh, don't tell me you found a conscience!'

Roy, angry, leaned forward and said, 'You wanna get me killed? There's faces up the Mission from up west who say Paul Grint was a bit tasty back in the day when he used to sell hooky houses to immigrants!'

'So you thought you'd tell me and get me to give you a bed?'

'Not for ever.'

'Too fucking right it isn't!' Lee said. 'And it doesn't give you any sort of intro back into Mum's life either. As soon as I get some cash you can have a few bob and then piss off on your way.'

Roy shuffled uncomfortably in his seat. 'Nice.'

'Consider yourself lucky I haven't punched your nose off your face.'

Roy was a useless, selfish, vicious waste of time, whose information could be wrong or completely fabricated. But Lee did have an old girlfriend who lived with a bloke who worked for Barking council and he would give her a tug with regard to Grint's new church. It may or may not come to anything, and even if it did it wouldn't earn him any money. Roy had never helped Lee earn a penny in his life. Lee looked at his watch and wondered how Mumtaz was getting on and whether she'd be back in time to see her new client at three.

Everything had gone. The Clarks box, the filth that surrounded it, the blood on her hand. The TV was still on and she was watching some chat thing about people who suffer from sex addiction. It was as if she'd faded out of a nightmare and then faded back into life but it was fuzzy and diffuse. She was also thirsty and her head hurt.

Some time passed, Maria couldn't tell how much, and then the doorbell rang. She didn't want to answer it. What if it was just a parcel? Or Jehovah's Witnesses? Or somebody selling something? But then what if it wasn't? What if it was the solicitor or Betty? She stood up and immediately felt dizzy and sick. She sat down again. She looked at her hand and couldn't believe it was so clean, so dry. Every small piece of evidence of the horror she'd experienced had just gone. The doorbell rang again and Maria put a hand over her mouth to stifle a scream. What was she going to do? She stood up again and then looked back at the sofa she'd been sitting on and saw that it was covered in a thin layer of her own hair. Had she been sitting there for days without moving or was her hair falling out now? She wanted it to stop. But only telling the absolute truth could even begin to make that happen and she was alone. The doorbell rang again.

And then she heard a voice that she recognised. Pastor Grint called through the letter box, 'Maria? Are you all right?' And then suddenly it was OK. Still unsteady on her feet, Maria nevertheless made her way to the front door and let Grint in.

'Oh, my dear,' he said when he saw her, 'what on earth is the matter?'

And then the dam burst and she cried. When she finished crying and she could speak again she said, 'Pastor, there was a box of blood. I put my hand into it!'

Paul Grint looked around the room and then began to speak, but Maria cut him off. 'I know it's not here any more, but it was.'

'Was it?' Paul Grint moved closer to her. 'I'm not disbelieving you, Maria, but did it ... did it mean anything ...'

She managed to say the word 'Yes' just once before she

started crying again. Try as he might, Pastor Grint could not get Maria to say what that meaning was.

Baharat knew that look. 'There's no point in being angry,' he said to Sumita who now stood, stock-still in front of her cooker, raging. 'The child is sick, Mumtaz can't just leave her.'

'That girl should go back to her own family!' Sumita said. 'Why should our daughter have to do everything for her? And after what her father did!' She shook her head. 'Mr Choudhury's son won't wait for ever. And what will people think?'

Mumtaz had told her parents that she couldn't come to dinner because Shazia was ill. What she was ill with, wasn't clear, but Baharat firmly believed that his daughter was making excuses. She'd met Aziz Choudhury once and it had been quite obvious that she hadn't taken to him – who would? But he had money and the Choudhurys were a respected family. Allah alone knew what Hanif Choudhury, the hajji, would make of it all! But neither he nor Aziz were now coming to dinner. They'd have to share the food with the boys, their wives and the grandchildren. Baharat just managed to suppress a smile at the thought.

'Mumtaz is no longer young. Soon no one will want her and then what will she do?' Sumita had been planning and then working on the meal for days. She was deeply disappointed.

'She will carry on working,' Baharat said. 'She has a house to pay for. What else can she do?'

'She can take an offer of marriage from a decent family!'

Baharat shrugged. 'Mumtaz was always an independent girl. She's a clever girl. Neither of the boys could have gone to university if we'd held guns to their heads. But Mumtaz—'

'No husband, no children, her life is a disaster! A waste.'

Baharat was a very even-tempered man. But this he would not take. Not about his Mumtaz. 'Sumita, my wife, if our daughter's life is a disaster it is partly because of us,' he said.

She made a noise in her throat like a squeak and then she moved forward, her hand raised as if she wanted to hit him.

But Baharat retained his calm gravitas, as well as his anger. 'We married her to that man because he was rich,' he said.

'Yes, but he wasn't rich, was he, he was—'

'He was rich, so we thought, he was good-looking and he came to me with all sorts of nonsense about how he was such a good Muslim, such a nice, nice man for my daughter.' Just the thought of it made Baharat suddenly shout with fury. 'But he lied! The bugger lusted for our girl only, he treated her badly, he was a gangster and a criminal and if he was still alive now and I knew what I know, I would kill him with my own hands!'

'Baharat—'

'How do we know that Mr Choudhury's son will not do the same, eh? A man of nearly fifty, never married . . .'

'He has been waiting for the right girl,' Sumita said. 'Everyone says.'

'Everyone?' He looked at her, remaining harsh in spite of the tears in her eyes. 'Gossiping women? Mr Choudhury has only lived here for a year. What does Mrs Khan or Mrs Dar or any of these women you speak to know about it? Eh?'

Silent for a moment, Sumita was simply reordering her argument and Baharat knew it.

'Well, you were just as keen for Mumtaz to meet with Mr Choudhury's son at the start.' she said.

And he knew that was true. He also knew that quite early on in the process he had changed his mind, although why, exactly, he didn't know, but suddenly it had all seemed like a very bad idea. Baharat got up from the kitchen table, picked up his mobile phone and walked towards the living room. 'I am going to watch the news on the television,' he said. 'There are protests, apparently, about the man who was killed by the police in Tottenham. There have been some riots. Some families have such terrible tragedies to bear.'

Sumita wanted to say that their own family was one of them, but she didn't. She just looked at all the pans on the cooker and shook her head in frustration. So much chicken! So much lamb!

XXVII

Maria prayed. Betty was with her and they had the television on with the sound off, but the images that played out on the screen were horrific. Suddenly, London had just erupted. Only two days before, a man had been shot by police in Tottenham and now people were rioting all over the city, from Barnet to Croydon, from Ealing to Barking.

Pastor Grint, having seen Maria through her tears, had gone to the church to meet with other members of the congregation to see if there was anything they could do. Buildings were burning, shops were being looted and kids who looked not much more than ten years old were hurling bricks at the police. It was a world of anarchy, of lack of respect, of frustrated opportunism. It was a world that Maria and her smart, comedy mouth had helped to fuel – so she believed.

Her tears had made her feel no better. Pastor Grint had just sat by her side. He hadn't punished her. But then why would he? 'What,' he'd quite logically asked her, 'am I supposed to be punishing you for?' She had to reveal whatever this sin was that appeared to be ruining her life and he didn't know what that was unless she told him – and she wouldn't speak. Besides, only God should punish, not man. She had tried to take Jesus into her heart, she had tried to repent and deny the devil but it wasn't enough. As she knelt on the floor in front of her TV she felt sick. She looked at the pictures on the screen and she wondered why all these kids who were rioting thought that smashing up shops was such a good idea.

She looked away from the TV and into the corner and there was the Clarks box again. Large as life, but without a speck of blood in sight. She looked at Betty and wanted to ask her whether she saw it or not, knowing that she didn't want to know the answer. The kids breaking in to PC World and Phones 4u didn't have a clue either. No one did. Not even Pastor Grint. She was alone. But then it had always been that way – really. It had always been that way and now it had to end.

Eventually she managed to say to Betty, 'You know I want to be with Len.' And Betty had looked at her and she'd smiled.

'Oh, my goodness, what a nice surprise!' Mumtaz felt her face flush. It was the shock. Out of the blue, Mark Solomons had phoned her.

'I got your number from your dad ages ago, when I heard that your husband had died, but then I didn't call. I am such a moron!' she heard Mark say.

'You're busy.'

'I'm a moron,' he corrected. 'God, Mumtaz, I was so horrified to hear about your husband. Fuck, man, to just be killed like that! And you were there, I—'

'So, Mark, your shows are amazing!' Mumtaz said. She didn't want to go over Ahmed again. If it were ever humanly possible she never wanted to even think about it. 'All that stuff we learned at uni really sank in, didn't it.'

There was a pause. He couldn't understand why she didn't want to talk about her husband. But then, almost audibly, she sensed him reasoning it out, coming to a conclusion that had to be wrong but which worked for Mark and his chain of logic.

'Yes, the show,' he said. 'Psycho-magical-behaviourism.'

She laughed.

'David Blaine without the sense of humour bypass,' he said. 'I'm lucky.'

'You're clever.'

'Yeah, but *you* know how I do it, don't you.'

'Oh, not always. Not now.'

'It's been a long time.'

'Yes.'

Neither of them spoke. There had been a kiss, just the

once, long ago. It had sat between them ever since, not knowing what to do. It had unnerved them both.

'So . . .' She gesticulated, trying to find the right words. 'Why the call?'

'Why now? I'm at Mum's,' he said.

Mark's mum lived at Gants Hill, just a couple of miles down the road. Mumtaz felt her blood pump at his closeness.

'I live in Cornwall now,' he said. 'Mousehole. It's fantastic. Good for a so-called magician too. Lots of legends and all the King Arthur thing and of course loads of crazy hippies and pagans running around wearing bits of trees and stuff. But Friday I'm off to Germany, for a TV thing, and I'm catching a flight from City Airport. So I thought I'd spend a few days with Mum.'

'That's nice.'

'Tazzie, if you've got any time, I'd love to see you,' he said.

No one had called her 'Tazzie' for years. Only Mark and her old uni friends had ever used that name. She didn't see any of them any more.

'Oh, Mark, I have a job . . .' She also had Shazia and she covered her head and there were . . . problems too. What would he make of her now?

'Oh.' He sounded disappointed. Mumtaz was disappointed too.

'And anyway it might not be safe,' she continued. She

was disappointed but she was also afraid. 'These riots . . .'

'Yes! Shocking! Looting and everything. But then if you build up people's material expectations and then tell them they have to face redundancy . . .'

'You think the riots are about the recession? What about the man who was shot by the police?'

'Poor bloke, but it's gone way beyond him,' Mark said. 'Fuck knows where it's going. Tazzie, I could come over and see you. I wouldn't expect you to come here. Forest Gate, isn't it?'

It was all too much! Her three o'clock appointment had been a lady who needed evidence against her violent, straying husband, yesterday if possible; then there was all the drug chaos with Shazia, the weird neighbour and then there was also . . .

'Tazzie?'

Lee had told her what his brother had said about the Chapel of the Holy Pentecostal Fire. He'd said that Roy could very easily be lying. He didn't trust him in the slightest. But what he'd told Lee had very much played into Mumtaz's fears about the church. The psychology on show had gone beyond the 'ordinary' for a religious service. Why? Mark had had a particular interest in cults and what was known as the 'group mind' at university. Should she maybe take him into her confidence, or was she just finding an excuse to see him again?

'OK.' She thought she heard a sigh of relief. 'But I work

in Upton Park – Green Street. Could you meet me there?'

'I could.'

'I should finish at five tomorrow,' Mumtaz said. 'I could meet you at the tube station. We could ... Look, I've got a stepdaughter, my late husband's child. I have to get back for her but I can spare an hour.' He didn't answer. Had her apparent coolness put him off? 'There's a pie and mash shop we could go to ...'

The pause continued for a while and then he said, 'Sure. Yes, that'd be great. Yeah, brilliant.'

'So I'll see you then?'

'Upton Park at five? Looking forward to it.'

They both said goodbye and then Mumtaz put the phone down. Mark had sounded disappointed at being given so little time with her, but she couldn't help that. Between work, Shazia and the police operation to trap Martin Gold there was a lot to do. Apparently neither of Shazia's friends were going to speak to her again once it was all over. But then youngsters got angry very quickly and then changed their minds even more rapidly. Not that that observation had stopped Shazia bursting into tears and going to her room with no food inside her. In her mind her peer group had just gone at a stroke. The fact that neither she nor any of the other girls was going to be arrested seemed to make no difference. If Shazia did but know it, the whole situation could have been so much worse.

Mumtaz went into her kitchen and made a cup of tea,

picturing Mark's face in her mind. Not conventionally handsome – he was far too thin and had hair that was way too mad for that – the thought of seeing him again nevertheless made her shiver with anticipation.

Vi reached down and picked the young man up off the pavement. She tried to ignore the fact that he looked like a total twat but it was difficult. With his 'ironic' old school blazer, several sizes too small, plus his expensive old-man brogues and his waxed handlebar moustache he was the epitome of a local tribe some called 'hipsters'. Rare in Newham, these privileged middle-class youngsters were common in Hackney, especially around Mare Street, parts of which were now on fire.

'Come on, mate,' Vi said as she pulled him to his feet, 'up you get.'

'Oh,' he said, clearly shocked, 'you're a woman.'

Vi had been at Lakeside with Shazia for just under an hour when she got the call to say that all leave was cancelled. She'd had to dump Shazia home, get to the station and it was then that she was bundled into a van to come over to Hackney. Now on Mare Street in full riot gear, she'd already had a chair leg chucked at her head and these bloody posh kids were just getting in the way.

'A boy took my bike,' the young man said. 'What are you going to do about it?'

A rubbish bin burned brightly on the opposite side of

the road. It was surrounded by girls who all wore over-sized earrings and swore, loudly.

Vi looked at the young man and sighed. 'Description?'

'He was wearing a hood.'

'Oh really?' Vi put her hands, one of which held a riot shield, on her hips and said, 'Go home. Sir.'

'Yes, but my bike . . .'

Something, possibly a car, exploded down near the library. A great cheer went up. 'Look, just fuck off, will you?' Vi said to the young man and then she headed off in the direction of the explosion. As she ran, she was passed by what looked like a whole family making off with a massive flat-screen television. A man had been shot, cities were in flames and all people cared about was the size of screen they watched *EastEnders* on. Vi wanted to take it off them but there was a fire in the middle of the road and so she had to just let them get on with it.

Two coppers with northern accents ran alongside her and one said to the other one, 'I was thinking of trans-ferring down south. Don't think I'll bother.'

A bottle containing what smelt like piss hit the ground in front of them and sprayed all over Vi's boots.

She called herself 'Sita'. It was a Hindu name which had the double advantage of both hiding her true identity and being a bit of a two fingers up to who she really was. A Muslim girl from Ilford, her real name was Saida and, as she always told the other girls she worked with, 'I ran away from an arranged marriage to a big fat slob so I could dance for other big fat slobs instead.' Sita was a lap dancer and she'd just finished her shift at the Pussy Palace down on Dace Road, on the edge of the Olympic site.

Sita lit a cigarette as she made her way down towards the canal. She lived over on Abbey Lane, Stratford and so crossing the canal and then heading up the Greenway was her quickest route home. It was late, but she wasn't tired; punters had been thin on the ground, partly because it was early in the week and partly because large parts of London were experiencing riots. Even the eastern European construction workers from the site had stayed away. If only to get a break from the grim hostels and bedsits they all lived in, they usually turned up whatever the day of the week. But people were scared. As she walked across the bridge over the canal, Sita strained her ears to try and catch any noises of violence, but there was only silence.

The ramp up to the Greenway on the other side of the canal was obscured by bushes and at night she didn't much like it. But Sita also prided herself on her courage and so she made a point, even in the dark, of not rushing up it. As soon as she got to the top she'd be able to see the new stadium which would have a load of workers clustered round it, and so her risk was a calculated one. Sita sauntered. She could do little else in what she liked to call her 'tranny shoes'. Six-inch stilettos in red faux snakeskin, her mate Tammy said they had a very 'seventies cross-dresser vibe' which had made Sita laugh. That said, they were bastards to walk in. As she began her ascent of the slope she made a mental note not to forget her ballet pumps to walk home in next time. And then suddenly, from the left, almost in her face, was a man's penis.

'Oh, what the—' Like everyone in the area she'd heard about the Olympic Flasher. Oh God, how on earth could she be a bloody victim of him! Unafraid, she pushed the small, pale member out of her way with her handbag. 'For fuck's sake . . .'

She had expected him to run away immediately. The Olympic flasher had not, after all, actually done anything to any of his victims to date. But he didn't move and for a moment Sita felt her heart begin to speed up. What if she was going to be the exception? What if she was going to be raped? Well, if that was going to happen, she was going to get a bloody good look at him first. Sita lifted her head and stared him straight in the face. She just saw him before he ran. And when she did see him, she realised why he'd paused after she'd slapped his knob away. He'd seen her face too.

Sita took her tranny shoes off and began to run after him. 'Oi you,' she yelled as she got to the top of the ramp. 'I bloody know you! Stop!'

XXVIII

Mumtaz spent the morning sitting in Lee's car outside the house of a woman known only as Pat who may or may not be entertaining a man called Hardev Singh. His wife, a very capable, organised and yet deeply hurt Sikh lady had been Mumtaz's three o'clock the previous day. Pat's house, which was on Browning Road, East Ham had a front garden full of old mattresses and some dead pot plants by the street door.

Mumtaz looked at her phone for what felt like the hundredth time and then put it back down beside her on the passenger seat again. Like all the Met Police officers, Vi Collins was now on riot duty for the foreseeable future. Even the officer who had been watching the house next door had left halfway through the evening to go off some-where. Policemen and -women were coming to London from all over the country, trying to stop what seemed to be unstoppable. None of this helped Shazia, alone in the house and miserable. Mumtaz had left her that morning, apparently asleep, but she knew that Shazia had spent most of the night ranging around the house crying. How could that dreadful old man, Mr Gold, make her do such a thing?

In return for telling no one about their smoking habits, Mr Gold had blackmailed Shazia into keeping the curtains and windows open in the living room while they all got stoned. Out in the garden, hidden by the trees, he'd happily masturbated. It was disgusting and it meant that not only had Shazia been forced to smoke dope by her friends, she'd also been suckered into putting them and herself inside some sick old man's fantasy. Shazia, if at a distance, had been abused and that was a very difficult thing for Mumtaz to think about. Albeit through her busyness, Mumtaz had let Shazia down.

Lack of movement around Pat's house made her mind wander. Mr Gold was one of Maria Peters' tenants and so when it all came out, that would mean more trouble for her. Mumtaz's phone began to vibrate and she saw that it was Lee who said, 'My old mate's boyfriend at Barking Council says there's no building conversion or planning permission or anything in the name of either Paul Grint or the Chapel of the Holy Pentecostal Fire,' he said. 'There's nothing coming up for any Christian place of worship.'

'So the new church, if nothing else, is a lie?'

'Seems like it,' Lee said.

'So where do we go from here?' she asked. She thought about Maria and how sick she'd looked whenever she'd seen her recently and she wondered what they, this faux church, were doing to her.

'With all the coppers on riot duty, nowhere, right at the moment,' Lee said. 'But I will give Vi the nod when I can. I'll see you later.'

Mumtaz put her phone back on the passenger seat and went back to half reading the newspaper she'd bought that morning. But it was full of pictures of people in hoods waving Adidas trainers about like trophies which made her feel sick. Was it any wonder that people were attracted to religion, even if it was extreme and manipulative, if this was the alternative?

Mark had been fascinated by religion and what some psychologists called 'group mind' experiences. The particular example Mumtaz always remembered was that of Fatima in Portugal in 1917. Three children claimed to have had visions of the Virgin Mary which culminated in seventy thousand people 'seeing' a miracle. At the behest of the Virgin, the sun had 'danced' in the sky, pinwheeling across the heavens and flashing with every colour on the spectrum. Seventy thousand people. That was some religious fervour.

When she'd run to Maria in that church when she collapsed, things had been very fervent. It had been difficult, Mumtaz recalled, to keep at a distance from it. Something Mark used to say when they played with hypnosis, explored its properties and its limits was, 'Don't join'. By this he had meant that to adopt the rhythms of the hypnotic state, particularly in a group, to enjoy and to participate was a recipe for losing yourself inside the suggestions that lived in the sounds and behind the sentiments of what was being said. One had to be at what Mark always called a 'mental step' away and even as a Muslim in a place that was not of her own faith, that had not been easy for Mumtaz. In the past she had always been strong when it came to hypnosis and suggestion. Mark had wondered, at one time, whether in fact she was susceptible at all. But in the end, she had been. To him.

Mr Allitt had come and he'd gone but he hadn't been happy. Maria hadn't been dressed, she'd smelt of booze and her eyes had been puffy and red.

'Is there anyone I can call for you, Mrs Blatt?' he'd asked her. 'I know we both have the church, which is a comfort, but ... A relative perhaps?'

Years ago she would have tried to get away with not handing his lovely Mont Blanc pen back to him, but she was a different person now. She gave him back the pen and the papers, signed. She'd said, 'I'm fine.'

But she could see on his face that he doubted her. She wondered why, but once he'd gone she forgot all about him and just took comfort in how much better she suddenly felt. Doing things right was just common sense as much as anything else. If you did things right then everything in your life was orderly and under-standable.

It was a warmish day and so Maria went to sleep on the sofa with the French windows open. When she woke up Betty had arrived and let herself in through the side gate into the garden, then through the French doors. She was going to stay with her until Pastor Grint arrived. Maria had asked him to come because finally she was ready to remove the obstacle that still existed between her and eternal salvation.

Martin Gold was feeling confused. Young Shazia's friends hadn't come round the previous afternoon and he was beginning to wonder what was up. Since the school holi-days had started back in July, they'd been round most weekdays, smoking.

He blamed DI Violet Collins. Rough old tart! Somehow she'd wheedled her way in with Shazia's mother and she'd even taken the girl out in her car when Mrs Hakim had gone somewhere or other the previous afternoon. Odd comings and goings in that house made Martin wonder if they were about him and so, just after he had lunch – a cheese sandwich – he climbed through the hole he'd made in the Hakims' hedge and confronted the girl, who he knew was alone in the garden. When she saw him she took a step backwards.

'Where are your mates, Shazia?' he asked. 'I was expecting you all yesterday.'

Her thin shoulders trembled, which he liked. 'Mum's friend came round and then Mum came home from work early,' she said.

'Your mum been friends with DI Collins for very long?' he asked.

'A while. Why?'

He shrugged. Then he said, 'Girls coming round today, are they?'

'No.' She had her hands on her shoulders now, hugging herself.

Martin was furious and his eyes blazed with it. 'Why not?'

She didn't say anything. He could almost hear the cogs of her brain ticking over, trying to find something to say. Eventually she said, 'We haven't got any weed. We've run out.'

He moved towards her. 'Bad planning. But don't they just want to come round for a chat? A muck about?'

'No.'

'Have you asked them?'

'Yeah . . . No.'

'Well, don't you think that, given what I know about you, that might be a good thing to do?'

Oh, he'd got used to a high level of eye candy since the holidays began! Martin needed his fix.

Shazia walked backwards towards her house. 'Hilary's gone out with her mum and Adele's . . . She's gone to, er, to . . .'

'I know you're lying, Shazia, and I'll be honest, it's making me cross.' He frowned. 'You know, if you're not nice to me, I won't be nice to you. If your mother knew—'

'Oh, please don't tell my mother, please!' It had come out automatically but then that was a good thing. Vi wanted to actually catch Mr Gold in the act but she was on riot duty together with every other officer in London. In the meantime Shazia had to behave normally until the old man could be caught.

'Well, you'd better get your friends . . .'

'But they're not coming over today. I wasn't lying! It's just me today.' And then Mr Gold smiled and suddenly Shazia felt very alone indeed.

Martin Gold was suspicious but he was so used to having 'fun' that he really felt he couldn't possibly do without it. He thought about it for a moment and then he said, 'Well then, I suppose I'll just have to make do with you, won't I?'

'What do you want me to . . . Oh . . .' Her eyes filled with tears and Martin began to feel himself become very aroused indeed.

He smiled. 'Oh, don't worry, my little thing,' he said. 'You won't have to do anything except watch – I promise.'

* * *

369

Roy flung Lee's front door open and called after the man who was running hell for leather down the garden path. 'Oi!'

But Roy wasn't wearing anything on his feet and so there was a limit to how far he could pursue the bloke. When he got to the garden gate he looked once down the street, but there was nobody about. Roy stared down at the fat envelope in his hands and turned it over twice. It was addressed to Lee and he had absolutely no right to open it, but Roy could smell money through the envelope. He went back inside the flat and sat down in the living room with the envelope still in his hands. The mynah bird was asleep, as it so often seemed to be. But Roy looked at it anyway, just to make sure that it was really out for the count. People said that they were very bright, mynah birds, that they could interpret human actions and know what they were doing. Roy slid a finger underneath the envelope's seal. To him it sounded really loud but it didn't wake the creature.

Lee had said that he could stay for a week, but then what? It was all very well for his brother to say he couldn't go back to their mother's place, but where else was there? He couldn't go back to the hostel and if he turned up at the happy-clappy church they'd probably give him a good hiding. Legging it with the collection hadn't been his best move, but he'd been so fucking bored. Playing at Jesus just to get a bit of food and tea did not address his needs as a man who liked a drink. And anyway, if Paul Grint did get to know he'd overheard him talking to the black geezer, Roy wasn't sure that was going to be a safe situation for him. He could of course have hung about and tried to blackmail the pastor, but people who knew Paul Grint of old all talked about how tasty he'd been in terms of violence in the past and Roy couldn't take that. He couldn't take on Lee these days. He watched the ten tenpound notes slip out of the envelope and into his lap. There was a note with them which said, *What I owe you. Bob.*

Roy looked at the money and he felt his mouth begin to go dry. A nice pint of Kronenbourg and a couple of vodka chasers would soon fix that. Then a quick hop over to Paddy Power and a little flutter and if there was an R in the month and the moon was blue he could make back what he'd spent out of this ton and more. He'd be back before four with the money and Lee would never be any the wiser. Roy hadn't had a proper drink for weeks. He ran into the spare bedroom and got dressed without washing. As he made his way to the front door, whistling as he went, the mynah bird woke up, looked at him and squawked, 'Own goal! Own goal!'

Mark had a tan, just like he did on the TV. It wasn't makeup and it suited him. Mumtaz watched as he amazed three young Sikh lads with a trick that had him apparently taking bundles of playing cards out of their clothes. In spite of the conversation she'd just had with Shazia, Mumtaz smiled. The girl had been in bed when Mark had phoned and so she hadn't seen her before she'd left the house to go to work. Then she'd forgotten all about it until Shazia had called to ask her where she was.

'I have to meet someone,' she'd told her. 'It's business,' she'd half lied.

'Oh.' It had been more than just disappointment.

'Shazia? OK?'

'Yeah. Yeah, I'm fine.' She too had lied, Mumtaz thought. 'I'll be home as soon as I can.'

''k.'

Shazia had ended the call. Trying not to think about what that catch of anxiety in her voice might mean, Mumtaz crossed the road and walked towards Upton Park Station and the little group of boys that surrounded Mark. Intent upon his various sleights of hand, he didn't notice her until one of the boys said to her excitedly, 'It's Mark Solomons, man! Off the TV!'

Mark had looked at the boy and then at Mumtaz and he'd beamed. 'Ah,' he said, 'my dinner date!' He reached forward to take her hand while putting his deck of cards back in his jacket pocket. The boys looked a little shocked to see a white man take the hand of a covered Muslim woman but none of them said anything. As Mark walked through the little crowd to get to Mumtaz she saw him take another pack of cards out of one of the boys' pockets. When they'd gone, she said, 'I see your thief skills are still sharp.'

'As are your eyes.' He smiled. He knew better than to kiss her even on the cheek in a public place, even though he wanted to. The pie and mash shop was just opposite the station. Mark gestured towards it with one long, thin hand. 'Shall we?' he asked.

It wasn't her kind of food at all but Mumtaz knew what Mark liked and, for the moment, it was all about him. 'Let's,' she said.

Like two well brought up children, they crossed Green Street at the traffic lights. Mumtaz noticed that the pie and mash shop was quite empty save for the woman who always served in there. She looked out of the window into the street with an expression of almost terminal-looking misery on her face.

'What are you doing here?' Lee tried to walk past the girl and get into the flat without having her follow him, but Foxy was young and quick and she was in before he could stop her.

'I've always had a thing about older men,' Foxy said.

Lee looked into the living room and tried to see if Roy was about, but seemed not. He didn't want to be in the flat alone with her.

'But I haven't got anything!' Lee said. If his own daughter

and her mates, only a few years younger than Foxy, were anything to go by, if he didn't have money she would soon lose interest. Not that his impecunity had stopped her before.

She put a hand on his crotch which he instantly whipped away.

'I'm skint, darling,' he said, 'boracic, potless, without funds.'

She laughed. 'You give good orgasms.'

You give good orgasms! What a mad, women's magazine thing that was to say! Lee could feel the age gap opening up between them like the Grand Canyon. He'd have to be rude.

'I don't want to have sex with you again,' he said.

But she just laughed. 'Yes, you do.'

'I don't!' If his dad's old mates up at the Boleyn could've heard him they would've been scandalised. Lee Arnold turning down a bit of hot totty like Foxy? But he didn't want her. They'd had sex, it had been a laugh but now it was over.

She walked towards him, making him feel as if he was being stalked.

'You should get home,' he said. 'There could be riots again tonight.'

She put on a baby voice. 'But I could stay here.' She jumped on the sofa and laughed.

'Oh, no you can't!' Suddenly angry, he reached down

and pulled her up by one of her arms. Chronus, who up until that time had been silent, opened one eye and mumbled, 'Own goal.'

Foxy looked at the bird and then at Lee. 'What's he say?'

Years of living with the bird had taught Lee that Chronus only ever said *Own goal* in one circumstance, and that was when he didn't like someone. Lee pulled Foxy across the room towards the front door. 'I didn't invite you here. You have to go,' he said.

'Why? I can do everything that porn stars do!' she said. Her massively high wedge-heel shoes made it difficult for her to move very quickly and so Lee just picked her up and carried her. 'Ooh! Ow!'

He opened the front door and put her outside. 'I know you can do all those things and very well too,' he said. 'But, darling, let's face it, that's all you can do, isn't it?'

Foxy looked genuinely shocked. 'What else is there?' she said.

'If you have to ask the question, darling . . .' Lee shut the door literally in her face. Then he muttered underneath his breath, 'The bird didn't like you.' But when she pretended to cry he didn't know who to feel more sorry for, her or himself. Then her tears turned to anger and she stood outside calling him a cunt for a while and then she left. Clingy people. Who needed them?

Lee checked the flat just to make sure that Roy was actually out and then sat down on the sofa next to

Chronus's perch. Gently he rubbed the bird's head and said, 'She's gone now, mate. All back to normal again.'

But then he remembered that the first time Foxy had been to the flat, Chronus hadn't said *Own goal* at all. He looked at him frowning. 'You change your mind about her, did you? Know something about her that I don't?'

The bird didn't speak.

Then suddenly, from nowhere, Lee said, 'I wonder what you'd make of Mumtaz Hakim.'

He actually felt his face heat up and so, even though it was only himself and Chronus in the room, he looked away quickly and pretended that he was fixated on the radio in the corner of the room.

XXIX

Mark had one plate of jellied eels and then he had another one, all smothered in vinegar. His love of eels had been one of the things that Mumtaz had never been able to understand about him. They were cold and slimy and they looked as if they possessed the consistency of rubber. Drinking tea and limiting her own food intake to bread and butter (she'd eat with Shazia later), Mumtaz had already told Mark about some unnamed church where hypnotic ceremonies took place. So far, so straightforward.

'What I don't understand,' she said, 'is how one particular congregant, a woman, comes to be attracted to such an organisation.'

'Why not?' Mark shrugged. 'You're religious yourself.'

'I worry she's being manipulated by them,' Mumtaz said. 'She's got a lot of money. And she has strange experiences – objects appear as if by sorcery in her home. She claims to see things, people.'

Mark's smile dropped. 'Why are we talking about your

work? I thought we were going to catch up for an hour. Mark and Mumtaz, remember?'

She looked down, suddenly ashamed of what she now saw was her own little bit of manipulation. 'I'm sorry.'

He smiled again. 'So tell me about your stepdaughter.'

Now Mumtaz smiled. They spoke about Shazia – but not about Ahmed – about Mumtaz's parents, mutual friends, about all the places he travelled to with his show. His favourite city was Prague. It was somewhere he knew she'd like too.

'The Czechs seem to almost instinctively love magic,' he said. 'It's going on all over the city.'

'I thought we weren't going to talk about work,' she said.

He looked out into the street, at people rushing home from the daily grind. People who had someone to rush home for. He didn't. He sighed.

'So tell me about this woman,' he said. 'This rich woman involved with this . . . cult?'

Although only in profile, she could see that his face was sad. He'd wanted her to rush to him when they'd met outside the station, her hair streaming out behind her like a black sheet. Like it used to be. But that was impossible.

'They didn't seek her out,' Mumtaz said. 'She picked up a booklet about the church and then went along of her own accord. She was recently bereaved, and I suppose looking for some answers. At the church she met an old schoolfriend. They hadn't seen each other for decades.'

'So that's when all the weird shit started happening to her?'

'Yes.'

Why had she launched in about Maria so quickly? They'd just sat down and she'd started immediately. Now she was on again, splurging it all out at him. He probably felt used and hurt and she didn't blame him, but in the instant that she'd seen him fooling around with those boys outside Upton Park Station she'd realised that she no longer loved him. It hadn't hit her either suddenly or hard because she'd really known it inside for some considerable time. But it was still a loss.

'The preacher, or whatever he is, at this church was convicted of fraud years ago,' she said.

'To commit fraud you have to lie.' He looked at her. 'And you know what I always say about that, don't you, Mumtaz?'

Mark's magic was constructed from a range of elements that included hypnosis, suggestion, sleight of hand, misdirection, charm, criminal intent and lying. In his opinion the magical act, which was truly a most mysterious product of all the other elements, popped out like some sort of miraculous child provided the trick, illusion or effect was properly executed.

'This man clearly understands, if only in a rudimentary way, the power of hypnotic suggestion . . .'

379

'Oh, I don't think it's rudimentary, Mark,' she said. 'I saw him put this woman under.' She described the technique she'd seen Grint use in detail. 'And there are pictures all over the walls, underlining his message.'

'And what is his message?'

'It's about Jesus Christ. It's also about giving.'

'Christianity, as far as I can tell, is about giving, isn't it? What else?'

She thought.

'It sounds to me as if this woman is suffering from some sort of delusory state. That's the most obvious answer,' Mark said. 'So she's involved with a church that's run by a man who's a bit dodgy, who pulls the old "hallelujah, brothers", getting everyone hyped up and a few hypnotic tricks? That's religion. So she . . .'

Mumtaz lowered her head and her voice and she said, 'But Mark, I saw him put her under. He's a pro and she looks ill. She's with them all the time now and she looks really sick. She didn't look ill before, what are they doing to her?' She didn't care what Lee's brother had said about some sort of 'job' Grint was planning – as long as it didn't involve Maria. That feeling she got from her of someone so locked up inside she was like her own prisoner was horribly familiar.

'If she's rich they could be trying to get money out of her,' Mark said. 'It wouldn't be the first time some religious nuts have tried to get money out of a rich person. History's littered with instances of it. In fact—'

'But she went to them!' She had to cut him off before he really started on a protracted rant about religion. Mark actively hated it; he called it a 'cancer'.

'And they took advantage of her. What do people expect from organisations of mass delusion, like the church?' He drank from the huge mug of tea the woman who served in the pie shop had made him and then turned to wink at her. 'Lovely cuppa!'

She was all of sixty-five, but she blushed. It wasn't every day she had a famous man in her gaff. It wasn't often she had anyone.

'So she went to them and they took advantage of her. Caveat emptor,' Mark continued.

'Her husband had died ...'

'You said she was vulnerable. Classic.' He drank some more tea. 'You should know about that.'

She ignored his last comment. 'As I said before, it turned out she knew one of the congregants.'

'Even better.'

'But Mark, she hadn't seen her for years. The way this woman tells it, she just one day decided to seek out God.'

'From a leaflet or a booklet or something?'

'Yes.'

'Have you seen it?'

'I've seen a leaflet but not any sort of booklet.'

'And so this other woman was sort of her gateway into this church? In terms of introducing her to people.'

'Yes.'

'And you think there's something concerning about that? You, who belong to a faith that also evangelises?'

'I do.'

In spite of all the trouble with Shazia, her work, her lack of money as well as the spectre of Mr Choudhury's son, an idea had been growing in Mumtaz's head about Maria Peters that she had told to no one in its entirety. It was the sort of idea she could only really put to Mark.

'I wonder if her entry into the church was engineered,' she said. Then she looked away as if she was ashamed. 'I wonder if her continued involvement is being engineered too.'

She heard Mark breathe in sharply. 'It's possible, but it would take a bit of doing outside of a controlled environment.'

'I know.' She looked back at him.

'Tazzie, *Wedding List* was a TV programme. It was entertainment and it took one hell of a lot of planning.'

Back in 2008, Mark had created a one-off TV show called *Wedding List* where he had successfully filled a warehouse with goods as listed on a secret wedding list belonging to a couple who were due to marry the following year. It had been a sensation and it had catapulted Mark into the foremost rank of stage and TV magicians alongside the likes of Derren Brown.

Mark lowered his voice. 'I had to get extensive intel on those people and the work that went into organising the suggestions leading up to the writing and sealing of the list were time-consuming and costly.'

'And it's something people write books about now.'

'My methods? No.'

'About suggestion, about influence, about advertising,' she said.

'Yeah, but not everyone can do what I do, or make what advertisers produce,' he said. 'And anyway, why this woman? Is she *that* rich?'

'She's rich but I don't really know how rich.' She whispered. 'The church is not all that it seems, that is known. There's evidence of strange financial dealings, of lies told to worshippers, and they do need money. They owe money.'

'So you think that they found themselves a pliable cash cow.'

'I fear it.'

He nodded his head and for the first time, Mark actually looked grave.

'She has no children, no husband,' Mumtaz said. 'There is no one to look out for her.'

'Except you.'

She smiled. 'I have a boss, a good man, Lee ...'

'Except you and Lee.' Then he sighed. 'That's nice.' He wasn't being facetious. 'But Tazzie, you know that whatever

we may have learned about cults and hypnosis and psychological programming at uni, out in the field it's always
more complicated. People who appear on my shows want
to comply. You're talking about a character or group of
characters who you think want to part this woman from
her money. And that's not always easy.'

'Why?'

'Why? Because most people don't want to give their
money away to anyone,' he said. 'Not you, not me, not
the dogs' home, not some cowboy builder, not even poor
children in Africa. They might give a bit, but not much
and especially not in this kind of financial climate. Look
at these riots. People want to grab what they can, not give
it away!'

'Yes, but she's rich.'

'Yes, and they're the worst!' he said. 'People are duped
every day, Tazzie, but in the scheme of things it is rare.
If, as you think, these people are after this woman's money,
I believe they have to have a much bigger lever than just
Christian charity.'

Mumtaz frowned. 'What kind of lever?'

'The kind where they've got something on her,' he said.
'The kind that makes pulling her into their web and then
milking her worth their while.'

Mumtaz was about to say *But she's such a nice lady* but
then she stopped. There was that thing inside Maria that
seemed to agitate and unsettle. A thing unresolved, a thing

that maybe both fuelled and jeopardised her once-famous comedy act. Was it something she was? Something she'd done? Something she hadn't done?

'But she likes these people. How can you like people who are effectively blackmailing you?'

'Maybe she doesn't know she's being blackmailed,' Mark said. 'Or rather, maybe she doesn't know yet.'

'His family lived next door to my family for years,' Sita said. Leaning on the toughened glass that protected the police station's front desk and its officers, she wanted to speak to someone in charge. 'Can't I speak to a detective or someone?'

The officer was only young and so Sita actually felt a bit sorry for him. He probably wanted to hit the streets and have a go at the rioters. 'We're a bit short-handed,' he said. 'There's some trouble ...'

'Kids looting the Carphone Warehouse, yes I know,' Sita said. 'But I have to get to work, you know?'

She knew she should have reported the incident on the Olympic site as soon as it had happened. But she'd been knackered. Her feet had hurt and when she'd finally got in she'd just fallen asleep. Now she had to be at the Pussy Palace in just over an hour and time was short.

The young copper went away and spoke to someone else for a bit and when he got back, he let Sita in beyond the front desk and took her to an interview room.

'I'm afraid I'll have to take a statement from you tonight,' he said.

'No detective?' She looked miserable. Then she said, 'Oh, well, you'll have to do.'

She gave him her details, her real name, her profession, her age. He was quite shocked she was as old as she was.

'If I were twenty I wouldn't be here,' she explained. 'I would be too frightened that my parents would come and take me back. But they're dead and my brother went back to Pakistan in the nineties.'

'Tell me about this man you alleged flashed at you, madam.'

'Back in the nineteen eighties I was living at home with my parents in Ilford. Cowley Road, near Valentines Park,' she said. 'I was a teenager then, a girl from a very traditional Pakistani family.'

The young copper was white and he smiled in a rather embarrassed-looking fashion. Actually, Sita was paler than he was but she knew that trying-to-be-racially-sensitive smile when she saw it. The boy began writing.

'My mum and dad wanted me to marry a shopkeeper from Barking, a great lump of a man with a limp.' She pulled a face. 'I ran away and discovered I could make money out of dancing, but that's another story. While I was still at my parents' house, we had these neighbours. There was a father, a mother, some old granny, four daughters and one son. Last night, up on the Olympic site, the son showed his penis to me.'

'You recognised him.'

Sita pulled a face. 'He was always getting himself out in front of me when I was a child. I hated him,' she said. 'Dirty bugger! A typical buttoned-up hypocrite. All religion and all that. If you ask me, he's your Olympic Flasher.'

'Do you know if he, this man, still lives in Cowley Road, Ilford?'

'I haven't got a clue,' Sita said. 'I haven't been back there since 1989.'

The young officer continued writing and then said, 'So what's his name, this man?'

'His name,' Sita said, 'is Aziz Choudhury and when I knew him back in the eighties he was training to be an accountant.'

The house was silent now and dark. Everyone had gone and she was alone with her thoughts, her feelings and the knowledge of what she had already done and what she now had to do.

Pastor Grint had just sat like a stone when she'd told him. Betty had gone white. That wasn't surprising. She'd finally told them everything, testified, confessed. She'd expected them to walk out, maybe even resort to violence. And who could have blamed them? But they'd just let her finish, no doubt having to listen hard as she burbled her confession through tears.

Because she'd been a Catholic she'd expected some sort of penance, even though she knew it wouldn't be in the form of so many Hail Marys because Pastor Grint thought that was nonsense. That was like treating God like a simpleton. But she had imagined that Pastor Grint would take her to the police station. She'd begged him to. But then he'd said, *Maria, what you did was a terrible thing. But man cannot hand out punishment, that has to be for God.* And he'd meant it.

But how was she meant to atone if there was to be no punishment? At last she'd managed to find enough courage and strength to confess and so open the way to finally be right with Jesus, only to find that her sin was not going to be punished. The slate was clean, she was saved and it was unbearable.

Betty hadn't helped. Clearly appalled, she'd nevertheless said that maybe Maria had already been punished. What about Len's death? What about the depression she suffered from? But it wasn't enough and Maria had become angry. What about an eye for an eye, a tooth for a tooth?

That, Pastor Grint had said, *comes from the Old Testament. Jesus is love, Jesus doesn't require eyes or teeth, just souls. He wants your soul, Maria, that's all. And now you've given it to him.*

Again and again she'd asked what else she could give

in order to atone and time and again he had told her there was no need. Then he'd blessed her, hugged both her and Betty and he'd gone. Then she'd been left alone with Betty. They'd talked.

Decisions had already been taken and telling Betty had been a risk. But she'd done it. Maybe she would tell Pastor Grint or even the police, but ultimately that wouldn't change anything. Documents had been signed in the presence of a solicitor and what was bequeathed would get to its ultimate destination whether that was this week, next week or next year. However, here in the darkness and the silence she feared that someone might knock at the front door and then break it in. But many hours had passed already and they still hadn't. Maybe Betty was being true to her word? Betty knew that what she was going to do was right and as time ticked on, Maria realised that she would not, if she so desired, be seeing her again.

XXX

Shazia lay on the living room sofa with all the curtains pulled and the lights off. Some news programme on the TV showed pictures of policemen and -women stomping around the streets of London, Birmingham and Manchester looking hard. The rioters, so far, didn't seem to be as thick on the ground as they had been the previous night. But she didn't care. She just wanted Amma to come home so that she could tell her about Mr Gold.

He'd made her watch him masturbate and it had made her feel sick. But what could she have done *but* go along with it? He didn't touch her or make her touch him and even though it was gross she hadn't been hurt. Conversely, if she'd lost her nerve and told him to bugger off or something, Mr Gold might have become suspicious. As far as he was concerned, Amma still knew nothing about her dope smoking and so he still had a hold over her. But what he'd made her watch had been gross. All sex was gross. Shazia never wanted to have it. Not again.

The riots had prevented the planned arrest from

progressing. Shazia had yet to suffer the humiliation of having Ady and Hilary in the house, pretending to smoke dope for Mr Gold. She hadn't seen or spoken to either of them since the police had gone to their houses and talked to their parents. Hilary had sent her a nasty text telling her she was 'sick' and 'a user'. That was good coming from her! But nothing from Ady. They'd been such good friends. Shazia, very softly, cried. Oh, where was Amma? She'd said she was going to a meeting and surely that had to be over now?

Shazia called Mumtaz's mobile number for the third time and for the third time it was switched off. She was generally very strict about phones being off during meetings at work, and even when they were just talking about something important together at home. She thought that having phones on all the time was rude and intrusive. Shazia didn't think so and neither had her father. In that respect, if nothing else, Shazia had been in agreement with him. What a pity that tiny similarity had been the only positive thing they had shared.

Shazia looked at her watch and decided that she wouldn't try and ring again for at least another half an hour. But then she did it just one more time and found that Mumtaz's phone was, as before, still off.

'Own goal!'

Lee looked from the squawking mynah bird to his

brother and found that he tended to agree. Chronus was sounding the mynah bird alarm with very good reason. Roy was utterly arseholed.

'Where have you been?' he growled. 'And where'd you find the money to get tanked up?'

Roy hadn't even made it to Paddy Power. The Duke of Edinburgh on Green Street was a pub he knew Lee never went to and so he'd gone straight for it. Some of the windows had been smashed by rioters the previous night and so it had been dingy and comforting in there. He'd had a few pints and then the barmaid had let him sit out the back by the barrels so he could smoke in peace.

'Leave me alone,' Roy said as he made his way from front door, to sofa, to steadying himself on the dining table. He wanted to get to bed, go unconscious and stop the room spinning.

'If you chuck up in this flat I'll heave you out into the garden!' Lee said.

'Oh, fuck off!'

'I mean it! Useless tosser. Why did I let you back into my life, eh?'

Roy didn't reply. Intent upon getting to the bed Lee had given him he veered to the left when he really wanted to go right and almost crashed into the kitchen.

'For fuck's sake!'

Chronus, in full agreement, moved his head up and down wildly and yelled, 'Own goal! Own goal!'

The cacophony of sound together with the stench of booze on Roy was all too much for Lee. 'Wind it in, will you, Chronus!' he said to the bird. Then running over to Roy he grabbed him just before he was about to barrel into a glass cabinet. With a roughness even he hadn't intended, Lee grabbed his brother by the shoulders and then hurled him into the spare bedroom. To his credit, he did manage to get Roy onto the bed but only just. Half his body hung off the side, an empty packet of fags, Lee's front door key and an old envelope fell out of his pocket and onto the floor.

Lee, more in the spirit of fanatical home tidiness than care for his brother, picked them up and put his key in his own pocket. It was then that he saw that the envelope was actually addressed to him.

No one appeared to be at home. All the lights were off and all the windows were closed. But Maria's car was in the drive and when she'd rung the bell, Mumtaz had thought that she'd seen a distant smudge of a figure cross the darkened hall. But if Maria wouldn't open up, what could she do? And why was she there anyway? It wasn't as if her conversation with Mark about Maria had come to any sort of firm conclusion. Even if she was in, she wouldn't want to talk to anyone about the church she clearly loved, at least not in any sort of negative fashion. What, if anything, did Mumtaz hope to achieve?

She didn't know. Mark would have called her a loony if he'd seen her ringing the bell and trying to see over the side gate into the back garden, but then the little meeting in the pie and mash shop had proved to her just how far apart they had become. All tan and trickery and funky, flip secularity. He was still a very attractive guy, and nice – underneath it all – just not for her. Mumtaz walked over to the side gate and tried the handle. Predictably it was locked. There was no gate on the other side of the building, just a small, metal garage that Maria never seemed to use and anyway both its doors were locked. Then she remembered that Maria also had an Edwardian coach house at the bottom of her garden. In the old days carriages would have swept down beside the house, where the gate was now, and the horses and the vehicles would have been accommodated in the coach house.

Clearly that was no longer happening, but maybe there was some sort of access to the coach house behind Maria's garden? Although frequently taken over by land-hungry householders, there were still a few back alleyways down which coal and other supplies would have been delivered to the properties years ago. One still ran along the back of Mumtaz's house. She walked to the end of the road but she saw nothing that even vaguely resembled the opening to a back alley. Continuing into the street behind Maria's, she walked past a heavily bearded Muslim man who looked at her with what she felt was a judgemental expression on his face. What was she doing roaming about on her own without a man? What indeed. The man's disapproval made her think about Shazia and she wondered whether she should call her. But she was only minutes from home, she'd call her when she knew whether Maria was in or not.

All the properties, like Maria's, like her own, were detached, double-fronted and huge. Some had lush, flower-choked gardens, while others were paved over to make hard standing for multiple cars. Looking down the sides of these properties wasn't always easy and one place, which was actually a small *madrasah*, was even protected by large, electric gates. When she did eventually find an old access alley, it was down beside the only empty house in the street. Semi-derelict and quite forbidding, the old house hadn't been touched for years. Making sure that no one actually watched her go onto the property, Mumtaz ran lightly to the entrance to the alleyway and immediately had to hop over a bag full of reeking disposable nappies.

Bindweed and endless stinging nettles were things that Mumtaz had expected. Fortunately she was wearing thirty-denier tights and so her legs were reasonably well protected. What she hadn't been expecting were the three old fridges, half a washing machine and at least eight bags containing empty beer cans. It was a depressing and messy journey but it did, eventually, get her to a piece of rotten fence between Maria's garden and that of one of her neighbours. As she threw a leg over, a strut thrust a splinter up into her thigh and so she had to stop for a moment to roll down her tights and take it out. Where the skin had broken, it bled but she ignored it. She was sure she'd had a tetanus jab at some point.

As she made her way out from behind the coach house and into Maria's garden she saw that the French windows were open. So she was in. Maria would probably go berserk if she just walked straight in, and with good cause. So when she reached the open doors she just stood beyond the step up into the house and said, 'Hello?'

Maria swallowed the pills in her mouth and then leaned back in her chair, pushing the paper bag that had been on her lap behind her.

'You're trespassing, get out,' she said to the shady, head-scarfed figure framed in the doorway out into the garden.

'I'm not here on behalf of the agency,' Mumtaz said. She stepped over the threshold. 'I'm here because I'm worried about you.'

Maria said nothing.

'Whenever I've seen you, you look ill and thin. I don't know what's happening in this house but I see your friends in and out all the time and I don't understand.'

'What don't you understand?' Maria said.

'How they can bear to see you looking so ill while doing nothing,' Mumtaz said. 'Have you seen a doctor?'

'I see my doctor.'

'Then maybe you should see another one. He isn't taking care of you. You take a lot of medication, Maria ...'

'What?' She stood, shakily at first.

'I've lived here, I've seen your medicine cabinet.'

'You had no right to pry.'

'Maybe not, but I did it. You're not well, Maria. You need help.'

'You mean, I'm nuts!'

'No, I mean—'

'God will punish or God will heal. You're a Muslim, you must understand that!'

'And as a Jewish friend of mine always says, "God helps them who help themselves",' Mumtaz replied. 'I can't just walk by and not do anything, Maria, you're a nice woman ...'

She laughed. 'What do you know? Nice? Mumtaz, if you really knew me you'd beg me to let myself rot!'

Mumtaz shook her head. 'Why do you think that you should be left to rot?'

Maria said nothing.

Mumtaz toyed with the notion of asking her whether her new friends at the church thought she should rot – it was the kind of thing stupid jihadi boys said to people they thought 'immoral' – but she decided against it. If Grint and his people were effectively in control of Maria's mind now she would not take kindly to questions about them.

BARBARA NADEL

'I want you to leave,' Maria said.

Mumtaz didn't know what to say, or do. Even peering intently through the gloom she could only just about see Maria's face. Details of the room she was in were sketchy. A whooping noise from what sounded like a youngster mucking around or maybe even looting over in Manor Park caused her to flinch. But then the silence came back again and the sun disappeared into the west and that which had been grey turned towards black.

'You must go now.'

'I can't.'

Mumtaz wanted light. She couldn't remember where the switch was on the wall for the overhead chandelier. Maria liked to use lamps. She moved forward into the deeper gloom and it was then that she heard a crunching noise and then a gasp. There was, she knew, a standard lamp somewhere near the fireplace. For a moment she just flailed her arms around trying to find it by touch. Then she heard a whimper.

She stopped. 'Maria?'

No reply came. Mumtaz put her hand on the mantelpiece and from there she found the standard lamp. She switched it on. Maria lay slumped and apparently unconscious on the sofa. On the floor at her feet were dozens of pill boxes and bottles.

*   *   *

'Where's my fucking money?' Lee yelled. 'God Almighty, the fucking bird was trying to warn me about you, wasn't he? Not the girl, you, you waste of skin!'

But Roy, in spite of being manhandled out of his bed, was completely dead to the world. Lee let go of his brother's throat so that he fell backwards and banged his head on the floor.

Lee put a hand up to his own head, which was pounding with fury. 'But why am I asking?' he said to himself. 'Why?' Then he looked down at Roy who very briefly grunted and then drooled. 'You've drunk it. You've drunk all of it because you're a fucking selfish twat!'

Although he'd never had very high hopes of getting any money back from Bob the Builder, he'd known that it was at least possible. And a hundred quid would have come in very handy. Lee briefly rifled through Roy's pockets to see if there was any cash left over, but there wasn't. If nothing else it would have paid one of the outstanding utility bills on the office. But now it had gone. Disappeared down the neck of a useless drunk who just happened to be his brother. Lee didn't know what to do. He didn't know whether he wanted to walk away from Roy, close the door behind him and try to forget about it or continue to kick the shit out of the bastard.

He went back into the living room where Chronus, agitated by all the shouting, was cawing and squawking. Lee walked over to him and tried to get close enough to stroke his head. But the bird was having none of it. 'Own goal!' he croaked as he pulled resentfully away from Lee's hand. 'Own goal!'

'Yes, yes I know I should never have let him in but he's my brother, what could I do?'

Chronus eyed him with distinct suspicion. Lee shrugged. 'What?'

The bird put his head underneath his wing as he did whenever he wanted to just cut off from anything he didn't like. Lee, trying not to feel rejected by Chronus sat down and put the television on. Flicking onto the BBC news channel, he saw that the riots, such as they were, seemed to be small and sporadic, so far. He was glad of that for all sorts of reasons, not least of which was that he knew that Vi was on duty. Although whether he was more afraid for Vi or because of what Vi might do, he didn't know. She was not, and had never been, a woman to shy away from a scrap.

He'd just managed to get into some strangely compelling cookery programme when a shambling figure, reeking of piss, staggered into the living room. 'I don't half need a glass of water,' Roy said.

Maybe if he'd then shuffled off to get the water himself, Lee might have let it pass. In spite of the piss. But Roy just stood as if waiting for Lee to go and get it for him. Chronus, who'd woken up now, gave a warning squawk, but Lee ignored him. The red mist of fury descended and he launched himself at Roy.

'You fucking cunt!' He took hold of Roy's filthy, greasy hair and pulled him by it across the room.

'Fucking hell, Lee!' Roy's face was red and scrunched up into a ball of unshaved fear. He stumbled and fell to the floor.

Lee took hold of his brother by his neck and pulled him along the carpet towards the front door. Chronus, beside himself now, cawed at the top of his voice.

'Shut up!' Lee looked down at his brother's scarecrow-like body and opened the front door with his one free hand. 'You can kip outside,' he growled at him. 'Like the piece of junk you are!'

Roy was too drunk and too sodden with urine to resist. Lee heaved him over the threshold and then kicked him into the front garden. He would have spat on him too had the couple from the flat upstairs not been looking out of the window. From inside he could hear Chronus still yelling like a maniac and jumping up and down on his perch.

'Shut up, bird, for Christ's sake!' Lee shouted. Then he went back inside and closed the front door behind him. Roy groaned once, and then became unconscious again.

'Maria?'

Mumtaz went over to the sofa and took one of the woman's wrists between her fingers. While she established that Maria had a pulse, Mumtaz looked at all the half empty boxes and bottles of tablets on the floor. Just at a

glance she could see antidepressants, painkillers and tran-
quillisers. She moved one box with her foot and found an
empty strip of sleeping tablets.

'Maria!' Mumtaz tapped the side of her face and Maria
Peters groaned. 'Maria, have you taken all these pills?
Which ones have you taken?' She didn't answer and so
this time Mumtaz slapped her. 'Maria! Tell me which
tablets you've taken.'

Although Maria Peters' eyes were opening sometimes,
she was clearly going in and out of consciousness and
Mumtaz was afraid. She'd never dealt with anyone who
had tried to take their own life before. She felt in her
pocket for her phone and then realised that it was in her
handbag which was on the floor by the French windows.
She shook Maria's shoulders and said, 'You've got to try
and stay awake. I'm going to call an ambulance.' She shook
her again. 'Stay awake!'

She was about to leave Maria and go and get her bag
when suddenly the comedian's eyes flew open and she
lurched forward, her face red and swollen.

'What is it? Allah!' Mumtaz helped her to sit up. 'Maria?'

Maria Peters looked at her with what Mumtaz inter-
preted as horror in her eyes. Then under pressure from
what was in her throat her mouth opened and a vast
deluge of pills, liquid and undigested food hit Mumtaz in
her face and spattered across her chest. Instinctively she
pulled back, taking a step away from the sofa but into

the back of the coffee table. Her leg jarred and then twisted and she pitched backwards over the table and onto the floor. As she fell, her back caught against the side of the table and she screamed. But when her head hit the floor with an audible crack, Mumtaz went silent.

For several seconds, Maria Peters just stared at the awful wet vomit that was all over herself, her sofa and her coffee table. But then when she felt able to stand she looked across the upturned table at the woman who was lying on her living room floor. The pale grey headscarf that Mumtaz had been wearing was stained with blood. It was a stain that was growing. Maria put a hand up to her vomit-covered mouth, her eyes widening in terror.

XXXI

Vi heard the news over her radio. Some old half-dead detective from Shoreditch nick had gone to a house in Fashion Street, just off Brick Lane, and arrested a man on suspicion of being the Olympic Flasher. The old tec had to be half dead because anyone else with a pulse who could even claim to be a quarter of a copper was out on the streets. Riots were no fun in anyone's books, except the rioters, but they did provide some very tasty overtime. As she walked down an unusually quiet Atlantic Road, Vi kept her eyes and ears open but she also allowed herself to think a little bit about how she might now be able to pay for at least a weekend break somewhere hot. So far the streets, if not quiet, were much calmer than they had been the previous night. Maybe the fury over the Tottenham man's death that had provoked incidents all over the country since the weekend had finally blown itself out. *That, or,* Vi thought uncharitably, *all the scumbags have nicked all the tech stuff they could ever want from Currys.*

As she walked past Brixton tube station and began trudging along Railton Road, Vi wondered where this news about the Olympic Flasher left old Martin Gold. If this apparently Asian man from Spitalfields did turn out to be the flasher then Martin was off the hook – for that. For what he'd made Shazia Hakim do was another matter. He had old habits and they were dying hard, if at all. It was fitting, Vi felt, that she should be thinking about old habits as she walked down Railton Road, Brixton. Back in the late seventies it had been known as the Front Line. This was because it was where the police and the local Afro-Caribbean community had always clashed. Vi remembered it well, not because she'd policed the area back then but because she'd had a mate who'd known a black guy who used to have what they called 'Blues' parties. Blues had been noisy, crazy, rum-fuelled and the sort of hash that used to get passed around had been second to none. Minus the violence and having two small kids at home and a useless husband, Vi remembered that time with affection. In the late seventies, Martin Gold had been inside.

'I'm really sorry to bother you, Mr Arnold, but is my mum with you?'

Lee looked at his watch. It was nearly nine o'clock. Mumtaz had gone to meet up with her old college mate at five. 'She's not here, Shazia,' Lee said. 'You've tried her mobile, right?'

'Loads of times! It's not even like her to switch it off for such a long time.'

'You at home?'

'Yes. Amma . . . Mum said she'd be back by seven at the latest. I'm worried, you know?' She sounded it. And frightened.

Had Mumtaz gone off with the famous magical sensation, Mark Solomons? Had she been seduced away to some swanky restaurant in the West End followed by tickets to some up-market magic club? Lee couldn't believe that for a second – even though Shazia wasn't her biological child, she treated her as if she were.

Lee was knackered after his altercations first with Foxy and then with Roy, but Mumtaz being on the missing list was worrying and so he said, 'I'm coming round, Shazia.'

'Oh.' There was some anxiety but also some relief in her voice. She was sixteen but, even so, being in that great big house on her own in a city that was tensed for more riots couldn't be a nice feeling.

Lee put his shoes back on. 'It'll only take me a tick,' he said.

'Thanks.' She cut the connection.

Mumtaz and Shazia lived less than five minutes' walk away. Lee turned the TV off and glanced briefly at Chronus who was asleep again. Then he wondered whether Roy was still stacked out in the front garden, not that he cared. But when he opened the front door he saw that the garden was empty. Roy had either wobbled off to pastures new or someone had dragged his body over onto Wanstead Flats and either mugged him or beaten him up or both. Lee began walking towards Mumtaz's house.

Betty had arrived very quickly after she'd called her. Maria still felt woozy but she was no longer drifting in and out of consciousness. She took Betty into the living room and pointed at Mumtaz on the floor.

'Is she dead?'

Betty walked over to Mumtaz's prone form and took one of her wrists between her fingers.

'It was an accident!' Maria said. 'I was sick and then, she ... She, I was sick in her face. You couldn't make it up!' And then just for a second she laughed. 'She fell over. Over the table. Went down like a, like ...'

'Marie, I'm trying to feel for a pulse!'

'Oh, sorry. Sorry, sorry!' She sat on the sofa. On the mantelpiece the clock ticked, the right cats, Gog and Magog, sat motionless in the grate and everything felt more normal than it had been for a long time. Except for all the tablets and the woman lying in her own blood on the carpet.

Maria sat back down on the sofa and tried not to breathe in the smell of her own vomit. She'd thought that because she took a lot of medication anyway, it wouldn't make her sick. But she'd mixed over a hundred pills up in that bag and swallowed over half of them.

'Did you eat anything?' Betty asked, still holding on to Mumtaz's wrist.

She had. She'd eaten so little for such a long time and the fridge had been full of chocolate she'd had for months. The inner comedian, rearing up suddenly, had said *what the hell?*

'You did, didn't you?' Betty said. 'That was really silly, Marie. Food'll just make you sick.'

'I know.'

'Do you still *really* want to do this?'

Maria looked at the vomit all over her clothes and her furniture and then she looked at the woman Betty was squatting down next to. 'Is she OK?'

Betty looked up and Maria felt her face pale. *Oh, God,* she thought, *please not again!*

Then Betty said, softly, 'She's dead, Marie.'

The scream that came out of Maria had a life all of its own. Betty tried to cover her mouth with one of her own hands but the scream just kept coming. Even when she slapped her around the face, it only abated for a moment. She shouted through it, 'Oh, Marie, look, you just have to carry on! It's the only way! Jesus knows you didn't *mean* it, but . . .'

Nauseous again, Maria vomited bile over herself and over Betty. If nothing else, that brought the screaming to an end.

'Oh, Marie!'

'What are we going to do?' she said. 'Bet, we have to go to the police!'

Once he'd made sure that Shazia was OK, Lee took a walk around the neighbourhood. The leafy Woodgrange Estate, as the area where he and Mumtaz lived was called, was quiet and very desirable but it was also full of bushes, little deserted bits of garden, railway tracks and a cemetery – all places where people could, and did, get mugged. Heading down towards the top end of Green Street, he passed Maria Peters' house, which was in darkness, and then turned into the road behind hers and wandered slowly in the direction of Woodgrange Road. There were a couple of deserted houses in that street and he wanted to just check them out.

One of them, which had, he recalled, always been known as the Wilde House, was in a terrible state. Most of the roof had collapsed and the gap where the front door had once been looked like that black obelisk from *2001: A Space Odyssey*, probably one of the most boring films of all time. Lee pushed the battered garden gate to one side and marched straight into the black obelisk. As he put his feet down on the rotten floorboards inside they groaned underneath his weight. These old places all had cellars; he'd have to be careful not to go flying through.

Back in his coppering days, he'd come across the Wilde

House a few times. An old man called Paddy Wilde had lived there. A recluse, Paddy Wilde eschewed the modern world and lit his home with candles and warmed himself by an open fire made from wood he cut from trees or nicked out of skips. As Lee recalled, he'd died intestate and then the house had been found to have subsidence problems. So now it just mouldered and splintered, waiting for some sort of house death.

'Lee?'

He turned. The voice was familiar even if the figure that stood outside the front entrance wasn't.

'Sam?' He walked back outside and found himself looking at a tall man wearing what Lee always called 'all the Muslim gear'. A heavily bearded man of what he knew was his own age. 'Samir.'

The man smiled. 'Long time.'

They embraced, naturally, but also in what both of them would have described as a very manly way.

'What have you been doing?' Lee asked.

Samir drew away and then smiled. 'I teach now, man,' he said. Then he pointed to the building with the big electric gates. 'That *madrasah*, loads of others all over the East End. You still in the filth?'

Lee shook his head. 'No, mate.' He struck a boxing stance and said, 'Private detective.'

Samir laughed. 'Blimey! Still keeping the streets safe though, eh?'

'Could say the same for you,' Lee said. 'Teaching. Keeping the kids out of mischief.'

'Caring for their souls.'

Lee looked down. 'Yeah.'

An awkward silence passed between them. Samir and Lee had never agreed about the utility of religion, even when Sam had still been in the police with him over twenty years ago.

'So, what you doing in the old Wilde house, man?'

Lee sighed. 'I'm looking for someone,' he said. 'My assistant. Should have been home hours ago. Her daughter's worried.'

'A lady?'

'One of your ladies, actually, Sam.'

Samir looked confused.

'Her family come from Bangladesh,' Lee said. 'She covers her head.'

'And she works for you?'

'It's a long story. But look, I'm worried about her,' Lee said. 'You haven't seen a lady, thirty-two, beautiful face, grey coat and headscarf, on her own?'

Samir nodded – somewhere deep inside there was still a copper who didn't miss much. 'She went down the side alleyway,' he said.

Lee felt his heart jolt in his chest. 'When?'

'About half an hour ago.'

'Did you see her come out again?'

'No. But I had to go and counsel this kid,' Samir said. Then he looked down at his watch. 'And now I've got a meeting.'

She heard Betty help Maria take more tablets. Before, apparently, she'd swallowed them with water. This time it was port. Even though she couldn't speak or move, Mumtaz knew that Betty had lied to Maria. Not only was she still alive, she could feel her blood moving strongly through her veins. She also knew that she could at the very least open her eyes even though she didn't dare to do so.

'I'll stay with you until you go to sleep,' she heard Betty say to Maria.

'Are you sure? I didn't want you involved. But maybe until I become unconscious.' Was that a note of panic in her slurring voice? 'What about her?'

'I'll deal with her,' Betty said.

'How?'

'I don't know.'

More drinking happened. She heard what sounded like a vocalised shudder.

'It was an accident,' Maria said. 'Maybe just leave her there?'

'Maybe. Would you like me to pray for you, Marie?'

'And the child? And her too?'

'And Mrs Mumtaz Hakim? She is a Muslim but yes, if you like.'

Seemingly the feeling of paralysis was just an illusion, a product of the shock her body had sustained when she'd barrelled over the table and smashed her head on the floor. She had a headache that was in a class of its own, but she could move and now she risked opening an eye, just a very little.

Amid watery vomit, Maria Peters lay down on the sofa while Betty Muller crouched beside her with her eyes closed. 'Dear Lord, accept the soul of this sinner,' she said, 'this murderer of children. An eye for an eye, a life for a life . . .'

Killer of children? An abortion? Had Maria had an abortion at some point? Born-again Christians didn't approve. And now this Betty and probably Mr Grint and the solicitor and who knew what other church members were trying to make her atone by killing herself. So that's what they'd had on her. How had they known? Had she told them? Betty's eyes slowly opened as she gently rubbed Maria's temples.

'. . . and knowing that your glory can only be attained via sacrifice . . .' And then Mumtaz's eyes met hers and Betty stopped talking. Mumtaz unable to prevent it, blinked. Time suspended for both of them until Maria groaned and said, 'What's the matter?'

Mumtaz saw Betty's mild eyes harden and she said, 'Nothing. Go to sleep. Go to Jesus. He's waiting.'

XXXII

'No he isn't, Maria! Jesus isn't waiting! Suicide is a sin!'

But Maria Peters didn't move. Mumtaz tried to get up but found that she couldn't. Betty rose to her feet and began to walk over to her.

'Why are you assisting this woman to kill herself?' Mumtaz said. 'Has she left you her money?'

Not even in the wildest reaches of Ahmed's violence had he ever kicked Mumtaz in the face. Betty Muller did not have such scruples. 'Unbeliever.' It wasn't even said in anger.

Mumtaz's jaw shifted to one side and then seemed to right itself again. She ran her tongue around her teeth to see if she'd lost any. She hadn't. Betty turned aside and went to one of the chairs over by the French doors.

'Why did you tell Maria I was dead?' Mumtaz asked. She could feel her face swelling as she spoke, her words beginning to distort. 'You must have been able to tell I had a pulse!'

Betty didn't answer, but Maria made a noise that could indicate that she could hear.

'Maria! This woman has lied to you!' Mumtaz said. 'Whatever has happened, whatever you've done, God will forgive! Allah, God, He doesn't want people to kill themselves, truly!'

'That from *you*!' Betty flung herself down on top of Mumtaz and showed her the cushion in her hands.

'How do you hope to—'

'They'll think she killed you,' Betty said.

Mumtaz looked over at Maria whose eyes were now open again. And then everything went dark as she breathed in the scent of velvet. As the smell of velvet cushion began to suffocate the life out of her.

For a moment she didn't even feel as if she had any sort of strength with which to put up a fight against this woman. She was on top of her with a cushion over her face, smothering her. There was a thought in her mind that if Maria deserved to die then so, in a sense, did she. Except that she couldn't because, unlike Maria, she had Shazia. That girl had suffered enough. Allah, but the pain of not being able to breathe was just hell! She tried to move her head from side to side, but this just made Betty Muller press down still harder on the cushion. Then she realised that one of her arms wasn't pinned to the floor any more.

Eyes had always been a problem for Mumtaz. When she'd had to study sight and perception at university, she'd been excused the video the lecturer had prepared for the group about eye surgery. But this woman was trying to kill her and so Mumtaz made herself slam her hand around Betty's face until her fingers found her eyes.

The scream the woman made sounded like a dog being whipped. A loud, piercing yelp. She let go of the cushion and flung her head backwards. Her hand now free, Mumtaz pulled the cushion from her face and then looked at her fingers just to make sure the woman's eyes were not hanging from her nails.

But then Betty, her eyes red but very much in her head, launched herself at Mumtaz and the two woman began to tear at each other's faces and bodies on the floor. Decidedly the weaker party, Mumtaz felt all the breath leave her body again as Betty pinned her to the floor and began to claw wildly at her face. The woman said nothing, not even making any noises, which was strange and, as it went on seemingly for ever, eerie. Trying to get at Mumtaz's eyes, Betty's fingers prised her hands away from her face. For a moment, when her arms were flung sideways and her face was uncovered and vulnerable, Mumtaz saw the clawed fingers come for her. And then, just before they reached her face, they pulled back. Sharply.

'Lee!'

He'd punched Betty Muller once on the side of the head and was now standing over her.

'Mumtaz!'

'Lee call an ambulance!' she rasped.

'What's gone on here?'

'Lee, just call an ambulance!' It was difficult for her to speak. Her jaw and her throat felt as if they'd been stamped on.

Lee called an ambulance and the police. The place looked like some sort of drug house. 'Pills?'

Mumtaz pulled herself across the floor towards the prone figure on the sofa. 'Maria's swallowed a load. Sit her up.'

Lee left Betty Muller on the floor and hauled Maria's slack body up into a sitting position.

'Lee, we have to make her sick.'

He knew what to do. It wasn't the first time he'd done it. 'Shit.'

Maria Peters said something unintelligible and Mumtaz shouted, 'Just do it!'

He stuck his fingers down the back of the comedian's throat and felt her gag. He did it again. Some water dribbled from her mouth and then he did it once more.

It all came out of her on a river of booze. And once again it flew straight in to Mumtaz's face.

'Oh, Christ!' Lee held Maria's shoulders. 'Mumtaz!'

'Don't worry about me!' She wiped a hand across her swollen jaw and her nose and then heaved herself up beside the comedian and held her arms. 'Go and make sure that Betty Muller doesn't get away.'

Lee looked at the small body on the floor. It wasn't moving and so he went over and felt for a pulse. He'd hit her hard. When he'd seen her trying to kill Mumtaz he'd just done what he'd had to.

'How is she?'

There was a pulse and it was strong. For once Lee was grateful that he was no longer twenty-five. 'She's OK. What *is* this?'

Then they heard the sirens.

Maria Peters, breathless and exhausted said, 'I killed my daughter.'

Epilogue

XXXIII

The police picked Paul Grint up at a boarding house in West Ham; they found Pastor Iekanjika at home at his devotions. DS Tony Bracci got a message over to Vi Collins in Brixton and she returned to Forest Gate as quickly as she was able.

Waiting their turn to be interviewed after Betty Muller and the preachers, Lee and Mumtaz sat in the soft interview suite nursing cups of coffee. Shazia had been taken to the Huqs' house in Spitalfields.

Mortified to be wearing the awful white jumpsuit the police had given her, Mumtaz was nevertheless relieved not to be covered in sick any more. They sat in silence – Mumtaz's jaw was very sore and speaking was hard – side by side, not looking at each other or touching until, eventually, Vi came in.

She stared at them for a few moments until she spoke. 'So no church in Barking,' she said.

Lee looked up. 'Council say no,' he said.

She nodded. He knew what she was thinking. Perhaps

if he'd passed that snippet on sooner some of what had just happened could have been prevented. But she also knew that in itself it hadn't been much. It hadn't been looting and rioting.

'I'm interviewing Grint,' she said.

Lee nodded.

'Someone'll come for you to take statements.'

She walked back towards the door and then she turned. 'Maria Peters'll live. You did some good vomit work there, Arnold.'

'You're lying.'

DS Bracci shrugged. 'Am I? I'm not.'

'That man, that private detective, assaulted me,' Betty said.

'You had a cushion over another woman's face. You were trying to kill her,' he countered. Lee Arnold had smacked her good and proper but she'd been seen by a doctor who'd said she was well enough to be interviewed. 'I'm not lying about there being no church in Barking, Betty.'

'I've seen the site. Paul took me. He would never lie to me.'

'Paul took you somewhere,' Bracci said. 'But it weren't to no site he'd bought, rented or had planning permission for. He's a conman.' He watched her eyes mist. 'Paul Grint always was and he always will be. God has not, Betty, saved his soul.'

She said nothing. Tony Bracci didn't know what was more painful, the look of her bruised eyes or the crushed look on her face. She'd loved Paul Grint. All the God-squad stuff aside, that had been the bottom line.

'I want to know why you tried to help Maria Peters kill herself. Was it for money?'

'Of course not.' She looked up sharply. 'That woman killed her own child!'

Tony leaned back in his chair. 'Tell me about it.'

'It was a long time ago.' She looked away.

'Obviously still bothers you.'

'I was her best friend. At school and then until . . . it.'

Tony didn't speak. He just waited.

She tilted her head up sharply. 'I was married. She was trying to get into comedy and I went to her first audition with her. But she was sick because she was pregnant. Not that she remembered me being there. Just thinking about herself! That was always Maria! Just ran home after the audition – just left me. She had a baby, a little girl, in a toilet, and then she strangled her.' She cried, hugging herself. 'She put her body in a Clarks shoebox and left it on the mud at Wapping Stairs!'

'How do you know all this?'

'I knew some of it already. But she told me and Pastor Grint the rest of it today.'

'Why?'

Through tears Betty said, 'Because she wanted to be saved! Because Jesus was sending her terrible signs!'

Tony had imagined a tale of abortion.

'But, maybe because of guilt, she couldn't part with the little one's body,' Betty said. 'She went back and got the box off the mud and she kept it. I went to the flat she got when she left her parents' place once and while she went out to get milk for our tea I looked around. There was a terrible smell and I wanted to know what it was. Then I found her, the little one, rotting in that box. That box that God made appear to Maria all these last months to force her to confess her sins ...'

Tony Bracci had heard some things in his time ... 'What are you talking about?'

'She came to our church. She knew she had to. Jesus had called her and then, when she came to church, he began sending her signs to make her testify.'

'She found you, not the other way around?'

'Yes.' Then she leaned across the table towards him and said, 'She arrived at church one day, alone. It was meant to be. Jesus wanted us to meet and he wanted justice, for her child.'

'And had you, before Maria arrived, ever told anyone else about what you'd seen in her flat all those years ago?'

'Marie had been in the papers some months before, making her comeback. When I saw it, it made me cross. So much fuss about her! But it made me sad too. No one knew of her shame except me, and I knew she had to be heavily burdened and she was.'

'And so you told Pastor Grint about your old friend, did you?'

'I thought she'd had an abortion and then just kept the body,' Betty said. 'I didn't know about the murder until today.' She put her head down. 'And of course I told Pastor Grint and he tried to help her, as I knew he would. I've always told him everything. But Maria wanted to die. She wanted to.'

'And did you tell Pastor Grint that too?' Tony asked.

'Of course I did,' she said. 'Why wouldn't I?'

'I didn't tell anyone at the time.'

The duty psych, a blond, middle-aged man with a nicotine-stain streak in his hair, said, 'Why did you kill the child, Maria?'

'Because I wanted to get away. From home. I couldn't do that with a child.'

She hadn't had to talk, it was the middle of the night and she was still in pain. But she'd wanted to.

'It was easy. I put her body in a shoebox and I took it down to the river. That's what people used to do in the old days when abortions were still illegal. They got a shoebox and they put the foetus in it. I got a shoebox of my own. It was the right thing to do, the right thing to put her in.'

'And you got on with your life.'

'Yes. I made jokes.'

He put his fingers up to his lips; he was confused. She was so cold. For a woman who had just tried to take her own life because of this incident, she was very cold.

'I switched that part of my life off.'

'Until?'

'What do you mean?'

'When did you start to think about it again?' he asked.

For a moment she looked confused and then she said, 'Always.'

'You just said, Maria, that you switched that part of your life off.'

'I switched the guilt off.'

'So what made the guilt switch back on again?'

'God told me I needed to be guilty. He sent me signs. He stalked me.'

'What signs?'

'Omens. Things that nudged my conscience.'

'What things?'

'The shoebox I put the child's body in, full of blood.'

The psych cleared his throat. 'So the memory of killing your child never left you.'

'No.'

'So when the tide took her body away . . .'

'Tide didn't take her body away.' She looked up. She

saw him frowning and then she said, 'I couldn't leave her there.'

It was hot and stuffy in the day room, the psych wanted a fag and he knew he was beginning to sweat. 'So what did you do?' he said. 'With her?'

'I took her home,' she said. 'And then I moved out and I took her with me. I always took her everywhere I went. It wasn't her fault that her father raped me, was it?'

'Who raped you, Maria?' the psychiatrist asked.

'My baby's father,' she replied, 'was Father Fernandez. He was a priest at our church and my mother and my sisters all loved him. What could I do?'

In spite of his dodgy past, Vi hadn't actually envisaged Paul Grint as a bit of a geezer. Maybe it was because he originated from up west?

'The church?' he shrugged. 'Yeah, I'll give you that. The Barking place doesn't exist, never did. Doesn't mean it wasn't going to. The Lord provides and I did get that short lease over the Olympic site.'

'And then you moved to Canning Town.'

'I had to keep my congregation together,' he said. 'Church is important to them, to all of us.'

'So what was the plan, Paul?'

'Miss Peters helped, she gave us the money. She was giving us more.'

'Was she.'

'Her idea. Drew up legal contracts for it with a proper solicitor, Mr Allitt. No pressure from me or anyone. Totally kosher. Ask him.'

'Had Miss Peters also written the Chapel of the Holy Pentecostal Fire into her will?'

'That was part of it,' he said. 'But she was turning some money over to the church straight away, to clear our debts.'

'Did you ask her to do that?'

'No. It was all her idea, she offered.'

'So you didn't want Maria Peters dead?'

'No!'

'So why did Betty Muller who, my colleagues tell me, is obsessed with you, try to assist Miss Peters to kill herself earlier this evening?'

'I've no idea. Ask her.' He smiled and then his face became grave. 'Inspector, Betty and Maria have a history. Neither woman is particularly stable.'

'Oh, no?' Vi raised an eyebrow. 'So why'd you spend so much time with Betty, eh? As far as I can tell you're part of her problem. She's a bit *too* religious, isn't she?'

He smiled but said nothing.

Vi looked down at her notes. 'And this history between Miss Peters and Miss Muller,' she said. 'Anything to do with a baby Maria had back in 1980?'

'You'd have to ask her.'

'Who? Maria or Betty?'

Again Grint said nothing.

'Maria Peters gave birth to a baby girl in May 1980,' Vi said. 'I know you know this, because both Maria Peters and Betty Muller have told us you do. Mr Grint, did you use this knowledge, in any way, to try to manipulate or get money out of Maria Peters?'

'Did I blackmail her? No.'

'I didn't say blackmail,' Vi said. 'What I'm talking about is you sending her out of her mind. She had some strange experiences. Boxes filled with blood, mysteriously appearing.'

'God can prick your conscience.' He smiled.

Vi lost it. 'Oh, for Christ's sake, Paul, it was you! I know you're bankrupt! Or you were. I know you're a conman.'

'Not any more, I've found—'

'Jesus. Yeah.' Vi sat back in her seat and looked down at her notes. 'Just like Maria, you're a lapsed Catholic, aren't you?'

He said nothing.

Vi persisted. 'So some notion at least about the Catholic mindset. Maria had been religious. You'd know how that would work, wouldn't you, Paul? You'd know she'd have a need to be punished in some way. You have a key to her gaff, did you? Betty give it you, did she?'

He didn't reply to the question, but said instead, 'Money isn't everything, DI Collins.'

'It is if you haven't got any,' Vi said. 'And you really haven't, have you, Paul. And this brings me to one Pastor

Iekanjika and why you keep on giving him IOUs for seven grand a month.'

'That's rent.'

'No, it isn't, Paul,' Vi said, 'that's well dodgy, that is, and you and I both know it. What we both also know is where the three million quid just recently landed in the Chapel of the Holy Pentecostal Fire's bank account came from too.'

He smiled. 'Maria's generous gift to help with our expenses.'

'Your new life, where was it to be, Paul, Spain?' Vi smiled. 'I know you knew she was planning to kill herself, Paul,' she said, 'because Betty told us so. She told us she told you everything.'

But Paul Grint just carried on smiling and then he said, 'But she's a nutter, DI Collins. Prove your allegations or let me go.'

It was almost midday by the time Mumtaz got home. She invited Lee in for some lunch and then spoke briefly to her mother on the phone. According to her mother, Mr Choudhury's son Aziz had been arrested by the police. She had no idea what for or why but the local community was buzzing with the news.

'And to think that you were so mad keen on him, Mumtaz!' she'd said. 'We will have to find you someone else.'

Mumtaz made tea and tuna sandwiches and took them in to the living room. Lee, his eyes half closed in what had once been Ahmed's chair took a sandwich and said, 'Ta.'

For a while they ate and talked about other things; their children, the riots, the weather. But then suddenly there was an awkward silence into which Mumtaz said, 'When do you think we'll hear anything?'

Paul Grint, Betty Muller and a Zimbabwean preacher called Iekanjika were still being questioned by the police. Maria Peters was in hospital.

Lee shook his head. 'I don't know.'

'Grint manipulated those people in his church.'

'Mumtaz, you and me'll never agree on this but all religion is manipulation.'

She said nothing.

'All Vi told me was that they found a key to Maria's front door in Betty Muller's bag.'

'Maria said she didn't give anyone a key.'

'Can we trust the word of a woman who tries to top herself, albeit with help? And what about Betty having a duplicate cut without her knowing? Didn't you say one of your brothers did that once?'

'Yes.'

'Could explain all the feelings she had about being watched, about the peacock feathers and all that other stuff just materialising. Betty nipping in to drive her bonkers.'

431

'It could.'

He looked at her with narrowed, doubting eyes. 'Don't tell me you prefer a weird, supernatural explanation.'

She smiled. 'Lee, I prefer a psychological explanation.'

'Same difference.'

This time she laughed. 'No it isn't. A person's state of mind can produce strange effects.'

'Like peacock feathers.'

'No! But guilt, which Maria has in spades, can haunt a person. People can produce conditions of fear to punish themselves or others, if they know their weaknesses and can exploit such things. Betty Muller was assisting Maria's suicide because she felt she needed to be punished for what she had done.'

'And for her money.'

'We don't know that yet.'

'No, but—'

'Lee, both Maria and Betty are vulnerable women. They are both alone and one of them, it seems, had a terrible secret. Things can happen to such people. To some extent they anticipate it.'

He didn't really know what she meant, but Lee just ate his sandwich and then he said, 'Oh, one of the blokes told me they've caught the Olympic Flasher.'

'Oh, that's good.'

'A bloke called Choudhury,' Lee said. 'Aziz Choudhury.'

So that was why he'd been arrested. Mumtaz felt vindicated in her low opinion of Aziz Choudhury but also a little bit sick too. Although she didn't usually go in for a lot of exposition about her priviate life unless she absolutely had to, she told Lee about her brush with the Choudhury's. He smiled and said, 'So you had a narrow escape then.'

Pastor Marius Iekanjika's lawyer was a Mr Riordan. As Iekanjika was big and dark, so Mr Riordan was small and pale. Vi Collins knew him of old. She knew his fearsome reputation as a pocket legal Rottweiler and she ignored it. Fixing her eyes on Iekanjika, she said, 'So, Mr Iekanjika, what's this about these seven-grand IOUs you have from Mr Paul Grint?'

Iekanjika turned aside to quietly consult with his lawyer. Vi looked at Tony Bracci and rolled her eyes. The rich and powerful were always like this, in her experience – not moving a centimetre without their advocate.

George Riordan cleared his throat. 'That's a private matter between my client and Mr Grint.'

Ignoring Riordan again, Vi said to Iekanjika, 'We believe that Grint may have been involved in extorting money from one of his wealthier parishioners in order to pay you – amongst other things.'

'No comment.'

Vi shrugged. 'Why so much for a dump like that old pub, Marius? You've got other properties. Why that pub in particular, eh?'

The Zimbabwean looked away.

Tony Bracci said, 'Mr Grint tell you why he needed that particular pub, Mr Iekanjika?'

Iekanjika said, 'Because he needed a place for his congregation to meet. A temporary place. He has a new church that is being built over in Barking.'

'No he doesn't,' Vi said. 'But then I think you know that, Mr Iekanjika. I think this because yesterday Mr Grint authorised the bank that holds the church's account to pay you what he owed you plus another hundred thousand pounds. He was going to do a runner with the rest, wasn't he?'

'He paid me what he owed me.'

'He paid you a hundred grand over the top,' Bracci said.

Mr Riordan put his hand on Iekanjika's arm, as if to restrain him. 'My client was owed more than just back-rent by Mr Grint,' he said.

'Oh? What?'

'That is a private—'

'A private matter?' Vi leaned forward. 'No it isn't, Mr Iekanjika. The woman who gave Mr Grint several million quid, as you probably know, tried to kill herself last night. Know who she left the rest of her ten million fortune to, do you?'

Neither Iekanjika or Mr Riordan said a word.

'Oh, yes, it was Mr Grint, wasn't it. A member of Mr Grint's church tried to assist this woman to kill herself, which is an offence in this country,' Vi continued. 'It all smells bad, Mr Iekanjika, and you know what? I think you picked up the stink well before I did and I think you exploited it.' She took a copy of an e-mail out from underneath the papers on her desk and placed it in front of him. 'From Shepherd's Bush nick,' she said as Iekanjika looked down at the document. 'You used to do a bit of enforcing over there, didn't you, Marius? Helping Mr Grint to "sort out" people who complained about being sold houses by him that he didn't own. He went down, while you just went home for a couple of years.'

'We've got evidence' – although whether Roy Arnold would actually testify to this as no one seemed to know where he was – 'that you and Grint planned this little job on this lady between you,' Vi said. 'Personally, I think that the death of Jacob Sitole may well be in there somewhere too. Matthias Chibanda tell his old mate Jacob about your plans, did he?'

'Matthias Chibanda killed Jacob Sitole for his mobile phone.' Iekanjika looked up, his eyes hooded and threatening.

'Oh, right, silly me.' She smiled. 'Mind you, I do have to have a chat with your mate Reverend Manyika at some point. Because on the twenty-second of April 2011 he visited you at your home in Silvertown, didn't he? And you may recall, Mr Iekanjika, that one of the things Reverend

Manyika said to you was, "What kind of Christian allows killing".'

'So what? How do you know that?'

'So I think,' Vi said, 'it's very possible that Reverend Manyika may well tell us a story that doesn't quite fit with Matthias's confession.'

'No he won't.' Iekanjika narrowed his eyes. Vi noticed that Mr Riordan appeared nervous.

'Why not?' Vi asked.

Iekanjika didn't answer.

'Because you can call on some hard nuts back in Harare to come here and do him in?' She leaned forward and said, 'I know exactly who and what you are, Iekanjika. And unless you start telling me the truth I'm going to have to think about handing you over to some people who are expert at finding out just what kind of hold those involved in promoting, shall we say, the interests of their nation to the detriment of their own people here in the UK, actually have over those they claim to help and "enlighten".'

'Matthias Chibanda confessed, he killed Jacob Sitole.' He laughed. 'This is ridiculous!'

'Oh he killed Jacob, all right,' Vi said, 'but he didn't do it for Jacob's phone. He didn't do it because he wanted to – those boys were friends. He did it to keep you safe from discovery, Pastor. Matthias isn't a bright boy, as you know, and so he told his mate Jacob about how you and Grint

were going to get a load of cash off one of Grint's parishioners. But then you found out, didn't you? Sadly for you,
by that time Jacob had already told Reverend Manyika.
Now if you were not an anti-opposition agent for your
country . . .'

'So you go to your Reverend Manyika and you ask him
then,' Iekanjika said arrogantly. 'He will reiterate what I
have said today. He will retract what he said in my house
when, apparently, you were listening. Trust me.'

XXXIV

The body of Leonard Blatt was exhumed exactly one week later. Vi Collins spent a night out with what some back at the station called the Ghouls, the forensic scientists, in East Ham Jewish cemetery. They found the tiny bundle of bones just where Maria had said they would be, inside what remained of Leonard's suit jacket. It had been full term, so the boffins said, although exactly how it had died was less obvious. But its spine had been broken at some point.

Vi wandered the sad, wet cemetery and wondered what Maria's girl would have been like if she'd let her live. She'd be over thirty. The child of a trusting youngster and a manipulative priest. Father Fernandez was dead now, Vi had checked. Poor Maria, she'd given birth, alone and quickly in a public toilet. People coming in and out all the time. She'd killed the baby not only to silence her but also because she didn't know what to do with her. Had the 'good' Father encouraged her to do so? Maria said that he hadn't. She said he'd never known about the baby.

Kids got in to messes and twists. They couldn't, or rarely

managed to, think calmly about what might be best. Kids were little animals, reacting. Some got away with it, others didn't. Shazia Hakim had done a silly thing, letting dirty old Martin Gold wank in her garden while she and her friends acted silly on dope. Of course the sly old sod's solicitor would argue that Shazia's involvement with Martin had been consensual and she was, of course, sixteen. But Vi would argue that he'd blackmailed a nice Asian kid who didn't want her mum to know she was smoking dope, or that she was being bullied into it by her friends. Adolescence was, Vi felt, still a fucking nightmare for kids in spite of ChildLine and all the anti-bullying initiatives that schools put in place these days.

Maria Peters hadn't been able to leave her daughter to be taken away by the Thames. She'd kept her in a box. Its awful smell had alerted Betty Muller to Maria's secret which Betty'd kept for over thirty years – until she fell in love with Paul Grint.

But what of Maria's husband? Vi looked over her shoulder at the tent that had been erected over Leonard Blatt's grave and she wondered. What had he known, if anything? Vi suddenly felt both very alone and sickened. What she needed was a good shag.

Paul Grint was on bail – courtesy of a parishioner. He was still staying at his shonky old boarding house in West Ham. Lee imagined it to be similar to the sort of place where Roy fetched up from time to time, except that Roy wasn't in any hostel now. He was back with their mum. Lee frowned.

Mumtaz saw this but she didn't make any sort of comment. Business was slow and Lee was worried. She ate her sandwich in silence at her desk until her mobile phone beeped to let her know that she had a text. It was Mark, he was back from Germany and he wanted to meet up.

'That church Grint was signing massive IOUs for has been shut down,' Lee said as he looked at a news story on his computer. 'The bloke who ran it was taking money for all sorts of old shit: exorcisms, identification of witches. There's also evidence, from one of his own countrymen apparently, that he was spying on his own people for the folks back home.'

'For Mugabe?'

'A lot of the Zimbabweans over here are dissidents. Must have been a brave sort who dobbed him in.'

'Is that why the boy from the other church died?'

'Because he found out?' Lee shrugged. 'Who knows? The Chibanda boy still sticks to his story it was all over a mobile phone. All the coppers can do is close Iekanjika down, lift whatever cash he's taken by nefarious means and deport him.' Then he changed the subject. 'How's Shazia?'

'She's fine.' She smiled. Now that Mr Gold was out of her life, on remand, she was much happier. She'd also decided to leave school and do her A levels at the local sixth-form college, far away from Hilary and Adele. She was making a fresh start, which was also much more financially advantageous for Mumtaz. No more skiing trips or expensive uniforms.

Mumtaz sent a text to Mark inviting him to dinner.

Betty Muller, alone, was actually in custody for assisting in Maria Peters' attempted suicide. She wouldn't give Grint to the police – she'd retracted her statement that he'd known about Maria's desire to kill herself. But he had to have known! Betty had always told him everything – one always told a loved one everything.

In addition to the three million pounds she had already given the church, Maria had left all the rest of her money and property to it in her will. There was no evidence to suggest that the solicitor, although a congregant himself, had forced her to do that. In fact the small amount of written correspondence between them indicated that the lawyer had actually counselled Maria to think long and hard about such a bequest. But she had ignored him.

And now, locked away in that hospital out in Essex, she was only talking to her psychiatrist.

Her phone beeped again. Mark replied that he could come over, but the best night for him was later that evening. Mumtaz thought about it for a moment and then sent him her address. She'd see him at eight.

Betty had tried to call Paul on several occasions but his mobile number was always unobtainable. However, even if she had managed to get through she wouldn't have been able to talk to him properly. Not with all those terrible, criminal women behind her clamouring to use the phone. Was this her life now?

The divinely manifested signs that Marie had experienced had led her towards suicide. The police thought that she and Paul had put them there to drive Marie out of her mind. She hadn't and he wouldn't; it had been God. Betty had seen them too. The police said she'd had a key to Marie's house in her handbag. But they must have put it there because she'd never had such a thing in her life. When Marie had called her that last time she'd rushed out of the house and rung Marie's bell and waited for the groggy comedian to let her in.

The police talked about manipulation but no earthly agency had manipulated Marie. When Paul had taken over the old pub in Canning Town, he'd done so because God had led him to that place. Another Christian, Pastor Iekanjika had been willing to rent it to him. It had been written. God had wanted Marie to have to face that location where her sin had first become apparent to her. Paul had said so.

Betty had never been to an audition before or since. Marie had been frightened, so she'd gone with her. Then Marie had collapsed and that awful man had laughed and said that she was probably pregnant. Marie hadn't said anything and Betty hadn't asked her. But Betty had noticed that she had put on weight. Then Marie had moved out of her mum and dad's place and got a flat, but there was still no baby until Betty had found the box. That awful smell and all the flies, she'd thought it was the drains. Marie had gone out to get milk for their tea and Betty had found it in that box – an abortion, or so she'd thought. Betty had left immediately. The next time she'd seen Marie had been when she turned up at church. Paul had said it was a miracle for Marie to just appear like that. He'd said they'd have to support her while she came to terms with what she'd done. They'd have to do it gently, at her pace, as the realisations came to her. Because she had to want redemption. If not, then why had she come?

Paul was the only person she'd ever told about the terrible thing in the Clarks box. The only one she'd ever trusted, the only one who'd understood. But when Marie had first arrived it was as if the whole thing had never happened. It seemed she'd forgotten – everything! But then as Paul had said he would, God had taken a hand.

At the end, Marie had wanted to die. It had been her choice, her way of atoning. Betty had only been doing what Marie had wanted. After all, why should a child murderer live? Betty would have loved that child and let her live wherever she had come from. Why hadn't Marie given the little girl to her? The bitch! Why didn't anyone understand this?

Anyone except Paul.

XXXV

'Maria sought out the church,' Mumtaz said.

'Did she?' Mark smiled. It was late and he'd already spent hours talking about his show to Mumtaz's step-daughter, Shazia. Now she was in bed and they were alone. Mumtaz had just told Mark about Maria Peters, about Betty Muller and Paul Grint.

'You think she didn't?'

'I think I could make someone seek me out with very little trouble,' Mark said. 'Mr Grint's a conman, so he's an amateur psychologist, that's what conmen are.'

'You mean by putting leaflets, booklets, et cetera in her way?'

'Maria Peters was back on the circuit and so it wouldn't have been difficult to find out where she lived. Then it was subliminal. I don't need to teach you this stuff, Tazzie! Grint pulled her in and then gradually, using what he'd been told about her, including her old religion, he pushed her latitude of acceptance until she was believing that God was either putting stuff in her house or making her do it to herself – driving her mad. God was stalking her.

'Pushing Betty's name or her image in front of her may have helped too,' Mark continued. 'From what you've said, that woman was obsessed with Grint. He could easily have taken her photo or put her name on his literature. She would've been flattered. Churches like that, leaflet all over the place.'

'We actually got one at the office,' Mumtaz said. Then she frowned. 'I'll have to see if I've still got it somewhere.'

'Grint engineered a trigger or triggers that set off Maria's memories of Betty and then he just waited for her to turn up.'

'Unless she really did just seek Betty out of her own volition?'

He shrugged. 'I'm telling you how a magician would arrange it, and I'm assuming Grint's guilt. Sure, she could have just sought that particular church out. But if, as you say, Maria seems to have no memory of Betty at that audition in Canning Town, then why seek her out to splurge her guilt? To some extent she was blocking it out. After all, back in 1980 Betty just legged it out of her life. Maria must have found that confusing or frightening, especially if she thought she might've found the dead baby. Maybe she went into denial? And anyway if Betty – who I accept had a key to the place – didn't put all those objects in Maria's house, leave her all those notes, who did? And don't say God.'

'Grint.'

'Of course. Grint or Betty, Grint manipulating Betty.'

'But Betty maintains Grint's innocence.'

'Because she's a desperate, middle-aged, divorced, child-less woman.'

Mumtaz looked down. In her own eyes she wasn't much different from that and Mark knew it. He put a hand on her shoulder. 'And she is besotted with Grint,' he said. 'Getting at Grint through her will be tough.'

He didn't know what the gynaecologist Ahmed had taken her to all that time ago had said. Mumtaz understood Betty Muller better than that woman would ever know.

'Grint wanted Maria's money and he got a tidy piece of it.'

'So how do we prove any of this, Mark?'

He shrugged again. 'If Maria won't ask for the money back and Betty won't dob him in, I don't know. As far as you know, did the police find any of Grint's leaflets or booklets in Maria's house?'

'I don't know,' Mumtaz said.

'I'd check. And I'd see if you can find that one you got at the office.' Then he paused for a moment. 'Grint didn't turn up on any CCTV footage, did he?'

'Of Maria's house? No,' she said. 'There is a shady figure in the garden on one of Maria's own tapes, but half the time she didn't even switch the system on in latter months.'

'But he or someone had to have planted those notes and those objects,' Mark said. 'Did things sometimes "appear" after there'd been a lot of people in the house?'

'After prayer meetings?' Mumtaz said. 'Yes.'

'Because as you know it's easy to slip something in a corner when you're in a crowd,' Mark said. 'CCTV just records a mob. As for the note she received which was—'

'Printed on computer. Notes actually; apparently she found one at her husband's grave, where the child was buried. Some other allusion to her dead daughter, I believe. But she threw that one away. The one the police still have only had Maria's fingerprints on it.'

He shrugged. 'Easy enough. Betty or Grint could have asked Maria to hold onto something for one or other of them for a second. They made sure they were wearing gloves. Simple.'

Mumtaz poured more wine for her guest and then drank some Coke. 'What I really don't understand is how Maria could have had seemingly full knowledge about the child, which she kept, but be in total denial about Betty's knowledge of it.'

'She blocked it out. Maybe,' Mark said. 'Maybe she just didn't mention it to Betty because she was so ashamed. You'd have to talk to her psychiatrist. But I think that when her husband died something gave inside her. To finally give up on her daughter's body was a big sacrifice for her. And yet at the same time by burying Leonard and the baby together she was putting the child into the care of a man she'd loved and trusted. Only later on, out on the circuit doing all the knob gags and whatever, did the double bereavement and the guilt really hit her. She was back in the old days when all she did, all the time, was rip people apart to keep her own demons at bay.' He shrugged. 'In my opinion, that is.'

She smiled.

'She also took a lot of psychiatric drugs, some of which Betty gave her,' Mark said. 'Psychiatric patients do give each other their drugs sometimes, it's well known. Maybe she did it at Grint's suggestion, which may not have been overt. I mean, we know he has hypnotic skills. Do you know if all the objects she told you about were real?'

'I saw them,' Mumtaz said. 'I still had the peacock feathers, I gave them to the police.'

Mark took a sip from his glass. 'From what you've told me she was in such a mess at the end, anything could have gone on. If Grint did plant suggestions in her mind then she could still have those in there. But unless that happens and somebody sees it, or unless she fingers Grint, if she even knows what he was doing . . .'

'Grint gets away with it.'

Mark frowned. 'In this world, Tazzie, the world of faith, magic and illusion, anything's possible.'

* * *

Lee opened the front door and saw Vi Collins standing on the doorstep.

'It's half past one!' he said. He hadn't been in bed, just dozing in front of the telly. 'What's going on?'

'Nothing.'

Vi pushed past him and entered his living room. As usual it was squeaky clean. Lee looked at her with sore, bleary eyes. 'Vi?'

She walked over to Chronus, asleep on his perch. 'Came to see the parrot,' she said.

'You've too much time on your hands since you caught that Olympic Flasher,' Lee said. 'Vi, it's the middle of the night and Chronus is a mynah bird. What do you really want?'

She raised an eyebrow.

'Oh.'

She flared, 'Well don't drown me in your enthusiasm, darling!'

Chronus opened an eye and looked at her. 'Well at least I woke *you* up,' Vi said. Then she turned and stared at Lee. 'I'm not going to beg.'

'Vi . . .'

She raised a hand. 'I'll go.' She stroked Chronus's head, smiled and began to walk back towards the front door. But just before she got there, Lee put his hand on her arm. She stopped.

'Stay,' he said. 'The bird likes you.'

She took a step towards him and he placed his other hand on her hip.

'I'm sorry . . .' he muttered. 'It's been a long time.'

'Last century.' She moved in closer, so that he could feel her breath on his face.

'Not exactly rushing into anything, are we.'

She kissed him and Lee Arnold became silent.

Maria wrote what she felt in the notebook Dr Black had given her so that she could record her thoughts. She read the entry she'd just written.

Paul Grint and Betty Muller are innocent of any wrongdoing on my account. I want Paul and the church to have all my money, all my property, all my goods. I am the only criminal. I killed my own innocent child. Please don't blame any of the nurses or the doctors for this.

And then she signed it.

The door creaked open. Maria put her notebook underneath her bedcovers. Nurse Julie smiled. 'Try and get some kip, Maria, yeah?'

'Yeah.' Maria slid down so that she was lying in the bed.

'Night.' Nurse Julie left.

Maria got out of bed. She was on fifteen-minute observations, what some still called 'suicide watch'. So she had fifteen minutes . . .

She took out of her knickers the tie the woman who'd prostituted her own children to buy drugs had sold to her in the dayroom and tied it around her neck. The woman said that if you managed to tie the other end round the door handle and then loll your head forwards you could be dead inside fifteen minutes. She quickly tied the other end around the doorknob and leaned forwards with all of her weight.

Mark had gone. In the morning the rubbish would be collected and so Mumtaz filled the wheelie bin up with the last of the waste from the kitchen and then pushed the whole thing out onto the pavement. Mark's visit had been nice but also upsetting. Because of what he'd told her about Grint, Betty Muller and Maria. It was possible Grint never was going to pay for what he'd done to those women. Try as she might, she couldn't find that leaflet that had come to the office. Given time, Grint would engineer another scam, try taking other people's money.

She was walking back down the darkened garden path when she heard a noise behind her. She turned and saw the Silver Prince standing by her gate, his trademark trainers shining in the moonlight.

'What do you want?' Her heart was pounding.

'Your husband still has a debt,' he said.

Shaking, she nevertheless walked towards him. 'My husband is dead,' she said. 'Is that why you've been following me? Because Ahmed had a debt?'

He didn't reply.

'Well, you're out of luck, I'm behind with the mortgage,' she said. 'I have nothing.'

'I don't think that's strictly true. I've been watching you for some time, remember? You have a job, parents, friends.'

She moved still closer to him. 'Get out of my garden,' she said. 'Leave us alone!'

'Oh, I'd love to,' he said. 'But my boss, a man Ahmed Hakim was deeply indebted to, is still owed money by your husband and now you'll have to pay, I'm afraid. You're a solvent lady and my boss has decided that you have inherited Ahmed's debt.'

'Debt for what? And who is this boss of yours?' Mumtaz asked.

'Ahmed, amongst his many vices, liked a little flutter on the roulette wheel,' the man said. 'He was absolutely rubbish at it, just as he was absolutely rubbish at paying what he owes.'

For a second she didn't know what to say. Ahmed had been many things, but a gambler was a new one on Mumtaz. She swallowed. 'I'll go to the police,' she said.

'You can't.'

'I can. I can tell them what you did to Ahmed.'

'And explain to them why you didn't give me to them before?'

'Yes!'

And then he said, 'You could, but you wouldn't want

452

young Shazia to go through what her father did to her
again, would you? Anyway, you owe my boss, Mrs Hakim,
for stopping Ahmed raping you – and the kid. You are
going to need some friends in high places if you want to
get that girl married off well, without her virginity. So I
would pay up, if I were you. We'll discuss terms in the
next few weeks.'

Every bone in Mumtaz's body vibrated with fury. How
did this man know that Ahmed had abused Shazia? No
one knew that. Had Ahmed told him? Boasted about it
maybe? 'I'll see you dead before that happens!' she said
and then she walked through her front door without
looking back.

The man in the silver trainers smiled. He knew when
women were attracted to him and he knew they often did
it in spite of themselves. He also knew he had Mumtaz
where he, and his boss, wanted her.

It was amazing what the mind did sometimes. Sometimes
it just woke up. Betty Muller sat bolt upright on her prison
cot and she knew exactly how Maria's key had got into
her bag. She'd seen him do it! That last day at Maria's
house, Paul had slipped it into her bag and then he'd just
smiled at her.

She'd only told him by phone what Maria was about to
do later that afternoon. So how had he known? Had he
set her up as an accomplice to that act? Had he wanted

the police to think she'd been terrorising Maria? That had been God, hadn't it? Oh, if only Maria had taken the gift of a child that God had given her and been grateful! *She* would have been. *She* would have done anything to have a child. Anything. How she'd hated Maria for that. Hated her!

All she had to decide now was whether she was going to tell anybody about what Paul had done. She tried to have a little practice to see what it sounded like. But when she said Paul Grint's name, she found that, try as she might, she could only say nice things about him.

Acknowledgements

This book would have been impossible without help and input from the following people.

For loving the whole idea of the Arnold Agency I must thank my agent, Juliet Burton, my editor at Quercus, Jane Wood and my Quercus publicist, Lucy Ramsey. You really got behind it, and me, and I thank you so much for that.

Comedy help came from Warren Lakin, Hattie Hayridge and Susan Murray. You all taught me so much about a profession that almost defines the word 'guts'. Thank you.

For accompanying me on seemingly endless jaunts around the Olympic site, the Thames shoreline, in and out of ruins and cemeteries, as well as feeding me, putting me up and putting up with me, I have to thank my good friends Kathy Lowe, Jim Reeve and Sarah Bancroft.

Help also came, as usual, from the wonderful Newham Bookshop in Plaistow, from Stratford Circus and from arange of local people, some with names and some without as well as from familial and other sources who prefer to remain anonymous.

Equipment advice was provided by Lorraine Electronics Surveillance of London E10 and much thanks to them for that.

Finally I'd like to thank my family and my friends, particularly my husband, my son and my mother. And, although she is sadly no longer with us, I'd also like to thank my friend and fellow author Gilda O'Neill who loved the east end and knew so much about it and its people. I hope she would have liked this book.

T   T